Hostile Takeover

"Let's see what the sneaky bastards are up to," Rofert said as they reached relative zero and started moving back. "Control, Engineer One stating intent to change trajectory and proceed ante for scheduled observation."

"Engineer One, Control confirms, proceed."

The docking pylon, then the melted regolith moved a hundred meters below, punctuated with ports and structures of the lodge, of old construction locks and the control tower and his residence. It really was a tiny station, and a tiny nation. It couldn't be relevant to anyone, and long term it was doomed anyway.

There was nothing significant visible as they passed the irregular lump that marked the arbitrary equator, but then . . .

"Holy crap," he muttered. "Did you see all this, Paul?"

The entire ante polar region had been built on. There were scaffolds, gantries, three docked tugs he could see in addition to the regular boat. There were a lot more than a hundred personnel here, too, because he could see close to that many swarming around building stuff.

In one way or another, it was a hostile takeover.

Then everything went black.

From "Starhome"

BAEN BOOKS BY
MICHAEL Z. WILLIAMSON

★★★

To purchase any of these titles in e-book form, please go to www.baen.com.

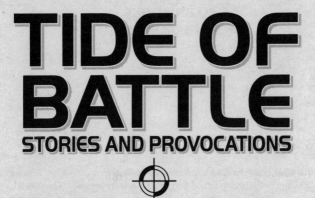

TIDE OF BATTLE

STORIES AND PROVOCATIONS

Michael Z. Williamson

TIDE OF BATTLE

All short story characters and events portrayed in this book are fictional, and any resemblance to real people or incidents is purely coincidental.

A Baen Book

Baen Publishing Enterprises
P.O. Box 1403
Riverdale, NY 10471
www.baen.com

ISBN: 978-1-4814-8419-0

Cover art by Dominic Harman

First printing, July 2018
First mass market printing, August 2019

Library of Congress Control Number: 2018015166

Distributed by Simon & Schuster
1230 Avenue of the Americas
New York, NY 10020

Printed in the United States of America

10 9 8 7 6 5 4 3 2 1

DEDICATION

To my fans,
who support my family
and my gun collecting habit.

CONTENTS

✥

TIDE OF
BATTLE

STORIES AND PROVOCATIONS

HOW I DROLL

WELCOME to my second collection.

I believe my short story technique is improving.

I used to struggle with them to great frustration.

It was after my first couple of novels I figured out how to address this problem. In a short story, character, setting and conflict have to be defined fast, and resolved quickly. At one level, you have to strip the story down to essentials, but without losing depth and richness. I do believe practicing this makes one a better writer for longer works.

As with longer works, I try to write the ending first, so I know where I'm going. The story is a journey, but it does have a destination, not a random trample across the landscape. The ending may change, but it has to be there for me to work properly.

Of course, I know writers who free-form it entirely, and others who start at the beginning and right to the end with no gaps. I can't do that. I write key scenes, vivid scenes, plot scenes, then cut, paste, smooth and dress the set.

At this point, it's about twenty years since my first paid publication. I've gone from literally a few bucks every few months to a novel that was half written in the back of my store, to being a full-time author with a part-time store, and now pretty much a full time author, though I sell at a few SF conventions a year mostly for fun. After thirty years, I don't know how to quit being a convention vendor.

As with any art, writing requires a thick skin. It's not the negative reviews that hurt. There are legitimate reasons for a reader to dislike even a well-written piece.

In fact, it can be instructive. If multiple readers didn't get, or misinterpreted a point, it might mean the author didn't present it well enough, or isn't matching message to audience.

The reviews that are frustrating are those where the commenter isn't criticizing the book the author wrote. Instead, they are criticizing the book they wanted the author to have written, whether as a strawman target, or out of a desire to read a different story. Some of the choicer ones include comments like, "If the characters would stop arguing we could get on with the story," about a story that is character driven, and complaints about events that don't actually occur in the story. "If your idea of fun is to toss flashbangs at your buddy while he performs first aid in combat, you will like this book . . .", which I sincerely hope no one thinks is fun or appropriate. And yes, the reviewer genuinely thought he read that scene in *The Weapon*, and that it was hilarious.

I recall one comment about *Freehold* to the approximation of, "Characters change implausibly. In the second half, Rob is revealed to be an ace fighter pilot, when there was no hint of this in the first half." Other than the fact that "I'm a pilot" are almost the first words out of his mouth, and him taking Kendra aboard for a training flight, and him flying characters around in several scenes. Other than that, no hints at all, no.

We refer to these types of reviewers as being so far off they're "not even wrong."

However, one can't worry about the seeds on rock not bearing fruit. At the other end are the people who do get it, despite flaws in writing.

Several years ago at a convention, a woman walked up to my table, pointed at *Freehold*, and said, "I despised the politics, and I couldn't put it down."

I replied, "Thank you. Then I did my job."

Some say the sincerest flattery is money, so thank you. Your continued support feeds my family, puts a roof over our head, and lets me continue writing.

Though perhaps that's inaccurate and there are better forms.

In the introduction to my previous collection, I wrote about my status as an immigrant, and as a veteran of the US military.

Shortly after that, two people sent me similar short fan letters, with the same phrase:

"Welcome to America. Thank you for your service."

Few authors can receive such a comment, and I was genuinely touched. I can only say, thank you very much, and you're welcome.

I've received numerous emails from war zones, where troops acquired donated copies, or purchased copies of my books in the Exchange. Several have the recurring theme of, "I stayed up too late to finish it, and if I die on patrol today it's partly your fault."

No, Soldier (Sailor, Airman, Marine, Contractor), *please* get your rest, the book will wait. As flattered as I am, I wish you health and further reading.

I make a point to send them a copy of anything recently finished and awaiting publication, to help the remaining deployment time be somewhat less boring between bouts of excitement.

Then there are specific, notable interactions.
Below are only a sampling.
There are many others.

Mr. Williamson:

A friend I've known for more than two decades was diagnosed with inoperable brain cancer last week.

While brainstorming for ways to lift his spirits, the idea surfaced that an email from yourself wishing him well might be quite effecatious (sic); he is quite fond of your work, beginning with *Freehold*. (He used the same book to hook me.)

His name is [redacted]. He'll be fifty on the 15th of this month, barring any additional accelerations in the growth of the glioblastoma.

Should you choose to fire off an email to him, I will print it out and read it to him, as the tumor has caused his vision to be rather iffy when he tries to read. (Reading aloud to him is far preferable to watching one of his headaches intensify.)

If this idea does not appeal or your schedule prevents,

I thank you for your time in reading this missive, and further wish to express both his and my appreciation for your work.

My response was:

Dear [redacted],

Sorry to hear you're not well. I always wish my fans the best.

I'm glad you're a fan of *Freehold*, though I always have mixed feelings about it. It was my first, and rather angry and vital, but not necessarily my best written. That seems to happen a lot. I liked the middle of my Sniper series best. The fans liked the third one.

I've attached my upcoming novel, "Rogue," and a couple of short stories I hope you'll be able to enjoy, even if in bed. They're not fully proofed, and I had five deadlines at once, so they may be a bit stark in spots.

I'll hope for a good outcome for you. Three years ago, I came back from the Middle East choking to death. Therapy helped, but it seems my body finally got around to dealing with it, and my breathing's mostly improved. I've always hated medications, but sometimes they're a necessity. I've tried to be cheerful about 2000 allergy shots in the arms, but it does get tiresome now and then.

I wish there was more I could offer than good luck, and hope for the best. A positive attitude never hurts, and frequently helps.

All best
Mike

And then there was this one:

Michael,

You may remember me from a few years back when we shared dinner together in Atlanta, GA during Dragon Con. I really enjoyed our meeting and learned that I should NEVER accept a table next to the waitstaff station. No matter the case, this year I was in the hospital hoping to die, and your book "Rogue" gave me what little hope I have. I was well prepared to end my life, but your character not ending his because he felt responsibility to his daughter gave me pause. I will live a few more years because you created a character who would not abandon his child. I thank you for the lesson.

    Very respectfully,
    [redacted]

I have to say, that is humbling to read, and worth more in personal capital than any number of terrible reviews.

Then, last year, I reconnected with a close associate I hadn't seen in some time.

We got along well enough, and discussed our mutual interests.

But as I left, they thought it important to say:

"Look, it's obvious you can write and have a following, but you got to admit, the subject matter is pretty naive."

No, I don't believe I have to admit anything, actually.

I didn't bother asking for further explanation, because

it was obvious, even without years of interaction, that this person really didn't think the same way I did.

One could criticize the writing style. It's certainly not as polished as my current style. I hope I've improved in a couple of decades since I first penned *Freehold*. I wouldn't write the same book now. At the same time, it continues at about 87% sellthrough rate (percentage of shipped copies sold vs shredded or returned), and I sold my first novel on my first submission to my first publisher, which is a strong statement in the industry.

I suspect the criticism was of the politics, or what they perceived were my politics. While I find my creation fascinating, it wasn't exactly my "dream" society then, and my thoughts in general have changed in a couple of decades. See above about my presentation of same.

It was possibly about the science and technology (this associate is professionally trained in the hard sciences). Here we run into two issues. First, this person isn't a sci-fi reader, and, like any genre, one must have or learn a grasp of some cultural assumptions to "get" SF. Frequently, unreal science is a necessary workaround to create the environment necessary for the setting we wish to place the characters in.

Then, there are reasons within my universe for the apparently low advancement of tech over the present day, much of which a student of politics or war can deduce. Eventually, some of that will be covered in other works, and some of it has already been alluded to.

This brings us back to my fans. In addition to the above specific examples, my fans include numerous members of the military and civil intelligence communities, including a counterterror investigator with several "hits" and apprehensions of active hostiles. Some are professional security, in IT, police and military investigations, or for diplomatic protective groups or are department chiefs for major banks. I've been given challenge coins by members and support crew of SEAL Teams and Special Forces units. I have law professors and political scientists among my readers. I have hard scientists, including researchers who head projects you read about in the news (neural implants and prostheses, for example), as well as stellar scientists among the numbers.

Given that, I don't believe I have anything to admit, nor to be ashamed of.

Remember what I said about having a thick skin?

Sorry, Associate, this time you're wrong.

But perhaps there is a naïveté, or merely a lack of background in our discussion, and it's not mine.

And my intent is to become a better writer with every project.

As for those of you who do enjoy my work, despite any real flaws, perceived flaws, or disagreements, it's a privilege to wake up every day and know I'm appreciated.

I thank you.

TIDE OF BATTLE

STORIES

THE DIGITAL KID

This came about when Kevin J. Anderson put out a call for SF writers who were fans of Canadian rock band Rush. I've been a fan since I heard the Signals album on QFM 96 in Columbus in 1982. In fact, they were the first hard rock (for the time) band I liked. I have all their albums, enjoy most of their songs, and have a few bits of memorabilia. SF pretty much owns prog rock, or vice versa.

This started out as being based on the song "Analog Kid," with a dash of Heinlein's "Starman Jones" thrown in. However, it went in a different direction, as stories often do. "Digital Man" worked its way in there.

If you're reading my stuff, I of course hope you'll like the story. If you're also a Rush fan you'll likely notice this uses a lot of the Signals album as background.

If you're a hardcore Rush fan or even geek, you'll probably be able to pick out references to "Subdivisions," "Driven," "Red Barchetta," "Mission," and some hints of

"Anagram," "The Pass," "Jacob's Ladder," "High Water," and Geddy's solo tune "My Favorite Headache." There's one clear hint at "2112," and you might recognize some background from my own Freehold universe.

If you enjoy the story, but are not familiar with any of those songs, I enthusiastically encourage you to look them up.

There was a brief disagreement with the editor over this story, a theme you'll see repeated later. The editor, who did make some very good line corrections and even a couple of factual and background suggestions, decided the entire book should be in Imperial measurements, except where it was "sciency," and metric would be okay then. My story wound up with a bunch of mishmash, including a correction from an engine with 7 liters of displacement to 7.39 quarts. The note in the margin made it clear the editor didn't understand engine displacement, and was confused as to if that was a lot of consumption, but was okay leaving it in there. I stetted it to 7 liters, and snarked to myself that if one doesn't understand engine displacement, one shouldn't comment on it at all.

Poor Larry Dixon's story ("Marathon," involving auto racing) wound up with all his car masses, lengths, distances and separations taken from even centimeters and kilometers, to decimal inches and miles. That got corrected back too.

I commented online that at some point I was going to write a story with "arshins" and "cho." I encouraged Michael Massa to do that in the Freehold anthology, with *a story during the Russo-Japanese War. You'll just have to search online for conversions.*

Still, minor production issues aside, I enjoyed writing it, Kevin Anderson accepted it, and his acceptance email was almost a fan letter, and the editor otherwise did a good job of finding things to polish.

Here it is.

⊕

THE EARLIEST SCENE Kent remembered from when he had real eyes was a meadow in the mountains. It sloped away on three sides, was surrounded by trees, and looked over the edges of a city below. It was hundreds of kilometers from home, and Mom or Dad had to drive them there. Sometimes they'd camp in a tent behind the cabin.

He couldn't remember who owned it. He did remember Joey and Atilla helping him build a treehouse. They had three platforms, a rope ladder, and had even stocked it with rocks to fight off "others." Looking back, he couldn't remember what others they'd ever need to fight, and Atilla had used twine instead of the rope he bought to haul the bucket of rocks up. When it snapped, it had gouged Kent's head open. He still had a scar from the stitches. At the time, that had seemed the worst pain imaginable. He'd since learned otherwise.

One summer, he remembered the trees down the hill being chopped to the ground and shredded by machines. Then an oval tower got built. It seemed out of place, growing out of the hill. Argosy Apartments, it was called. They had ads out about the gorgeous view, except they'd destroyed his gorgeous view to do it. They'd also destroyed the tree house. At night, he could look out over the geometric sprawl on the plain below, and the rushing lights of distant streams of cars.

Even here, the glare interfered with stargazing. He begged Dad to drive him over the peak at 2 A.M., so he could catch a meteor shower.

He and his friends continued to play there, but he tried to face the other way, uphill, so he wouldn't have to look at the concrete. He wanted to imagine he was exploring the wilderness, not surrounded by millions of people.

"You seem frustrated," Mom had said one evening.

"They put a building on the hill," he said. "It was all rolling trees, and now there's apartments."

"I saw," she said. "It's not the same, eh?"

"No."

"We noticed it, too," she said.

He remembered the next year, when he sat in the back of the car as they drove for the summer house.

"Don't we take this exit?" he asked.

Dad said, "We're going to a different summer house."

"Oh?"

"It's a surprise."

They drove up and over the mountains, looking down on a valley full of spruce trees. He had his wilderness back. There was a house here, too. They were two hours from the grid around the city, but here was wilderness.

The new house was all log outside, all wood panels inside, with rails and deck around it. It was like something out of a western movie.

His father said, "This was your uncle Travis', but he said he wasn't going to use it much, so he let us buy it from him."

"Can Joey and Atilla visit?"

"If their parents say so, yes."

He and Dad nailed timbers and plywood to make another tree house, in the thick lower limbs of a larch. It shifted in the wind, which scared him at first, but eventually became fun, then soothing.

Overhead he had vivid blue sky by day, and black nights scattered with buckets of stars. He'd sleep out under them, unafraid of the blanket of night or the animals passing through. He stared at the stars, knew every constellation, and watched until late became early, for glimpses of meteors. That was where he was bound. No one could build apartments to block that view, if he could get into space.

Far down the hill, the high-speed train wrapped through the valley. He could only see it occasionally, and the road not at all.

It wasn't until later he realized Mom and Dad were rich. So were several of his friends. He showed pics of his summer house to kids at school. Reggie Hanaway grabbed him at lunch one day.

"It's kinda not cool that you have a second house. A lot of the kids here don't even really have one, just apartments."

"I just like it," he protested. "I'd live there all year if I could. I don't care about money."

"Well, it isn't fair," Reggie insisted.

He guessed money mattered to people who didn't have it. Just as space mattered to him. There were three companies building ships to explore other stars. He wanted to be on one.

"You'll need lots of math," Dad had said. So he started reading sites on geometry and trigonometry, and used his chore money for proctored tests.

When he was sixteen, his parents let him drive some of the trip. It was tiresome, across the flat prairie and up into the hills, then the mountains proper. It had seemed so much shorter when he was young.

"I never realized what a thousand-kilometer trip actually was," he said.

"Ain't it, though?" Dad replied. "The turn off is just around the bend here. Slow for it."

"I got it," he agreed.

His uncle had died two years before. They owned the cabin outright now, and the barn of tools and equipment. They also had one of his old cars. It wasn't like modern vehicles. It had no fuel cell. The engine was over seven liters and guzzled gasoline. The brakes and suspension were a lot softer and slower than a modern car, and it had no navigation or feedback. You even had to change gears manually. It was simple in mechanism, and he learned how to maintain most of it with the shop tools. He watched old videos and read books on how to handle it on the road.

In between he lay in the grass and watched deer, elk and bobcats amid the waves of grass. At night he looked at the stars.

The next year he took the van down into the town for a container of gasoline.

"Hi, Kent," he heard. It was Sheriff Okume.

"Hi, Sheriff."

"What do you need gas for?"

"I got my uncle's old car working."

"That old Hemi?" the Sheriff said with raised eyebrows. "Watch yourself. Those things were damned near uncontrollable."

"I will." He knew every bolt of it.

It took some time to clean the engine up and get gas flowing, but it fired with a cackle.

They probably shouldn't have let him take it, he realized later.

It's my turn to drive, he thought.

The car swayed on turns. It was gorgeous, but heavy and ungainly. In a straight line it was like a rocket, and he loved the acceleration pinning him to the seat. He could imagine he was lifting for space. He nailed it on every straight. It didn't like turns, though. He'd studied inertia. This was a good example.

The curves came up fast, and he was scared. The tires whined on the edge of their envelope, and it took real strength to muscle around the bend, even with power steering. It held, though.

The next curve surprised him, and he braked, double-clutched and downshifted. The tires skittered, and the car grabbed. He was learning it, becoming one with it. He would master it.

As he thought that, the road wound up before him into an inside turn that gave way to a tight outside bend. He recognized it. He hadn't realized he was that far up the mountain already. He slammed the shifter, stomped the pedals and heaved the wheel. He felt the car understeer and skid across the road, then gravity dropped away as he sailed into the open air over the spruces below. He had a moment to think about how pretty they were, and that he was flying, before they shot past him like feathery spears and a crashing bolt of pain ran up his spine into his head.

"Kent, can you hear me?"

"Ayeh." That wasn't the right . . . what was . . .

"You're safe. You're in hospital."

That was . . . what it?

"No . . . eyes . . . work . . ." he muttered. The . . . words. Words. Hard to get.

"You suffered some brain damage from the accident. It will take time to recover. Do you understand?"

Of course he understood. He wasn't . . . wasn't . . . that word . . .

He started crying. He felt someone hold his hand, then lean against him. It was Mom.

"Physcal therapost?" he asked.

"I'm a helper while you learn how to move again."

She sounded pretty. He wished he could see her.

He felt her hands and someone else's steady him upright and pull his arms onto rails. He clutched at those and managed to stay upright. He locked his elbows and let his lower body dangle.

"We're going to work on trying to walk today," she said. "It won't happen all at once. For now, just get used to being upright again."

He knew how to walk. All you did was walk. Except his

legs didn't do anything when he tried. He tried to talk and made gargling noises. The words had stopped again.

"Remember, your left leg is a replacement," the helper said. "It might take some time. It's normal."

No, what was normal was walking. He looked at his legs and couldn't see them.

He thought really hard. Think, walk, think, walk. Sweat started rolling into the bandages on his face, and he started crying again. He was clenching his jaw, and his teeth hurt. His shoulders hurt.

Think, walk.

The helper reached over and put her hand on his, and gently pulled his fingers off the bar.

Think, walk!

His left leg moved a fraction. Then another. Then it slid forward the length of a foot. He could tell by where his knee was.

He heard her gasp something.

She'd said, "Already?"

He strained and growled and clenched until his teeth felt like they were being stabbed. Then his real foot slid forward to join the left.

His arms went numb and he fell, landing in a heap and busting his lip on the bar.

"Did it," he said.

When he woke up he was back in his room.

He knew when the doctor came in. He'd already learned to identify people by the sound they made and their presence in the room.

"How are your words, Kent?"

"Better," he said. "I can remember a lot of them. What happened again?"

"You had a concussion and traumatic brain injury. Sections of your brain died. Do you remember what today is?"

"Eye day. New eyes." He was frightened, but he needed to see.

"Yes. We can't transplant. Your optic nerves were too badly damaged. We'd have to put artificial nerves in anyway. So your eyes are artificial, too."

"Yeah."

It took a long time for his eyes to come back, because they weren't eyes. He saw grainy upside-down images. Then he saw right-side-up images. Finally they colored in. He noticed that things focused perfectly in front, but not outside of a circle of direct vision. He could see better, though. There were colors here he'd never known before. He asked about it.

"Yes, the imagers are designed to cover the entire spectrum that's theoretically visible to humans, and a little more for harmonic resonance."

"What does that . . ."

"You'll learn later."

He saw things differently than before. His memory of lighted streets in veils of fog wasn't the same as what he saw now. Now he could see the droplets and tiny rainbows of light through them.

His senior year had him in tears, or would have, if he'd still had tear ducts.

He was still finishing junior year work he'd been doing at home, because he'd missed most of the school year itself. But more than that, he remembered he'd been a clocker in trigonometry. He'd been starting on calculus and gearing up for diff eq, in high school.

Now, geometry had him angry.

"But what is the answer?" he asked as Mr. Siles helped him plot another graph.

He followed with his eyes as Mr. Siles pointed.

"That. Minus fifteen to seven point three."

"But which one?"

"All of them, Kent."

He knew this, but he didn't. "How can more than one be an answer?"

"How many integers are between one and ten, not counting them?"

"I . . . Oh."

He'd been stupid. How could he not know that?

Mom and Dad didn't even mention the car, but it hung there, a subject never raised. It has been valuable, historical, and Uncle Travis'. All the additional support he'd needed on top of the medicine had cost them the summer house and land. In a shove of the accelerator, he'd destroyed part of his family's history. He was an apartment kid now.

He'd also destroyed his future. He was too far back in math to get into the programs he needed for space. He could dream, but he was trapped. He didn't want to work in one of the towers that blocked the stars.

"Hey, Kent, want to come cruising?"

"Sure," he said. He couldn't drive again yet, and wasn't sure he wanted to. But Marc had a sweet convertible, and it was a warm night. He needed to get out of the house.

He realized part of the reason they took him along was freak factor. At the Coff-In coffee shop parking lot, high school and college kids milled about. In shorts, his left prosthesis was visible. It almost matched the skeletal wheels, seats and window frames of Marc's Turbo V.

Shortly, a burning-hot blonde ran fingers along the door ledge, looked at him, and asked, "Did you get those shades to match the car, too?"

"Not exactly," he said, and took off his shades to show the metal orbits underneath.

"Oh, wow!" she said, more impressed than bothered.

Jackpot.

Yeah, it was shallow, and what did he care? He'd lost his real eyes and suffered a lot of pain. This was only fair.

"What's your name?"

"Casey," she said.

He could walk with a limp. He could see adequately. He'd even done well enough to get accepted to Avalon University, but that meant nothing now. His eyes especially needed ongoing tuning, and they occasionally aberrated enough to need a reboot. He wouldn't be going to space.

So he threw himself into cybernetics. There had to be a way to integrate stabilization protocols and circuits onboard. Then, of course, they'd have to be micronized.

Materials did funny things at that scale. Cryogenic cooling was not an option for an implant.

It was properly graduate work, but he didn't want to wait. Class, study, then independent research. The grad students were aloof; but finally accepted his determination. He thought some of that was pity for his "condition." That should irritate him, but if it got him where he needed to be, he'd swallow it.

His apartment mate kept nagging him.

"Kent, man, you need rest," Andy would tell him at four in the morning.

"I need study."

"You're going to pass."

"Passing isn't enough." He had to clock it.

And he had to get to the gym. The left leg needed to work like the right one, and he needed more muscle tone. He pushed weights until his entire body burned, and bulked.

He still talked to Casey, but they weren't dating.

She'd asked, "But what job are you going to get in the real world?"

"If I can't crew a ship, I'm going to one of the stations," he said.

And that was it. She wanted to remain on Earth.

The farm in the hills wasn't his anymore. Still, he made a point to drive up and take in the view from roadside, and from the public land further up. There was a quite nice meadow there, and the view was even more vivid, if slightly artificial, with his eyes. He even went in winter to see the endless quilt of snow. He drove cautiously, sedately, with all the automated controls engaged, wincing every time someone passed him and volted up the mountain.

♦ ♦ ♦

His sophomore year he got a spot of good news. The deep space projects changed the rules. They said they'd take certain prosthetics if they were stabilized.

That was his field. That's where he'd put all his effort.

His work was already known. CyRe Inc. and Omega sponsored some of his research and provided prototypes. He was in his second year of his doctorate when, completely apart from his thesis, one of his papers led to micronization of monitor and adjustment circuits, that just might be powered by bioelectricity. He received patent co-credit, and references.

A recruiter from CyRe called and offered him a position.

"Thank you very much, and I expect I'll take it, or something similar," he said. He'd probably have to. Better a rat in a race than in a cage.

"What would convince you?" she asked.

"If you had deep space operations," he said. "I put my life into this because I'd wanted to get there, and couldn't with the prostheses I had. I probably can't now, even with the improvements they're making, but I don't want to commit until I have to." He wanted the lights of space, not of an industrial park.

"I'm sorry that we don't," she said. "But I'd like to keep in contact as you get closer to completing your doctorate."

"Please do," he said. If he couldn't go, he could help others, whether they wanted to reach space, or just live normal lives. He wanted space, though.

An hour later, his phone rang again.

"This is Kent," he answered.

"Mister Eastman, my name is Najmul Hasan. I'm with HR at Prescot Space Resources. Ms. Luytens at CyRe gave me your information . . ."

He would have to make a point to visit Ms. Luytens. He'd never met her, but she was the most beautiful woman in the world.

Prescot even wanted to pay him. He promised to consider their offer seriously and respond within three days. He lasted two days before accepting, and barely avoided screaming that he'd do it for free.

He was going to space.

Prescot had heavy industry in the asteroids, and wanted to jump to other systems. They worked with JumpPoint, on theoretical physics he was only vaguely aware of. But they were going to space. They had a ship ready for trials, a destination, and wanted crew.

When he went to the mountains in August, he took a specially programmed sensor suite along. He hoped he'd need it.

This time he had control of the car. It was modern, safe, and handled any surface. It was better than his uncle's historical beast in every measure, but it lacked character.

Still, it took him along the road and up the mountain. He didn't let it get near the edge of control. Any time he felt traction feathering, he eased off. His future wasn't in race cars. It was in spaceships.

For the next two years he learned how to fly an interstellar ship. The math was simple, really. The tough part was adapting his eyes so he could control them with internal feedback, and learning how to do that. The lack of eyelids was still more hindrance than help. Then, some of the flight controls were operated by tracking the pupils. He had no pupils. Four cyberneticists created an interface that mounted to the side of his eyes, and used induced microvoltage to mimic tracking. He wasn't involved with that, because he was working on the ship's bionetic systems. He had to grit his teeth and trust in four strangers to make things work without ruining his eyes or bouncing him from the mission.

The tracking worked. The module was slim enough, but protruded from the sides of his head like bug eyes. He looked properly cyborg with those installed. That almost seemed fitting.

He was paired up with Lance Naguro for training. Together they worked on astronautic computers and onboard mission controls. They still had to learn to astrogate and pilot. The days started at 0500 and often went until dinner. They sat at consoles matching those of the *Seren Wrach*. The flight, with the Jump Point, should last about a month. They might remain in system for a year longer. These couches would be their work stations. They were smaller than any cubicle, but they'd be in space.

About a month in, Lance said, "Kent, if you'll pardon the terminology, you're a machine. Do you ever sleep?"

"Yes." Some nights he saw treetops and a dark void. Some nights it was a dark void with stars. Other times it was a cubicle in a building. That was scarier than the first one. "But I want to do this."

"There's no doubt," Lance said. "I think you're pretty well guaranteed to be Lead."

He shrugged, "Lead, Second, as long as I go. Or the

next flight. But I'm going. I'll volunteer to remain in place for the second mission, too."

Three months later, he got notice.

Lead Engineer, Astrogation and Project Control: Kent Eastman.

So then he had a crash course in flying, and cringed at the term. He went up in sailplanes and propeller trainers with instructors, then into jets, and finally, a converted military fighter. He discovered the loss of a leg let him pull more Gs—he had less extremity for blood to pool in. That, and his eyes worked past where flesh eyes grayed out from the same issue.

Parachuting terrified him, every jump. It took ten jumps to qualify for escape procedures, but he took ten more. It didn't reduce his fear. Falling would forever be his phobia. Gravity fell away, and he saw spruce trees.

It was only logical, he insisted to himself, that he buy a Hawkwing HangJet.

It did handle a lot like a hang glider. Then, if you dialed up the thrust, it turned into a tiny aircraft. You could drop from a plane, or throw yourself off a mountain. He knew he had to do both.

The drop from the jumpship wasn't as scary with the jet as it had been with a parachute. He pulled the lever that snapped the wing struts open, thumbed the igniter, and felt the engines shove. Here on the coast, he could see the endless waves of the sea. It wasn't space, but he felt there was a bond. He flew in broad loops around the dropzone, and stirred up a wave of leaves when he touched down.

After that first open-air flight, he loaded the kit into his car, and with Lance along, drove up to where the farm had been. It now belonged to some wealthy producer, who'd kept all the buildings, but had built a castle deeper in the trees. He messaged ahead to be sure he was expected, and welcome.

The police lights surprised him. Had he been . . .? Damn.

It was Sheriff Okume, who said, "Doctor Eastman, do you know why I pulled you over?"

The sheriff had helped save his life fifteen years before. He owed the man.

"I am so sorry, sir. I wasn't even paying attention."

Smiling and shaking his head, Okume said, "We already had one wreck this year. Slow down, okay?"

"Yes, sir. Have a good day."

Yes, he'd slow down. For now.

Lance chuckled, and he realized his fellow astronaut didn't know the details. He shrugged and drove.

He pulled through the electronic gate and bumped across the meadow.

There was his sensor pillar, with a hawk soaring down past it to snag a mouse from the grass. The pillar was untouched, and had two years of panorama. He pulled the pins mounting it to the steel post, and opened the trunk.

"Okay, Lance, you take it back down."

"You're sure?"

"Yup," he said, grabbing the hangjet, and closing the trunk. "I'll beat you down."

His phone rang. Even up here.

"Hey, Mom."

"Kent! What's the site for your interview? I want to make sure I catch it."

Indeed. That was in twenty minutes.

He told her, and started laying out his gear for his first earth launch.

The hawk watched him curiously from a half kilometer away. His eyes were slightly better than the bird's.

On cue, the stream channel called.

"This is Kent."

"Doctor Eastman, are you ready?"

"Sure."

"Okay, we'll start recording . . . now, and intro, and we're on.

"We're live with Doctor Kent Eastman, before he leaves Earth and heads for another star system. Hi, Kent."

"Hi, Alex."

"How do you feel about leaving Earth? Sad? Or eager to get away?"

"Well, both of those. I'll miss my family and friends, and my favorite places, but I'm leading the way where I hope others will follow."

"What are your final preparations before you leave Earth for several years, possibly forever?"

"I'm actually at a remote place in the wilderness, that's been an inspiration to me for a long time. I brought a stereo-holo-imaging setup so I can create a full surround image of it to take with me. It's been running for two years, so I can visit any season I want, or just let it run at its own pace. There's audio as well. I just wish there were some way to preserve the scents."

"So you're taking a bit of Earth with you?"

"A small bit that's very personal to me, yes. We have entire matrices of images, video, music and film, and we'll get updates as we go. But this archive is something for me."

"Can you take a listener question now?"

"Sure."

The voice was that of a teenager. "Doctor Kent, I had ocular implants two months ago. I've been blind since birth. I'm just starting to see things now and I guess it'll be years before everything syncs. It's almost dizzying. I managed without sight just fine, but now I realize there's that much more, and I will be able to see more than most people. How did you get from recovery to where you are now?"

He knew which eyes the boy meant. His research had helped create them. A small shiver of satisfaction ran through him.

"You have to be driven," he said. "Whatever you want to do, it has to be a passion that possesses you. You have to live it, dream it, wrestle it. If it doesn't mean that much to you, it's not your destiny, and you have to find what is. Never settle for less. Of course, it might take a long time to get there, and there might be detours. But you have to make the path."

He'd expected a half-hour-long interview. Those were typical. At forty minutes he realized this one was running long. He sat back in the grass and pulled his hat brim over his eyes. The evening sun was still bright in the clear sky.

After an hour, he got up and started prepping for departure. He had to do so before it got too dark.

A young woman in the Seychelles wanted to know what courses had been hardest.

"I had to take high school math twice," he said, as he

mounted the wings on the frame. "I had a traumatic brain injury from the accident that destroyed my eyes. It was so frustrating, I got so angry, knowing I'd learned all this and it was gone. Once I got through that . . ."

"The rest was easy?"

"No, not at all. But I knew it wouldn't stop me. All I did was math. If you're going into space, math and science are critical, even if you're in a social science. The more you can do to help the mission crew, the better." In fact, ballistic math had been easy, after all he'd done.

Alex asked, "So what do you think you'll find there, Kent?"

"I have no idea," he said. "Something different. Somewhere I've never seen." He realized he'd barely seen Earth.

"I understand that. Exploration." The interviewer concluded with, "Thanks again, Doctor Eastman, and good luck and safe skies."

"Thanks very much, Alex. Good luck down here."

He took one last long look around in the still, cloudy evening, smelling the spruce, the mountain grasses, the tang of the fuel in his jet.

He donned the harness, checked every item religiously. He'd never been gigged in training on that. He took the list line by line, every time.

The meadow dropped away to the east, sloping steeper and then down a shallow cliff to the land below. He'd chosen this spot from memory. It was a safe, almost perfect launch zone.

He gripped the controls, flexed the wings, and read the HUD.

He had the one booster for launch, so he had to make it count.

He started the turbines and heard them spool. With the auto-igniter engaged, he jogged, ran, sprinted for the slope, and leapt. The wings caught air.

The booster cracked and roared, and shoved him across the mountainscape as the turbines ran up. He angled slightly down to gain more velocity, watched the revs climb, and felt the thrust drive into sustained flight range.

He arced wide right, looking for the ribbon of old asphalt below. He found it, woven through the trees, and rose above it, looking . . .

There. That bend, those trees. That's where his journey had started.

He took a tight, banking turn around the bluff, feeling Gs increase as he drove into the thermals rising up the slope. The trees had recovered, though there was a visible dip where the car had shorn their tops down. The maples glowed red and orange in their fall livery. The wind whistled past his helmet, causing ripples down his jumpsuit and down his spine.

And now it begins again, he thought.

Leveling off with arms out, he made a long, smooth descent, until the treetops whipped past only meters below, and the wind scoured his cheeks. He kept his enhanced vision on the path ahead. It wouldn't do to crack up now. He had an appointment to make.

The clouds parted, and bright beams of golden evening sunlight drenched the landscape. The trees gave way to shaven fields, and he ran thrust-up until the wings thrummed in resonance, then eased off until consumption and velocity curves guaranteed he'd reach the landing zone. The sky ahead was indigo fading to a velvety violet. The sun was at his back, melting into the mountains.

It's my turn to fly.

The road unwound behind him. Before him were the stars.

End

SOFT CASUALTY

I was brainstorming and joking with my friend Rahul (Ray) Chatterjee, an Indian immigrant and US Navy veteran, about the war in the Freehold universe. Asymmetric warfare is a fascinating subject, and partisan forces are limited in the traditional weapons they can bring to bear. This leads to all kinds of creative approaches—bicycle caravans, sabotage large and small, ambushes. I mentioned a psyop idea I'd had, and Ray simultaneously laughed hilariously and swore in horror.

This one's for you, Ray. RIP.

Later, it was reprinted in the 2015 Year's Best Military & Adventure SF, and the reader poll voted this story the winner. Apparently, SF readers take notes about this sort of thing.

⊕

JANDRO HAUER waited in the hot, bright light of Iota

Persei for his shuttle to clear for boarding. On his forearm was a medication patch feeding a steady dose of strong tranquilizer. Above that was an IV line from a bottle hanging off his collar. He'd be in orbit in a few hours, and transferred to a starship home. Perhaps then he could calm down.

"Hey, Soldier," someone called. There were eighty or so people at this boarding. He looked toward the voice to see another uniform. A US Marine with a powered prosthesis on his right leg gave a slight wave.

"Hey, Marine," he replied. "Soldier" wasn't strictly accurate for the combined South American Service Contingent, but it was close enough.

"I noticed the meds," the man said, pantomiming at his own arm. "Are you a casualty? If it's okay to ask."

Jefferson was a beautiful city, or at least it had been before the war.

Jandro Hauer looked out from his quarters. This building had once been apartments for the middling wealthy. The enlisted people had a good view, the officers were lower down. That's because the locals occasionally fired a missile. Usually Air Defense intercepted it. Usually. Three floors above him there was a hole, and a sealed off area, where one had gotten through and killed two troops. That's why he was inside the window with the lights off, not out on the balcony. He could see the towers of brilliant white clouds rising over the coastal hills just fine from here.

Support troops spent a lot of time indoors, not interacting with the planet or its residents. It was safer that way. That, and it meant not having to deal with the bright local light, thin air, vicious fauna.

He still didn't get it. The former colonists were so willing to fight the UN and Earth they'd destroy their own city in the process, which would just guarantee whatever was rebuilt would look like all the other major colonial cities. Being independent had let them develop a unique architecture and style. That wasn't going to last with them reverting to Colony status.

It was 1900, but still full light here. The local day was twenty-eight and some odd hours. The UN Forces stuck to Earth's twenty-four-hour clock. That led to some really surreal days where it would be midnight at noon.

A chime at the door indicated his roommate returning. He stepped aside because . . .

Jason Jardine swiped the lights on.

"Off!" he shouted.

Jason scrabbled with the touch plate.

"Sorry," he said as the room darkened.

"Always check the window first, Jase," he said. Jase was a senior corporal in Finance, but had only been here a week. He was still adapting. It was his first offworld mobilization.

The man nodded. "Yeah."

Some troops even kept the windows opaque 24/7, or 28/10 here. That was safer, but it didn't let them have a view.

"Goddamn, it's a hell of a city," Jardine said, walking over to the window.

"It is. That concentration-of-wealth thing is pretty dang good, if you're the one with the wealth." He looked around inside.

Troops had scribbled notes, art, tags and names on the walls. There had been decorations. Even though war trophies weren't allowed, there were ways to get stuff out.

Jardine looked where he was looking.

He said, "Just pay some local a few marks to sign it over as something sold to you, and as long as it passes Customs, you're fine. The guy you replaced picked up quite a few neat things in town."

"It's that easy?"

"Depends. If they have kids to feed, they'll sell just about anything. You know prostitution was legal here, right?"

"I heard. Not just legal, but unregulated."

"Pretty much. So some of them are still in business, and others are freelance."

Jardine said, "Just wear an all-over polybarrier."

"Not really. Most are actually clean. That was one of the things they were very strict on."

"I heard they're cheap, too." Jardine stowed his day pack on a rack by the door.

"I've heard that. Never tried, not planning to. I also hear some of them made a fortune."

"Doing what?"

"Doing rich guys. Apparently when you have a lot of money, you want to spend it."

"Makes sense. Almost like a tax."

"Hah. Good." He hadn't thought of it that way. What would you do if you had all that money? "Heading for chow?"

Jase said, "Nah, I was wondering if we could go out and

eat? Into the compound area, I mean. I know there's vendors out there. Do you know much about them?"

"Yeah, why not. I've eaten at several. That will be a change from the chow hall. They're doing lameo chili again anyway." He hated military chili. It wasn't chili with paprika and rice and whatever else they put in to make it international. It was nothing like the chili he'd had when visiting Texas, or that you got in a restaurant back home. He'd also had enough sandwiches lately. He didn't want another bland burger thing.

He took a step, looked down, and said, "Let me change into casuals." He was still wearing a battle uniform, even though he never went out on patrol. They had orders to "support the battlefighters." That meant dressing up like them during the work day.

He went to his room, undressed and tossed the Battle Uniform onto the bed for later. It was a nice room. Most of the furnishings were still there and in good shape. The dresser was real wood of some figured sort. He grabbed a clean Casual Uniform from the top drawer and pulled it on. He was back into the common room in two minutes.

"Let's go," he said to Jase.

Six squares of this area was controlled compound, barricaded off with triple concrete and polyarmor walls. Inside that were military and UN contractors only. Outside that was another four blocks of restricted area, where local contractors took care of non-essential functions. Outside that, chaos.

Though even there, most of the fighting was subtle. It wasn't until you got outside of the metroplex that violence started in earnest. Here, they didn't even need armor. As long as it was stored in their quarters, it was considered "within reach."

They walked the two blocks to the inner perimeter and berm, scanned out through the gate, and entered the Gray Zone. It was patrolled by bots with cameras, and there were a few MPs rolling around in carts. He still wasn't sure how many, but there was usually a cart in sight. He looked both ways and saw one patrol. There were probably a hundred troops in sight, more around the rest of the perimeter.

The local sun was gradually going down. It was late summer, and it was merely hot, not scorching. It reminded him a bit of Rio, except for the thin air and higher gravity. The sky was clearer, though, and this city had a split personality. Most of it continued to function, its business and politics monitored by the Interim Government in this compound and in those two buildings to the south, protected by lots of heavy floater platforms, manned air support and ground-based lasers. Very little got shot at it these days, but occasional gunfire happened to little effect.

This area was a low-intensity war zone.

To punctuate that, his phone chimed a message.

He looked fast, wondering if there was something inbound, some political change.

It was from Kaela Smith at the MP station.

The screen read, "Jandro, the sniper casualty earlier today. Moritz got shot. Sorry. —Kay."

He didn't even swear, he just wiped the screen.

Jase asked, "Something bad?"

He realized he was tearing up.

"That sniper this morning at the West side? Got Sammy Moritz."

"I'm sorry. Were you close?"

"No, it's just . . ." he took a deep breath, because this was scary.

"Right after we secured this area and set up for the diplomats and provisional government, they shot some guy at the gate. Just dropped him from a distance and that was all. He got replaced by someone else. They got shot. Moritz was the fifth or sixth person in that duty slot."

"That's sick." Jase apparently hadn't heard about this yet.

Jandro said, "Very. They're not targeting battlefighters or staff. Just people at random, or in this case, not random. It's been six people in about three months in that slot."

Jase puffed out air. "Glad I'm not an MP. At least not that MP."

"It's creepy. I wonder which poor bastard gets it next." He didn't want to think like that, but he couldn't help it. One field unit kept losing cooks. Convoys got disrupted. They needed live drivers because automated ones got waylaid or hijacked. The enemy was outnumbered, but technologically smart and vicious.

He always wondered if they'd come after Logistics some day.

Jase asked, "Can't they rotate around?"

"They do. But they seem to follow the slot, not the location."

"Sheesu."

Tension came out in words. "These fuckers have no

sense of decency. We laughed, it was hilarious, when they abducted Huff, stripped him naked and made him walk back. But if you're a prole, you're likely to just wind up dead."

"Is that why the no fraternizing order?"

He nodded. "Absolutely. Outside the second line, nothing is safe."

"Almost makes me glad to be stuck in here."

Jandro said, "Almost. Would like to actually fight, though. Or support it. Something." He actually wasn't sure about that, but he kept telling himself that.

"Yes, but logistics is what wins wars," Jase said. "And my family's glad I'm safe," he added.

"Hey, at least you're here, doing something." They crossed into the plaza that had been a park of sorts. Much of the greenery was chewed up from troops walking and playing. One of the trees had been used for climbing until the CO stopped it.

Jase nodded. "You're right about that, and so was the captain. These people really don't want us."

He said, "It's resistance to change. In twenty years, their kids will love life and wonder why anyone lived this way." They were told that, and he wanted to believe it.

"I hope so. The poor people must appreciate it."

"So I'm told. I see interviews."

Jase gave him a disgusted look. "Oh, come on, you don't think those are faked."

He sighed. That hadn't come out right in English. "No, not at all. But everyone I've met locally has a couple of different things going. I've also read in history texts that civilians will tell occupying forces anything to keep them happy. And I can't imagine a lot of frustrated rich people are shooting at us."

Jase replied, "No, but maybe the people doing the shooting need money badly enough to do it for them. Or are held hostage some other way."

He said, "Or maybe they're just afraid of us from propaganda. Hate isn't rational."

"Yeah. Okay."

Good. Jase didn't like the conspiracy nuts any more than he did. Sure, there were problems back home, but no one started a war just for a political edge. Bribes, manipulated language, economic payoffs, but not wars.

"So what looks good?" he said. There were ten or so little carts and knockdown kiosks offering food.

Jase said, "Pizza's always good. Or I always like it. But it just doesn't taste right here."

He said, "They grow different grain breeds."

"That must be it. Don't they use real animals, too?"

"Yes, raised out in the open air and then killed."

"That's awful. It's so awful I want to try that, just to stare at people and tell them."

That was funny. "Hah. It was really trippy the first time. I got used to it. It's just meat. You realize that's in the dining hall too, right?"

"I didn't." Jase looked at him with distrust.

"All food has to be locally sourced. There's just no effective way to bring in that much meat from outsystem, process it in orbit and land it. So we get it here."

"Why don't they tell everyone?"

"It's inspected and approved. There's some sort of BuAg exemption until we can build enough facilities here.

So they don't mention the source in case it disturbs people."

"I guess I can see colonies needing that, but once you get to cities," he waved around at the surroundings, "shouldn't you be building vatories?"

"Exactly. So you've already eaten dead stuff, and these people either don't have a choice, or actually like it."

"The chow hall meat is a bit stronger tasting than home, I guess. Wow. Suffering animals. One more way we're tougher than civilians."

"You can't really brag about it. Someone will call a counselor."

Jase nodded. "I know. But part of it is knowing, and part of it is tossing it out there when someone wants to try to measure up."

He said, "There is that. I feel sorry for the grunts. You can't boast about being in combat. It's seen as some sort of moral and mental handicap. No wonder they all burn out."

"Six months is a long time. I've been here a week and it's getting old fast."

Enough talk. Jandro asked, "So what are you eating?"

"How's the bratwurst?" Jase asked, and pointed at a cart under a broad tree that was warping the plascrete walkway.

"Spicy and greasy. Occasionally there are small bone chips from processing."

"How spicy?"

He considered and said, "Middling. Hot for Europe, medium for Tex."

"Let's do it."

"Looks like he's closing, too. Better run."

They jogged over to the cart, and looked over the menu. It was posted on a scrolling screen in English, Mandarin, Arabic and Russian. Next to the screen was a tag certifying inspection and authorization to be in the Gray Zone.

The cook looked up and nodded.

"You're just in time. What can I get you?"

Jandro said, "I'll take a cheddar brat."

The man nodded. "Got it."

Jase said, "The 'Meatlog.' That sounds suggestive."

"I had one before. It's good. Savory and salty as well as spicy."

"Sure. That's two hundred grams? I'll take two."

The cook, Gustin, per his nametag, flipped three sausages off the grill, said, "That's all I had left. You're in luck," and rolled them around to drain on the rack. Then he rolled each into a bun, and pointed to the condiments. "What would you like?"

Jase considered and pointed. "Lemme get the dark chili mustard, onions, relish and banana peppers."

The man didn't stint on the toppings. Each boat-shaped bun was overflowing.

They paid him in scrip he could exchange later. It was supposed to cut down on black marketing, but Jandro had heard of so many ways around it. He wasn't really interested in scamming stuff, but it wasn't hard.

He pointed to a bench under another tree. It was made of wooden timbers locally, not extruded.

"I was on Mtali for a while, too, when I was just out of training," he said.

Behind them, the man closed his cart, unfolded the seat and drove off. It was a fueled vehicle, not electric.

"Oh?" Jase asked.

"That was much worse than this place. Here they're opportunistic. There, they were crooked."

"How crooked?" Jase asked.

"We had to open every package, test every delivery, and no local help at all. They'd steal it in front of you, toss it over the fence to a buddy, and insist they never saw it."

"Hah. Lameo."

"Very. It was pathetic. These people are creative at least." And scary. He'd swap that for incompetently dishonest any time.

"The food looks good."

Jase squeezed and stuffed the bread around the contents, angled his face and got a bite. He chewed for a moment, and flared his eyebrows.

"Damn. If all dead animal tastes like this, I could be a convert."

"Hah. Just don't say that around the cultural officers."

"Oh, hell no. But it's different from vat raised. Stronger tasting? Something. Good stuff."

The cheddar brat was good as always, and he tried not to think about dead pig. On the other hand, he'd seen pigs up close. They were pretty nasty creatures.

Jase took another bite and made it disappear.

"Is stuff like this why people stay in? Seeing all parts of the universe?"

"All parts we know about. It does cost a veinful to travel. We get to see the bombed-out ruins. Chicks in New York and Beijing and Nairobi pay good money for that."

He munched the brat. Yes, once you got used to the ugly fact of a dead living being, rather than one raised in a vatory with no head, they were tasty. Did the animal's emotions and life flavor the meat? That was a bit creepy, and bit taboo.

He bit something hard. There was something in it, probably a bit of bone. He worked it around and pulled it out with his fingers. It was gray. He wiped it on the boards and kept chewing.

There was another.

"Damn, they need a better butcher. I'm getting bone bits."

Jase took another bite and twitched, then pulled back with a confused look.

"What the . . ." He reached into the bun, grabbed something and pulled it out. It was a long, gray piece of polymer. It took a moment to recognize it, and then it was instantaneous.

It was a shredded dogtag, and it had been inside a sausage. That meant . . .

Jase screamed through the entire audio spectrum, then he vomited a meter, gushing and squealing and choking and trying for more.

A moment later it hit Jandro, and he puked and puked and kept puking. He realized he'd blacked out, and was leaning over the table. Then he heaved again It felt as if he'd emptied his entire tract, and he hoped he had.

Someone nearby asked, "What's wrong, are you alright?"

"Water!" he demanded. "Ohdioswater!"

A bottle was placed in his hand. He cracked the seal, rinsed, spat, rinsed, spat, gargled, and kept going.

Everything blurred out as two people helped him walk to the clinic. There were MPs around, and camera drones. Someone handed him two pills and another bottle of water, and he tried to swallow them, but spat the water out. The pills went with it.

He didn't want to swallow anything.

Someone waved an inhaler under his nose and he passed out.

He woke up in a bed, wrapped in a sheet, and a South Asian woman in casuals sat next to him. The lights were at half. He could tell that he was medicated.

"How are you doing, Alejandro?"

"I feel ill," he said. Very ill. He'd eaten . . . Oh, god.

"I'm Doctor Ramjit from Emotional Health and Wellness. You're safe here."

"I know. I'm just . . . it was awful. Jase pulled out that tag . . ."

"What do you think it was?"

"A shredded dogtag."

"The investigators say they're not sure of that."

He sat up and shouted, "*It was a maldito dogtag!*" As she recoiled, he added, "Ma'am." If he wasn't careful, he'd wind up in some long-term facility.

She reached out and offered a hand. He took it and clutched at it.

She said, "It may have been. If so, it may have been a prank."

"I hope so." Yes, that was entirely likely. Like stripping

the General, or the doped sodajuice one time. The locals wanted to find ways to screw with the troops. He hoped that was it.

"Did they get the vendor?"

She hesitated a moment.

"No, and he's not responding to contact."

"I feel okay otherwise. How long am I here?"

"When you feel fit you can leave. We will do trace analysis on the regurgitate. We'll let you know what we find."

He wasn't sure they would. If they said it was clean, would he believe them?

"Can I get something for the stress?"

"Yes. I've prescribed some tranquilizer patches. You're welcome to come talk to us any time, or the chaplains. You're on quarters for tomorrow so you can de-stress."

"Thank you," he said.

He gave it a few minutes, decided he could walk, and signed out. He made his way back to the dorm, and slipped inside.

Jase's room was dark, but the door was open.

"Jase?"

"Yeah."

"How are you?"

"Sick."

The man didn't want to talk more than that.

He went to bed, and the tranquilizer did help him sleep. He woke up twice, hungry, but shook in terror at the thought of food.

He was still awake on and off, and a glance at the wall

said it was 0500. The chow hall was open, and he was hungry. He'd slept in casuals, so he wore those down.

He walked into the dining hall, and walked right back out. They had sausage in there, and pans of other meat. He couldn't do it.

He went to the dispenser in the rec room and swiped his hand. He went to select a bag of vegetable chips, and his hand froze. They were local, too.

Perhaps he wasn't hungry yet.

Two hours later he was back in the clinic.

Doctor Ramjit saw him at once.

"Please tell me," he said. "I have to know what you found."

"The sausage contained human flesh," she said evenly.

He'd known it would be bad news, because he couldn't have trusted the good. He closed his eyes and felt dizzy, as if spinning.

"It was only a trace amount," she said. "Probably a piece of muscle tissue. The identag was deliberately placed to draw attention to it. It was intended to be morally horrifying, and it was."

It was intended to be morally horrifying. What she didn't seem to grasp is that it really was, and what that implied. The troops knew what had happened, and everyone had been eating local food for months. There was no way to be sure how much of it was contaminated with their buddies, and there was no way to be sure how much wasn't.

It was worse than that.

That was the moment Jandro knew there was no line the rebels wouldn't cross. They'd spent a year and a half escalating the moral outrage, humiliation and fear. The executions of the MPs, and this, had been a message.

We will hunt you down relentlessly, remorselessly, tirelessly. Regardless of your power and the damage you inflict, we will violate the sanctity of your mind. We will make you question reality and yourselves. And we will never stop.

He wanted to go home. There was nothing here but hatred, no one to be liberated, no one to be brought into line with modern thought. They were atavists and savages who could not be reasoned with.

The UN Forces alliance had come here to save them from rampant repression. He'd seen some of the poor in images from patrols. Out of the city only a few kilometers, some people lived in shacks without power or plumbing, because it was cheap. No one should be forced to make that "choice." There wasn't even a right to due process. That had to be paid for in cash, in an annual tax that they insisted on calling a "resident's fee," even though it was a tax. Fail to pay, and you had no status.

Yet, when the Forces arrived to help them, dirt poor and super rich alike homogenized into one people, intent only on fighting them.

"Whose tag was it?" he asked.

She blushed and stammered.

"I don't have that information."

"You do," he said. "It was a real person's tag, wasn't it?"

"It was," she nodded, looking queasy herself.

"Who?"

"Binyamin Al-Jabr. The first MP shot at the gate."

His head spun again.

"That's not for release," she said. "At all. But I'd rather you had the truth than a rumor."

It was orchestrated terror. They'd shot the man and taken his body. They'd shot everyone who replaced him in the last three months. The MPs were near rioting in terror. Then they'd chopped him, or parts of him, up and fed them to Jase and Jandro.

He really didn't want to know what part of the body they'd used. Nor how many batches they'd made.

"I can't eat," he said, and erupted in tears. His lips trembled as he mouthed, "I have to go home."

"I will arrange it," she said. "I've documented both emotional trauma and post-event trauma. We'll get you home. We've got other people distressed as a result, though of course, none had the direct experience you and Senior Corporal Jardine did."

"I can't eat," he said again. "Please hurry."

Doctor Ramjit seemed compassionate, but someone in the chain didn't believe him. A sergeant from Commissary took him over to the kitchen, to watch the food being prepared. It arrived in ground and cut form, and he watched a steak go from freezer to grill. He could smell it, too, dead meat. But the cooks were all contracted locally, brought in every morning and searched. A couple of them stared at him, then there were a couple of giggles.

"Didn't you see that?"

"See what?" his escort asked.

"They're laughing at me."

"It's fresh steak. Or you can choose a vegetarian option." Though the man looked unsure himself. He kept glancing furtively at Jandro, and at the cooks.

"I . . ." He had no ability to trust them.

The smell caught him. Somewhere there was pork, and he remembered bratwurst, and there it was again. He ran from the kitchen.

They took him back to the clinic and dosed him again. He felt needles, and they said something he didn't follow.

He almost limped, almost staggered back to the dorm, escorted by a medic. He carried a case of Earth-sourced field rations. He had that, and sealed bottles of expensive, imported spring water. That would have to suffice until he left.

Jase wasn't there. He was probably at the clinic, too. He might even be worse off, since he'd gotten the whole dogtag.

That set him reeling again, and he quickly brought up some landscape images from Iguaçu National Park.

Two hours later he stared at the open packets before him. He'd even placed them on a plate and microheated them, so they'd look more like real food.

He couldn't.

He knew it was perfectly safe, packaged on Earth, and was real food, but he couldn't.

Maybe in a day or two.

The door chimed and opened, and Sergeant Second Class Andreo Romero walked in quietly.

"Hey, Jandro."

"Hola."

"Jase is in the Emotional Health Ward. They reassigned me here."

On the one hand, he needed company. On the other, he knew a suicide watch when he saw one.

"How is he doing?"

"Not good. Homb, they officially haven't said anything, but there were witnesses. Everyone knows what happened."

"Did they find the vendor yet?"

"No one knows where he is."

"Not even the other sellers?"

"They say they've never heard of him. They're also gone. No more local carts. All food is going to process through the dining hall now, for safety."

It might well be. But Jandro couldn't eat it. He pushed back from the table and left the food there.

"Is Jase coming back?" he asked.

Andreo shook his head. "No, he's pretty much sedated and prioritied to return home. He took it pretty hard."

"I took it pretty hard."

There was awkward silence for several moments.

"Well, if you need anything, I'm here. They say you're on extended quarters until tomorrow, then you're on days."

"Days" didn't really mean much here, since each shift would be four-plus hours out of sync with the local clock. It was a gesture, though.

Andreo said, "The cooks are all going to be offworld contractors, too. Pricey. We put in a RFQ already, and have some interim workers from BuState and elsewhere. The chow hall is going to be substandard for a while, but that's better than . . ." He faded off, and shivered.

Jandro nodded. Lots of people had eaten from the local vendors.

Andreo asked, "Can I finish that ration if you're not going to?"

"Sure."

At least someone could eat it.

That local night, another MP was shot. Officially they were told counterfire had demolished the sniper's hide, along with a chunk of that building, but he didn't think it would matter.

He twitched all night, between wakefulness and dozing. The next morning, he was ravenous. He opened another field ration, and managed two bites before nausea caused him to curl up.

It's from Earth. It's vatory-raised chicken. There's eggs and vegetables. It's guaranteed safe.

Maybe lunch.

He walked into the Logistics compound, into the bay, and got greeted.

"Hey, Jandro. Good to see you back."

"Danke," he said. Johann Meffert was German.

He had materiel to process. Three huge cargotainers sat in the bay, pending sort. This shipment was ammunition, spare parts, tools, generators and nuclear powerpacks for them. He had units and their transport chains on cue, with quantities needed. Those always exceeded quantity available. He broke them down by percentage, then applied the urgency codes to adjust the amounts. Once the captain signed off, the loader operators would dispense it to be tied down and depart for the forward bases.

He ignored Meffert's periodic stares. Everyone was doing it.

"Ready for review, Captain," he said into his mic.

He sat back and stretched for a moment. It did feel good to do something productive.

"Looks good so far, Jandro. But those KPAKs need sorted, too."

He looked at his screen. He'd missed four pallets of field rations.

"It's not my fault!" he shouted at the bay. "I didn't plan to eat him, I didn't want to eat him, and I didn't put him in the food!"

He stood up and walked out, back to the clinic.

"You really must try to eat something," Doctor Ramjit said. "Vegetables should be fine. I've switched to that myself. It's perfectly understandable that you don't trust the meat."

He sat in a reclined chair, surrounded by trickling fountains, soft images, and with a therapy dog for company. It responded to his scratches with a thumping tail.

"They're from on planet," he said. Had they urinated on the plants? Grown them in poison? Fertilized the ground with dead troops?

"How are you managing with field rations?" she asked.

"Better," he said. "I've eaten part of one."

Her frown was earnest. "That's not enough for three days. You've already lost weight."

"I know," he said. "But I can't. I just . . . can't." He hoped she understood.

"It's not just the food," he continued. "It's this place. All of it. I can't be around people like this. The cooks were giggling. Our people stare at me. They get the gossip.

They all know. Jase has already gone. Please send me, too."

"I'll try," she said. Her frown came across as pitying. He didn't want that, either.

He untangled from the chair and dog and left in silence, though she said, "Good luck, Alejandro. You have our wishes."

As he entered his room, his phone pinged a message. He swiped it.

"Alejandro, you are scheduled to depart in fifteen days. The clinic will fit you with a nutrient IV to help you in the interim."

"Yes," he said to the Marine. "I'm a casualty."

"Good luck with it, then. I'm sorry, at first I'd figured you were a base monkey. They don't know what the point is like."

"No, most of them don't," he agreed. He looked around at the other people on the rotation. Some were military, some UN bureau staff, some contractors. They might know what had happened, but they had no idea what it felt like. Thankfully, none of them recognized him.

The Marine said, "But I saw that," pointing at the IV. "I hope you're recovering?"

"Yes. It shouldn't take long. Good luck with the leg."

"Thanks. They say three months."

He boarded the ship and found his launch couch. The shuttle was well-used, smelling of people, disinfectant and musty military bags. He settled in and closed his eyes, not wanting to talk to anyone. They bantered and joked and sounded cheerful to be leaving. He wasn't cheerful, only relieved.

When they sealed up, pressure increased to Earth normal. He breathed deeply.

The acceleration and engine roar took a faint edge off his nerves. Soon. Off this nightmarish hellhole and home.

The tranqs worked. He had a scrip for more, and a note that said he should not be questioned about them. Doctor Ramjit had said that wasn't unusual for some of the Special Unit troops, and even some of the infantry. "The ship infirmary should be able to refill you without problems," she'd said. "Especially as we've put out a bulletin about personnel generally suffering stress disorders. We haven't said why."

They even helped with launch sickness. He felt blissfully fine, not nauseous.

He zoned through nothing until the intercom interrupted him.

"Passengers, we are in orbit, and will dock directly with the *Wabash*. Departure for Earth will be only a couple of hours. Final loading is taking place now."

Good. He eyed the tube on his arm. He could have them unplug this, and he could eat real, solid food from safe, quality-inspected producers on Earth.

Well, he'd have to start with baby food. Fifteen days of the tube had wiped out his GI tract. He'd have to rebuild it. That would be fine. And he'd never touch a sausage again.

He unlatched when the screen said to, and waited impatiently. He wasn't bad in emgee, knowing how to drag himself along the couches and guide cable. Several passengers didn't seem to know how, and some of them were even military.

Shortly, he was in the gangtube, creeping along behind the Marine and a couple of contractors rotating out.

There was a small port to his right, looking aft along the length of the ship. He looked out and saw the open framework of an orbital supply shuttle detach a cargotainer from the ship's cargo lock, rotate and attach another in its place.

He flinched, and nausea and dizziness poured into him again.

The cargotainer was marked "Hughes Commissary Services, Jefferson, Freehold of Grainne."

He fumbled with his kit, slapped three patches on his arm, and almost bit his tongue off holding back a scream.

End

STARHOME

Micronations have fascinated me for a long time. The world really doesn't like independence, and the inherent nature of government is to find predictable consistency. A plurality or even a majority of political figures believe they know what's best for everyone, if only we'd do as they say.

I've actually formed a hypothesis on this. Typically, national leaders are brighter than average, but not so bright they can't connect and communicate with average people. Bona fide geniuses find this hard to do, because they do see the larger picture and get frustrated by those who don't.

However, the ones who are smart enough to lead, but not smart enough to see second-, third-, or even fourth-order effects often equate themselves to the real geniuses, failing to grasp the actual shape of that bell curve.

And so they cause at least as many problems as they solve.

The only solution from that point of view is consistency. If there is no dissent, the problems go away.

Politicians often manufacture mythical bogeymen to draw attention away from the fact they're not actually doing anything about the real problems, and to scare the populace into giving them more authority.

Back to micronations: Quite a few present-day ones handle banking of questionable assets, offer tax shelters, and . . . flexible . . . legal platforms. Some of their clients are criminal enterprises, but others are people or groups who wish to avoid the above games, be left alone to pursue their futures, and not be pigeonholed.

This is one of the running threads in the Freehold universe, but it works at different levels . . .

⊕

ONE DIDN'T have to be involved in a war to suffer, nor even in line of fire. Collateral economic damage could destroy just as easily.

First Minister Jackson Bates looked over the smallest nation in space. From the window of his tower, he could view the entire territory of Starhome up above him. Centrifugal gravity meant the planetoid was "up," but he was used to it. It was a rock roughly a kilometer in diameter, tunneled through for habitat space, with its rotation adjusted to provide centrifugal G.

The window was part of a structure that had once been Jump Point Control for Earth's JP1. As orbits and jumplines shifted, and as technology advanced relentlessly on, it became cost-ineffective to use the station, and it was too small and antiquated for modern shipping. A new one was built, and this one "abandoned to space."

When the UNPF made that final assignation, his grandfather took a small ship with just enough supplies to let him occupy and declare it private territory. The tower became the family home and offices, and the control center for their business.

Agencies on Earth panicked, and there'd actually been a threat of military occupation. The UN courts had ruled the abandonment made it salvage, and the Bates' occupation was that salvage. The family owned a hollowed-out planetoid of passages and compartments, and could do with it as they wished.

At once, the bureaus of Earth protested. BuSpace, BuMil, BuCommerce all took their shots. If they hadn't been so busy fighting each other, they'd have wiped out Starhome a century ago.

The family's entire livelihood was fringe, marginal and unglamorous. Actual smuggling would have made them a valid threat to be attacked. They were information brokers, dealing with untraceable data that was useful to someone, encoded heavily and carried through the jump point directly. Eventually, legitimate cargo transshipment began, since their docking rates were cheaper, just enough for the additional flight time to be offset for certain classes of ship. Tramp freighters came by, and finally a couple of fleets contracted gate space.

All of which had evaporated when Earth's war with the Freehold of Grainne started. The UN bit down hard on tramp freighters, anything with a Freehold registry, and then started more in-depth monitoring of every jump point it could access directly or by treaty.

The last ship had docked a month before. Little was

moving, and what was tended toward huge corporate ships who wouldn't waste time on Starhome. What were docking fees to them?

For now, Starhome had food and oxygen. When it ran low, they'd be forced to pay for direct delivery at extreme cost, or ultimately abandon the station and return to Earth. There'd already been inquiries from the UNPF to that effect, offering "rescue."

Jackson Bates wasn't going to do that. He might go as far as Jupiter's moons. He wouldn't step foot on Earth again if he could avoid it.

His phone chimed.

"Yes?" he answered. All forty-three staff and family knew who he was.

Engineer Paul Rofert said, "Sir, if you're not busy, I need to show you something at the dock tube."

"On my way," he said.

Starhome's docking system was a long gangtube with docking locks protruding. It was axial by design, so ships had to be balanced with each other or counterweights. In practice it was "mostly" axial. Over a couple of centuries, drift happened. That was a known issue, and he hoped that wasn't the problem now.

It took three minutes to run a trolley car down the tower, to the axis, and along it. He knew every centimeter of the route, every passage and compartment. Those had once been quarters for visiting VIPs, when just visiting a station was novel. That had been rec space, and still was, officially. There weren't enough people to make proper use of the gym, so some of the equipment had been relocated over there, to what was once commo gear for jump control. Everything a century or more out of date was aging in either vacuum or atmosphere and quaint at best. But, it was his home. Apart from four years in college in Georgia, this was the only place he'd ever lived. There was room enough for hundreds.

Rofert was waiting at the hub before the dock tube, which was still empty. Jackson's executive, Nicol Cante, was with him. He unstrapped from the car and shoved over in the near-zero G to give her more room.

"Chief," Jackson greeted and shook hands. Paul Rofert was tall, black with gray hair, and had worked for the family for three generations. He knew every bolt and fissure in the place.

"Sir," Rofert said with a nod and a firm shake back. "I hate to deliver more bad news, but . . ."

"Go ahead." It wasn't as if things could get much worse.

"The axis drift is worse than we'd anticipated. It has precessed enough the tube can't be considered axial anymore. We'll need to adjust rotation."

"Can our attitude jets do it?"

"No, we'll need external mounts and a lot of delta V over several days to avoid lateral stresses. And it has to be done soon or feedback oscillations will rip the dock apart."

"Then I guess we're out of business," he replied. He was surprised at how easily he said it. Apparently, he'd known the outcome and just been waiting for the cue. "We can't afford that."

Rofert said, "Sorry, sir."

He sighed. He was glad his father wasn't here to see that. They'd lasted two generations as an Independent Territory. Now they were done.

"I'm Jackson to you, Paul. We're friends even when the news is bad." He continued, "My personal craft can take twenty if we have to use it. That will be the last one out. See what transport you can arrange, Nicol. Call Space Guard if you must, but I'd prefer we leave with dignity."

She swiped at her notepad. "On it, Boss. When should we plan for evacuation?"

"Part of me wants to get it over with, and part wants to hold out until the bitter end. Use your judgment."

"Got it."

Her judgment was exceptional. She had degrees in physics and finance. She'd offer him a grid of windows, costs and movements and guide him through the decision. That ability was why he'd hired her. No doubt she'd find other employment, but he felt he was cheating her by asking her to plan her own evacuation.

He'd sounded depressed and defeated. She'd been calm and solid.

Nicol's suggested schedule meant they'd start leaving in a week. There was one in-system charter willing to haul most of the staff at that time, and that would clean out much of the available credit. They were that deep in the hole. The command staff would go with him, as would a Demolition Crew, who'd strip cables, metals, food, anything aboard that could be salvaged. It would either go aboard, or in a planned orbit. Mass and material were commodities in space. At least with that and the proceeds from selling his boat he'd be able to reestablish on Titan, or if he had to, on Earth, somewhere reasonably still free. Chile, perhaps. Sulawan. New Doggerland.

He still wouldn't be in space then, though, nor independent.

Nothing had docked this week, either. Nothing was going to, even if they could have. The dock and davits were silent, the workers helping tear out non-essential materials for recovery. What had been the old gym was now a pile of iron and aluminum for reuse, for the little value it held. The hatches were sealed, the oxygen recovered to stretch what was used in the working space.

His phone chimed, breaking his musing and his mood.

"What?" he answered.

"Inbound vessel, sir. Very stealthy. And it came from out and forward, not from the point."

He realized it was astrogator Marie Duval in Docking Control. His estranged daughter in law by the son of his estranged wife. His wife and son were both back on Earth, just not the type for space. Marie had stayed.

A vessel? Not from the point?

"Human?" he asked as he started swimming that way, grabbing a loop on the cable that wound endlessly between hub and DC, as a cheap elevator.

She said, "Yes, it seems to be. Forceline propulsion, but tiny."

"Phase drive for interstellar, then?"

She replied, "No indication of that, no."

"I'm on my way across," he said. Centrifugal G increased as he was pulled outward.

He needed to see it. He worried without a conclusion until he arrived, pulled himself through the hatch, and looked at the monitors.

There it was, tiny and dark.

Marie said, "I tightbeamed them, sir. No response. Should I try laser?"

"Go ahead. How far are they?"

"Six light-seconds. We saw them about six and a half."

That was close. No one had seen them until now?

A minute later she said, "Laser response, sir."

The audio said, "We are a private ship, offering trade."

Jackson responded with, "Approaching ship, be aware our docking facilities are compromised and unsafe. You cannot dock directly. Who are you and what are you offering?"

"We will avoid the dock tube. Please stand by for our arrival."

He shrugged. "Well, they're human, and talking. I can't imagine anyone wants to hijack this place."

Duval said, "That is a warship, though, sir."

"Based on the stealth?"

She nodded. "Yes, sir. It's stealthed stupid. No one tries to stay hidden in space without a reason."

"You're correct, but we can't do much. Prepare to zip a request to Space Guard if we have to."

"It's already queued, sir. The ship will be here in under an hour. Space Guard is at least four hours away after we call."

"Understood. I'll wait here for any updates." They could call him, but he wanted to show his support, and it would be faster if he could see screens directly. He made himself some coffee and found the cookie stash. The chairs were good, this being one of the few places with decent G levels. They were half a century old, repaired multiple times to avoid excess costs.

It was definitely a human ship, and it maneuvered in slowly. It had to have been en route at low thrust for a long time, or the energy signature would have shown.

It had no markings, no IFF. Active radar and other scans showed almost nothing, just bare ghosts. It was a hole in space as far as sensors were concerned.

It moved in almost to contact, then opened a hatch, deployed a line, and tethered to the base of the dock assembly. Three figures came out in V-suits, entered the maintenance lock and cycled through.

Jackson and Nicol had time to get placed to greet whoever it was, and four security personnel stood at angles with shotguns. "Stood" in near zero G by hooking to stanchions. It didn't seem there'd be need, but there was no proof there wouldn't be.

It was cold in the terminal. There was no reason to heat it, with no ships inbound.

The lock unlatched and swung. The three inside were youngish, fit, definitely human, and unarmed. They doffed helmets.

The woman in front said, "Greetings. First Minister Bates? I'm pleased to meet you and apologize for the circumstances. I'm Doctor Hazel Donahey. This is Doctor Andrew Tyson and Assistant True Hively."

"Doctor," he agreed and shook hands. "This is my executive, Doctor Nicol Cante." If they were going to use titles, so was he.

He asked, "What can I do for you?"

Doctor Donahey said, "We need a research base for stellar and deep space observations. You have a habitat that's unfortunately rather quiet, but that suits our needs."

She didn't look threatening, and certainly could be an academic. Space-short hair, no jewelry, no wasted movement.

He wanted to accuse them of being vultures, but he didn't have a great bargaining position.

He said, "It is quiet, and I wish it wasn't. I regret that I don't even have functional facilities anymore."

Donahey said, "Our budget isn't large, but is under-written, and we can provide a certain amount of oxygen, food and power beyond our own needs. We'll also have available people with technical training to assist in overhaul."

So what did they want?

"You said you need observations?" He gestured for them to follow. There was no imminent threat, and there were frames at the edge of the bay.

She spoke as they pulled themselves along. "Yes. Sol is unique in many ways, including the still-elusive intelligent life. There are several competing theories on its stellar development. Then, drive research is notably concerned with terminal effects around jump points. The deep space, but still heliospace is critical, and again, this is a very convenient place to operate from."

Nicol asked, "Why not just use a leased liner? And who do you represent?" She draped across a frame with the casual sprawl of someone who had spent years in space.

"Liners have tremendous operating costs. We're from Brandt's research arm. We are strictly private."

He said, "And we're supposed to overlook that Brandt is based in Grainne, the UN has occupied your system, and you're magically here near a jump point for 'observations'?"

Donahey shrugged and tucked into the frame, as did her assistants. "Science is about knowledge, sir. This is a project we've worked on for a long time. I can make the data files available if you wish. We were using a remote site in Salin, but there's a significant difference in stellar environments between a K Three and a G Two star."

He hung from one stanchion, just to have some sort of base. He noted Nicol wasn't in the same orientation as the rest. She liked to get angled views on things to spot discrepancies.

On the one hand he wanted to believe them. On the other, they had a stealth ship, probably military. On the other, he really owed nothing to Earth at this point. They'd tried everything they could to kill his family's dream. On the other, there was a difference between not owing Earth and assisting possible espionage. On yet another hand, he needed operating cash even if he was shutting down, and the food and oxy they promised would close out two costs on his accounts.

"Let's go to my office," he said.

They were experienced spacers. They followed easily in low and no G. Everyone was quiet on the trolley, and he was embarrassed at the worn, out-of-date seating. He was glad to get to his office. That wasn't more than a decade out of date, and it had enough G.

He offered his restroom so they could change into shipsuits and shlippers instead of V-suits and grips.

When they came back in coveralls, he asked, "May I get you anything? Hard or soft."

"Hot tea with lemon would be very nice," Doctor Donahey said.

"Two."

"Three, please."

He nodded. Even a short EVA could be cold out here. The terminal wasn't kept warm anymore either, relying on waste heat from equipment to heat it and now the equipment wasn't in use.

"Tea all around, and drinks later, please, Frank," he said to his grandson, the Factotum On Duty. That was a fancy title for "gopher." Though they did more than just gophering.

His title of First Minister was a fancy way of saying, "owner." It just gave a political spin. In reality, his leadership was smaller than any but the tiniest rural villages on Earth. But the volume of nothing he commanded . . .

"You do understand I'm nervous, with the war on," he said.

Donahey said, "Understandable. If you prefer, we can negotiate with Earth and occupy after you leave. The only problem is it would take several months to get approval, but since we're a recognized research institute, they'd eventually consent. And of course, you wouldn't be benefiting."

Yeah, there was that. Everyone had plans for the station, when he finally left. It made him stubborn.

Frank brought back the tea, and he took the moment it was being served to signal to Nicol, who asked, "So what do you think of Carnahan's hypothesis on jump point eddy currents during the reset phase?"

Donahey said, "That's more Andy's area."

Andrew Tyson said, "Bluntly, the man's deluding

himself. Those currents occurred twice, during a specific combination of ship and point, and similar but far smaller effects were identified with the same class ship in an earlier generation of the same point mechanism. It's purely an artifact of circumstance, not a general effect. But that is the sort of thing we want to test."

Nicol nodded and asked, "What was the Delta X on that ship?"

"Well, it was forceline propulsion, so the Delta X was almost entirely within the hull. Induction field harmonics are more important, and it was under a k-value of six."

"Fair enough," Nicol said. "So you at least understand physics. Would you mind if I observed your findings?"

"By all means," Donahey said. "We'd want an NDA for discretion, but you're quite welcome to observe the process."

Jackson caught her signal back.

So, they were legitimate, just here in odd circumstances.

"What do you need and what specifically are you offering?"

She said, "We'd need lodging for ourselves—there are twelve—and boat crews as they come through. We'd need access to two divergent points—the end of the dock assembly, and the antipodean point on the outside. We'll be occasionally pulling a lot of power from your reactor. We'll make up the mass."

"And what do we get?"

"Oxygen, food, fuel, metals and organics. Everything a small habitat needs, since we need it functional too. We assumed occupancy and support for a hundred."

Jackson thought about asking for money, too, but that really was a generous offer. It was twice current crewing level, so should last a bit. He hated being forced to take it, though.

"Our docking gantry is no longer axial, and in danger of catastrophic failure from oscillations," he admitted.

The three looked at each other and seemed to swap expressions.

True Hively said, "I should be able to coordinate that. It's a significant amount of reaction mass and maneuvering engine, though."

Donahey said, "We'd consider that our top offer."

Really, it was fair, in that Starhome would remain functional for as long as this took, and docking facilities would be back online.

It wasn't fair in that it only prolonged the inevitable.

Since he'd be returning to Earth's economy even on Titan, and taxed again, he wondered what kind of write off he could get for donating the rock to them.

"How long is the project?"

Donahey said, "Our current funding allows seventeen months."

"Deal," he said.

It gave everyone seventeen more months of employment and distance from Earth. He'd have to keep paying them from shrinking capital, but he wouldn't have to turn them out.

Donahey said, "Then we'll return to our ship, and arrange to move into your ante section, as you called it. Thank you very much for your hospitality. And you, Doctor Cante."

Right after the visitors were escorted out, he got notice of an incoming transmission from Space Guard. It was an offer to evacuate his people now, pending acceptance of . . .

"Nicol, do we have some sort of demand from the UN?"

"It just came in," she said. "Apparently these idiots can't even coordinate their own memos."

"What is it?"

"It's a salvage price offer to buy you out and relocate us."

"Bastards."

He took a moment to calm himself, and said, "I wonder if Prescot will pick up my request. It seems like the scavengers aren't even waiting for us to die."

The scientists and crew started moving stuff at once. They had supplies for themselves, crates of technical gear. They took accommodations in the other privately owned lodging Starhome had already sealed off, and brought it back online themselves. Their ship transferred reactor fuel cells.

They double sealed the passages to that section by physically locking airtight hatches. They requested no one approach the ante pole during outside maintenance, either.

"We can do that for you," True Hively said. "Our sensors are easily disrupted."

A week later, a freighter arrived with cargo pods of oxygen, food and attitude engines. It was good to look out his office ports and see a ship again. Even only one ship.

It approached in a long arc to dockside only, which was costly in fuel.

"I don't like it," Nicol said.

Jackson said, "It's all from Govannon, and all properly marked. Legitimately purchased."

"Yes, and I suppose they may have phase drive to explain how they came in the back way. You haven't asked about that."

"I haven't," he agreed. "I wanted to see if the deal was real, and if it would help. We have a year and a half to hope things turn around, or to withdraw in stages."

She said, "I'm still bothered by a heavily stealthed boat from deep space, and the lack of advance notice. So is Marie. They really don't want to be seen."

"Their credentials checked out with Brandt, didn't they?"

"They did," she admitted. "Then I messaged my friend Travis in R&D over there. He's never heard of them. Corporate says they're legit. Operations isn't aware."

"I suppose it was classified research."

She said, "And if so, it was for Grainne . . . who we are now at war with."

"We are? Earth is. We're neutral."

She said, firmly, "Boss, neutral status goes away if you aid a hostile power."

"Have they done anything illicit?"

"No. They really are making solar observations, but you realize they could be tracking ships, habitats, commo and anything else as well, right? They're in-system, with shaky credentials and sensors that can image fireflies in Iowa from here."

Jackson was enjoying really good French bread, baked by his staff using wheat that came in aboard the researchers' supply ship.

He checked off points. "Grainne's jump point with Earth is down. No one is going to let them jump warships around. They had phase drive of course, since Brandt is located there, but only a few ships. They can't stage an attack here, they no longer exist as an independent system. Even if these people are spying, it's not going to do any good."

Nicol said, "I more wonder if they contracted to NovRos or even the Prescots. The UN is building infrastructure everywhere against other independence movements. The Colonial Alliance can't do anything the UN doesn't want to allow. It's more likely corporate or political espionage than military."

"Exactly."

She said, "Either way, we'd still wind up in jail for life for helping. Even if they've locked us out of our own habitat, we can't claim we didn't know."

"Do you want out?" he asked. This was important.

She shook her head. "No, Boss, I'll stay. I'm curious. I just wanted to make sure you realized the risks."

"Always," he said.

She said, "At least I have work again, monitoring our guests. They pass down the axis daily and are making observations. I'd sure like to see their other end, though."

"Have they furnished the data for you to review?" he asked.

"They have. It's too detailed and esoteric for my skillset, but looks real, and even if I understood it, I'm holding with the NDA unless it's relevant to our safety."

"Well done, thank you."

He couldn't run the place without her.

The next ship was a week later, with more supplies and more personnel. They graciously offered other upgrades, those sponsored by Prescot Deep Space in Govannon. It irritated Jackson more. Prescot had refused a previous deal, hadn't responded to his new one, but were willing to send stuff if someone else paid for it. That defined his status.

The station rumbled with the low hum of reaction engines nudging it back into alignment, with a promise that the docks could reopen in less than two weeks. Assuming, of course, there were any other ships.

Doctor Donahey visited his office every two or three days. She was on the schedule for today.

"Good morning, Jackson," she said on arriving. He'd been clear he was not "Sir" or "First Minister."

"Good morning, Hazel." He pointed to the tea.

"Thank you," she said and took a cup. "I just came back from the sensors at the end of the docking tube, and checked with True on my way. Did you see your terminal should be online next week?"

"I did," he said. "I appreciate it greatly, even if we never get to use it. At least we won't be abandoning the place."

"I like it," she said. "It's old, but has character. Have you thought of asking Prescot if they could use it?"

"I have. They're not interested."

"That's odd," she said. "I thought they'd find it useful, especially as they built it originally."

She seemed bothered.

He asked, "Can you tell me about your project? I'm an educated layman."

She took a deep breath and said, "Well, we're working on several things. In my case, we're watching the chromosphere currents and variable fluctuations of the Sun, and running hefty simulations backward on how it was at the time life first evolved, and the varying radiation there would have been. That's to see if any of it might be significant to stages of the evolution of life. So far, we've found lots of habitable planets to terraform, a handful with their own life, and few that have any advanced organisms. Any number of factors could affect it. So I'm a physicist, dealing with life scientists. Mine is all 'how?', theirs is all 'what if?'"

"What cycles are you tracking?" he asked, and had some tea. That was an expensive import here, too.

"Milankovitch, Rujuwa, the neutrino flux variation, among others."

"Interesting. Are you religious at all, Hazel?"

She shook her head. "Not at all, but I would enjoy exploring outside influence on it all, if there was any way to determine its existence. Are you?"

"No, but I often wonder."

"That seems to be human nature—and how the supernatural came to be created. Humans recognized a pattern, couldn't find a reason for it, so created one."

"How is Andy doing on his projects?"

"He has a lot of people building processors and setting sensors. Still. What he's looking for is very subtle, and it's annoying having to work around it. That's why we sealed the entire ante third of the station."

He said, "Yeah, I signed off on that, after a lengthy tour. As much as I want to help, being locked out of my own home is a tough call." He also had Paul using an abandoned conduit to check on them. The engineer reported everything to be good.

She replied, "It affects my observations, too, but even though I'm nominally in charge, both Prescot and Brandt want his data. So I have to make do."

"What do I need to know about anything upcoming?" he asked.

"Well, once you can operate again, Andy has a clear zone we really need kept free of trajectories, if you can manage it at all. He's very firm on this, but of course, it's your station. Keeping in mind if his team pulls out we have to renegotiate our terms." She seemed embarrassed. "There's another large pod train coming in with additional gear, stocks for you, and a few more personnel."

"Understood. As long as Operations has it, I have no problem. It's not as if it's an astrogation hazard. One other question, if I may."

"Go ahead."

"Why did you arrive in what's essentially a stealth military vessel from deep space?"

She made a face.

"Andy's work, again. They were explicit that we not disrupt space any more than necessary so we could get a clean baseline for examining forcelines and other structures. We were towed around by a tug, and he made them detach further out than I was comfortable with. The boat is secured against as much leakage as possible. It's basically the equivalent of a clean room.

You notice the supply vessels only come in from the docking pole vector."

"So am I even going to be able to resume docking ops, then?"

She looked really embarrassed.

"Yes. Andy will be very unhappy, but at that point, he has to make do. We've accommodated him as much as we can. That decision's up to me, and that's why I'm in charge even though his research has priority."

"Administration and politics," he said, feeling empathy for her.

"Exactly. Thanks for the tea. Shall I check in on Friday?"

"That should be fine."

He didn't bring up that Brandt wasn't clear on their status. He'd save that a bit longer.

After she left, he called Rofert.

"I have a favor for next week," he said.

"Yes, Boss?"

"Can one of your inspection tugs make an orbit around the station?"

"Not an orbit per se, in any reasonable time, but we have enough juice in one to pull a loop, yes."

"Thanks, I'll get with you."

He thought about contacting Space Guard and reporting on events, but he was officially a neutral nation. Contacting them put him more under Earth's thumb and less in the independent category. As curious as he was, he was still a head of state. If Earth stepped in, even the courts might revoke his status.

They were demanding a response to their previous offer, too. The UN Bureau of Space Development understood he controlled a station, etc, and were pleased to extend an offer of salvage cost for the low-use asset, etc, in lieu of further action to assess a bunch of issues that could result in fines.

He needed something soon or they were just going to show up and drag him to Earth.

Could Govannon or Brandt run some public ships here and put up a pretense of interest?

He called back, "Paul, and Nicol, we need to have a meeting on this."

Rofert replied, "On my way."

Nicol said, "Right here." She stepped through from her office.

With everyone seated in G, and something stronger than tea to drink, he opened the discussion.

"The UN, Earth specifically, is trying to hurry us into abandonment. They don't seem to be willing to wait, and they're pestering us. Govannon hasn't expressed interest, but is happy to support a Brandt operation here. We've got speculation that Grainne, if they remain this 'Freehold,' is interested. I need input."

Paul Rofert sipped whisky and said, "Prescot has plenty of resources and might like a remote maintenance facility. You and I have discussed this. If that offer wasn't good then, it doesn't mean it might not be good again soon. They value privacy, too."

Nicol said, "The problem is, they have everything they need on their side. On our side, Frontier Station isn't presently doing enough business to get in the way of maintenance docking, and they have lease agreements for dock space."

"And Grainne?" he asked.

Paul twisted his mouth.

"That all depends on them surviving a war and remaining independent."

"Yes," Jackson said. "The same applies to us. We're smaller, and even more readily occupied. But I don't want to throw in with what may be the losing side."

"Will almost certainly be," Nicol said. "They don't have the infrastructure to fight for long. The UN, meaning Earth, is stupidly focusing on the planet more than on space resources, but still, they can't do it."

Paul said, "The guests are straightforward to deal with. But the scientists can't speak for the government, and what government they had is in hiding."

Nicol said, "That still may have been a warship they were in. It was probably repurposed, but I still don't trust them."

"Why not?" he asked.

"Business as usual, oh, and by the way, can we set up clandestinely with you, right next to our enemy? I don't like it."

"Any more word on their bona fides?"

She said, "The scientists have written peer-reviewed papers and appear to be legitimate, but I'd be hard pressed to say they have the seniority for a mission like this."

"Meaning?"

She said, "Meaning they could have been hired as a front."

Paul said, "Possibly they were the only ones available?"

She shook her head. "You'd still send them, but someone with more field time would be in charge."

Jackson said, "The issue is, this is our only income at present, and while it covers some essentials, we're not making any money. I'm paying everyone out of company capital. I can't do that for long. So we still come down to, do we close shop now, hold out until this science mission runs out and hope something comes along, or do something else?"

Nicol said, "You've been up front with everyone about when it might roll over us. Don't worry about that."

"But I do," he said. "Stringing it out isn't fair and doesn't make sense, unless we have a good chance of succeeding."

She said, "I suppose I should be honest and admit I sent my resume to Prescot for any relevant position."

"I don't blame you," he said. He didn't, but damn, if she didn't see an out, and he didn't, it was all over. "I guess in that case, when you get an acceptance, I take that as the turning point and close up."

Paul sat very still and said, "I'll remain until the end. There's nothing for me on Earth."

Jackson remembered that Rofert had been in space since his family died in a "pacification" conflict. All cultures were equal on Earth. But occasionally a culture was deemed troublesome and "reintegrated."

He looked at his engineer and lifelong friend. The man had been working here before he was born. "You will ride with me, and we'll go to Titan. And I guess I know what I have to do. Nicol, tell everyone we'll resume departure plans. Paul, your people will need to stay. And I still want to make that survey. Call it nostalgia."

"Understood."

"Got it."

The incoming ship did have a lot more supplies, and more personnel.

It was getting very suspicious. What did a group of researchers need with so many technical assistants? Yes, they'd helped do a lot of equipment overhaul, even to the point of surface treatments and duct cleaning. But why?

If they wanted a hostile takeover, this was a slow way about it, and what point would it serve? If tramp freighters didn't need his station, no larger group would. Few corporations had the funds to waste, and those would have just offered to buy him out and grant him a bunch of favors. The actual governments just wanted to ignore him or exercise eminent domain.

He was going to make that orbit, and Andy's research be damned.

Later that day, Jackson realized he needed a new V-suit. He hadn't gained much weight, but a decade had changed his shape. This one pinched and rubbed. It would last the trip, though.

Rofert personally flew him. They had to inspect the docking array anyway. They ungrappled and slowly accelerated out from the axis.

Pointing to the dock through the port, Rofert said, "It's aligned within very close tolerances, about point five mils."

"Impressive," he said. The visitors' work was honest, no matter what else was going on.

"Now aft and ante," Rofert said.

They overshot the dock while decelerating, got a good scan of the outer terminal and beacon, then slowly moved back. There were workers in the pools of illumination on the scaffolding, some his, more of them visitors. There were over fifty of them now, and it made no sense.

"Let's see what the sneaky bastards are up to," Rofert said as they reached relative zero and started moving back. "Control, Engineer One stating intent to change trajectory and proceed ante for scheduled observation."

"Engineer One, Control confirms, proceed."

The docking pylon, then the melted regolith moved a hundred meters below, punctuated with ports and structures of the lodge, of old construction locks and the control tower and his residence. It really was a tiny station, and a tiny nation. It couldn't be relevant to anyone, and long term it was doomed anyway.

There was nothing significant visible as they passed the irregular lump that marked the arbitrary equator, but then . . .

"Holy crap," he muttered. "Did you see all this, Paul?"

The entire ante polar region had been built on. There were scaffolds, gantries, three docked tugs he could see in addition to the regular boat. There were a lot more than a hundred personnel here, too, because he could see close to that many swarming around building stuff.

In one way or another, it was a hostile takeover.

Then everything went black.

Rofert said, "I'm afraid I did, sir."

"'Sir'? Are we down to that, then?"

Sweat suddenly burst from him. It was a sellout, and it was hostile. Paul had been in on whatever it was.

"We're not low on power," Paul said. "We've been disrupted." He pulled out a rescue light and started flashing it, just as something obscured the view.

It was a stealth boat, bay open, maneuvering to intercept.

"Paul . . . this was not cool. Not at all."

"Hold on, please, sir. You need to see this." He sounded earnest and urgent.

The invading force, because that's what it was, had turned the rear third of his castle into a combat operations center. He'd seen what he needed to.

He kept quiet, because his life might depend on not irritating anyone. He'd let them have the rock, as long as they let his people go, even if it meant detention for a while first.

Detention, at least, would still be in space. Arguably better than being "free" on Earth.

Whoever was in the boat was cautious and careful. It was long minutes before they were ensconced in the bay. It closed, blacker inside than out, the stars and station disappearing.

There were bumps, and lights came back on. Hanging off the davit holding them were several armed troops.

The one in front waved for attention and spoke through a contact mic. "Mister Bates and Mister Rofert, if you will please open and disembark, the atmosphere is safe."

Rofert looked at him, shrugged and unlatched the hatch port.

They were allowed to maneuver to the forward end of the bay, where actual deck was, and tie to stanchions.

When the bay was pressurized the others unmasked, so Jackson did, too.

The nearest man said, "We apologize for the circumstances. We'd hoped to delay this a bit longer." He looked Hawaiian in ancestry. And broad. About fifty. His accent was from the Grainne Freehold Halo.

Jackson replied, "I'm sorry to have hindered your war."

From the other, "Who said anything about war?"

"It's obvious you're from Grainne and using my home as at least an intel base. It's already set up for that, and I don't have any way to stop you." He should be furious. He'd had suspicions and at this point, it didn't change the outcome of losing his livelihood. Both sides could die, for all he cared. And Paul . . . had obviously seen this in his conduit crawl, and why hadn't Jackson insisted on going along, too?

He turned, "Paul? Why?"

Paul said, "Sir, I know you don't want to abandon your home. Earth would kill you whether intentionally or not. I promised your father I'd maintain it and keep it. This is the only outlet we have, for now."

The officer said, "We intend no violence against you."

He asked, "Do you intend violence against Earth?"

The man responded, "At present, we are gathering scientific information."

"That doesn't answer my question."

"How many questions about the data you transfer have you answered? Or even asked?"

That was valid. He knew much of the data they handled was questionable, if not outright illicit. This, though, pushed the envelope of plausible deniability.

He said, "I acted in good faith. Even though your presentation was questionable."

The man said, "You acted in your own self-interest. You still can. The scientists are doing so."

"So you're funding them?"

"They're funded by Brandt and Prescot, as they said. We're furnishing labor and transport."

He'd accuse them of being cheap, but he knew what charter transport would cost.

The man added, "We're also providing your supplies, at present."

There was the offer. "What do you require me to do?"

"Nothing at all. Just tell no one. We'll continue to cover your operating costs, and we hope the war will end shortly. At that point, you resume being a private exchange and transshipment point."

He believed that was true and honest. He wasn't sure it was something the man could realistically promise.

He replied, "So I have to choose which side I take, in a war I didn't want any part of."

"I guess that's up to you," his counterpart said. "When a landslide starts, the pebbles don't get a vote. The war has started, but the hostilities haven't reached here yet. You not only get a vote, you must vote."

He could be their ally, or their prisoner. Either way, Earth would regard him as hostile and treat him accordingly. They'd wanted Starhome back from the moment his father claimed it.

"I'd have to tell my exec," he warned.

The man nodded. "Yes, just face to face. No transmissions, and none of the inside staff."

It wasn't as if he could call anyone. If he managed to get a message to Earth, even if they believed it, they'd destroy everything his family had, and likely charge him anyway.

Earth had attacked a small nation with a lot of resources because it offered political leverage against others. They in turn had occupied his home because it offered leverage back.

"I wanted to be neutral," he said.

Very seriously, the man said, "So did we, sir."

The parallel was ironic.

Jackson said, "I have nothing to lose. At the same time, I have nothing to gain. What bargaining position do you have, sir?"

The big officer flexed as he moved. It wasn't intimidation. He was just that big with muscle. He pulled out a flask, took a swig, and offered it.

"Silver Birch. Some consider it our finest liquor."

It was informal, but they were in a cargo bay, on deck surrounded by loading equipment. He accepted with a nod, took a drink, and damn, that was smooth. He'd heard of it, but even the head of state of a rock couldn't afford such imports.

"Very nice," he said.

The officer said, "For now, I can increase cash payments somewhat, to cover our 'maintenance facility.' And I assure you only noncombatant craft will dock here for the duration. That's to our benefit and yours. If you'll tell me what you need for payroll and other overhead, I can approve it."

That was a significant shift. However, if he was selling out, he wasn't going to sell out cheap.

He asked, "What if I am attacked by the UN forces?"

"We'd be attacked as well, in that case."

"Yes, but what is my status?" he prompted.

"At that point, you are an engaged ally, and we'd do our best to defend you as well. Since we'd need the facilities for retreat and repair."

Jackson said, "I'll have my exec draft that as a formal agreement, if you don't mind, holding you to tenant status." He wanted his people drafting the agreement on his terms.

"Fair," the man agreed.

Yes, but . . . "And after the war, then what?"

"What do you want?"

"First refusal on docking rights for any Freehold-flagged freighter."

The officer shook his head. "That would be impossible to enforce, given our legal system."

"What instead, then?"

The man said, "We can strongly recommend that our vessels use your services. If you've studied our culture, we're very big on social connections and support of friends."

"Well and good," Jackson said. "But I need something stronger than recommendations."

The man sat and thought for a moment, and Jackson let him. He looked around. The other personnel were still on alert, ready to react to orders. He figured this guy was the officer in charge of the project.

Finally, the man said, "I can guarantee ten years of baseline support of your operation at its present size. Expansion is up to you."

That did it. He was subsidized and beholden, but still independent. They hadn't taken, hadn't threatened, and hadn't tried to buy him out. They respected his sovereignty and circumstances.

First Minister Bates addressed the foreign officer officially. "Reluctantly, and under protest, I accept this pending signature, and offer you continued sanctuary, with the expectation that my people will be given proper treatment as both noncombatants and nonparticipants in our agreement."

"Then, sir," the man said, extending his hand, "you have my word as a Freehold officer."

He shook, and wasn't sure what to say next. He turned to Paul and said, "Whether we live or die, Paul, it will be here, in our home."

His friend grinned back. "That's the only way it should be, sir."

End

HATE IN THE DARKNESS

*I'd been wanting to write more actual space warfare in
my Freehold universe, and Tony Daniel requested a story
for an anthology* (Star Destroyers, *from Baen). This one
ties in referentially to some of the events in* Angeleyes.

*The big problem space combat is going to present is
that not only is there nothing to hide behind, but energy
signatures from a powerplant that can move a ship at
respectable velocity are huge and easy to detect. Barring
a significant change in our understanding of space, even
advanced non-reaction drives will use and emit gobs of
power.*

I enjoyed the challenge.

$\oplus$

SPACE IS DEEPER than most people can grasp, even
those who work and live in it. Star systems are islands.
One can hop between those islands in days, with enough

power, and a jump point or phase drive. Doing it the long way requires even more power, and literal decades to centuries of time.

Which means those vast gulfs of scattered dust, subspace matter and scarce chunks of rock or frozen gas are devoid of anything of interest to anyone not of a specific class of scientist.

Except a fleet of military ships hiding for their lives.

Freehold Military Ship *Malahayati* departed the remotest berth in human history, isolated in interstellar space at a location provided only to two of her officers, with instructions to scramble and destroy the data if the ship were captured. The idea of capturing a ship was ridiculous, except it had happened twice, both times to the enemy from Earth. One had been threatened into submitting, the other boarded through subterfuge by an elite team, and turned back on its former owners, until being claimed by yet a third party.

She was a destroyer, equipped with her own star drive, not dependent on a tow from a fleet carrier. She could operate independently, but would be woefully outnumbered and outgunned anywhere in UN space. She wasn't going to fight head to head.

Instead, she was going to live up to her nickname of *Hate*, and strike hard and fast in enemy territory.

Earth's fleet was numerous and well-supplied, though limited to and bottlenecked by the jump points between systems. The Freehold ships were few, with little backup, no major resupply and no defensible bases. The war wasn't being fought head to head.

Until now, *Malahayati* had ferried stealth intel boats

around, using her phase drive. She could go virtually anywhere, though there were few places worth going that weren't covered by jump points. It did mean she was less predictable, however.

Then the astro engineers had built a clandestine base, in deep space, where no jump points reached and only a phase drive ship with the proper astrogation could locate. It was nowhere, near nothing, with cold, distant stars the only scenery, and four warships the only company. Fewer than ten officers present knew where they were.

Astrogator Lieutenant Malin Metzger was one of them.

He was on this mission because of his mathematical skill. The proposed mission involved rapidly evolving four-dimensional geometric zones. After the strike, whatever Earth forces were available would try to hunt and kill the Freehold ship. They had to fight, but they dare not lose any ships if it could be avoided. On the fly, he'd have to calculate zones of threat, velocity, evasion. He would be de facto commander during the operation.

Once clear of the station, *Malahayati* boosted long and hard at 1.5G, building up velocity to use later. Crews cycled through watches as she accelerated endlessly, her powerplant humming near full power. A supplemental fueling craft, precious and necessary, ensured she had full capacity once at speed. It detached and braked for reuse.

Captain Commander Hirsch was half-visible through the display tank in the pie-shaped C-deck. The command crew all had the battle display to share, and their own overhead displays for task-specific matters. Technical staff were a half deck below.

Hirsch said, "Proceed with mission." He wrote his

departure order into the log, and it appeared on Metzger's display.

Warrant Leader Jaqui Tung on the helm said, "Sir, I am ready."

The captain flashed his maneuvers to her display, and she took it from there.

"All hands prepare for transition . . . Phase entry imminent . . . Maneuver commencing."

There was really little to see or say. She had her sticks and display, and she made the warship move. Metzger felt a momentary odd sensation, very deja-vu-like, only over his whole body, as they entered phase drive. That was it.

All the drama would be at the terminal end, and most of it merely mathematical figures.

Metzger reviewed his op-plan. It was content-heavy, and filled his screens, the hologramatic space in front of him, and the chart display. There would hopefully be minor updates in-system, but what they had was what the assault was based on.

More important than the assault was the evasion and escape phase afterward. He'd instruct Tung if he could. He might have to take instantaneous control or engage the AI to avoid eating all the missiles he was sure any Earth ships would throw at them.

He then closed and darkened his station, and reclined in his G couch. He'd spend most of the mission lying in it.

With medical help he slept. It was productive sleep, but not enjoyable. It was a military necessity and felt like it. Three divs, just under eight Earth-hours later, his system woke him.

Captain Hirsch said, "Welcome back, Metzger. Are you ready to commence?"

"Sir, I am. I have the Deck and the Conn."

"They are yours."

They precipitated out of phase drive far from Earth's normal routes, deep in the Kuiper Belt. They'd planned their original acceleration to give them the velocity they needed here. They were near four percent of C, devoid of most emissions, plunging in-system fast enough to wipe life off a planet if they didn't mind sacrificing themselves in the process.

They'd prefer not to do that. Nor would Earth, any inhabited planet, or major habitat let anything in such a trajectory impact. But that depended on detecting an approach, which was based on the assumption such an object would be reflective or under power, not a mostly black body against a mostly black background. Only planets had enough sensor area for that kind of defense. Habitats were vulnerable.

They fell in-system, taking only Earth hours to transit what would normally take days.

As they shot in, ship systems were reduced in power. The engines were shut down, reactors at standby, generating only enough for life support and basic operation, thermal leakage radiating aft. They needed to conserve energy for later, and minimize any outputs at all now.

Hate wasn't invisible. Her outer hull was going to radiate at some temperature warmer than 3 K. Part of the mission profile, while they weren't under thrust, was to put minuscule puffs of liquid nitrogen and helium out on the hull to cool that spectrum.

Playing the odds on someone else's sensor skill was part of the operational planning. It didn't make Metzger any happier . . . even if the inverse square law worked in their favor.

For now.

Metzger rested again under mild tranqs to maximize his function time later.

He woke on schedule, went below and refreshed himself and ate, and dragged back through the passage to C-Deck.

Once ensconced, he donned headset, visor and touch gloves, brought up his screens, then waited. He attempted to appear casual, but was tense inside. This was it. And there was the time tick. It pinged all the command crew, and the ship came alive, even if not under power.

"Battle stations, battle stations. All hands as assigned and stand by for low-emission protocols."

Metzger settled further into his G couch. Even at their current insane velocity he expected to lie here most of a day, with a very quick head break or two, and food delivered.

If they'd miscalculated, he might very well die here.

The first part was intellectually easy, morally tough. It was a declared war. The target was a military terminal. It was unquestionably a legitimate attack.

It was also, practically speaking, a rear echelon facility that never expected anything beyond sabotage. A major combat strike wasn't anything they were prepared for.

The trajectory was clean, their ship all but invisible. The captain's orders gave Metzger final approval over launch, because it used his figures. The attack had been planned by himself, Hirsch and the Strategic Office aboard the station. Everything that followed, though, was done with his calculations and his input. The execution was his.

He was about to kill a lot of people.

Their people had killed a lot of his people in his system, even if these individuals hadn't personally done it.

But they hadn't personally done it, and they were the ones taking the punishment.

It was time. He stomped on the quandary, secondarily unlocked everything the captain had already unlocked, and brought up his imaging displays.

He sipped water. He was thirsty now. He had no idea how he'd feel later.

"Separation," he announced. He thought he could detect a fractional change in the ship's balance as the drone, munitions and impactor mass detached, but it was probably just a psychological effect.

Then it was back to waiting.

The station's active search functions should detect the Freehold weapons at a given radius, and not before. They were optimized for the standard range of orbital debris. Any runaway or sabotage ship was expected to show boost phase and be readily identifiable. *Malahayati* was a fuzzy nothing with near no emissions in the primary search band, as far as sensors went. They should not be detected. The infalling mass, however, would be, eventually.

Metzger turned command back over to the second officer, lay back to tranq out for a couple of more divs.

It was near midnight shiptime when he woke, examined the image display, and checked status.

A dot showed their position, other dots showed the

station, two known patrol ships, several in-system cargo haulers and the Freehold weapons' assumed positions. Slowly, as he watched patiently, the positions changed.

It was another long div of him staring and doing little before anything significant happened.

Next to him, but separated by a divider, Sensor "Officer" Doug Werner said, "They just went hot. Their threat warnings are live. Subjectively." Werner was in fact a contractor who'd been conducting training aboard ship when the war started. Their regular sensor officer was somewhere unknown.

It was important to remember that what they saw had happened long seconds, entire Earth-minutes previously. The decision cycle would get shorter as they got closer. Though even distant exchanges might be unavoidably lethal, giving them only more time for regret.

The station's first response was fast and reasonable. An energy battery fired, and seconds of travel time later, a massive energy flux vaporized the incoming threat.

Which flashed into chaff that curlicued across space.

The second projectile was masked by the cloud, and didn't become visible to them at once. When it did, the battery fired again.

Then there was activity and reset as one of the drone-launched missiles arrived on a completely different trajectory. Another battery fired, and another plasma flare lit the space. It was an expensive decoy, almost a ship itself, but the growing background clutter was degrading the station's ability to respond.

It was obvious to the station command that this was a deliberate assault. They sent out an open broadcast.

"Station Control to all vessels, we appear to be under attack. Remain clear of the Docking Control Zone and stand by to provide support. Gather any intel available and forward."

Watching their defense collapse was fascinating but tragic. Their tactics assumed rogue space debris or a critically damaged ship on collision course. There were plans in place to deal with a sabotage or suicide mission. There was no way they could yet have prepared for a non-jump-point entry by a warship that evaded all interception options.

The entire strategy of system defense was being rewritten right now.

Then the third frontal warhead arrived, too close for them to do much. They tried to destroy it, but it was designed to and did detonate close enough for a wave front that lit their shields with overload and scattered more metal dust. It was probably beautiful and terrifying up close. Here, it was numbers and icons in the airspace of Metzger's display.

The decoy's trailing booster stage detonated, a pure dummy, but close enough to require more reaction. Then a mass of lithic warheads, rocks, hammered down from behind the chaff screening, followed by one last warhead.

This one was a killer. It was an anti-matter-triggered fusion device visible all the way out here, with a detectable radiation front. It flashed in the entire spectrum, even in visual range. It detonated close enough to melt some of the superstructure, and drive that vaporized material through the rest of the station.

What had been a UN spacedock was melted vapor and

shattered debris. Thousands of people and three ships still docked no longer existed. Hundreds died within the next several seconds, some few having just enough time to cry "Mayday!" into the void. Then silence reigned. The debris disappeared from sensors as it cooled into slag and ash, dispersing into the Kuiper Belt.

At least it was a clean death, he reassured himself. They might have had time to be scared. They probably wouldn't have felt a thing when it actually happened. Boiled, crushed or overloaded by enough radiation to cook every neuron instantly. Anyone else suffocated within seconds.

Captain Hirsch said, "Well done."

"Thank you, sir," he agreed. For warfare, it was well done. It was also something they could probably do again. Until the UN had phase drives installed, they couldn't use the tactic, as they'd found out disastrously when they tried to "clandestinely" enter the Grainne system proper through the jump point.

He'd just killed several thousand people who had no idea they were combatants.

The next few Earth-minutes were mass confusion as two patrolling ships lit their drives hot, started trajectory for the station, then powered down as pointless. If anyone had survived, they'd be dead before any rescue could reach them.

Probably, no one had survived.

Then the ships turned power onto active sensor sweeps and detailed analysis of all space around them. They would attempt to backtrack trajectories on the impactors and reduce their search cones.

The problem with space was that there was nowhere to actually hide. The second problem was the power outputs of a major ship's plant were significantly more detectable than distant stars, or local planetoids.

Captain Hirsch asked, "Sensors, can you get any commo?"

Werner replied, "Minimal. It's tight beam, little bleed, and encrypted. Senior Ustan is doing traffic analysis and looking for indicators."

Hirsch said, "So we wait."

Their current trajectory would have them safely out of system, well into deep space, and in prime phase-drive options in ten days.

"I need a break," Metzger said. "Helm, please resume control."

Tung said, "Sir, I have control."

"Thank you. Captain, I need to walk a bit. May I have your leave? I'll be in the gym."

"You may. Thanks for your plotting so far. Please be ready for any notice."

"Yes, sir."

Metzger pushed and pulled his way aft, into the gym, and into the centrifuge. He could walk in endless loops, but it would work his muscles and burn off some stress. Being cooped in a G couch for most of a day was exhausting.

He wasn't the only one walking, but he took a brisk stride that had him slowly lapping two others. He recognized one of the engineers, and one of the weapons maintenance techs. They all politely ignored each other.

He'd just vaporized thousands of people, most of them not direct combatants, but support.

The UN was going to try to kill him and everyone he served with in response.

Hell, they were already trying to do that.

Was it worthwhile? Or would it just escalate to more nukes and kinetic weapons back home? Was it worth winning if there was nothing left?

Fatigue hit hard. How long had he been at it? Eight divs, almost an entire day cycle. Yeah. Rest and calculate, that was his life at present.

He was about to ping the captain for permission when an incoming message ordered him to rest. "If unable, report to the medical officer."

Moral quandaries aside, sleeping wasn't a problem. He made it to his cabin and collapsed onto his bunk with just enough consciousness left to fasten in against maneuvers.

Captain Virgil Ashton, UNPF, aboard the frigate *Laconia* twitched at the alarm. His first glance at the display showed nothing untoward in the vicinity. Helm was steady. Nothing looked out of line.

Then he saw the transmitted report.

Station Roeder was being hit hard. In the display, warheads and mass piled in bright flashes, overloaded its screens and smashed it to vapor.

Distress calls and beacons disappeared in cries and screams, then lonely silence.

Twelve thousand people had just died.

He tried not to twitch as adrenaline shot up his spine and he broke into a feverish sweat.

"Where the hell did that come from?"

Ahead and right of him, Reconnaissance Operator Alxi

said, "Sir, everyone is searching now. All ships, all stations."

It had to be the Grainne Colony, and it was a violent, mass attack far inside Earth space. And why hadn't Space Force acquired phase drive as soon as it was proven? It allowed things like this. Whichever ship had done that had avoided the jump point entirely.

Where was it?

The tactical display showed a trajectory that intersected the station at one end, and dissipated into space at the other. Somewhere along that arc, that attack had been launched.

Another image lit, the potential cone the hostile had taken after launch.

Fleet commed in. The Admiral came on personally. Ashton straightened.

"Ashton, are you ready for pursuit?"

Ashton replied, "At once, sir. We have the track and can boost at once."

"Go. Frag order will follow."

"Yes, sir. We are in pursuit." He turned. "Navigation, Helm, maximum safe boost."

"We're on it."

Warnings sounded and *Laconia* accelerated.

Helm Operator Rao asked, "Are there any survivors, sir?"

He scrolled through the messages piling on his display.

He said, "There may be a handful in a tumbling section, and some in rescue balls if they can be reached fast enough. They were in the dock section."

"Does this count as a terror attack?"

Twisting his neck, he said, "Technically it is within the Law of Armed Conflict. They hit a military target during declared hostilities."

Rao snapped, "That's a BS technicality. Maintenance and support aren't combatants."

It had been inevitable, really, as soon as the UN had dropped KE and nuke weapons on Grainne. Sending second-rate troops for occupation hadn't been smart, either.

Ashton said, "Either way, we pursue."

"And then vaporize them." The man sounded enraged, his teeth clenched.

Ashton nodded. "Once we have that order, yes."

The Grainne ship was somewhere in that cone in the display. For now, their best pursuit trajectory was a shot down the middle.

Intel came in bit by bit.

Alxi summarized the Fleet Intel report verbally for everyone, even though it was in the display. There were a lot of things in the display, and they could be easy to miss.

"There was a lot of mass in that attack. The conclusion is it's one of their destroyers. Big enough for phase drive, but not one of their fleet carriers. Those are too valuable and too fragile. A compact, phase-drive equipped ship with mass load. One of their Admiral class. We've previously destroyed one, that leaves three."

Ashton said, "Good. I know their capabilities. Got them for review?"

"Yes, sir. Best known are on the display."

Malahayati was a destroyer, phase drive conversion, twenty-five years old. Their frames were smaller and more compact than UN ships, mainly built around jump point defense. It was still a bigger ship than his frigate. It theoretically packed missiles and beams, but wouldn't have been able to resupply easily. Two previous known engagements. It hadn't been seen in months. It was likely low on everything.

Ashton said, "Now we have to figure how much fuel they used, still have, and can spare."

This had to be punished, and *Laconia* was in a good position for it.

Rao reported, "*Quito* is astern, but can boost more. They're joining."

"Excellent, put me through. Shema, Ashton."

Captain Grade 2 Shema said, "Hell of a thing, eh?" She looked wide-eyed in shock, not fear. It looked odd on her North-Asian face.

Ashton replied, "Yes. Are we going to try to bracket?"

Shema said, "First I want to parallax all our sensor info. There might be something that will show them to us. I've got your trajectory. I'm going to deviate slightly outward, just on a hunch they'd rather be on the outermost track to space they can use."

He said, "That makes good sense. Should I launch drones or waste a platform for intel?"

She shook her head. "I advise against it. We'll throw that at them when we find them. There are other ships that may be able to cross our scans and find something."

"Understood. I just hate to chase without knowing what I'm chasing."

She said, "For now that's all we have, but it puts us in a better position when we do find them."

"It does. Yes, ma'am. We'll funnel everything to you as we get it. *Laconia* out and listening."

"*Quito* out and listening."

Alxi said, "Sir, I may have something. An occultation of a star, and a rough trajectory, but it's barely outside the estimated envelope."

"Can you reconstruct a track?"

"I can." It appeared in the display. It didn't match either the estimated launch point or the current search cone, but it was too fast to be any kind of debris.

Alxi was good. She'd known where to look and found something.

It was his call to make. He made it.

"It's close enough to assign it as Unknown One. See what *Quito* can find."

"Yes, Captain."

Metzger felt he'd barely closed his eyes when an alarm woke him.

"Report to C-Deck."

He staggered to his feet and stumbled up the passage.

He was going to need a head break soon, but what did they have?

"They have us IDed," Werner said as Metzger walked around the catwalk to his station.

Second Astrogator Yukat was on duty, and she cleared the couch as he approached.

This was his mission, his plan, and he had to furnish the options to the captain.

He settled in to the still-warm couch and squinted until his gritty eyes focused and his muddled brain tracked. The trajectories showed as equations, charts and graphical loops in the system 3D sim. The tracks were beautiful ballistic curves against gravity and real motion.

They all had potential intercepts.

Metzger addressed the captain.

"Sir, our options are decoy and evasion now, or continue ballistically until any pursuit closes, then conduct decoy and evasion. I had planned for a momentary diversion in trajectory towards jump point."

Hirsch said, "I recall. Do the latter. Any energy they expend now we won't have to fight against later."

"Understood, sir. Helm, my console has command."

"Understood, sir," Tung agreed.

He wanted to appear discreet, while being just noticeable enough for them to respond. This was why space warfare took segs or even days.

The correction for the jump point was simple. A huge solution set would accomplish that. This part of the set would actually get them there with enough fuel for a jump. This second choice would do so discreetly enough not to be seen. This one would just let them be seen, and give him the option of more visibility while still meeting the proper terminus. He mathematically shaved down a geometric shape until he had maneuvering options, minimum loss of fuel, and plenty of open space for evasion.

"All hands stand by for thrust," he warned, and pinged the message through text, audio and klaxon. Thirty seconds later, his correction started. The ship boosted softly, 0.2154 G according to his figures, and held it for exactly 436 seconds. It then cut back to micro G.

Then it was back to waiting.

"Sir, request permission for induced sleep."

Hirsch said, "Absolutely. I'll need your brain at its best. Helm, take control."

Helm responded with, "Aye, sir. Helm has control."

Metzger shuttered his couch, pulled a darkened visor over his eyes and ears, and watched hypnotic red waveforms drift across his vision. His brain tried to calculate their shapes, while he felt warm and ensconced in his couch. He'd just figured out the saw-sine expression of one when it changed to another, and . . .

Aboard *Laconia*, sorted data piled up.

Rao reported, "*Mirabelle* just came through jump. They're on an almost crossing vector, actually a very good position for an intercept, though tougher to get a good shot."

Mirabelle was a destroyer. She was almost as fast, closer to the hostile, and had better weaponry.

"Got him!" Alxi said. "Sir, cross-referencing ours and *Quito*'s scans with those from *Mirabelle* has him marked. Also, we apparently had a stealth boat behind orbit?"

Ashton replied, "We did? I wouldn't know. They don't talk to anyone."

"Well, they're talking to me now. Or rather, they're sending a very tight, burst-encrypted message to *Mirabelle*, who then tightbeamed us. So we're hopeful the enemy can't crack it."

The "Enemy." That term hadn't been used much. They were the "opposition," the "resistant colony." After this, they were finally the "Enemy."

"Is it in the display?" he prompted.

Alxi said, "It is now."

The enemy ship was moving fast, but unpowered, and that was a very well-designed trajectory. It took them far enough from the jump point or habitat to minimize visibility, but not so far in-system to increase their flight time or expose them to in-system sensors or weapons.

Ashton called down to Engineering Deck. "Powerplant, how much over max can we handle for a few hours?"

Commander Basco paused a moment, then said, "I can support ten percent over. Fifteen is probably safe but you'll need to sign for it."

"Fifteen it is. We're chasing this asshole down."

Another shape came on the display.

Navigator Mafinga said, "Assuming full fuel bunker, that's his possible trajectories to deep space. Once he hits the edge of that, he's clear."

"How much overlap do we have on intercept?"

Mafinga ran a cursor through the image.

"Currently over two hours."

Ashton twisted his lip. "Not a lot, but enough. Will higher boost help?"

"Sir, it will not. We'll eat through our own fuel."

"If we plan to wait for a recovery vessel, how much can we close?"

Mafinga swiped and tapped for calculations, and said, "That opens up options, but sir, I'd rather save that fuel for any course changes. We don't know how accurate these initial findings are, or what weapons they'll throw."

Ashton nodded. "Valid. They'll throw missiles, the

same as we will. He can't risk being seen and can hide missile drops easier than a beam. We can't pour enough energy into a beam for potshots. When are we in range for a firing solution?"

Tactical Officer Shin said, "Only about ten minutes to max range. But we'll have a much better shot in thirty-four."

"We'll wait if we can," Ashton decided.

Shin added, "I have an ongoing solution updating, sir."

"Closer means a larger warhead, correct?"

"Yes. It doesn't make a lot of difference normally, but in this case, the weapon mass is an issue."

He asked Shin, "Can we overboost the warheads?"

Shin said, "We can fake it with some additional jacketing. There will be more emission, and higher velocity fragments, but we'll lose some to the blast."

"Any hit will be a good hit. A few minor delays and he's stuck in-system until we slag him. Do it."

Shin tapped info and swiped his display. "They're on it," he said.

Ashton tapped for his orderly.

He said, "Please have food brought to the bridge crew. Have our reliefs on mandatory rest waiting. This may drag out." He turned back to the command crew and said, "Rest breaks will be one person every fifteen minutes, with a junior officer filling in. We want to keep our information flowing smoothly."

"Let's fry this clown."

"I'm awake," Metzger said at once, before he realized there was an alert sounding in his ears.

He glanced at the displays surrounding him as the captain brought him up to date.

"They're in pursuit. I need your expertise."

"It looks like they corrected to match my anticipated course, and have deduced the shift since then. I'm determining any discreet evasion will be impossible. They've got us dialed in fine based on energy signature."

Captain Hirsch said, "That was my conclusion. We'd hoped to be further out before detection."

Metzger said, "We might have been better taking a burn as soon as they IDed us, but we'd then be juggling fuel, too."

"Do you have a scenario to cover this?"

"Sort of. That one I discussed with you. Alpha three Alpha."

The nature of forceline propulsion meant the ship had zones of speed, much like surface vehicles would reach speeds where energy to overcome friction increased dramatically to another plateau.

For now, Metzger made a course adjustment and applied a steady, low thrust to get them to deep space as quickly as possible. The math was simple. If they reached interstellar space before pursuit reached them, they were free. If pursuit reached them, they had to fight. If they had to fight, they had limited maneuver margin before they'd have to go ballistic and drift into position for phase drive. If they ate too much into their safety margin, they wouldn't have any star drive capability.

To fight, they had a modern electronic warfare suite, but once within range of mass or beams, they had six and only six configurable warheads against their two pursuers.

"Okay, I assume I'm going to have to lead on this since it was my calculations. I'll need food, induced sleep between activity, and the medical officer to keep an eye on me. If that meets your approval, sir, it should be a half seg before they manage to do anything relevant. I'd like to drop under again. If they close within those parameters or seem to detach anything that might be a weapon, wake me at once. With your permission, sir?"

"Do so. I'll have a cook on call for whatever you'd like when you wake up."

"Right. Thanks. And first, head break."

He took care of business, returned and snuggled back into his couch, and waveformed back into unconsciousness.

He knew he'd been asleep, but all he saw was increasing waveform complexity and modulated tones. The machine was pulling him back awake.

Then he was conscious and removed the mask.

A glance at the displays showed a third ship, a picket destroyer, closing, though not yet in range to be combatant.

"Captain, I'm aware of the display. Are there any other updates?"

"You have all the data available."

"Understood. Helm, maintain your control for the present."

"Helm retains control, understood, sir."

It was embarrassing to be surrounded by what were effectively servants. Still, it was for his benefit as he drove this beast alone.

He stretched in place and probed at an itch under his shoulder where a fold of uniform had irritated him.

He recognized the Chef Assistant in one of the couches for support staff and observers, and said, "Chief Lalonde, I'd like a cocoa, please. Double dark, regular cream, splash of butter and half-sweet. A dark smoke ham roll with smoked gouda and peppered egg filling."

"At once, sir," Lalonde agreed, and hoisted himself aft.

He turned to the surgeon, Lieutenant Doctor Morgan.

"I feel okay, a bit groggy. Is there anything you can give me for focus and attention without affecting my ability to sleep, ma'am?"

She took his thumb, pressed it against a metabolic probe, then checked the data.

"I will formulate something," she agreed.

"Thank you. Captain, I'm ready to resume."

He checked the plots and trajectories, looked at the astro-sims for possible corrections. Those were based on the available energy consumption figures for those ship classes, and *Malahayati*'s exact figures.

"Sir, I recommend we continue. I expect they'll shortly get a firing solution. I want to launch in return, wait for that incoming weapon to get to a precise point, then use that as maneuvering screen. If I time it right, ours will detonate after theirs, and that will be a second screen. Two maneuvers well-hidden in fuzz should dramatically increase our chances with little waste of available bunker."

"You're not going to hit them with it?"

"I think a near miss is achievable. I expect they'll simply evade if it gets too close, and we lose any effect. If I can judge when they'll maximize their evasion, I can detonate just before that."

"You're playing chicken with fusion warheads."

"Exactly, sir."

"Proceed. Mr. Metzger?"

"Yes, sir?"

The captain spoke very carefully. "If you believe you have failed and we are pending destruction, please do not make any announcement. It won't make any difference. We fly until we win or die."

Metzger said, "Yes, sir. Though I'm quite sure I have the odds on this one."

"Excellent."

He'd better stay awake for now. He'd likely need more drugs before this was over.

Had it been most of a day cycle already?

Right then, the assigned surgeon returned.

"Here is your cocktail," she said.

"Thank you." He took it, she gestured, he chugged it. It tasted like slightly bitter grape juice. Not bad.

"I may need to drug heavily in a div or so. To stay conscious."

"If you do, I have that standing by."

"Thank you."

Werner reported, "I believe the new arrival at the jump point is another destroyer. Warren class."

"Correction time?" he asked.

"We are roughly six light-seconds from the point."

"Understood."

The data showed on his display, as did the lag time. Whatever he saw had happened 5.94 seconds previously. That also would change as vectors closed.

Well, that limited his maneuver options. He didn't dare get closer to that ship. That was probably part of their plan. He blacked out an entire chord of possible trajectories.

Now he had to think about decoying that one, at approximately the same time.

It wasn't just the three craft in play. It was the light-speed delay in sensor response, then the much slower craft response. If any of them saw his maneuver, it would be a wasted effort.

Both trailing craft could be screened if his warhead detonated there, relative. He set that to remain a "fixed" variable, maintaining optimum position.

He could screen the other one in that fuzzy locus there. He might only achieve a partial obscuration. Damn.

"Surgeon, I need you to consult with the senior engineer. Specifically, I need to know how many frames aft we need to clear, and what shielding we'll have, regarding how close I let their incoming warhead approach before I evade. Captain, do I have your permission?"

She asked, "You are trying to avoid casualties by the narrowest margin?"

"That is correct. Microseconds and meters may help."

Hirsch said, "Please proceed."

Morgan nodded to them. "I will find out."

"Please hurry, ma'am," he added as she clattered around the catwalk. "They just launched. Subjective. It's on the way. Appears to be less than six hundred seconds to impact. Captain, please tell the engineer I need to know our maximum safe energy level on a single maneuver, and our maximum power output. Stress the comparative urgency."

Boy, did that sound calm.

At least it would be over quickly.

The captain barked, "Engineer Major Hazey, I need you in this discussion now."

Metzger returned to his task. If they'd launched, and he was getting a refinement on the missile because it was under full boost, he needed to drop his . . . then. Unpowered. By not boosting, his would be harder to detect, even if they expected it. That increased his probability. They needed a hit, he only needed a screen.

Really, at the far end, if he maintained sufficient fuel, or reached clean space seconds ahead of any pursuit, they won. The enemy only won if they hit him.

A blinking notice showed in his panorama, yellow and coded as Engineering. He opened it.

It looked as if everyone could move to Frame 70, and he had a shield rating factor for the best field they could cast astern, plus internal ballast blocking. That allowed him to create a variable depending on the size of the warhead inbound. For output, the note said, "Emergency rating is 130%, but I'm willing to support 135% under the conditions, if it's under a ten-second burn."

He had to assume pursuit would want to send the most powerful warhead they could for area effect. They also needed it fast, however. Judging from that motion, he wanted to say it was on the high end of the spectrum. If it was weaker, he'd have less screen to hide behind. If it was more powerful, they were all dead.

I'm basing it on assumed flight characteristics of a missile we've never seen in combat, he thought.

That was all he had. He should drop the device . . . now.

Then a VDAM—Volume Denial Dispersed Mass Weapon. It was only tungsten jacks, but the relative velocity would make those into potentially deadly projectiles. Most likely, the UN shields would block the debris, but the particles might score hits, and they might deny chunks of space to support craft.

Both were blown out by hyper-pressurized nitrogen, and had a gas "jet" for movement. It was little delta V, but it meant they would be harder to trace to source, and slightly closer to pursuit. They'd engage thrust momentarily before impact.

Captain Hirsch asked, "May I assist in any way?"

"Not at this moment, sir, though the tube crews should keep the warheads live and be ready to change delivery."

"They will."

He needed to actively fire at that third picket. It needed to be the dirtiest warhead they had.

"Can they sheath the next warhead with something to increase the fuzz?" he asked.

"Stand by," the captain asked and turned to query.

He said, "Standing by. I will be maneuvering on momentary notice. All crew should be restrained."

A few moments later, the captain said, "Munitions says it's as dirty as it can get. Characteristics on screen."

He wasn't a munitions specialist, and he wasn't really a sensor expert. He tapped both officers into the display.

"Advise me, please," he said, and flashed figures.

Werner said, "You want to keep them behind the sixty-two percent mark of the radius. Assuming their gear is what it was last time we did an exchange."

Munitions Officer Hadfield lit into the display and said, "This isn't dirty in the radiation sense. It's remarkably clean. The sheathing will create all kinds of high energy fragments that will be a temporary cloud. You'll have perhaps point two seconds. After that, we'll be brighter than it, at that boost."

"Thank you. That really doesn't help my calculations. I'll be playing by ear."

He regretted saying that, especially that way.

He added, "Your advice is valuable. I'll do my best with it."

He launched the second missile and let it burn for the target. They knew where he was and would expect him to shoot.

The tumbled warhead astern was still functional, and pursuit seemed to be willing to risk it, or unaware of it. They were at full thrust, possibly six G.

"Our maneuver is going to hard, violent, multi-axis and hot. I'm momentarily going to use all power for thrust and kill everything else."

Captain Hirsch said, "The crew are informed."

In the sim, vectors closed. That explosion would hopefully shield *that* cone, and overlap with that explosion and the other cone.

He set the system to implement his maneuver on that exact time tick, and stood by to override.

No, it was going to be right now.

Astern was a danger-close explosion. *Malahayati* creaked and popped as the reactor drove at 140%. Everything went black as power surged undiminished to the engines. They shifted, heaved and rolled, G pulling him in three directions at once. The straps cut into him and he bumped his shoulder on the couch frame. Then everything went still as thrust stopped. Lights and enviro came back on.

They hadn't blown up, and the enemy hadn't blown them up.

"Stand by for round two," he announced.

Two more ticks crossed each other, the warheads he'd launched hopefully blinded pursuit, and as the debris clouds cooled, the engines hummed again, at 136% of rated capacity. It felt even rougher, with the vectors combining to make it very uncomfortable.

They were in a slightly longer, but much faster arc for clear space, and down a measurable percentage of their available maneuver margin.

"Well done, Lieutenant," the captain said.

"That's only the first, sir," he replied. "My options were limited. Slower or longer trajectories would expose us to more fire, so I had to choose faster or flatter, and they know it. We've gained seconds, possibly Earth-minutes. All three are still in the chase."

Ashton watched the displays. A creeping caret represented their missile, seeming to crawl toward the enemy's probable mark. Only when one realized how many thousands of kilometers each centimeter represented did the speed become apparent.

Alxi said, "There was possibly a very faint change in motion. It could be jettison of mass for moment gain. Or it might be a launch."

"A loiter missile, I assume?"

She nodded. "It would have to be. There's nothing showing yet, and an immediate launch would paint them."

"Understood," he said.

The other ships would have firing solutions, soon. One of them was bound to score a damaging shot eventually.

It was a pointless war, with the numbers the way they were. Grainne couldn't win. As brave as this attack was, it was worthless, suicidal and only serving to piss more people off.

"Sir, our missile has positive lock."

"Good! Let's see what we're about to kill."

Data came back. Yes, Admiral class. *Malahayati*. The fact it was named after a famous Earth commander just made their claims of being independent even more ridiculous. Trajectory, thrust, likely fuel load available. Now the track matched very closely to what they had from the attack. And damn, she was burning. How did they get to 0.049 *c* and still have maneuvering margin?

The missile finished and detonated. There was a ripple of approval among the crew.

Shortly, the combined sensors should tell them what if any damage had been done.

Alxi said, "Sir, we have vector on incoming threat. I think—"

A massive explosion showed in the display, on the view screen and on sensors. *Laconia* trembled from the wave front against her shields, and several loud bangs echoed and clattered.

Someone said, "Son of a bitch, the fuckers hit us."

Chief Engineer Basco said, "Damage report: shield

containment needs flushed. Minor rad damage in forward sections, including Control. Outer hull breaches, count three, contained. Minor damage to drive antenna two. We've lost about point two G of boost capability."

That was an amazing shot. On the other hand, the UN ships weren't playing hard to see so were easy targets. The damage, though, would slow *Laconia*. *Quito* would have to take lead.

"Status on the enemy?"

"Unknown, sir. We've lost them. They apparently maneuvered after either or both detonations."

That bastard.

"Someone else should have data," he demanded.

"Sir, *Quito* was in our thrust shadow, and *Mirabelle* also took fire, though only close enough to act as a screen."

"That devious bastard," Ashton said in respect.

He addressed his staff. "Make your best guess on cones of potential and I'll do the same. We'll compare. Start scanning immediately. They may be damaged, too."

"Yes, sir."

Metzger studied the available sensor information. Light-seconds mattered.

"Bogey One is down slightly but measurably in acceleration. I think we hurt them with something."

Engineering reported by audio and display to him and the captain.

"C-Deck, I cannot authorize any more boosts over one hundred thirty percent. I was serious on my limits, and we've strained containment. You'll have to expect that to drop on future high-energy burns, too. I'd say I'm not happy, except I want us to win. We have to be alive to do that, though."

"Understood, thank you, sir," he replied. Yes, it had been a risk. They'd needed everything they could get.

Gods, he was tired. His eyes were getting gritty, and his guts sour.

"I need something mild to eat."

"Banana?"

"Yeah, thanks."

He took a moment to color-code all his envelopes to make it easier to grasp them at a glance. If . . . once . . . they got to green zones in those fascinating shapes, they'd be safe from intercept. They had the velocity advantage. Earth had three ships and less need to save power. They could call for refuel. Though much farther and they couldn't. They were reaching their own recovery envelope.

Worst case, we might take three more ships with us, the hard way.

They were incrementing toward green on Bogey One. It was going to get passed by Two shortly. If the UNPF was smart, it would stay in the race as recon, and he'd still have to deal with it.

He had three warheads, and three pursuers. He could drop five more VDAMs, and it was possible that had been what damaged Bogey One, though it could have been the warhead or even internal overload from the pursuit.

Someone handed him a banana. He ate it in three bites, then sipped cold tea.

Captain Hirsch said, "I would like to suggest you consider if further damage to Bogey One will cause

Two to stop to rescue, and take both of them out of the running. Do you have anything against that?"

The captain was politely saying he was about to give an order.

Think. Think.

"Sir, unless we are able to damage life support or structural integrity, they can batten down on minimum and wait for rescue. I don't think we can reliably plan to effect that."

"You are correct. If that becomes a viable option, do take it."

He said, "Sir, I intend to cause as much damage as possible as we depart."

Hirsch replied, "And if we don't, I will cause them even more."

"I understand, sir."

Really, capture would probably be worse than death. Out here, very few civilian craft would detect anything. The UN could claim destruction for both PR purposes and cover, then do whatever it took to get intel out of every member of the crew, probably starting at the bottom. After that, space was an unfillable graveyard.

He asked, "Munitions, what effect would a VDAM have if detonated fractionally before and next to a warhead?"

Lieutenant Hadfield asked, "Are you trying for more ionization fuzz?"

"I am."

"It's not efficient, but it will work. You will get some congealed particles afterward, as well, but they will only be fractionally efficient for impact kills."

"Please configure the remaining warheads for that.

That leaves us two more VDAMs I can use to jack off."
The tungsten pellets were tetrahedrons, not quite jack
shaped, but the joke was obvious and common.

"Now I am hungry," he suddenly realized.

Lalonde asked, "What do you need, sir?"

"I know it's off schedule, but any chance of that pot
roast soup from last week?"

"I think I can have something in a few segs."

"Please."

At least he'd eat well as a condemned man.

Bogey One was going to drop out and be only a recon
source. There was no reason for them to play a game, and
they were farther back in the engagement envelope.
Bogey Two was continuing to advance, and would
eventually move out of envelope, if they didn't detect
Malahayati. So far, so good.

Bogey Three's course was going to bring them a lot
closer before receding. It was unlikely they'd avoid
detection, even with the oblique, almost skew trajectories.

He ran sims on when that detection might happen, and
what Two could do in response. Would it be best to
maneuver again the moment they were seen? Or use
incoming fire as another distraction?

He realized Lalonde had a stew bag at his shoulder,
and mumbled "Thanks." He squeezed out a mouthful and
resumed figuring.

Calculations showed that given their own fuel margin
and established trajectories, any further maneuver would
slow their escape. The obvious fast curves would be
attacked preemptively. If he waited for incoming, his
available volume and options would shrink a lot.

"As soon as they detect us, we have to maneuver again. Realistically, that will be our last maneuver."

Hirsch demanded, "Elaborate, please."

Metzger ran through his reasoning and figures.

"An immediate maneuver gives us the broadest envelope and them the widest search volume. If we wait, we have fewer options, and they will be slightly but relevantly closer."

"Understood. Maneuver as you see fit. After that, what is your call?"

"If they detect us after that, we're on a very tight fuel margin. We need enough to get us into phase, and to somewhere we can precipitate and expect help." If they dropped into normal space light-years from anywhere, it would take years for any message to get out.

"Please keep me advised on that margin," Hirsch said.

"Yes, sir."

If they couldn't do it, the captain was going to try to take at least one pursuer with them, the hard way.

Really, there weren't any other options.

Metzger was the only one aboard who could prevent that.

"Sir, I think I can drop a loiter mine onto Bogey Two. The problem is, the residue of the detonation, microseconds as it is, will be enough for them to track this trajectory. Even with onboard maneuvering."

"Save it until you believe we're exposed."

"Understood. That increases the probability of a miss, however."

Hirsch acknowledged, "Yes."

"Confirmed."

Engineer Hazey reported, "Astro, we're losing efficiency. Adjustments require shutdown, so you need to assume loss of acceleration and efficiency. I've got a chart for you."

Metzger looked at the chart and clenched his jaw. He added the figures and reassigned everything. The envelopes changed and narrowed.

Werner said, "Incoming fire."

Metzger scanned the tank. There it was . . . "From where?"

Werner said, "Unknown. Bogey Four assigned, not identified."

"Stealth boat," he said. "There's no reason they don't have them the way we do."

That meant another set of sensors they had to evade.

"So the good news is, I can not bother evading behind their detonation fuzz. We can boost freely, then go silent after our screen."

Hirsch said, "I'm going to work with you on this. We need as much boost as we can get without shorting ourselves on the phase entry, but we also need to appear to not be concerned about energy consumption. That keeps their search envelopes larger."

"I agree and thank you, sir."

The Captain asked, "The next question is why they revealed that boat by firing."

Good question.

"I expect it's a loiter missile. They want us to think the stealth is there and waste resources. But it doesn't matter where it is. Just that it can ID us."

Werner said, "That may be, but I'm doing everything I

can to find emanations or occultations that might show their maneuvering . . . and I think I have."

Bogey Four showed in the tank. It would have come from forward of the jump point, even forward of the UN base there.

"So they have a secondary base we didn't know about, and most of them don't either."

Werner continued, "They also have really good missiles. It seems to have IDed us and locked."

Hirsch said, "And that's why they revealed the asset."

Werner replied, "Has to be expensive."

Metzger asked, "Do I need to waste a warhead?"

Werner wrinkled his brow. "I think you can stop it just with jacks. Add in flash and reflection chaff."

"Agreed, and done."

The charges were dropped in soft, deep vacgel that would make their signature even less visible than everything already was. All combatants were looking as much for dark holes in space where none should be, as they were for emissions.

Captain Hirsch said, "I have a boost solution for you."

Metzger looked at it.

"That only allows us two more evasion burns."

"Yes. I'm trying to draw them into wasting power in pursuit, and minimize our exposure time. If they think we're in more of a hurry, I'm hoping they get careless."

His eyes were beyond gritty, stung with sweat. He could barely visualize the equations. Everyone here had stayed on with him. The entire combat crew had to be wired. Chef Assistant Lalonde kept bringing food and beverages, Morgan brought stims. In between, some of them got combat naps. No one was going below decks at this end.

"I have no reason to dispute it, sir. Just noting we're limited on future evasion."

He brought thrust online and the frame hummed.

Twelve seconds of light lag time later, Werner said, "They're boosting in pursuit."

"Good. Now we see if it works."

The burns had been carefully selected to this point to align them with Jump Point Two. This was to encourage the UNPF to concentrate forces on each side of the point. The four pursuers were hoping to chase them into a blockade.

It was likely, though, that someone had assumed the possibility of phase drive, since several Freehold warships had it, which freed them from the fixed points.

Now was when they'd find out. If the enemy all planned to converge near the point, it would increase the safety envelope when *Malahayati* deviated further from that course.

Captain Ashton saw the emission blip. "We have them. Thank *Gemdi* for the assist. Cut to minimum shipboard expenditures and chase those bastards down."

Rao asked, "Why would they head for the jump point?"

He shrugged. "Maybe they were towed in-system. Or damaged."

"Would they still have jump drive after a refit to phase drive?"

He shrugged again. "We don't know. I think that's more likely than them not being converted."

Engineer Basco asked, "Could they have ripped the phase drive out to reuse it, and plan to either lose this ship or slam the jump?"

That was a good speculation.

"Also possible. *Mirabelle* is going to cover the route to the point and prevent transition."

Alxi said, "Well they're visible now, and we're getting a lot more data. They can't win."

"No," Ashton agreed. "But they can't surrender, either. They're probably convinced we'd torture them to death or something, and they have to know we can't trust their intentions and will shoot to kill. So they may try to take someone with them. Between our ships, we have enough missiles. Fire when you have a solution."

"Will do, sir."

"Sir? They're firing."

Metzger was brought into a discussion between the captain and the engineer.

"Commander Hazey, is there any way at all to recover some of our drive power?"

Hazey said, "The only way to improve efficiency is to send an engineer aft to the reactor, under power, to make adjustments. They will die. And I guess if you're going to give that order, I'll do it, because I can't morally order anyone else to."

Metzger said, "I understand. We will try hard to avoid that." No, he could not request the captain give that order, not if there was any other choice at all.

"Thank you."

Metzger said, "Then I guess it's time to make our last

screen and burn, drop a loiter mine through the fuzz, jack off with everything we have left, and hope we power enough to clear system."

Hirsch said, "I see your envelopes. I have nothing productive to add. It's your mission, Astrogator."

"Understood, sir. We will initiate this maneuver on my mark. Countdown on screen."

Klaxons alerted the crew. Reactor power. Acceleration and boost. Danger close detonation. Stand by.

The weapons rolled out, improving their mass ratio fractionally. The screening warhead detonated, and boost cut in.

Engineer Hazey was going to be furious. Metzger had entered a Command code to bypass the locks Hazey had set in place. The program pushed the reactor to 141% of max, well over emergency max of 115%, and his warning of 125%. It was all or nothing.

That boost tapered down to 125%, then 120%, then stopped. They were still inside the debris sheath from their own detonation. Metzger itched. It was psychosomatic, but he was inside a fusion explosion, or at least the edges of it.

"They'll track us out of that, eventually," he said. "Hopefully, they first think we scuttled, then draw some wrong assumptions."

Engineer Hazey came into the net.

"I want Command to understand I am very, very unhappy with my recommendations being ignored. It should be noted at this point, if another vector change is needed, I will have to sacrifice a member of this crew to effect reactor repairs. I hope it was worth it."

Hirsch intercepted the call.

"I authorized it as an emergency measure, and felt it best not to alarm anyone with the status, in case of failure."

Damn, he was a good commander. All he'd said was for Metzger to proceed and Metzger hadn't said how far he was pushing it.

Hazey said, "Understood, and I comprehend the circumstances. Now please log my objection for the record, because this poor beast is going to need an overhaul if we survive."

But Bogey One was now out of reach, and Bogey Two was losing vector. Unless they had boost they hadn't exploited, they were probably out of it. Bogey Three could still potentially intercept, though they'd strain any known limit and need recovery afterward.

Bogey Four was still unknown, but a stealth boat likely didn't have the fuel ratio for any kind of chase like this.

Werner said, "Our loiter missile just went live. Intel on Bogey Four and Bogey Three. Not a lot, but it improves the estimates. Bogey Two is now evading."

And with that, Bogey Two dropped completely out of the race. No matter what they boosted, nothing known would let them pull enough G to intercept.

"Well done, Metzger," Captain Hirsch said.

"Thank you, sir, but we still have Number Three."

Ashton clenched his jaw against very negative feelings. Anger, frustration, fear, all boiling over.

They'd evaded the contact envelope of the enemy missile, and in doing so, lost any hope of catching that ship. *Quito* had maneuvered around it, being that much closer, but between fuel margin and the vector changes, she was unlikely to catch them, either.

He muttered, "Damn whoever is flying that bucket. He's in league with gods, or devils."

He saw the updated data in the display and said, "It's bad, but *Mirabelle* has them. Exact current trajectory plotted. She'll chase them down and slag them."

Helm Operator Rao asked, "Sir? How deep have you ever gone? Because we're going a lot deeper before this is over."

He looked at the plot.

No ship he knew of had been this far out. They were well beyond the heliopause.

"It's been an impressive chase."

Rao asked, "Are we going to offer them terms?"

"Those terms would be war crimes tribunals. They might win on a technicality. I doubt they want to risk it. They're going to run until we kill them. If they run low on power, they'll probably scuttle. I expect that ship is stripped to nothing."

Rao gritted his teeth. "Makes sense. We can't let them get away or they'll do this again."

"Exactly that. We'll keep scanning. Every bit of intel we get helps stop them now."

Bogey Three was moving further into the green.

Metzger said, "We have a single warhead, sir. And a minimal amount of energy margin. We're already likely to need a tow and refuel on arrival home."

Hirsch said, "I see the figures." The two of them were the only ones with the coordinates of their base.

Hirsch continued, "Strip out any gram of mass we can spare. Dump oxy, water, anything. We'll use that missile as we leave."

The Operations Officer, Commander Cortes, said, "Yes, sir, though we already stripped almost everything."

Across the deck, Metzger could see the captain's gaze. "Then strip more. Uniforms. Underwear. Crew can manage in a single coverall. If we have to, we'll dump that. Shlippers only. Unclamp any backup equipment and have that standing by. We might need that more, but if it'll save us, it goes. If it can serve as reactor mass, get it in there. If not, queue it to jettison."

"Sir."

The order was given, and below, crew feverishly abandoned personal clothing and items, ripped out spare equipment, dumped containers. Reaction mass crept up slightly from a handful of material that was usable as fuel without reconfiguring the process. The rest showed on a graph, which corresponded to increase in fuel margin.

I've spent the last two day cycles staring at a screen full of math and coded graphs, Metzger thought. Most people would have no idea what they were looking at. To him, it was their life or death.

A short time later, Werner said, "Incoming. Can't ID the type, but it's got hellacious maneuver capability."

Hirsch asked, "Can you call impact time?"

"Estimate only. The thrust is shifting continuously and apparently randomly within a range, more as it closes. We can't run."

"Can we evade?"

"If we do so just before detonation, we might spoof it."

Hirsch said, "Then configure that last VDAM and whatever chaff and decoys we have. Metzger, you and Werner make the call. Blow, jettison and boost."

"Yes, sir. Werner, what's our call?"

Werner said, "We'll have milliseconds in the danger close envelope, and we need to call that conservatively."

"Can we evade now?"

"I expect it has enough range to track and follow. It's very active. We're zeroed . . . and now there's two more launches."

This was it. Either they reached that safe plateau in space, risked entry this close to the primary, or tried to evade high yield warheads at fractional c.

Forcing steely calm into his response, he asked, "Can you give me a range on its expected detonation?"

Werner said, "It's on your feed. Updating as we go."

The missile showed as a dot with a glowing marker over it, fading from yellow to purple.

"Well, I think we can take a full second on the window. How fast can we get out of the envelope, allowing for response time?"

Lieutenant Hadfield said, "I think point five is pushing it. You didn't want to max boost again, did you?"

"Do we need to?"

Hirsch said, "Given your figures, one two five percent will suffice. One three five is better."

"One three zero. Split it." *And hope we don't blow up our reactor, or just render it incapable of powering the drive.*

Werner said, "Well, we're about to find out. It's on you."

"Alert, jettison and boost."

Metzger clenched up. G kicked, the ship's frame creaked, something thrummed as a too-close detonation caught them from the aft port lower. The dot in the display flashed bright, and figures scrolled. It was 40% more than assumed, far beyond what they'd anticipated, and inverse square law was their friend as they fled.

Aboard *Laconia*, Alxi shouted, "Detonation. I think *Mirabelle* got them!"

She then added, "Damn. *Gemdi* reports boost."

Ashton asked, "They got out of that?" The enemy crew were demons.

"Sir, we believe they were damaged, possibly severely. That missile got close enough they were in the plasma sheath."

"But not a hit."

Alxi said, "No, sir. That class of missile has been having frequent problems. A factory defect."

"So the contractors screwed us over again. The enemy is still maneuvering."

Alxi said, "Yes."

"So they got away."

Through clenched teeth, the Recon officer said, "I admire and hate them at the same time."

Ashton asked, "What's the word on the rest of the salvo?"

Alxi looked at her display and carefully said, "Captain . . . nothing can reach them on their new track. All five will burn out and abort detonate."

"At least we haven't made it less safe with debris."

Oh, he was furious. They'd fired eight missiles and possibly caused some damage. Four ships were scattered across the Kuiper belt and would need support craft to recover, taking weeks in which they were known to be unable to protect assets. His ship was damaged. Station Roeder had been lost with all hands, three ships in repair, nine boats in dock, over thirteen thousand casualties.

And the enemy was now at an insane $0.06\,c$, too far out for anyone to reach with anything. By the time any updated sensor info reached the in-system defenses, even those powerful beams would be too late. The request was sent anyway.

Then, as they watched, the ship contorted inside a phase field and disappeared.

"Command is demanding a report."

Ashton felt a ripple of cold adrenaline.

"I'll take that in my cabin."

Command would probably understand. The media and the public would not. Captain Virgil Ashton and his peers were going to be crucified in the press.

Captain Hirsch said, "You're keyed in on damage report."

The report tumbled in and Metzger caught the important parts.

"Eight dead . . ."

"Fifteen critical injuries . . ."

"Reactor feed damage, containment shaping defect, max power down to eighty-nine percent . . ."

"Frame damage, hull damage, contained . . ."

"Life support holding . . ."

Completely out of context, he asked, "Captain, what's the fastest you ever traveled?"

"I'm guessing you're about to tell me."

"We're at almost point oh six c."

Even with a modern, well-tuned forceline drive, that took enough energy to power one of Earth's continents for a year only a couple of centuries before.

Werner said, "Three more launches. Tracking five. On your display."

Metzger looked. The five all showed as colored marks, vectored toward their own tag.

None of them had carets in the green zone. None of them could reach *Malahayati*.

"We're clear," he said. "Barring something our intel didn't find, farther out than anything else they have, we're clear. Sir, I request permission to secure and sleep until phase entry."

"Granted. Well done, Astrogator. You are relieved. Don't worry about phase entry. Second Nav Miquelon and I can handle it."

"Thank you, sir. And all of you."

He rolled painfully out of his G couch and staggered aft. The surgeon assisted him to his cabin and onto his bunk.

With battle damage, short power and massive velocity to counter, they barely made it. *Malahayati* precipitated rather farther from the base than Metzger intended. They were four light-hours out. It would be ten days on minimal power and half rations before anyone would reach them.

Four hours was 1.5 divs. It was that long again before a response came to their report and request.

"Fuel and drinks on the way. Welcome home, *Hate*. Congratulations on your mission."

That nickname seemed to fit perfectly.

Captain Hirsch said, "Mister Metzger, I saved one bottle of sake for such an eventuality. Will you do me the honor of serving the command crew and yourself?"

"Yes, sir!"

End

A FLOWER GROWS
IN WHITE CHAPEL

Gail Sanders and Michael Z. Williamson

I was very happy with how the next pair of stories turned out. Set in Mercedes Lackey's Elemental Masters universe, an urban fantasy retelling of the early twentieth century, mostly in England. Our story is in fact set in London and surrounding areas.

Some of you may be aware I'm an immigrant, from the UK to Canada to the US. I understand several dialects. I also served in the US Army and USAF, so I speak those dialects too.

While writing this story, I wrote everything in English idiom—slang and colloquialisms for the time, spelling ("colour" instead of "color"), and so on. Gail kept fixing it to American standard when writing her parts, before we realized the conflict, and I took charge of final form.

Then the editors told us that while they appreciated the gesture, the standard from the publisher was American English.

Therefore, all these Brits are speaking like Yanks. Please be assured this is against my wishes and under protest. Twits.

ISABELLE HELEN HARTON, Headmistress of the Harton School for Boys and Girls was in her office when Karamjit knocked discreetly.

He said, "There is a child at the entrance, Memsa'b. The guardians want to speak to you."

She knew by his tone and phrasing that these were not the usual nursemaids or concerned parents that normally came to the doors of her school.

She closed her book, stood and said, "Thank you, Karamjit. I'll be right there." She rose from her chair and walked downstairs.

When she opened the door to the chill, damp, February air, she gasped and stared. There was indeed a child, but the guardians holding her hands so carefully were elementals.

It wasn't uncommon for waifs to be dropped off at police stations, orphanages or churches.

It was quite rare for one to be brought to the front door of the Harton School by earth and air elementals. In fact, it had never happened before.

Gathering up her astonishment and sitting on it hard she spoke with at least the appearance of aplomb, and politely asked, "May I help you?" Protocol must be adhered to when dealing with elementals or unexpected things could happen.

"She is pursued. She is in danger. She is alone." The breathy syllables could barely be heard above the noises on the street. The sylph's feet did not touch the ground and of course she did not leave a shadow, but she gripped the hand of the little girl with desperation all too visible, despite the sylph's transparency.

"What pursues? What is the danger?" Isabelle's astonishment was giving way quickly to alarm.

"We know not. All we know is that it has consumed her parents, and reaches out for her. Will you take her into your charge? Knowing that there is danger?" This was remarkably formal for a normally flighty satyr. This was also alarming to Isabelle and she hesitated, knowing that the request was both a geas and a binding. Looking at the confused and frightened eyes of the small girl, she knew that she could not turn her away.

"I will take her into my charge and protect her to the extent that I am able."

"It is well," both elementals said in unison, before disappearing, one sinking into the ground and one fading into the air.

The girl collapsed onto the frosty front step, as if only the elementals had been keeping her going.

The child appeared to be far too small for the neat little room. Her dark hair spread over the pillow as she restlessly shifted, but she did not awaken. She had a faint Chinese cast, but was clearly mostly European.

What am I going to do with you, little one? Isabelle wondered as she kept watch from an overstuffed armchair. She had no idea what the guardianship of the elementals could mean and the prospect of danger was not new, yet she was used to having at least some information on from which direction that danger might come. She also knew that she couldn't have left the little one to her fate. She sighed deeply and then reached up to caress the hand that had appeared on her shoulder.

"Who do we have here?" Frederick Harton, Isabelle's soft-footed husband said in his quietly concerned voice.

"I don't know, but potentially a very great problem." Isabelle gestured over to the clothing that was laid out on the other small bed in the room. Neatly arranged was a skirt with petticoats, as English as would fit in any middle- to upper-class neighborhood, but next to them was a blue silk tunic of distinctly Asian design. The fabric was a bit worse for wear, with a couple of ragged tears.

She ran her fingers over the rich fabric. "It's a cheongsam. They're Chinese and in this quality of material are only worn by higher-class diplomats or families. I encountered a few Chinese merchants in India and they didn't wear anything this fine. The Chinese are very structured with strict laws on what each level can wear. Why would a European girl-child be wearing something that only a Chinese diplomat would be allowed to wear?"

He offered a reassuring squeeze but no comment.

She continued, "We won't know anything until she awakens. She was also wearing a red silk pouch around her neck. I left that alone. Even in her sleep she got very agitated when I touched it."

"Does she have a name?"

"Mei-Hua," she replied. "Which is also a puzzle. She's

clearly English, and her accent places her to Cheshire. Yet she offered a Chinese name in excellent Mandarin."

"Headmistress?"

If her office hadn't been so quiet Isabelle never would have heard the hesitant question.

"Yes, Mei?" She tried to project reassurance. The little thing was so self-effacing that she almost blended into the walls, even after being here for a month. She had no problems with the other children per se; it was almost as if they didn't know she existed. Everyone in the school was surprised when she spoke, as if by her speaking she had become real to them again.

"Agansing said I was to talk to you, please? About the garden?" Mei-Hua bowed deferentially and kept her eyes low, avoiding eye contact with Isabelle.

"What about the garden, child?" Isabelle had to work hard to keep a sigh out of her tone. To a woman used to cheeky Londoner children, this politeness seemed both extreme and worrisome. Combined with Mei-Hua's knack of remaining unnoticed, it spoke of unseen damage from whatever she could not remember—either in what happened to Mei's parents or how she came to the school.

"Agansing said that no one really has time to take care of it. So may I please? And may I have a pot and soil for a plant in my room?" Mei waited, her slender body seeming tense and anxious.

"That sounds like an excellent idea. Tell Agansing I gave you permission, and if you need anything for the garden, he can help you with it."

"Thank you, Headmistress." Mei bowed again and closed the door behind her.

Perhaps with a useful activity she will come out of that shell. With that thought Isabelle turned back to reviewing her students' progress.

Isabelle stared, and searched her memory. Yes, just a few days ago, this plant had been dry, sallow, wilted and near death. She'd noted the contrast to those around it.

Now, though, it was vibrant with color, flush with growth and taller than its neighbors, which also seemed to stand more proudly. The bloom atop it was perfectly picture-book symmetrical, and seemed to glow violet with a lip-red sheen underneath. It was beautiful.

"How did this happen?" she asked the girl.

Mei-Hua shrugged slightly and mumbled, "It was tired. I helped it."

"You most certainly did!" she replied, but the girl had turned shyly away and offered nothing else.

Within days every flower in season bloomed huge and bright, even those that barely budded in April. The stalks straightened, the leaves filled out. All the herbs in the garden behind the kitchen sprouted thick and healthy, and the food gained an extra little zest.

Two weeks later, Isabelle happened to pass Mei-Hua's room whilst on an errand. The girl was just coming out on her way to breakfast. Behind her, near the window, the pot she'd asked for sprouted a huge white peony.

It was impossible for such a blossom to bloom so quickly. Or was it? Clearly it had. Clearly also, Mei-Hua had a Talent for flowers.

The girl took her classes, quietly, and had no trouble with grammar, arithmetic or history. When not busy with schooling or chores, she spent most of her time out in the garden, caressing and talking to the various plants, all of which responded with straight, robust growth. The plant in her room remained in brilliant bloom, new flowers replacing the old.

Lord Alderscroft's carriage was familiar, but its arrival unexpected. It drew up in front of the school, and he debarked in a hurry. He reached the door as Karamjit opened it in surprise.

"Good day. I must speak to Frederick and Isabelle at their earliest convenience," he said as Karamjit took his cane and hat.

In minutes he was seated in the drawing room, and hot, fragrant tea placed on a table between them.

Isabelle gave a nod that indicated Karamjit was to leave them alone. This was clearly something under the rose.

Frederick remarked, "So David, what brings you to our little corner of White Chapel? It's hardly your usual haunt." He poured three cups of tea with splashes of milk and delicate sprinkles of sugar.

Alderscroft accepted his cup with a nod and spoke directly to the point.

"I bring tragic news. You heard the King has been fatigued of late. It has reached a crisis. Yesterday he collapsed unconscious and is bedridden. They aren't sure if he's in a coma or has suffered an aneurysm or something similar."

Isabelle widened her eyes. "There was no mention in

the morning news, nor have I heard anything from the stands."

"No, it is all word of mouth, to keep it from the tabloids."

Her stomach fluttered.

"Oh dear. They have no diagnosis?"

Over a sip, Alderscroft said, "Not yet. He is officially taking a few days' rest at Marlborough House and responding to a personal matter. You see, the reason I came to you is that I don't think that the doctors are going to find anything. I think that the reason for his collapse has something to do with magic—but not my sort of magic, not elemental magic. After his collapse, my contact at the palace was able to get me into his rooms. They were awash with, something. . . . I could almost feel myself going under, slowing down. But I could not *find* anything."

"And so you've come to us, for help?" Isabelle's skepticism caused David Alderscroft to flinch, just a little. "Don't tell me you've found something that your 'White Lodge' can't handle?"

"Actually, I was hoping that Sarah and Nan could have a look. I can get us into the Royal Residence, into the King's rooms."

She flared her nostrils and tensed up as she placed her tea down gently but with haste. "No! Absolutely not. David, you know how I feel using the children that way. Sarah Jane Lyon-White and Nan are still children and I will not put those children into danger."

"Love, I think we must," Frederick quietly interrupted her angry reflex with a hand on her wrist. She leaned back into her chair as he continued, "Will we be with them, Alderscroft?"

He nodded and placed his own cup down. "Yes, I can promise that much. And I'll have to go along as well. They won't let you in without me."

She unclenched her jaw and accepted the wisdom of the idea.

"Tonight then. I want time to prepare the girls."

They rode in Alderscroft's carriage to the rear of Marlborough House. He stepped out first and spoke at length to a military officer, a captain, probably of the Lifeguards, but in field uniform, not parade. The other men all appeared to be police. Marlborough House was a Royal Residence, but not the Palace. The informal presentation would help disguise the king's presence.

The captain frowned darkly, but acceded after several minutes of talk punctuated with gestures. He stepped inside, and spoke into one of those new-fangled telephone boxes.

With a command and a gesture, the two guards at the door snapped their rifles to port arms and stepped aside. That seemed to be assent to entry.

Isabelle was impressed. Not even two waifs with birds and three obvious foreigners with a less than fashionable schoolmistress caused them to be anything other than impassive statues.

Inside, a young man in a bespoke suit gestured for them to follow him up the stairs. Even the rear servants' staircase was broad and elegant.

Little noise was made and nothing was said. They

walked down a long corridor, the children uttering soft gasps at the sights but otherwise silent.

Another guard stood at a double door, its panels bookmatched of some highly figured wood. There was an exchange of gestures between their escort and the guard, at which he nodded smartly, opened the door and stepped aside.

Within was a private chamber, richly appointed and smelling of tobacco. A doctor sat beside a huge, soft bed. Nestled in the deep comforters was His Royal Majesty, Edward VII, clearly sick.

His eyes were closed and sunken, his cheeks hollow. Even his proud beard looked scraggly and weak. Looking up at this remarkable group of people, the doctor approached Lord Alderscroft and obviously started to make a fuss.

Words were exchanged, the doctor wide-eyed with raised eyebrows. He looked at the unusual party and then back at Alderscroft, opening his mouth to protest. Then somehow, with the addition of but a few more low words, the doctor quietly gathered his bag and let himself out. Isabelle's cynical mind suspected a method other than sweet reason had been used to get the doctor to at least temporarily quit the scene.

"He won't be gone long," Lord Alderscroft commented rejoining the rest of the group.

At once, Grey whistled low. *"Bad. Something here."* The parrot fluffed up her feathers and then spread her wings over Sarah's shoulders.

Even the humans could feel it. There was an aura of despair. It was if they were standing on the edge of a cliff, staring down mesmerized at the rocks below, just waiting for the pull of gravity . . .

Neville quorked loudly, startling everyone. The raven on Nan's shoulder had his feathers ruffled as well and looked as if he wanted to bite something, if he could spot it. Even with the warning Alderscroft had given them, they had almost been drawn in themselves.

Sarah looked up at Grey and then over at Nan. Neither one of them obviously really wanted to get closer to that feeling, but Isabelle knew it was the only way.

"Memsa'b, we need light. We need light to pierce the darkness around the King."

Isabelle's voice began a chant that the girls probably found a bit familiar. Sarah had heard that chant before when the girls had been trapped in a house haunted by something worse than any ghost. Nan reached out her hand and clasped Sarah's before joining her voice to the chant. The other members of the party joined in. Slowly a glow surrounded the two girls and they walked forward approaching the pillared bed.

As the girls stood by the bed, time drew out endlessly. Sarah and Grey appeared to be conversing with . . . nothing . . . or rather, with something that wasn't there.

The darkness got heavier and the two girls retreated.

Nan blurted in a forceful whisper, "Let's get outta 'ere. 'Tain't safe. Back to the school." Even though she was a child, no one felt the slightest inclination to argue with her.

They made a hasty retreat, and Isabelle felt safer the farther they moved from the King's bedside. When they reached the stairs, she was merely unnerved. By the time they entered the carriage, she felt adequate.

"Not a word until we are at the school," she cautioned.

When they arrived back home, Nan and Sarah seemed comfortable and secure enough.

"I think that we could all use a cup of tea. Agansing, could you please bring it to the parlor?" Isabelle briskly took charge and chivvied everyone in that direction.

Sarah said, "Please, but . . ."

"Yes? Go ahead, young lady."

Sarah hesitated only a moment.

"Memsa'b, before I tell you what I found out, we need Mei-Hua. She has to be here." Her solemn tone lent her a maturity out of place for such a young girl.

Mystified, Isabelle went and found Mei in her room, talking to her White Peony in a soft melodious voice, in Mandarin. Startled, the girl looked up as Isabelle entered the room.

"Mei, we have a situation that may involve you, please come with me."

Mei simply bowed and followed the headmistress. She did not seem at all surprised. She followed to the parlor and took the worn chair in the corner.

Finally, with all of them gathered Sarah spoke nervously. "The King is possessed. They seek his life force. That is why the doctors find no malady. It is almost as if his dreams hold him captive and out of his body. The longer this goes on, the weaker he will become, until the king dies."

"Who does?" Isabelle asked. "Who controls his dreams?"

Sarah shrugged in agitation. "I do not know. Only that he is held."

It was entirely possible the doctors couldn't determine his condition because of limits in their art. However, Sarah had been accurate in her spiritual sojourns before. Isabelle was inclined to believe her. She did have one question though.

"How do you know this Sarah?"

"Mei's parents told me."

Mei-Hua gasped.

"What do you mean my parents told you? My parents are dead and gone, I saw them die," Mei-Hua whimpered. "I saw them die," she repeated.

Isabelle was glad that Mei's memory was returning, but she was afraid that the shock could be too much. She leaned over and took the girl's hand in comfort.

"Please wait just a moment, Mei," she said gently. After a few moments of sobs and deep breaths, Mei-Hua nodded, and she explained, "Sarah can sometimes talk to the departed."

Turning back, she asked, "Is that what happened, Sarah?" She gave a pleading look, wanting Sarah to be gentle.

Sarah nodded around her tea.

"Yes, Memsa'b. Mei's mother was a gardener and Mei's father was a foreign minister. They learned of a plot against the king because of England's actions in Hong Kong."

"By whom?"

"They said it was some enemy of the Emperor Zuantong."

Mei-Hua said, "Xuāntŏng." She looked a bit more alert.

Frederick asked, "Could it be the last gasp of the Boxers?"

Fully attentive, Mei asked Sarah, "Did they mention guizi?"

Sarah nodded and said, "Yes, I heard exactly that."

"It means 'demon,'" Mei said. "It's what the Righteous Harmony Society, the Boxers, call foreigners."

Isabelle asked, "Mei, were your parents working on a treaty with the emperor?"

Mei shifted in the chair and looked uncomfortable.

"Well, it wouldn't be with the Emperor, no one sees him, but with Royal Ministers. But I don't know."

Isabelle tabled that for now, and turned back to Sarah. "What then?" she asked.

Sarah said, "There was a spirit attack in China. Mei's parents had come up with a counter to it. Then the spirits moved here."

Isabelle said, "If they couldn't succeed against the emperor, then the king would be the next choice."

"Yes."

Mei said, "So that's why we came back." She looked very unhappy, but sat erect and strong.

Isabelle said, "Then your parents were attacked," she didn't say killed, "in London, before they could tell of it. Once Mei was under the protections of the school, they couldn't find her. So, they've been at the side of the king, hoping against hope that Mei would find them."

"What is this plot? Who's doing the plotting?" asked Frederick.

"They didn't know. They were only able to find that it involved getting at the king through his dreams."

"And the counter?"

"It's my White Peony." Mei looked terrified and elated

at the same time. "The one in my room. It's from the plant my mother bred. It's like no other in the world. Its scent will protect the king from the dreams. We were coming to England to present it to the king when my parents died. Now I remember why they're dead." A tear crept down Mei's face. "Now I remember who they were."

Isabelle leaned over and carefully held the girl. Between the spirit attack and the shock of it, her memory had blocked it all until now. Its return would be painful, too.

After some discussion, they formed a new party, much smaller this time; Isabelle and Lord Alderscroft escorted Mei-Hua to the House. She carried her White Peony in a beautifully painted pot. With due ceremony, Alderscroft's carriage was let into the courtyard. They debarked and entered through the main foyer, and in daylight this time.

The doorman and guards let them through, and their suited escort showed them to the front private stairs. Alderscroft said something, and there was another brief argument, but their guide bowed briefly and departed.

As the three of them climbed the narrow stairs, Mei-Hua slowed, and then stopped.

"I remember this place." Her whisper was so quiet that Isabelle almost couldn't hear it.

With increasing concern, Isabelle knelt down and looked at Mei.

"How do you remember it? You haven't been here."

Mei couldn't answer her. Her eyes were wide and she was caught up in memories, trembling so hard she could barely retain her grip on the flower pot.

"We were here," she said. "It was on these stairs."

The fear in her eyes caused Isabelle to glance up at Alderscroft. His expression was one of mild annoyance at the delay, but behind him Isabelle noticed a gathering darkness.

"David! Shields, now!"

Alderscroft reacted at once to her commanding tone, and raised the shields of a Fire Master, shields of ethereal fire. Through their swirling flames they saw the darkness strike at them and rebound, and strike again. It resembled a swarm of insects in its glittering darkness, but with no actual discernible forms. Eventually, after long minutes, it drew back and waited, just beyond reach of Alderscroft's shields, leaving them in a black stairwell that sucked up all the light that entered it. It even felt dank.

With the initial attack rebuffed, Isabelle felt Mei still trembling.

"Mei, what else do you remember?"

The girl stared vacantly, gasping in whimpers. She knelt and hugged the flowerpot.

Isabelle gave her just a slight shake. "Mei, we need to know now. What else do you remember?"

Finally Mei focused on Isabelle.

"They were only able to protect me, to get me out. I ran and I ran and I didn't stop running. They died to protect me." Tears rolled unnoticed down her cheeks.

Remembering the elementals that brought Mei to her, Isabelle turned and said, "David, they were Earth and Air. Are your shields still holding?"

He nodded. "Yes, but we need to start moving. This is going to get noticed. We need a guide through the darkness."

"Will a Warrior of the Light do?" she asked, though it wasn't really a question. Firmly, she added, "Mei, take my hand. This time you're not running."

Isabelle's appearance changed with each step of the staircase. She began to glow with a light that pierced through the darkness and lit the way forward. Her stature grew and her aspect became that of an ancient Greek huntress, wearing a short chemise-like garment that would have scandalized proper society. At least, it would do so until they had seen her face, then they would have been terrified. Step by hard-won step the trio climbed the sweeping stairs, Isabelle coaxing Mei-Hua along while Alderscroft reinforced the rebounding shields. When they had reached the top, the darkness gathered itself up for one final blow. Sensing the increase in tension, Alderscroft changed tactics; instead of blocking the onslaught, his flames engulfed the glittering bits of darkness. The flames roared up as they fed and then muted back down on his command. The hallway stretched in both directions, silent. Any staff had vacated the area from either spirit influence or fear of the ethereal battle in progress.

"Mei, which door?" Isabelle wanted her to lead as much as possible, to keep her attention focused so she wouldn't have time to be scared.

"I think . . . that one, Headmistress." Mei indicated with a tilt of her head, as one hand gripped Isabelle's tightly, and the other clutched the peony's pot.

"Are you ready, David?"

He nodded and said, "Let me go first, I'm still shielded." It was also clear he was straining to maintain those wards.

Alderscroft opened the door to the King's chamber. The wave of despair was visible coming out of the room, but it never reached them. As it neared, it simply dissipated and became the illusion it really was. The White Peony worked. Seeing no more visible threat, Alderscroft thinned his shields until they were unnoticeable.

The trio approached the King's bedside. The attendant doctor looked as if he were coming out of a long sleep in the chair where he had been sitting watch. Already the gloom was lessening, the light through the gauzy drapes brightening.

Mei-Hua approached the bed, carefully cleared small items from a bedside table and placed her White Peony as close to the King as possible. She fluffed it gently with her hands, delicately wafted air over it, and whispered soothing encouragement. The plant seemed to stand tall and fan itself out.

As the fragrance permeated the room, the King's color began to improve, and the remaining dimness retreated in ebbing waves.

Isabelle and Mei stood close to each other, but back from the bed, holding hands and waiting. Alderscroft continued to be on guard, scanning the room for any new threat.

Finally, his eyelashes fluttered and opened.

As the last traces of gloom vanished, Mei-Hua's eyes widened; tears continued to run down her checks unnoticed, yet she stood straighter. They all stood straighter, as if the gloom had been pressing down on them physically as well as mentally.

There was a long pause, while the King stared at her, and she said nothing, only stared back. Finally she gathered her courage and released Isabelle's hand.

Deeply bowing she said, "Your Majesty, I bring greetings from my honorable departed parents, Special Envoys and Ministers Plenary to the Emperor of China, Henry Walsingham and An-Hua Walsingham, to His Royal Majesty Edward the Seventh, of the United Kingdom of Great Britain and Ireland and of the British Dominions beyond the Seas. May I present this flower on their behalf, in hopes it will keep you well."

The King stirred, seeming most fatigued, but raised a hand. She extended hers for him to take, and curtsied.

Finally, he uttered, "Our thanks to your parents for their service, and my personal thanks to you." His voice was gravelly and strained, but his smile clear.

Isabelle sighed. Needs displaced desires, but change, even for the better, was always a complication. She had finally accepted David's invitation to move to the estate he offered.

The country would be both healthier and safer for the children than London's often thick air. Also, she was concerned about Mei. Since the King had recovered, Isabelle was afraid that the unknown plotters would make another attempt at either him, or Mei-Hua. The King had Alderscroft's White Lodge to keep an eye on him, but Mei was Isabelle's responsibility, one she took seriously. At least Lord Alderscroft's offer of his estate out of London as a new home for the school would give them some distance.

His Majesty did have inquiries about the cause of the attack. It should be possible to determine the opposition, but it would take agents and ships and long weeks at least. In the meantime, they knew the threat existed.

The girl continued to improve. His Majesty and His Majesty's chief gardener had many conversations with Mei on the properties and history of Mei's White Peony, for His Majesty had developed a personal interest in the flower. For now, though . . .

"Come Mei, it's time to go." Isabelle briskly took Mei's hand. Mei was wearing her gift from His Majesty; He had arranged a cheongsam, in a shining white to match the Peony she had given him, brocaded in broad patterns.

"Where are we going, Headmistress?" Mei-Hua looked around avidly. There was still a shadow lurking in the corners of her eyes, but Isabelle was relieved to know that she was on the mend.

"We're going back to the School to finish packing. I'm sorry we can't remain longer, but you can visit again."

"Thank you, Headmistress," the girl said, beaming.

Isabelle took a final look around the Kew Gardens. The sculpted hedges made neat, geometric shapes around the controlled riots of colorful flowerbeds. But Mei-Hua's attention was focused on a new exhibit, the result of her work over with the Royal Gardener. It had taken many hours in the greenhouses and beds, and had only been made possible by Mei's Talent with plants. It was an exhibition on the White Peony, now named after Mei's parents: the Huawang-Walsingham Peony.

Mei-Hua Walsingham bent over the wide expanse of

beautifully blooming White Peonies, inhaled their fragrance, and smiled.

"I am ready," she said.

End

A PEONY
AMONGST ROSES

Gail Sanders and Michael Z. Williamson

Gail deserves credit for significant factors in this story.

The last story was in the reign of Edward VII. He was succeeded by George V. I chose that event for the plot of this story. If you look through some obscure history books, you'll find Mr. I.H. Burkill, the Pagoda and the dragons are all historically documented. Gail found all those. George V did ascend the throne on the summer solstice in 1911. So this really might have happened . . .

⊕

MEI-HUA WALSINGHAM gave a wistful sigh. She enjoyed her position at the Royal Botanical Gardens at Kew, working with the rainbow of flowers and riot of decorative shrubs. But sometimes she missed the Harton School. Sometimes, she missed it more than she missed her parents, which was distressing.

She took that uncomfortable discovery to her parents' shrine in the corner of her boarding room. Lighting some incense, she sat in front of the little Chinese table that she had so carefully arranged. It held a White Peony and the official portraits Mrs. Harton had located for her once her memory had returned.

"Mother, Father, it's not that I don't miss you, but I know that you're still here watching over me. It's just that you're not a part of my life and the school became my home after you both were murdered. I miss my friends and I miss Memsa'b and Sahib Harton. I found a place there, I'm still not sure that I'll find one here."

It had all come out in a rush, because she had to say it, and had no one else to say it to.

A little breeze caressed her cheek, but it could have been just from the open window. That it smelled of her father's pipe tobacco and her mother's White Peony rather than the London air was also surely a coincidence. Feeling strangely comforted she rose to her feet and prepared for her day.

She had challenges ahead.

Last May the King had died.

There was nothing to be done about it. He smoked heavily, and had been ill for months. It was not related to the previous elemental attack on his person, but she felt hurt just the same. He had been gracious to her, and he had offered the financial support and the position she now had, unheard of for a woman, much less one of mixed blood.

He had died clutching one of the Peonies she'd had

delivered to the Palace to protect him. They were the legacy of her parents and could ward against evil. They couldn't ward against simple ill health and old age.

In the present, her Peonies were being moved to a new location by the Pagoda. It had been built by an Englishman a century and a half before, and while it appeared to be a pagoda at a distance, up close it was obviously English and not Chinese. It was half native, half foreign, and out of place. Mei realized that description could apply to her, too.

She had to coordinate the move with Mister Burkill of the Herbarium. He wasn't trained in magic, and hadn't been given all the details of the Peonies' power, but he knew they were special and essential to the Royals, and accepted them as his charges. The Peonies weren't famous, but they were noted in several high circles. That was enough for the staff.

"Good day, Miss Walsingham," he greeted her. "Are we ready to start the move?"

"We are, sir," she agreed. "One plot every three days for the next three weeks."

"As you say, Miss." He was agreeing because he'd been told to. He'd rather move them all at once, and had said so. Mei was worried about a drop in the Peonies' energy if they were all to be uprooted and distressed at the same time. Mister Burkill was an expert botanist, and well-read, but what she did wasn't in any book.

"I'll manage it," she said with a smile. "It means they'll have plenty of bloom for the Coronation."

"Well, the beds are ready, by the Pagoda. I think that's a nice match, don't you?"

"It's alright," she said noncommittally. They all meant well, she realized. They didn't grasp the intricacies of China, and to be fair, most had never visited it and never would.

"Let's hope the rain holds off," he said, pointing up at the gravid gray clouds overhead.

The bed was nicely dug, the soil black and rich. The gardeners had their wheelbarrows lined up like taxicabs, and were carefully digging up each Peony, placing it in a pot, and laying it in a barrow.

By eleven, the entire first bed had been relocated, replanted, and she fussed along the rows, using the edging bricks as stepping stones. She made sure to touch each plant, reassuring them that they were as they should be. She told them to wait on blooming until they were ready and refreshed.

By midsummer, they should be fully recovered and lush, for the Coronation of King George V.

The transfer of the first bed complete, she moved on to her regular duties.

From the second bed she chose a full, healthy specimen, dug it up most carefully and transferred it to a large pot. That was placed in a wagon, and rolled off to be taken to the Palace. The new King didn't know why Peonies were always in bloom at his residences. He'd be told when the time was right.

A light rain rolled in from steely sky, and they sheltered in the Temperate House.

Burkill had tea served, and invited the laborers to join them. He was a middle-class, Cambridge-educated botanist, but he politely ignored some of the class rules and kept in regular conversation with the workers. He did sit at his own table, though, and chose who would join him. Mei was the only subordinate who gained that privilege.

"Your flowers are very strange, Miss Walsingham," he said. "I've taken to analyzing them. They're stronger than other peonies I've seen, but still very tender and delicate. I can't explain it."

"My mother bred them," she said. "I don't know exactly what she did."

"I see," he said. "Have you seen the Chinese delegation for the Coronation, Miss?" he asked. "They've been through the garden twice this week."

"Only from a distance," she admitted. "They wouldn't know me, so I have no reason to visit with them," she said. That, and she was a half-breed. Some English accepted her as a "Colonial," others as the daughter of a diplomat. A goodly number treated her as a foreigner of lower station. The Chinese nobles and Imperial servants would think no better of her. Her mother's exile and marriage to a foreigner would mark her just as outcast to the Chinese, if not more so.

Ironically, the diplomatic delegation were all wearing English-style suits in their visits and business. She wasn't sure if she was glad or annoyed that they weren't in Chinese dress.

"They might not be overly friendly, given your father's station," he agreed.

"I'm all English now," she said. If for no other reason than the forces she'd fought previously would be delighted to have her on their ground. She was here to stay, where elemental mages, her Talent and Peonies kept her safe.

And she did love the Gardens.

Her boarding room was in a house three miles from the Gardens' main entrance. She was glad of her bicycle, which made the trip much easier, though many of the new automobiles were a problem in traffic.

She arrived home at ten after seven. Mrs. Seton, her landlady, had baked fish on the table. The other residents were girls who worked as housekeepers or seamstresses, and weren't home yet.

"That smells lovely," she said. "But I have work to do. I hope you won't think it rude if I take it upstairs."

Mrs. Seton smiled above her slightly plump figure and said, "Of course, dear. But don't work too hard. You need rest and fresh air."

"I get fresh air all day, madam," she said with a smile.

"Yes, but what about the rest?"

"I will, thank you." She placed a slab of lemon-seasoned sole on a plate, with some fried potatoes, and took it upstairs.

Once in her room, she set the plate down and removed her shoes. She did intend to rest. She also did have to review the schedule for the protective Peonies. Several plants were dispatched to the Royal quarters biweekly. Out of season, they were forced to bloom in a greenhouse. As they wilted, they were brought back to be nursed into renewed vigor, and others took their place. The entire replanting matter was interrupting that schedule. Then, she was tasked with the water lilies in the same area.

Those would be moved next, to a new pond. She was less tense over those, though she still wanted their move to be gentle. It showed her priorities, she realized, as the lilies would require more care in the move than regular peonies would.

A beautiful formal garden was spread out beneath her. Mei could see two people in this garden. It was a hot and sunny day near the height of the sun and there was a quality to the air that told Mei that this was not in England, or even in Reality.

The man said, "Well, hulloo there! Gads, what a lot of beautiful flowers. Are these all your doing?"

The woman started, obviously not expecting to hear voices in the gardens at this hour of the day. Usually the workers did the rough tasks just after the daylight broke and the nobility, diplomats and bureaucrats preferred early evening.

She pulled her expression over her emotions, gracefully rose from her kneeling position, turned toward him and bowed. She obviously hoped that he would mistake her for one of the lowly workers and thus escape his presence and his memory. She had not figured on his English "arrogance" and his willful ignorance of Imperial "civilized" behavior. She was also not aware of his keen eye for details.

Henry Walsingham hadn't been appointed the King's Representative to the Emperor of China without proving his skills in a different pool of sharks than the Imperial court. The unknown gardener's grace and her expert and unobtrusive application of Earth Magic had actually gotten Walsingham's attention weeks before. However, mindful of the proprieties he was bending, he had waited until he was sure that they would be unobserved. After a quiet word to one of the Sylphs hanging around him to keep watch, he had enacted his ambush.

With a properly respectful return bow (to one who may be an equal) and a much-moderated tone, Walsingham inquired in perfectly executed Mandarin: "It is my imperfect understanding that your mastery is responsible for these humble gardens achieving their present grandeur. Would the Master Gardener consider imparting some of her wisdom to me?"

Visibly realizing that she had strayed from the polite blankness that was proper to astonishment, the young woman schooled her expression.

"If the worthy gentleman wishes to receive wisdom, he might try someone more appropriate to his station." With that, and another bow, she gracefully turned and walked away from him.

Walsingham was forced to concede the encounter but not the battle. The glint of amusement in her almond eyes was almost a dare for the war to continue.

Mei woke from the dream with a start. Why was she dreaming of how her parents had met? While she had been told the stories, these dreams were too vivid to be just a retelling of those stories. Shaking her head, still caught up in the surrealism of the dream, she looked around her small room.

She was still dressed, and her clock said it was near 2 A.M. She shivered slightly. She didn't remember how she got to bed, but she was atop the blankets and England could be quite chill even in summer. She slipped into her nightgown and under the covers.

Why that dream? It was almost as if she were watching it in person. It bothered her. Was she obsessing over the past? Was it some sort of coping mechanism? What was she missing?

She drifted fitfully back to sleep.

The next morning, she took tea, and toast with butter and marmalade. It wasn't the same as rice porridge, but she did like the contrasting flavors of the tart orange and the savory bread.

She reflected back on her dreams of last night. Why was she imagining how her parents had met? It was almost as if her parents were trying to tell or teach her something. Well, she would wait to see what developed. Signs from the other world came as they would, and couldn't be forced.

She pedaled her way to the Gardens. Today she had to supervise moving another bed of flowers, review the orders for compost and minerals, and then encourage the recently transferred plants. The previous bed was being converted to something else, but Mister Burkill would see to that. Her specialty was the Asian varieties that were becoming so popular now that England was promoting its Chinese connections, and above all, to keep the White Peonies for the Royals.

After rolling through the front gate of Kew Gardens she parked her bike and secured it with a lock. From there, she went on foot to her station. She reflected on how much she enjoyed her walk in the mornings. It might become unbearable come winter, but for now it gave her a chance to see the other plantings before starting work. She courteously greeted the planters and other gardeners and for every smile returning her greeting she received a frown or a hostile look. Mei sighed. She hoped that it wouldn't take long for the others to understand that she was no threat to their position or standing. For an empire that "the sun never set on," England's people had a very narrow viewpoint.

She walked down the path toward the Pagoda, and took the long sweep toward her beds. Then she gasped and cried.

The Peonies were blighted. Not only would they not make a proud display for the coronation, they might not survive at all. Nor was it just the new bed. The old beds were suffering, too.

She didn't understand. Flowers responded to her touch if not her presence. That was her Talent. She'd had her hands on them only two days before, but now they were wilting into a wrinkled, stained, soggy mess.

"Oh, no!" she cried, and ran forward.

"Miss!" Burkill shouted.

She stopped and turned.

"Begging your pardon, Miss, but the Director said you should stay back."

"Why is that?"

Reluctantly he answered "They're saying you did it, Miss, the Chinese diplomats. They're saying that you're out to get revenge because of your mother's exile from the Imperial Court."

"Mister Burkill—Isaac, do you believe that I would kill my mother's legacy?" In her desperation she broke both protocol and propriety. "These Peonies are the only gift I have from her."

"I know, Miss, but I don't know what else to do. I have to obey the Director."

Mei-Hua Walsingham drew herself up with dignity. "Yes, but I know who the Director has to obey."

It was time to make a telephone call.

"I don't know who you contacted, Miss, but the Director didn't half act as if he had seen a ghost." There was certainly a hint of both glee and astonishment in Burkill's voice.

"You'll have a chance to meet him. He's meeting us here to have a look at the Peonies. I'm afraid that there is more going on than meets the eye, and he sees deeper than most. Even if he spends most of his time in that silly Men's Club of his." That last comment was voiced tartly enough that Isaac raised an eyebrow and yet held his peace.

Mei and Mister Burkill didn't have long to wait. Shortly, they saw a very dapperly dressed man with a shock of white hair, almost like a lion's mane, walking toward them along the path. He plied his walking cane briskly and was within speaking distance after only a few minutes wait.

"Miss Walsingham," he said courteously.

"Lord Alderscroft. This is Mister Burkill. He is in charge of the Herbarium and this section of the Gardens." With a twinkle in her eye Mei went on to say, "He's a

Cambridge trained Botanist and sure to achieve Director himself someday."

"I don't know about that, Miss." He held out his hand to shake Lord Alderscroft's. "I'm just a simple gardener," Mister Burkill said a little stiffly.

"I'm a Cambridge man myself you know," and with that mysterious alchemy of attending the same College, even if in a different discipline, the ice was broken. "I recall we met once or twice in school, and your credentials prove you are no simple gardener."

After a few moments' courtesy talk, Alderscroft excused himself and walked slowly among the Peony beds, leaning over to examine several. He spent quite a few minutes wandering around, and the frown on his face deepened.

Eventually, his travails brought him back to her.

Mei looked questioningly at Alderscroft and raised her eyebrow. They had discussed the possibility of elemental interference on the phone when she had asked for his help. Alderscroft shook his head; there was nothing he could detect.

"No?" she asked aloud.

"I find no signs of any foul play," he said.

Her heart sank. She couldn't have done anything to harm them. She hadn't. All was as it should be. Except they were dying.

"Please let me look for myself?"

With Lord Alderscroft standing as surety for her conduct, Mei was allowed to approach the wilting beds. She knew that she should feel insulted by the need to have him here for that purpose, but she was too intent on the task before her. The conversation of the two men occasionally penetrated her concentration.

". . . they're making a lot of fuss over having the daughter of an exiled and disgraced Chinese high-caste family in charge of an Imperial treasure, by which they mean the Peonies . . ."

Mei felt the ground, it was sufficiently damp but it clumped oddly.

". . . there's a lot of people who don't have anything better to do than spread around what I put on the beds . . ."

She stroked the leaves and stalks. Tell me what is wrong, she asked the Peony. It responded slowly, as if through a fog, but it didn't know.

". . . the Director's not the only one listening. I hope she can solve this or there may be an Incident . . ."

The Peony couldn't tell her, but Earth and Air could. There was a vague smell that was neither Peony nor rot. Something had been added to the soil around the plants.

It was either poison or some kind of magical equivalent. Certainly the other side was eager to suppress the Peonies and their healing agency. But was this attack on them via elemental intervention or by simple contamination?

"It is either a poison or something that had been added to the soil," she said.

"You don't think it is a common blight?"

"There is an easy way to tell," she said. "We plant an unrelated species and see how it responds."

Alderscroft said, "We have less than a month until the Coronation. There isn't time." He emphasized the last word to remind her that they needed live Peonies at the Palace, within days.

"There is time enough for me. But I must be left in peace. I need a rose."

Alderscroft gestured. At a nod, one of the gardeners, Mister Higgs, came over to consult, then strode briskly to the greenhouse. For fifteen minutes, she and Alderscroft waited silently. He pretended to observe the garden. She used her hand to dig a small planting hole.

Mr. Higgs returned with a rose cane, its root in a burlap wrap.

"Thank you, Mister Higgs," she said politely, then turned and placed it in the ground.

Mei shifted her long skirt and sat on her knees in front of the rose, whispering to it and caressing it. It visibly grew as she coaxed it. She moved from sitting to squatting and back, keeping as comfortable as she could on the damp earth. Lord Alderscroft was nearby, she knew, checking on her every few minutes. She paid no attention. The plants needed her. Mister Burkill kept a more discreet distance.

When the rose was only an hour old, it was already a foot high with a tiny bud blushing through sepals.

The bud was dark-tinged and oozing.

Poison. That was what had happened. Nothing magical was involved, which is why no amount of elemental effort had found anything.

Lord Alderscroft cleared his throat. She turned and looked at him.

He asked, "Is that grotesque color what you refer to?"

"It is," she said. "Now, I need a lot of roses."

He raised an eyebrow. "If that's what you need."

Mister Burkill came over. His expression was neutral, but bothered. What he'd seen wasn't natural, and he clearly knew that.

Alderscroft still wasn't convinced, but was giving her the benefit of the doubt.

"How many is a lot?" Mister Burkill asked, less skeptical than Lord Alderscroft. He could see the effects of the poison for himself.

"Probably all we have. Have the planters run them in a line along the edges, right against the bricks. Then we'll need to run a hose and pump from the pond."

She expected to be told it was impossible, but Mister Burkill stood, stiffened, and took off at a smart walk, almost an ungentlemanly run.

Twenty minutes later, five gardeners Mei didn't recognize trundled over barrows containing a half gross of roses.

"Here, Miss?" one of them asked.

"There. All the way along, please. Just a hand's depth in will be fine."

They produced trowels and started digging.

"The water should be pumped slowly, just to keep the barest puddle on top," she said.

Another team of men arrived with a hose and pump on a cart, and unrolled it toward the water.

Mei felt guilty at what she was to do. The poor roses were a sacrifice. They drew more water, and would draw the poison with them, and she'd force them to strain unto death to do so. People told jokes about flowers feeling pain. They weren't jokes to her. But the Peonies were wards of the Royals, and the roses were the soldiers she intended to use to protect them in turn.

Alderscroft watched her, convinced at last she was right. And what power she had. Who would have thought a Talent over something as mundane as flowers could be so key? And now, it seemed that Talent could force entire fields of growth. But it was draining her.

He motioned for one of the staff. The man hurried over.

"Sir?" he asked.

"Please ensure Miss Walsingham has sandwiches and water. Some lemonade might be nice, too. If there is a parasol available, bring that as well."

"At once, milord."

She sat there all day, encouraging and stroking the roses—roses that visibly crept from mere canes to mature shrubs, then died. Each wilted, tattered rose represented poison drawn from the soil. Was it enough? As each rose wilted and died it was replaced by yet another immature cane brought by selected staff. Were there enough plants?

She grew tired and ragged, her eyes bloodshot. But by the time of the long dusk, she slumped alongside a row of dead English roses.

Inside that perimeter the Peonies stood proud, bright and healthy.

Mei woke hearing voices in the next room. Her surroundings were unfamiliar; she was not back at the boarding house where she was lodging. The room was bright and airy, featuring a floral wallpaper and late afternoon light streaming into the room. The last thing she remembered was the gardens and then darkness.

". . . Look, I don't care how she did it; it *could* be magic for all I care. Those peonies are now right as rain. Those so-called diplomats were wrong about Miss Walsingham and you know it!"

"The problem, Burkill, is that while I, King Edward and now you, all knew the value of those peonies, no one else does. Except whoever is trying to kill them off."

"The other problem is that King Edward is dead. King George is too busy getting ready for his coronation to even know what danger he could be in."

"That's my problem, Burkill. We can bring the King into the fold after things settle down a bit. Meanwhile, those peonies are additional protection until we can. They have to stay healthy!"

"I'm just a gardener, My Lord. Miss Walsingham and I can handle the flowers; you just make sure we don't have to deal with any of those deuced foreigners while we do so."

"A Cambridge botanist is not a simple gardener and Mei is one of those deuced foreigners in some people's eyes."

"Yes, that's the other problem—now, they're saying that maybe the peonies might have contributed to King Edward's illness. After all, there was one clutched in his hand when he was found . . ."

The voices faded off as Lord Alderscroft and Mister Burkill headed out of her hearing. Mei would have liked to have heard Alderscroft's reply; things would have been much easier if she knew what he thought of such rumors.

Well, it didn't matter. She had to get up and see for herself just how the Peonies were doing.

She was still very weak and being light headed didn't help her progress. They'd removed her shoes before covering her up. Bending over to lace up her shoes almost caused her to faint again. She had really pushed her Talent past her limits. Leaning up against the door she listened, then slowly opened it.

"Miss?" a female voice said.

"Yes?" she asked, turning.

"Are you feeling better? Mister Burkill said we wuz to take care of you."

"I'm alright now," she said. "Thank you. Is this his house?"

"Yes, Miss."

Taking her time and frequently leaning up against the wall, she made her slow and careful way to the front doors. She had to politely shoo the housekeeper away. She'd be fine. She just needed to get back to the Gardens.

She hoped the cabs were still running in this neighborhood.

The brief rest in the cab restored enough energy for her to walk with some semblance of her normal energy through the entrance to Kew Gardens. While she kept herself to a decorous pace, inside she could hear her Peonies crying out: "Hurry, hurry, hurry." She knew something was wrong. Everything in her felt it. There was a gathering of energy ahead, a swirling of air and a spattering of rain where the sky had been largely clear shortly before.

Undeterred by the weather she approached the Peony beds. The area was deserted as the visitors took shelter from the sudden storm. Weather had never bothered Mei. Even though she couldn't see them, her father's Air allies watched over her still. A quick pause to reach down and touch the Earth confirmed her feeling of something amiss. The Earth, too, was troubled and for the same reason that Air was troubled; Magic was stirring ahead— dark magic.

Quickening her pace as much as she could in her long skirts, she approached the Peony beds around the Pagoda. Those closest to her appeared to be unharmed and she sighed with relief. Reaching down, she stroked the leaves and flowers of the shrub nearest her. The Peony practically screamed into her mind. Shocked, Mei staggered back and then noticed a furtive figure skulking near the beds closer to the Pagoda.

Near the crouching figure there was a ripple of color running through the White Peonies. They were changing from white, to red and then to black. Without pausing to think, Mei approached the unknown figure. Straying slightly to the side of the paved path, she grasped a hoe one of the planters had left behind from the planting yesterday. With her steady stride muffled by the rising winds, the figure was too involved in whatever they were doing to notice her.

Hesitating slightly at the vague sense of recognition at the man's clothing and the touch of the magic spilling over, she stood poised above him with her hoe—and then she swung.

❖ ❖ ❖

*"Earth and Air, our daughter. Earth and Air will find
you. Earth and Air will aid you. Earth and Air will bind
you."* Mei-Hua Walsingham heard her parents' voices in
the caress of the wind on her cheek. She smelled her
father's pipe and her mother's favorite flower carried on
that breeze.

Then she was awake.

She looked around. She was in a tower looking out over
the gardens. She was in the Pagoda. How did she get
here?

A gust of wind slapped at her, and she turned while
clutching at the wall. She was on the top balcony, and the
man from the garden was standing near her.

"Mei-Hua Wang, you have been most aggravating," he
said in Mandarin. But his accent placed him to Shandong,
where the Boxers arose. "Your ancestors would not
approve of you consorting with *guizi.*"

Guizi. *Foreigners.* But she was English, too, caught
between worlds.

She wasn't sure if the wind had been elemental, but he
hardly needed it. He could loft her over the balcony in a
moment. If he was a Boxer, they were called that in the
West because they were skilled in Kung Fu.

He started chanting and staggered, almost as if drunk,
but she knew that was a fighting technique, and that it hid
spirit possession.

She leapt lightly back, and had to steady herself again
against the balcony rail. She needed a way back inside
the building, and then perhaps she could race down the
stairs.

A voice said, "We're with you, Miss."

She stole a glance over her shoulder to see Mister Burkill, with a pruning hook. He sounded nervous, but sure.

The Chinese man was in full fury now, swaying and waving and whirling. She understood some of his incantation, calling for spirits to possess him.

Then she heard Lord Alderscroft's voice.

"It is spirits you want? Then you shall have them, sir. Miss Walsingham, you must focus on the wooden dragon."

She wasn't sure what he meant, and cast her eyes about. There, at a roof joint above them, was a stub. At one time in the past it had been a carved dragon. Each roof peak had had one. They were rumored to have been gold and sold off, but they'd been lacquered wood, and rotted away.

Wood! But it was dead wood. She had no Talent over it. However . . . was that a hint of moss? A few vines?

She did focus on it, coaxing it, urging it to grow.

Trees were a product of Earth and Air, her parents' elements. This was dead wood, but there was plenty of air, and the decay under the moss was earth, and it was growing.

In a moment, the lump flowed and shifted, and she yelped in fear, but it resolved as a dragon's head with a twisting body and furled wings of moss and ivy: an Imperial dragon.

Her attacker staggered, and shouted, and the wind rose to a howl.

Then Lord Alderscroft said, "Air, sir, against a winged dragon? But I am a Master of Fire."

The dragon twisted and wove, blocking the space

between the Chinese mage and them. Then it snorted a breath of sulfur, and followed it with a scorching blast that singed her hair.

The heat rolled over her, with the smell of scorched and dried wood and fumes, and the wind dropped to a hot breeze, then to nothing, and the dragon evaporated into dust, fragrant with the smell of damp moss.

The mage had disappeared.

Mister Burkill said, "His goose is cooked."

Before she could make sense of the horrible joke, he continued, "So, this is what you do for entertainment, Sir and Miss, playing with spirits?" He sagged back against the wall and breathed deeply.

"I've partaken of spirits ever since you and I read together at Cambridge," Lord Alderscroft said. "But we should get Miss Walsingham to the ground, for some tea."

Yes. She found herself shaking in reaction and fear. But she felt a rush of relief under it.

The Peonies weren't precisely "featured" at the Coronation, but as the Royal Carriage rolled past, Mei could see a plant inside. It was one of her Peonies, contrasting against all the pageantry with its brilliant white. Here and there, men wore other flowers as boutonnieres, as did some ladies in their corsages. There were enough scattered about to dissuade any interference. The beds at the Gardens were in full bloom, and that much energy should shield the whole city for now.

There wasn't much to see of the parade. Her main reason to be present was to see her flowers, both from pride and duty.

Lord Alderscroft and some other ranking personages had explained the nature of elemental magic to the King, and advised him on several defenses, including the Peonies. Her work was to continue.

Back at the Gardens, Mister Burkill was congratulatory in his own calm way.

"The flowers look spectacular, Miss," he said. "You have done well, even better than I'd have thought possible."

"Thank you, sir," she said. "I wish there were more I could do. People are starting to grow more peonies in their gardens, and I hope it will be enough."

"I hope so, too," he said. "There has been some more work in that direction, though."

"Oh?" she asked.

Burkill said, "His Majesty has reviewed the events, and has asked that I take a post at the Botanical Gardens in Singapore in a year or so. That will give us a broader knowledge of your Oriental flowers, and their strange powers."

"In a year or so?" she asked.

"Well, Miss, first I have to learn what I can here, if you don't mind sharing your knowledge. And while ladies can't be awarded degrees, a study of natural science at Girton College in Cambridge seems like a fair exchange."

"And perhaps my mother's Peony could be brought back to China." It would be fitting, she thought, ending her mother's exile in a way. The next few years looked to be very full.

She had challenges ahead.

End

HOW SWEET THE SOUND

Morgen Kirby and Michael Z. Williamson

My friend Morgen Kirby wrote the original version of this for a planned anthology in an alien universe. That project didn't carry through, so she had good story with an unusable setting. It wasn't going to work in the Freehold universe. Magazines didn't want it. But it was a good story.

I did some minor tweaking to change the setting, and made suggestions. She changed the setting a bit more. I did some small edits, and advised on some others to fill in the new background. She did those and I polished a bit more.

This is mostly her work, and I served in a supervisory capacity, as they say, but I am proud of, and enjoyed being part of it.

For the record, while I am Scottish by parentage and ancestry, I don't play the bagpipes. But I own bagpipes. Yes, that's a threat.

⊕

DONAL FOUGHT HIS WAY UP from a nightmare of rains and flooding and desperation. Slowly the images faded as he clawed his way toward wakefulness, but the dream-induced shivering didn't fade. He was cold, painfully cold. Something about the entire idea felt wrong, and he shied away from examining it too closely. He started groping for warmth, warmth that should be right about there . . .

The warmth wasn't there. He woke a bit more and started groping, and found something else that felt wrong: Why was the edge of the bed there? *That's not right*, he thought, and opened his eyes.

He blinked sleepily at a dimly lit room. It was small and institutional and definitely not where he had expected to wake up. "Elys? Elys, where are you?" he croaked.

There was no answer, but he hadn't really expected one. The sound of his voice in this room reminded him of where she was. And every morning, as Donal cursed himself for a sentimental fool, he cried brokenheartedly for his dead wife Elys.

Idiot. I buried her, I watched her die, I couldn't do a damn thing to save her, you'd think I would remember it and not look for her every time I opened my eyes . . .

It only took a few minutes to cry himself out. He wiped his face with the flat of his hand, shoved the covers back and swung his feet to the cold floor. *And isn't that a shame, married forty years and it only takes a few minutes to cry enough to get you over losing her?*

"Forty-three years," he said aloud, answering the voice in his head. "Forty-three years we were married, and there never was a better woman on the face of the earth."

He went to the sink in the corner and splashed some cold water on his face to erase the tear tracks. His reflection stared back at him accusingly the way it did most mornings, or so it seemed to Donal. He didn't look too closely at it, and it repaid the favor by not looking too closely at him.

Elys had made Donal the happiest man alive when she'd said yes. She'd given him her great heart, her sharp mind, her skilled hands. She'd given him two sons, both gone now in the aftermath of the invasion attempt. She'd had patience beyond belief, but when you passed that she had a temper that had a lot to do with Scots ancestry and even more with bone-deep pride. Slim and strong and beautiful as the trees at harvesttime, all red and gold and glowing and spirited . . .

Go on, I was never all that, said a remembered, more-beloved voice from inside Donal's head. *You need to be getting to it. There's work to be done and dwelling on the past won't make it go away.*

She was dead, and he was living in a bunker that resembled and was called the Anthill. Earth had survived the invasion, mostly. The larger cities were still craters. The rest of them were abandoned. The alien landing sites glowed from whatever hellish power source they'd used, but wasn't strong enough to stop fusion bombs.

Fusion bombs, however, were less effective against bioweapons. The actual disease had been quarantined out of existence. The parasitic Riders, though, that dulled the brain and turned animals and people into zombies who'd attack any living thing were harder to beat. The timeframe had been months, then years, then tacitly assumed to be never, though now the experts said years again, as they devised new strategies.

And right on time the broadcast started up. He didn't know whose bright idea it was to start the day with little-progress bad news, but it had been there since day one and wasn't likely to go away any time soon. Donal scrubbed as best he could with a wet washcloth while listening to some no-longer-chirpy youngster asking the scavenging teams to look out for clothes and blankets, seedlings and plants with the roots intact, tools, and basically anything electronic. Hydroponics needed all the help they could get. Her co-anchor, an older man with what was supposed to be a reassuring voice, reminded everyone in the Anthill to make sure their radiation equipment and their weapons were well-maintained. Maps of known hot spots, he said, were available at the hatches.

The report from Commander Sheffield did have some actual new news in it. Some maniac out NORAD way had managed to capture a few Ridden feral dogs. They'd planned on studying them, maybe dissecting some. Those plans lasted for the first day. Luckily someone had kept cameras on the containment area for the whole time, and had caught footage confirming that the Riders were not only carnivores but viciously cannibalistic. The lone surviving Ridden dog had been too badly injured to last long, but it had gorged itself on its kills before dying. NORAD had also managed to remove a mostly intact

Rider specimen. Pictures would be available at the hatches, but in very general terms they resembled a squid with a main body the size of a plum. Tentacles infiltrated the brain and spinal cord through openings in the skull.

The sign-off was, as always, three things. A weather report. A sort of prayer, addressed To Whom It May Concern, that this end quickly. And a time estimate until humans could take back the surface.

Donal, who by this time had finished his wash, gotten dressed, and made his bed, laughed humorlessly at the estimate. "Five years? Yesterday it was seventy. If we're lucky."

Oh hush. People have to have hope. It keeps 'em working and brings that day closer.

Work wasn't outside anymore. It wasn't safe: the Riders had invaded a lot of the animal life big enough to support one of the parasites, and would gladly take a human. So no more of the farming he was used to, and harvesting wood for furniture-making was an unacceptable risk while there were metal and plastic furnishings still in storage. He couldn't even work at something that would tire him out enough to let him sleep decent, since the idiots that did the work detail had decided that he was "too old to perform strenuous duties." As he tied his shoes, Donal snorted at the thought.

"Sixty-three isn't old. I can put up a barn by myself if I have to."

I know it, love. God willing, when this is over you can put up another one.

Now they had him babysitting. He changed diapers, he

put on band-aids, he cleaned up spilled drinks, and he came home every day with a headache from the screeching. He frequently thought that some of the children would be improved by a swift swat to their hindquarters, but the room nanny had thrown a fit the first time she'd seen him do it. She'd watched him like a hawk ever since.

The walking stick he used now was in its usual place next to the door, and it clip-clopped along with him halfway down the hall before he remembered to go back and lock his door. He muttered a curse at the door, the lock, and himself for being forgetful as he worked the key out of his pocket and used it. He hadn't needed to perform that particular chore Before; his neighbors had all been honest. Here, it hadn't been a month before someone had opened the door and trashed his room. Luckily they'd not found his pipes, but after that he locked his door. Sometimes he even remembered to lock it before he started walking away. Most days he even remembered to take the key with him when he went out.

"Can't teach this old dog new tricks, I guess. A man used to be able to trust his neighbors. Now I don't even know who they are. Some neighbors."

And you've said boo to them?

His morning route took him down an elevator, along a couple of hallways, and into a room full of tables and chairs. The painted words above the doorway said "Cafeteria C." This was where Donal ate and spent time with his grandsons, which was about the only appeal the windowless institutional room had for him. He looked over at their usual table and there they were, the last family he had left.

Breakfast with the boys was the usual mixture of tragedy (the food, if it could be called that) and business. *I wouldn't have given this slop to the hogs, and now I'm eating it myself. If only Elys*—Donal choked off that thought.

Through breakfast the boys normally talked about their schoolwork, which seemed to be mostly out of some survival manuals, and Donal talked about his job of watching little 'uns, and all of them carefully avoided talking about anything from Before. Today the boys were acting tense, but Donal figured they'd tell it in their own time. Neither James nor Scott were the type of boys to get into trouble, and they weren't quite old enough to be interested in girls yet. Good boys, they were, and Donal was proud of them both.

The three bowed their heads and said their usual quick grace, with Donal's added thought *Thank you for enough food today, may there be enough tomorrow.* Today's breakfast, the fatty nameless meat and bitter coffee and stale toast and canned milk, not to mention the ever-present pile of vitamins, had vanished as fast as two growing-boy appetites could make it go. All that was left was the oatmeal with all the warmth and friendliness of paper pulp. James and Scott looked hard at it: they'd been raised to never waste food, but they clearly doubted whether the oatmeal counted.

"I don't blame you, boys," said Donal, putting as much syrup as he could on the dubious grey mass. "I've had tastier road mud. But your grandmother, God rest her soul, would say . . ."

". . . Eat it now so you'll have it when you need it,"

chorused the boys. They copied their grandfather and finished their breakfasts, scraping every last scrap out of the bowls. Donal finished his coffee and was about to stand up when the guilty looks the boys had been exchanging focused on him.

"Grandpa, can you come with us this morning? Just for a little while?"

"I suppose I can be late today, James. What's the matter?"

"Nothing. There's just something—"

"Something we want to show you," interrupted Scott in a rush, his freckled face blushing slightly.

Donal stood. "Lead on, boys. Let's get the dishes cleared away and I'm yours for a while."

The three got their trays, coffee cups, glasses, and silverware picked up and took everything over to be washed. They weren't ten feet from the table when the spots they'd been in were claimed, and other people were trying to eat their share of food that was nourishing enough to keep body and soul together but not tasty enough to make you like it.

The boys walked quickly toward their classroom, with Donal a step behind. The walking stick he carried wasn't something he needed for everyday use, but it did make a handy discouragement to the occasional group of thugs who thought honest work was something for someone else to do. Usually he could keep up just fine.

The boys joined a trickle of other people, their classmates and some parents and grandparents. Donal nodded to some he recognized. They filed into an open bay, originally meant for storage but now converted to a

dormitory. There were beds along one wall, scavenged
packing crates converted to makeshift foot lockers, and
folding chairs set up along the opposite wall. The floor was
clean enough to eat off, and there was a military
uniformity to it: though the footlockers were scavenged
packing crates and no two bunks had the same bedding,
every corner was carefully aligned. Everything was put
away neatly and the corners were sharp. Everywhere else
the windowless grey walls were depressingly generic: here
they were covered with charts and pages from various
manuals.

At a sharp whistle blast, the boys ran to stand beside
their bunks and stood at attention. Donal was impressed,
and surprised into taking a closer look at the boys. He'd
known they were getting taller, but James had filled out
and Scott was working on it. Maybe his boys were
becoming men, and he had missed it.

They can't be growing up just yet, Donal thought.
They're only . . . He stopped and thought about it. The
two boys, his grandsons, were twelve and fourteen. Not
even old enough to shave. And there they were, standing
like soldiers. Donal shook his head in disbelief.

A short stocky man closed a door firmly behind him,
startling Donal out of his thoughts, and walked to stand
in the center of the lines of chairs. He had a slight limp
and an air of authority that made the limp seem irrelevant.
He looked over the seated group and waited for silence
before filling the room with his clear spoken voice.

"I'm Sergeant Thomas. I've been training these boys,
your sons, your brothers, your grandsons. You've been
working on keeping us fed, clothed, civilized. Your boys

have been learning to keep us safe. They've done well in the classroom. Today, it's time to start the real-world testing. Starting today, we see if your boys have learned enough to be men."

Sergeant Thomas turned to face the line of painfully young faces. He glanced at each face, boys on the edge of adulthood, untested mettle, untempered metal.

"We're going to be sending you out on scouting parties. Two boys will go out with one of the regular patrolmen. They'll stay out for a week. I want you to bring back any info on Rider concentrations. Individual Riders of course are target practice. The scientists want a sample. I say hang the scientists, I want you back alive with all your equipment and whatever you can salvage. If you can't bring it back, map it.

"You know how to survive, boys. Time to prove it. Make me proud. Fall out."

As he turned and limped off the floor, the boys relaxed and came over to confer with their families. Scott and James were glowing, proud and as eager to please as puppies. Donal stood and hugged them fiercely, reaching up (and what a surprise that was, James was taller than he!) and putting an arm around them both.

James said, his voice hoarse, "We wanted to surprise you. We wanted to make you proud. Just like Dad did."

Donal, looking from one face to the other, smiled around the lump in his throat. "You did, boys. You always have."

Scott said, "We'll be leaving in the morning, Grandpa. Sarge has us heading north."

"I'll be ready to go, just tell me when."

The boys looked at each other, frowned. Scott, confused, said, "But civilians aren't supposed to—"

"I want to go see your grandmother, boys. I've been waiting until I could ask, one man to two men. It's time."

"But . . ." said James.

"Let's go talk to that teacher of yours." Donal was quiet but firm. "I want to go home, boys. Take me home."

Sarge had taken one look at Donal's face and thrown the boys out of his office. "Go pack," he said. "This is going to take a while." He closed the door firmly after them, then limped back to the chair behind his utilitarian desk.

Sitting back in his own chair, he looked at Donal appraisingly, while Donal looked straight back. After a few seconds Sarge chuckled.

"Okay, we're two old dogs sniffing and wondering if we're going to fight. I for one have better things to do. How about we have some coffee and you tell me what's on your mind?"

Donal chuckled as well, and relaxed a bit. "I want to take a trip back to my home. It's not far from here. I'll . . . probably be staying."

Sarge silently took Donal's measure, then unlocked one of the drawers of his desk. "This'll take something a bit stronger than coffee, I think."

Sarge poured a generous slug of bourbon into Donal's cup, and a little bit more than that into his own. There was a thriving black market in various forms of 'shine, and the vats could produce something that was vaguely like beer, in the same way that hard tack was vaguely like chocolate cake: most of the proper ingredients were there, but not enough to make it taste good. This was good bourbon, real bourbon from Before, and so both men paid devoted attention to the first sip of their drinks before focusing on each other again.

"Are you going to cripple those boys?" Sarge didn't sound as if it was anything besides a routine question. Donal didn't like the thought that it could become a routine question, but he'd started it and he had to finish it.

"Those boys've grown up fast. They haven't had any parents since this whole thing started. Except me. And I haven't been much of a parent, none of us had time. So they did it on their own, these last three years. Hell, you've been more of a parent to them than me." Donal sighed. "They don't need me anymore. If they don't need me anymore, then I need to get out of the way."

"You're not working?" asked Sarge.

Donal snorted. "They think I'm old, so they've got me doing the idiot stuff that doesn't take muscle, that isn't *work*. It's fine for the ones used to sitting. I'm not. I've farmed all my life. Sitting just makes me think, and the more I think the more I want to drink myself blind."

Donal brought himself back from the inside of his head and looked at Sarge. "If I drink, hell if I sit here and think much longer, I'm going to kill myself. If I kill myself here, someone will have to deal with it. It'd probably be my boys. Leaving a mess for them to clean up isn't right."

Sarge nodded and took another drink of his coffee. "You still haven't answered my question," he pointed out.

Donal sighed. "I know."

The two men sat as Donal thought. Finally he answered, "I don't think so. I think they're grown enough to mourn, but I think they'll understand."

Sarge nodded slowly, just once.

"You leave tomorrow at six. Don't take anything the boys can't bring back. I can't say I like it. But I understand it."

"Thank you."

"Thank me by not making your boys shoot your parasite-Ridden ass the way I had to shoot my parasite-Ridden mother." Sarge grimaced, gulped his mug of high-octane, shuddered. Donal topped off Sarge's mug with the bourbon, added some to his own mug, and the two men went to work on drowning past horrors.

The ancient Humvee bounced along the winding mountain road. The road wasn't in bad shape, considering. The passengers still had to get out every so often and move the occasional fallen limb or animal carcass while Jack, the driver, stood sentry. The test was supposed to have an outer limit of twenty-five miles, but the cabin was a little bit beyond that, so the boys and Donal were going to have an extra two days.

Jack hadn't liked adding a passenger, especially a last-minute one, but had settled a bit when Donal showed him where the cabin was. No radiation hazard and out of prevailing wind currents of the nearest one, up-mountain so water contamination would be minimal at most, no bridges to cross. Best of all to Jack's mind, there were three routes up until the last three miles. If they had to backtrack, they could. It wasn't going to be a day in the park, nothing was anymore, but it wasn't going to be a raid into downtown either.

Donal had an extra pack on his lap. It was not his gear but one precious reminder and remainder of his life Before: the satchel containing his bagpipes. He kept an eye out, watching the autumn-painted trees go by and thinking of Elys's copper hair. His fingers fidgeted with the clasp when they weren't moving in patterns of songs he remembered.

They all soaked in the feeling of sunlight on their faces, air that smelled like plants and not disinfectants, and wind that came from moving and not from a vent. The boys were nervous and kept looking up, flinching at birdcalls and rustling brush. Around and behind made sense: there'd been a hog farm around here, and a hog with a Rider was a fast and terrifying threat. But up?

"I'd forgotten it was so big," said James, and Donal winced. Another thing to blame himself for, keeping his grandsons in that damned Anthill where they couldn't see the sky. *God grant they'll have plenty of time to get used to it again, and soon.*

The one-story cabin that Donal had lived in most of his life was as untouched as a building left alone for a few years could be. The barn was in slightly worse shape, but there weren't any holes in either roof. Donal had built solid, built to last, and it had. The Laramie place, Donal's closest neighbors Before, had been raided a month before Donal had finally given in and gone to the Anthill. Donal had helped put up the house there too, and built just as solid, except for the picture window Betsy had wanted in the living room. A Ridden bear had broken it and eaten every man, woman, child and beast inside that solid house. He'd come back from seeing how much it'd cost to have the Jenkins bull cover his milk cow just in time to kill the bear with blood on its muzzle. One of the goats had gotten out of the pen and was shredded hair and bone all over the yard.

Donal shook his head, chasing away the old bad memories. Jonas Laramie had been a close friend, best man at his wedding, and he'd been best man at Jonas' wedding. Their kids had played together. Jonas had given him the carved wooden nameplate that still hung on Donal's front door.

Three last turns on the road, then there was the familiar driveway on the right.

While Jack and Scott kept watch, Donal got out of the Humvee and dragged his old keychain out of his pocket. He unlocked the door to the last true home he'd had, then took the nameplate down and handed it to James. "Put this in the Humvee, please. Your grandmother would want to know it's safe."

The biggest part of the inside was one low-ceilinged great room, as neat as it could be after standing empty for a few years. The shuttered windows in the front room had unbroken glass, but the window over the kitchen sink was long gone and the cabinets warped and mildewed.

The boys split up to search the house and block off any entry points. Jack, walking into the kitchen, called out, "Be careful, the floor's soft in here."

Donal smiled one-sided. "If you fall through, you won't go far. The basement doesn't extend under the kitchen."

Jack snorted. "That's reassuring. I'll only get my foot caught, not my whole leg."

"Yeah, pretty much." The two shared a black-humored laugh. By the time the boys had reported all windows blocked (to Jack, Donal was disappointed and gratified to see), Donal had cleaned enough of the living room to have a good place to sleep. Jack's scavenging through the kitchen had turned up jars with bulging tops, dry goods that no longer were, cans that by their dates might still have edible food, and a drawer that had held dishtowels and now had a very comfortable nest of mice. He didn't even try opening the fridge, claiming that "dealing with hazardous waste wasn't in his job description."

Donal had had better luck. The cedar-lined linen closet had escaped mouse habitation, and the coats in the coat closet had some wear left. He packed them carefully, sometimes stroking careful hands across an afghan Elys had made or something that she had worn and loved.

The four worked hard, with at least one sentry for every trip outside to pack things into the Humvee. Elys's cookbooks, Elys's pots and pans and knives, Elys's pictures, Elys's seed packets and sewing machine and everywhere Donal looked there was something of Elys that was being taken down and packed and taken away. The living room and dining nook and kitchen were slowly emptied, packed and taken out or packed and stacked against the wall for later retrieval.

It was too much like erasing his life, erasing Elys. Donal excused himself and went back to what had been their bedroom to be alone in the last refuge of her that there was. He sat on the tattered, rodent-eaten remains of the bed they had shared, letting his silent tears soak into what had been her pillow while the boys and Jack removed Elys from the rest of the cabin.

A knock on the doorframe startled Donal awake. Scott stuck his head in, announced "Dinner's ready," and then left without waiting for a reply. Muzzy-headed from sleeping during the day, stiff from leaning against the wall, Donal sat up and dry-scrubbed his face, then stood and stiffly walked down the short hall and into the main room. The other three men, sitting in the light of an old oil lamp, carefully didn't look at him as he sat at the table and ingested the travel rations they'd brought. Donal didn't pay too much attention to what he was eating: he wasn't sure he wanted to know what the food was supposed to be.

He woke up as he ate, and started watching the others who so-carefully were not watching him. They looked about as healthy as anyone could, considering. Donal mentally nodded: his boys could go on without him. They just had to figure that out.

After dinner, Donal got out his pipes for a practice session. The strains of Amazing Grace came sweetly, if a bit haltingly. Danny Boy followed, then Silent Night, A Rovin', Mood Indigo, Agnus Dei, She Walks in Beauty, Taps. A verse of the Wedding Song. Then Amazing Grace again, slow but sure this time, as always the song to put the pipes to bed. The silence as he did so was reverent.

Donal was almost done with his pipes when something crashed into the side of the house next to the kitchen. Jack grabbed his rifle and went to the kitchen window, moving aside the cabinet door he'd blocked the window with.

James snuffed the single oil lamp on the table and Jack opened the shutters slowly after he'd gotten his night-eyes. One carefully placed shot and whatever had been trying to crash through the wall collapsed on the ground instead. Jack latched the shutters.

"Small bear I think," he said. "Looks like it's alone, but there's not any way to tell without going outside to look. I don't suggest anyone do that. You said this place has a basement? We'd probably better sleep in it, if there is one."

"This way," said Donal, picking up his pipes and his pack.

Jack had set up a watch order, with James being first and Jack taking the hated midwatch. Jack left Donal out of the rotation "since it's not your grade up for grabs here."

The front and back doors had been barred and blocked, and the shutters hastily barricaded by bookshelves. Jack slept almost instantly, but Scott tossed and turned for a while before he finally dozed off. Donal laid on the floor of the basement and felt like he'd fallen off the Earth he knew to land on a different one. This was *his* house. He should be asleep in *his* bed, next to *his* wife.

Instead, he was asleep in his basement, and his fourteen-year-old grandson stood guard against the ghoulies and ghosties and long-leggity beasties and things that went bump in the night. Good Lord deliver us.

God, he prayed, *tell her I'm coming. I'll be there soon as I can.*

Elys's familiar chuckle filled his head. *Bit late, aren't*

you love? Or maybe a bit early. More likely early, knowing you.

Donal closed his eyes and pictured her face. *I had things to do, Elys,* he thought.

He could almost feel her stroking his cheek, as she had so many times. *So did I, love. I wish they'd been the same things.*

Donal smiled in his sleep as his lovely dream-wife helped him forget one more time.

Dawn came too early and too late, grey and cold and smelling of rain. Breakfast was a subdued affair with Jack keeping an ear out and the boys lost in thought. Donal, sitting for the last time in his chair in his kitchen, kept wanting to look for familiar homey touches that had been packed and removed yesterday. It was home, but didn't feel like home. But then, with the weight of what he planned to do that day upon him, nothing felt quite real. Not even the boys, boys he'd known and loved all of their lives.

Boys he intended to never see again. The thought felt like a gut-punch. *I'm leaving my boys. God grant me the strength to do it.*

Routine carried them all through eating, washing up, packing to go. Donal checked his pipes as he assembled them, wiping off a speck of dust, picking lint off the bag, checking the reed and the keys. His care was almost ritual.

"I'm going to take a look around before we go. There may be a group out there. Boys, I want you to cover me." After clearing the windows, Jack checked his rifle and went out, shutting the door carefully behind him.

The boys half-opened the shutters while Donal started a series of scales to warm his hands. He started soft and slow and gradually got louder and faster, enough to make what was left of the windows rattle. He closed his eyes and played the loudest, shrillest note he could, then quickly scaled down as deep as his pipes would go.

Outside, Jack yelled and fired a couple of shots. Scott fired through the window once while James kept an eye on the tree line. Donal, drowning himself in his music, barely heard the noises as he began Amazing Grace.

Jack said something that wasn't clear. Scott asked, "What?" and this time Jack's response was loud and clear: "You need to see this. All of you."

James closed and latched the shutters of the window he was at and crossed the room to keep Jack covered.

Scott's hand on Donal's shoulder startled him away from the music. "Jack found something he wants you to look at, Grandpa."

Donal set his pipes down carefully, then picked up his rifle and went outside. James, he noted approvingly, kept scanning the tree line even though curiosity must be eating him alive, and Scotty had resumed his post at the other window.

Jack was kneeling next to the corpse of the mountain lion he had just shot. All but one of the hits were torso shots: that one had taken it in the head, passing through and out the other side but leaving the face relatively untouched.

Well, at least the shot had left the face untouched. The mountain lion looked like it'd walked into a chainsaw: its eyes were gouged out and deep slashes ran from its forehead to its throat. The sides of its head were also deeply gouged and the flesh hung from its head in chewed-looking strips. Jack had slashed through the bulge at the base of its skull, making sure to kill the Rider as well as the beast it rode.

"Something got it good," said Donal. "Bear, maybe."

"It got itself good," corrected Jack. "The slashes run the wrong way. They're only on its head. And look at its front paws. It did this to itself. And come look at this one."

Jack moved over to squat beside the one that was in a heap against the wall of the cabin. Donal recognized it: once upon a time, it had been Will Davis' dog, a boxer/lab mix. Jack sliced the bulge on this one as well.

"Just like the other one. Looks like it tried to tear its face off, doesn't it?" Jack threw a quick glance at Donal. "I've never seen them do anything like this. Maybe those pipes of yours hurt their ears."

Donal snorted. "You're trying to tell me that they're not music lovers?"

"I'm trying to tell you that I don't know. But I'm going to be keeping a sharp eye out while you're doing whatever it is you came out here for. I watched that mountain lion claw its face off, and try and claw its ears out of its head. It banged its head against a tree a couple of times too. Then it charged the house. Anyone else talking about it, I'd'a laughed at them. Somehow, seeing it just wasn't that funny."

Donal said drily, "I hope that isn't some sort of comment about my playing."

Scott looked at Donal, mock-innocent. "Oh no, Grandpa. It's a comment about your singing." James snorted muffled laughter as Donal shook his head and muttered, "Smartass."

"Just for that, you can do the dishes for today and tomorrow," said Jack as he stood to go back inside. "You forgot the Eleventh Commandment."

Donal stood as well. "Eleventh Commandment?"

"Yup," said Jack. "Thou Shalt Not Get Away With It."

The walk uphill was tense. James and Scott had had good training, but didn't have the knack for slow sweeps yet. They started at every rustle, nervous as first-timers with buck fever. Jack, with a lidded bucket carabinered to a back belt loop, was slower and more methodical in his sweeps. Donal kept an eye on them as he played Nearer, My God, To Thee while they walked. He'd never seen the boys as nervous as now, and they'd grown up in those woods. *They'll settle*, thought Donal. *But settle or not, they're someone else's boys now.*

The final resting place for Elys's earthly remains was under an apple tree that Donal had planted for her when they settled in the cabin, and a few rotten fruit were scattered across the weeds covering the grave, all the good ones having been scavenged the day before. Jack took a few precious moments of attention to mark the tree on his map: fruit, fresh fruit, had gone from commonplace to desperately desired memory in the Anthill. Bringing back the location of a fruit tree would buy a lot of social credit. After he buried her, Donal had cut down and tarred the stumps of every tree within about thirty feet of her grave, so she'd be able to have the dawn light fall on her, but he hadn't been able to bear the thought of laying axe to that one tree.

Donal stopped playing and bowed his head. He prayed briefly to the God he'd been introduced to as a boy, the God that he'd never quite forgiven for taking Elys too soon, the God that at the end of the day was comfortable and comforting and there.

When he raised his head, Jack was making slow circuits of the clearing and the boys were clearing the spoiled fruit and weeds off of the grave. Donal heard their ragged breathing and knew that the boys wept. They had loved their grandmother deeply, as she had them. Donal ached to sleep beside his wife: the boys ached to sit at the table and help her make dinner, to be fed by her love as much as by her cooking.

Finally it was clean. The boys had weeded around the simple headstone, carved with her name, birth and death dates, and something Donal had said at the funeral. "She goes and takes the sun with her."

Amazing Grace. First, last, and always, Amazing Grace. Tears ran down Donal's face as he played for Elys. It had always been her favorite song. The boys sang in choked voices, and Donal soaked in their voices as best he could. It would be the last time, and he found that while he was tired and ready to lie down with his wife, he mourned for the boys who might someday understand.

Hallelujah (and wasn't this the coldest and most broken of hallelujahs?). Taps. Danny Boy. Good Night, My Ang

And then a shot, followed by a shout from Jack. "Boys! Incoming!"

Donal cursed himself for forgetting a rifle as James and Scott wiped their faces and turned to fire at the oncoming creatures. There were three of them, coming from different directions, all with clawed-up heads, all staggering blind and full-tilt for Donal and the two boys. Jack was in the way of one, and shot it in time to keep it from running over him, but the other two didn't seem to know he was there. They tripped over the stumps, slid on the apples, and still came on. James shot one while it was trying to get back up, shot it again to make sure it stayed down.

Scott had his rifle aimed at the last one, but didn't fire. It staggered toward him, fingers digging frantically at the ruined meat where its ears had been. Something dangled from a ruined ear, something that might have been tentacle. "Becky, stop!" he yelled, his voice shaky and cracking.

James heard his brother and whirled around. He charged the creature and swung his rifle, hitting it midback and slamming it to the ground. Scott covered it but still didn't fire, his white face showing his freckles in sharp contrast. It tried to scramble to its feet but couldn't seem to get its legs to work.

Jack called out, "Kill it, Scotty!"

"I can't!" Scott coughed out between harsh gasping breaths. "That's Becky, oh my merciful God that's Becky Laramie, she's only eleven, oh God . . ." He trailed off as the thing at his feet tried to drag itself toward him, and took a reflexive step back. James raised his rifle to his shoulder and aimed, but Jack barked, "No! Scott has to do it."

Scott turned a bewildered sick face to Jack, then to Donal. "Grandpa?"

"A man has to kill his own dog, Scotty."

The thing on the ground, dragging itself forward, grabbed Scott's ankle. Scott screamed and put a bullet in its head with panic-born speed. He threw his rifle down and pried frantically at the emaciated fingers, breaking one off in his haste. Once free, he backed away then turned and puked.

Donal walked over to the corpse and kicked it with all his might. The self-mutilated corpse rolled just enough to send Donal into a towering rage. He kicked it again and again, unaware that he had started screaming at the dead pile of alien-infested flesh on the ground before him.

Finally he ran out of breath and curses for the Riders, their ancestors, their siblings, and their livestock. His foot and leg ached like the devil, his throat was raw, he was sweaty and puffing and his ears rang. The corpse's ribcage was rather more concave than a ribcage normally is, and the remains of the head swung a bit more freely than heads normally do. There was stinking blood all over Donal's boots and his legs up to his waist, and the sticky filthy stuff was too much to bear. He took a few steps away, pulled up some of the long grass, and started scrubbing at his boots and pants.

Jack, cleaning his knife next to one of the other corpses, whistled long and low. "And I thought I hated those things."

Donal shook his head, still scrubbing the disgusting muck. "Those things. Ate. My sons," he puffed. "Chased. Me off. My land. Made. Me break. A promise. To Elys." He inhaled deep, held it, let it out slowly. One more, slow in and slow out.

"Those damned monsters are the only things that ever

made me break a promise to Elys. I promised her I'd play on her grave every year. I've been stuck in that damned Anthill and the last two years I haven't been out here to play."

Donal looked with loathing at the corpse of a girl he'd loved like his own. "That was Becky Laramie." His voice was soft and gentle and disconnected. "She liked blue flowers. She made Elys a wreath and got her to smile when the pain was so bad she couldn't think straight. She was a sweet girl. She liked listening to me play. I'd rather have died than have her be Ridden. And I don't even know if we've got time to bury her decently."

"We'll make time. Let me get this—" he thumped the bucket "—back to the Humvee and I'll grab a—Look out!"

Jack's eyes focused over Donal's left shoulder. James shot twice and Donal heard the body fall. Jack went over to look, leaving Donal to finish cleaning up as best he could. As Jack walked by Scott he patted the boy's shoulder and Scott looked after him with shamed gratitude.

"Grandpa, this one isn't clawed up," called James. Before the Riders, it had been a dog.

"Maybe this one doesn't have whatever the others had," suggested Donal as he limped over.

"Look at the back of its neck. It's infested, all right. I think your pipes drew the others in to stop whatever was hurting them, and this one followed them to the meat. We know they're cannibalistic." Jack shook his head. "I know dog whistles hurt dog ears, maybe this is more of the same."

"That's ridiculous. Flu, rabies, that I could believe. Anthrax. Allergic reaction to those damned parasites. Poison ivy, even. But bagpipe music?"

"Ridiculous or not," said Jack, rising from where he knelt, "we'll have to cut this short and head back as fast as we can. Even if it's not your pipes, I've got to get this head back to the Anthill. Somebody needs to know what's going on. What I wouldn't give for a working phone right now."

Donal shook his head. "I'm staying. I'm tired, I'm finished with what I needed to do, and I'm staying."

"Staying, Grandpa?" asked Scott. He had recovered his rifle and was trying to keep watch like his brother, trying to regain Jack's respect and trust, and all-too-aware that he'd just proven himself a boy.

"Scotty, being useless is a sin and a crime. I've got nothing else that had to be done. There's nothing left that can't be done by somebody else. I'm useless now, worn out. Time to throw me away. I'm done."

"But you're not—"

"Scott."

Scott looked at his brother, wordlessly begging James to back him up. James swallowed. "You're not staying, Grandpa," he said.

"Don't fight me on this, James. It's hard enough."

"Grandpa, either we all go, or I'm staying with you."

"Me too, Grandpa," said Scott, his voice cracking as he stepped up to stand with his brother.

"The hell you are." Donal glared at his grandsons.

James swallowed nervously but stood his ground. "If I'm a grown man, you can't stop me. If I'm not, then you're not done raising me."

"You listen to me, James Patrick McLeod—"

"No, you listen to me, Donal Thomas McLeod! Ask Grandma what to do. I know you still talk to her, ask her!" Donal was shocked to silence.

He's right, you know. Elys's voice was sober and quiet, and Donal shook his head and squeezed his eyes shut to try and lock her out.

That never worked before, love. It didn't work while I was alive, it won't work now. I'm inside your head, remember? The boy's got a point. Several. You need to go back.

Donal covered his ears and crumpled to the ground weeping. The much-beloved voice of his dead wife continued to echo in his pain-filled mind, telling him that it wasn't time yet, that he had to carry on alone for weeks and months and years and eternities yet. He didn't feel the boys hugging him or their scalding tears mixing with his own. He didn't feel the wet grass soaking his pants, or the rock under his right knee. His heart was breaking, and he had no time for trivialities.

He was dimly aware that he was being carried back downhill to the cabin. He heard the others talking, disconnected sentences floating around his head, occasionally stopping to make sense before wafting out again. "I've got the pipes." "Are they damaged?" "I don't think so." "How is he?" "Damned if I know." He . . . drifted.

It was dark when he woke up from being not-there. Donal sat up slowly, feeling cold and creaky and old, as he never had before. Jack, sitting by the basement steps, drew on his home-rolled cigarette and stubbed it out against the wall, then took a drink from the cup next to him. He didn't offer to help Donal up, and Donal was dimly grateful for that.

The boys had laid down one on either side of Donal, snuggled close and tangled in their blankets. As he extricated himself, they scooted in their sleep, seeking the missing warmth.

"You scared the hell out of us, old man," Jack said.

Donal, stretching and wincing, spoke to the air. "The last time I felt like this, I got thrown from a horse my neighbor's daddy had. Took the bruises a while to fade, and I walked funny for a while after that. I never did get on a horse again. Promised I wouldn't, and I never did."

Donal looked sidelong at Jack. "I never broke a promise to my wife. Not a single one. I went up there today, and I was going to send you back to that damned hole in the ground with those two boys while I stayed here with Elys."

Donal closed his eyes, cleared his throat, and swiped the hair back from his downturned face. "It was going to be the hardest thing I'd ever had to do. I only had the guts for once. I'll never be able to do it again."

Jack opened his mouth, closed it. Opened it, closed it again. The look of shame on his face was dimly visible in the lantern-lit gloom, and Donal met his eyes for a painfully intense instant.

Scott murmured in his sleep, wordless, and tried again to snuggle against the warmth that had been there. He touched his brother's hand and subsided. Donal bent down and adjusted Scott's blanket, brushing a hand against the sleeping boy's hair. James too got a gentle caress from a work-roughened hand.

"They still need you," Jack said. Donal stood with an effort, limped over to the stairs and started up them one at a time. His knuckles on the railing were white as he pulled himself up.

"They need a lot. I don't have it to give to them anymore."

The answer that Jack couldn't give was closed behind the door, shut away with the boys who represented Donal's present. It was the past he needed to be in now, the past he needed to come to terms with.

He went up to the kitchen, got a drink of water from the canteen with his pack, sat down in his chair at the table. The well-remembered room had only a few slivers of light through the shutters, but the light in his memory was enough to guide him to his accustomed place without hesitation.

There had been the salt and pepper shakers. There, the napkins. There, the scented candles that Elys had loved. And there, oh there had sat the most wonderful woman in the world.

No fool like an old fool, said the remembered voice.

"And your fool, always," was Donal's quiet answer.

The boys still need you.

"The boys are men now. What they need, they can get for themselves. I need you. I need to be next to my wife again. I can't do this again. If I leave now, I'll never be able to do this again." His voice broke with the confession that he wouldn't ever have the heart again to try and put a bullet in his brain.

The breath of memory-Elys's sigh held regret and exasperation. *I need you too. And I'll have you next to me again, you know that as well as I do. But you're not done yet. You know better.*

Donal closed his eyes as hot shameful tears burned their way down his cheeks. In his heart, he knew that Elys was right. Just as he had always known, and seldom admitted, that while the voice was Elys the words were nothing more than his conscience.

Now he stood accused, by himself, of cowardice and laziness and selfishness. Of trying to get out of doing the work he owed. Of not doing right by his boys. He could deny none of it, could apologize for none of it, and there was only one way to atone. Only one way out, and that was through the long lonely days ahead.

Finally the tears ran dry. Donal felt empty, and smaller somehow. Broken. But broken or not, it was time to take up his load again, and get back to the work that was left to him before he could rest.

The coffee was about ready when he opened the basement door. Scott and James in their sleeping-puppy pile stirred and stretched. Jack stared at Donal, took his measure, and nodded to himself.

"Come and get it, boys. We've got some walking to do today."

"Grandpa?" James looked like he was waiting to hear the bad news. Donal winced inside at the sight of the boy's face, hopeful and suspicious and already preparing for disappointment. Scott wouldn't look at Donal, but his whole body listened with painful intensity.

"Come and get it, I said. We still need to check out the Laramie place before we head back to the Anthill. And I'm pretty sure Jack wants to get rid of whatever's in that bucket."

James lunged up the stairs and tackle-hugged his grandfather tightly. Scott was half a step behind, and they clung together like castaways with the storm still raging. Donal's back and legs ached as he held the boys . . . No. He held the two men, his grandsons, close to his heart, and their tears washed him clean.

They gulped breakfast hurriedly, impatient to be off. Donal had cleaned his pipes while the others slept, and inflated the bag while the others put their backpacks on and checked their weapons.

"What are you doing?" asked Jack.

"Testing something. If I play while we march, and every single one of those damned things that we come across has tried to claw its face off, maybe I'll believe you."

"Fair enough. Going to try playing music this time?" Jack asked.

Donal grinned evilly. "Oh, I'm sure I could remember some polka tunes, if I tried hard enough."

One last look around the main room and they left, Donal patting the door as he secured it behind them. The boys and Jack spread out a bit, and as the four men walked away from where Donal's home was, he played one of the last pieces that he had left of that home.

"Amazing Grace, how sweet the sound, that saved a wretch like me . . ."

End

HOW DO YOU SOLVE
A PROBLEM LIKE
GRANDPA?

This is in John Ringo's Black Tide Rising *universe.*

I've always noticed, when I consult on disaster preparedness, a segment of society who are flat-out jealous and angry at those who are prepared. They're condescending, mocking and demeaning all the way along. Then, when trouble actually happens, and it does—an earthquake, tornado, ice storm and power outage, what have you—they proceed to almost blame those with foresight, while expecting those individuals to provide for them.

A lot of us discuss the number of clueless, hopeful twits who say, "If the world ends, I'm coming to your place."

That's nice. How do they plan to get here? And why do they assume they'll be welcome to consume my resources?

And how will they respond to a big fat, "I told you so"? or "Get off my lawn"?

⊕

ANDY THOMPSON was tense. Going to see his grandpa shouldn't be a meeting. It should be a visit.

This was a meeting.

The house was a nice brick split, well-maintained. The grass and trees were trimmed and pruned, but there was no other landscaping. It was plain, and clean.

Grandpa Thompson had always liked guns, hunting, the outdoors. His collection of knives and guns had been amazing. Now it was full-on hoarder. The man had crates of MREs, racks of cans, drums of water, god knows how many military rifles. He'd blown through most of his income and savings, keeping just enough to pay the bills.

The man did pay his bills, and his food, and his taxes, but there wasn't much left over, and the next progression in behavior would be past that point.

If they could resolve it now, he wouldn't have to try to put Grandpa in a home. Although, with Grandma gone, that still might be something to discuss later.

James C. Merritt, his attorney, was graciously coming along on a very modest fee, and Doctor Gleeson was along to gently advise. Grandpa was as areligious as Andy, so there was no point to a clergyman.

Grandpa met them at the door.

"What's wrong, Andy? A lawyer?" Grandpa said after a glance. He was still sharp. "And who's this other gentleman? Come in, sit, please."

"Grandpa, Doctor Gleeson's been mine and Lisa's marriage counselor. Good man. He's along for support."

"I hope no one's died. Is Andy Junior in hospital?"

"No, everyone's fine, Grandpa. This . . ." he looked at Gleeson, who nodded. "This is about your spending, and the guns."

The cabinet here in the living room contained high-end hunting rifles, behind armored glass to protect them while showing them. That case had cost a couple of thousand dollars. It was also the wrong background for this discussion, because those were valuable and personal.

"What's the issue? Everything that needs to be papered is. I have a lot of them in trust for you and the great grandkids. I don't spend more than I have. I'm pretty sure my debt's less than yours."

The old man wasn't angry, but he was certainly alert.

"Grandpa, it was fine when you had a dozen, or even a couple of dozen, but you've got what now, a hundred?"

Grandpa leaned back in mock relaxation. He was tense.

"Since you ask that way, none of your goddam business. Andy, I don't want trouble with you or anyone, but how I spend my pension and my wealth is really not your concern. You've seen the trust and the will, and even if I was cutting into those, which I'm not, that would be my choice while alive. But I'm not. You don't have some notion of trying to declare me incompetent, do you? I have lawyers, too, and probably better ones, with no disrespect intended to you, sir," he added to Merritt.

This was not going well. He nodded to Merritt.

Merritt said, "Sir, my client is concerned about your assets, and has asked that I act in advisory capacity. While I assume you are completely within the law, your collection has been mentioned at the city council and elsewhere. They've got concerns."

"Mentioned by whom? I don't generally advertise." Grandpa's gaze wasn't getting any more relaxed.

It had been Andy's younger brother Sam, who meant well, but wasn't very good at these things. He'd gotten a bug up his ass, decided the government would know what to do, and gone to see the mayor. It was a small town. Word got around. They all knew the old man needed to stop "collecting," but that hadn't helped. Although, that had gotten the action they had here, if it worked.

Merritt was good. He answered the old man's inquiry with, "You've been seen at various gun shows, stores, swap meets. Someone took an interest and started following you."

"Stalking me, you mean."

"Legally it has not reached that level. They are free to observe, as you are free to buy."

"And everything I have is legal. If the cops show up with a warrant, they'll find exactly that."

Merritt said, "I'm quite sure, sir. But if the police do show up, they'll confiscate everything on at least a temporary basis, and then there will be articles in the news. You know how they paint gun owners."

He followed with, "Sir, I'm on your side. I've got a safe full of ARs, an early Russian SKS, an FAL—"

"Metric or Inch?"

"Metric. Imbel. Imported back before you had to chop barrels and sub parts."

"Nice. Do you know the Empire ones can take metric mags as well as their own?"

Merritt nodded. "I'd heard that."

Grandpa twisted his mouth and shook his head. "So you're saying some asshole is pitching a fit about me being a collector, and if I don't want my collection ruined, I need to divest."

"There's more nuance than that, but that is the rough summary, yes, sir."

"Goddamit."

Grandpa sat staring from man to man for about three minutes. Andy said nothing.

"And what will convince the concerned idiots I'm not some sort of deranged Nazi or whatever?"

"I don't think there's any specific number on it. But some of the racks of MREs and such, and ammo, and the scarier guns. One AR is not an issue. Five different ones, I can make the case that they're for different target shooting, or collectible. Once you get to a dozen, people start to freak out."

It was another three minutes before Grandpa said, "I'll think about it."

Andy felt like crap. Grandpa had taught him to shoot, and he'd enjoyed it. He just never got into it the way the old man did, almost an obsession. If Grandpa had fifty cars, it would have been the same, or if he'd been binge-buying collectibles on eBay. Even if he wanted to be safe against disaster, four or five guns was enough. He had taken that one trip to Africa, and a couple of the hunting rifles were really gorgeous.

But adding in all that food . . . it was hoarding, and it had to stop.

Doctor Gleeson was soothing, and feigned interest in the details, or maybe he was interested, but he kept the discussion moving about liquid assets that could be accessed in case of illness. That tack seemed to help.

While everyone was busy in the living room, he took a surreptitious look in the garage, at the rafters above it. MREs, canned goods, toilet paper, plywood, pallets of something. Down in what had been bedrooms were a couple of racks of rifles, three gun vaults, another pallet with boxes stacked on it, and some footlockers. The closets had various camouflage clothing and a lot of things like parkas. They were mostly different, but there were dozens of them.

Maybe they should try to coax the old man into a retirement home. Otherwise, he could open his own surplus store.

The other bedroom contained more varieties of knives, machetes, axes and clubs than he'd ever known existed. Some were on racks and stands for display, which was either awesome or creepy, depending on the presentation.

At least the front room was a perfectly normal office, with computer, filing cabinet and bookshelves, until he realized the books were all about gunsmithing, emergency medicine, and survival, with military manuals and a bunch of woodworking and craft books. At least the latter was normal.

He knew that a lot of people raised in the Depression hoarded stuff out of habit. Grandpa had been born after World War II, though, and had a middle-class upbringing, then had worked as an engineer after Vietnam.

It could be something war related, or maybe he was just old and obsessive.

Andy wanted to help the man live to a healthy, normal old age.

Reggie Thompson looked around his living room and sighed.

He'd reached a deal with these pansies that involved selling his collection slowly. As long as his numbers were going down, the limpwristed little shits felt better.

He really didn't care how they felt, but the world being the world, they'd make life hell on him. If he had a choice, he'd just move fifty miles out and tell them to go piss up a rope. He needed to be near the hospital, though, in case of another problem with his lungs. No good to live in the boonies and die from something treatable. He also suspected as soon as he was in hospital, stuff would start disappearing. Even if he had a spreadsheet for reference, he'd be told he was crazy and steered toward a home.

This was how his grandkids repaid him for all those hikes, fishing weekends and range trips.

He thought about calling John and his wife but his son was out in Oregon, and they'd had some words over that idiotic election. That was partly Reggie's fault. He was a blunt, unrelenting son of a bitch, and he knew it.

He looked around. It really was a collection, not just prep. He'd had one of every pattern of AR, from the original ArmaLite AR-15, to the first USAF issue, first Army issue Model 602, that he'd carried in 'Nam in '65. Then he had the A1 he didn't care much for, the A2 that was better, A3 and A4, several M4gery variants including the Air Force's. He'd paid to have the proper markings on them, even if they were semi-only civilian guns.

One of the buyers had about gone apeshit at the "BURST" markings. The next had taken a quick look at the internals, saw they were all legal, and grinned. He'd paid a decent price.

So now he had five. The old school, the functional civilian modern one, and three carbines.

Those didn't hurt so much. They could be bought anywhere. He'd been willing to take a few-hundred-dollar loss overall. He'd probably have to. Which one did he really need? One of the carbines would have to do.

But they wanted to thin out his Mausers and Lee Enfields. Those things were appreciating in value, fast, and were both pension and his grandkids' inheritance, though he got the idea that little bastard Sam was the whiner about it, or at least one of the whiners.

Those would have to wait a while, as would the H&Ks. He didn't care for them much, but their fan club sure did. Okay, so those before the classics.

He really hadn't made a big deal about them, but he did sometimes load a dozen gun cases into the van to go to the range. This area was increasingly young liberals moving into older homes for the atmosphere. What were they called? Hipsters, that was it. He thought about the irony that these days there was no one *under* thirty you could trust.

He had a month's worth of food now, the rest donated to charity, sold cheap to the Scouts for camping, and most of the MREs sold on Craigslist.

He'd sold the suppressors, but still had the M60. That was worth a damned fortune, and more all the time unless they reopened the Registry. With .308 running what it did, the Pig cost $200 a minute to shoot, but that really wasn't a bad price for an orgasm.

Fuckers.

That would be near the end. He could milk out this sale for a year or more. Hell, he might be dead by then.

When the last of the AR rack sold on Gunbroker, he had some AKs to start listing. And then all the mags.

He'd still have the tents and winter gear.

He was almost certain Sammy had been the problem. The boy had never really got into guns. He'd been a video gamer from the '80s on. Not shooting games, either. Then there was his wife, who'd constantly talked about, "Endangering the children."

"I'd hoped to leave some of the antiques to you and the great grandkids," he hinted.

Sammy seemed to be choosing words very carefully when he said, "That's a kind gesture, but we wouldn't really know what to do with them."

Andy didn't have kids, and his interest in guns stopped with a Remington 870 he'd last used, as far as Reggie knew, a decade before.

Dammit, there was culture here, and craftsmanship, and collectible value, and they just didn't care. They were the same kind of people as Maxwell's kids, who had no interest in his classic '64 1/2 Mustang and '69 Cuda. He'd watched the man sell them at auction. He got good money, but they were gone and he'd never see them again. The man had slumped as he handed over the keys.

This was his estate, his life, his heritage, and they just didn't care.

That was the unkindest thing he could imagine.

What always pissed him off in these arguments, first online, now here, was that the hunting rifles in that case packed two to three times the power of the so-called "assault rifles." Hell, if they knew what the Merkel .375 double rifle put out, they'd need Depends. You could use that on charging rhino. 5.56mm wouldn't even puncture the skin on one.

But the lawyer and the counselor had been correct. If he tried to fight this, the little bastards would just dial up the press, the soccer mommies, and the panty-wetters until someone came along and took everything for "examination" and tossed him into a don't-care facility.

His plans didn't allow for that. They did, very reluctantly, allow for this.

But he still hated the ungrateful, nosy little bastards.

Andy sat with Sam in Chili's, drinking margaritas and waiting for fajitas.

"That spreadsheet was impressive," he said.

"It was creepy," Sam replied.

"Yeah, but it listed everything."

"That's what's creepy about it," Sam said as he licked salt and took a drink. "Guns, magazines, cases, slings, cleaning tools, every goddam screw that might go on a rifle. And hell, he had more stuff than the local police."

Sam probably didn't know what the police actually had, but there had been a lot.

"Well, I got him into a good mutual fund. It's near a hundred thousand now."

"It's obscene. A hundred thousand dollars on guns.

How rich would he be if he'd put it into something useful?"

"It wasn't all guns."

"Right. I forgot. Enough food for a year, like he's a Mormon or something. Even they don't do that anymore."

"Well, he's smart enough. I think it's partly our fault."

"Huh? How?"

"Dad lives in Oregon now. We should have been visiting a lot more often, especially after Grams died. He needs company. I doubt there's much of a dating scene for seventy-five- year-old widowers."

Sam frowned. "Oh, there probably is, but I doubt he cares. He did love her a lot, and he does miss her I'm sure. But you're probably right. We should visit at least once a month, maybe even swap off."

"And take the kids."

Sam said, "Monica isn't comfortable around him. You know how she voted. Grandpa is loud about it, even online. She feels he's angry enough to be scary."

"I hate being critical of your wife, Sam, but she needs to remember she joined this family. We visit hers, she needs to return it."

"It's not that easy."

It probably wasn't. Sam had never been the strong one. He read a lot of books, sat in the corner, and even now, he sits in an office writing corporate reports. Andy actually traveled and looked at the sites he was insuring, ladders, hoists, the works.

He hated to think his little brother was a wuss, but in many ways, he was.

✧ ✧ ✧

The screen showed a dozen people, naked and vacant-eyed, suddenly turning angry and charging toward the camera. Then there were rubber bullets, then tasers, and cops wrestling with angry, snarling, biting people.

Reggie wasn't sure what to make of the video. It could be drugs, like Krokodil or bath salts, but it was a lot of people. It had to be some sort of disease. So he'd need to start quarantine protocols. He'd also need to make sure he had plenty of diesel for the generator.

He pinged his friend Kevin in the State Department, for any info he might have, and Ted, who was a neuroscientist. Both had private emails that didn't go through official servers.

Ted didn't reply. Kevin's response was very short. "It's real. Global. Duck and cover."

He stared at the screen for a few moments, then composed a new message.

"My place is available. Ping if you're inbound." He addressed it to six people and pressed send.

He felt bad that none of them were family.

He slammed the locks into the doorframes, and he was glad the kids had never seen those. Steel doors with internal crossbars were proof against a lot of things, and they were kevlar lined with light ceramic backing.

The windows, though, on the ground floor especially, were going to be tough. He had the sandbags. He needed to fill them. There were a lot of them, and the fill pile was at the bottom of the yard, nicknamed "goat mountain."

The video from the cities got worse over the summer. There were rampaging mobs of naked, insane people, and someone used the "Z" word. Zombies. Whatever it was

was communicable and nasty. He was going to have to secure things as best he could.

The food, more than the guns, would be useful now. He had a well out back, and there was a seep from the cornfield that he could filter. It might contain a few fertilizers he couldn't neutralize, but that was less important than not going near anyone communicable.

He took to ordering all his food online, and having it delivered to the garage. It was all packaged, and he ran them under the UV light, spritzed them with bleach, then rinsed them off with the hose. Then he put on his paint respirator and used tongs and gloves to shelf stuff. After several days, he dated each item with a Sharpie, then placed them into regular storage. They'd still need to be rinsed again, though. He'd need to be rinsed, actually, and it was hot enough a shower was a pleasure.

At his computer, he ordered a lot more bleach, soap and respirator filters.

He also realized that he might have to triage his own grandkids, if there was a risk they were contaminated.

As he was thinking that, he heard a car out front. He stretched to look out the window. It was Andy, pulling into the driveway, still doing about thirty. His wife was with him.

He sprinted and strained up the stairs to the door, before they were out of the car.

Andy called, "Grandpa! I called in sick at work. Do you have room?"

"For what?"

"Have you seen the news?"

Yup. That was it. "Yes. Why did you come here?"

Andy spread his hands and said, "Because you have all that food and gear."

Oh, he was going to make them sweat.

"I see. So now that you actually need help, you want me to take care of you. After you already told me I didn't know what I was doing and made me get rid of most of it."

Andy looked ashamed and embarrassed. "Dammit, I'm sorry, Grandpa. We couldn't know."

"And what are you bringing?"

"Uh?"

"What do you have that's useful? Skills? Food? Ammo?"

"Uh . . ."

"Did you even bring your shotgun?"

"No."

Reggie gave the young man The Look. It was the look all old timers kept on hand for these occasions. Tommy Lee Jones did it perfectly. Reggie had practiced while watching him.

"Grandpa . . . please."

He tilted his head. "Go out back. I'll send out a tent, and it even has a heater. Park the car down the street and walk back slowly so you don't scare people."

"Tent?"

"Quarantine, for a week. Then you can come in."

Andy gaped. "Are you serious?"

Reggie was serious, and had to make them believe it. Besides, he owed payback on Andy for helping Sammy cut back his preps.

With The Look, he said, "Don't make me shoot you. Park, then 'round back."

The man did so.

So, was Sammy going to come running up with his brats? Reggie had been gentle with John, John had been downright wimpy with Andy and Sammy. And once it got to Sammy's boys . . .

Andy parked, but he walked back awful briskly. It was obvious he was tense. Reggie noticed he didn't bring anything from the car. Not even sunglasses.

Meanwhile he called his neighbor Wendell.

"Hello?"

"Hey, old man, seen the news?"

"Only a bit. Some drug gang or something?"

"That's what I thought, but it's worse. Quarantine is in effect."

"Crap. You're serious?"

"Yeah, my friends in State and elsewhere say it's depopulating chunks of Africa and Asia already."

"I ain't got more than a couple of weeks of groceries."

"I still have you covered."

"Thanks."

"Any time, brother. But when did you last go out?"

"Two days ago."

"So you stay there five days, and don't answer the door or get close to anyone. Then you come here on Saturday."

"Will do."

Wendell had far less preps, but the man had skills. He'd volunteered for a second tour before Reggie was drafted, and had real decorations from it. He still knew how to shoot, too.

Andy squealed and sprinted as he reached the driveway.

"I saw one!" he said.

Reggie looked up the street. Yeah, that was a naked old man, soggy and flabby, who seemed aware enough to track Andy and follow him.

Reggie reached inside the door, grabbed the rifle he had there, and took two shots. The second one dropped the man.

"It's started," he said.

There were eyes at curtains and windows around the neighborhood, and he saw Davis across the street in his front porch, holding a rifle. Davis had been Navy during the Cold War, but he knew how to shoot.

Andy set up the tent with difficulty, but managed. They had an airbed, blankets, an electric heater for night, extension cord for laptop, and his wireless. He put food outside the French window every meal, and they took it. He handed out a box of bleach wipes, and they dug a slit behind the hedges. Reggie wished he'd stocked lime. If they were contaminated . . .

Sammy arrived the next day, with Monica and kids. He pulled into the driveway and parked, fussed around, then got out.

"Move it down the street," Reggie said.

"That's not safe."

"It's in the way there."

"Why? You're in the garage."

He sighed.

"Anyone getting close can hide behind it. It needs to be moved away from the house."

"But the—"

Reggie sighed because he already was responding to what the boy was starting to say.

"Leave the others here, and *move it*."

Monica tried to run for the house.

He pointed his M4 at her.

She just stared, then started screaming at him.

"I knew you were an all out right-wing gun nut! You—"

"Shut it, woman."

She gawped and stared.

"Now listen closely, because your life depends on it. I've got a second tent. You will take it to the bottom of the back, a hundred yards from Andy. You will camp there for a week. You will not touch, get close, or even move near Andy and his wife, or they have to wait as long as you do. I'll put food out. You'll have heat and internet. Or, I lock this door right now, and shoot you if you try to go near them. Whatever this disease is, it's a killer, and I'm not taking chances. Otherwise, I wish you luck, you can have a shotgun, a box of shells and a crate of MREs, and you go elsewhere."

Sammy didn't argue. They stared each other down for five minutes, in silence, and the boy said, "Okay." He turned and let the kids out of the car, spoke carefully, and pointed around back.

Reggie said, "I'll do dinner in an hour."

"Ya got macaroni 'n cheese?" Jaden asked. He was five. He looked scared because the adults were arguing.

"Sure do." He looked at Monica. "I can make that for them. And just soup and sandwiches for the rest of you."

Sammy barely parked past the property line, and

sprinted across the yard. Reggie sighed. It would have to do.

Up the street were several more wandering naked bodies. They went to the first house and started breaking in the front windows. The widow Mrs. Lee's house.

To Sammy, he said, "I took you shooting when you were young. Did you ever stay with it?"

"Uh, no."

Reggie stood another rifle outside the door.

"Then you learn again now, and fast. Keep that in your tent. Wait until I'm inside."

He looked back to Mrs. Lee's house, where the three might-as-well-be-zombies were still breaking in the glass. He raised the rifle, aimed carefully, and squeezed off a shot. He hit, but not solidly. Again. Torso, and the man started to slump. The second one took three bullets.

Because he couldn't leave Mrs. Lee like that, he dropped the last of the three, but knew he couldn't waste ammo like that again. The distance wasn't impossible, but moving targets made things a lot tougher, and he didn't have enough ammo.

He pointed at the rifle for Sammy, then went inside and latched the door bolts.

He didn't have her number in his phone. He called Wendell.

"Wendell, can we get Mrs. Lee?"

Wendell said, "I dunno. Maybe Davis can help. Anyone else coming?"

"Yeah, my friends, but I don't know when. I'll check."

"Okay. I'll tell Davis to check on her. Anything else?"

He thought for a moment and replied, "Yeah, if they

can move out to the country, they should. Much as I'd like to form a neighborhood watch, people want to vote on things, then they vote for what they want, not what they need. Imagine that in 'Nam."

"No thanks. I'll tell them. I'm not sure they'll do it."

"No, but we have to try."

During the days, he fastened barricades inside the windows, and bars outside, drilling into the masonry. He ducked inside when the mailman came past, and waved off some salesman or other. They got lots of them around here.

Wendell came over after six days. On day seven he let Andy and Lisa in. He was going to make Sammy's family wait an extra day plus, just to make sure. He thought the car had moved slightly and the boy had made a late-night burger run or something. He couldn't entirely blame him. The five-year-old and three-year-old were bored and angry.

Every major city was now reporting outbreaks. Once the infection took, people got violent and vicious within a few hours.

Things started falling apart.

Lots of people were trying to quarantine, few had enough supplies.

Andy and Lisa came in, and he pointed to the bathrooms.

"You should shower. We have hot water for now. The food won't hold out for long with all of us here," he said. "It would have, but . . . and you know what I'm going to say, right?"

Andy flushed and said, "You told us so. But how the fuck could we predict zombies?"

"Zombies, commies, Nazis, angry native tribes, aliens, mutant bikers, something, sometime, will require the use of guns and food. Remember that, you little shit." He wanted to smack the boy.

"Yes, Grandpa. I'm sorry."

Reggie turned and said, "Wendell, I think it's time we started stacking stuff."

Wendell said "Roger that," as he walked into the room.

Andy blurted out, "You're black."

"And?" the man replied. He was about Grandpa's age, carrying that civilian variant of the M14 with a scope on top. He looked pretty damned fit and lean for someone near seventy.

"Nothing." He had no idea why that had come out. Inadvertent racism? This was a bad time to even discuss that.

Wendell jogged upstairs and went into the garage.

Grandpa said, "I have friends coming. They're bringing more stuff. Then we're going to see about moving further out, where there's less people and more food."

"Farming?"

"Maybe. Farming takes fuel and effort. Depends on how many people die. If it's enough, we just hunt and plant a truck garden."

That was a frightening thought.

From upstairs, Wendell shouted, "And we have another bunch, up the street."

"Okay, after this, we get out the backup supply. Andy,

Sammy, grab the rifles." Grandpa snapped his fingers and pointed. Andy did so. Sam hesitated, but he did as well.

"Outside, on the porch."

Andy asked, "Shouldn't we fight from in here?"

Wendell said, "No, we fight where we can see and maneuver, and lock up later. Those gooks aren't even visible from the house."

It was scary to be outside, but Grandpa made sense, and there were four of them with rifles.

He stood on the porch, which now had a couple of planters and some sandbags around it. The old men had been busy. Up the street was a nightmare.

Four filthy, naked, raging men were beating on a car, trying to break into it, and the passengers inside.

They were people, and they were sick, but they'd kill him if they could. He lined up sights and shot, and missed. Sammy went through five shots before he hit one, a creepy-looking guy with a beer belly, who drooled. The shot was into the leg and tore a hole that just seemed to make him madder.

Behind him, Grandpa said, "It's always tough the first time you shoot a man, but you need to get over it fast, because we're not getting any resupply."

"Sorry," he said. He took two more shots to hit one, who clutched and screamed and thrashed around on the ground before stopping. Dying.

He shot at another shambling body. There were a lot of fat people around here, it seemed.

Then Grandpa and Wendell started shooting, and that hurt his ears.

As he winced and cringed, Grandpa said, "Yeah, hurts, doesn't it? You little fuckers made me sell the two cans for the rifles. I guess you get to deal with the noise. It's not like my ears matter anymore."

The rifles cracked, and bodies fell.

Come on, he thought. *What were the odds?*

He shot. Another went down. Then he froze, because the next was a pretty young girl, under the stains of blood, dirt and waste. But he couldn't do anything to save her, and she was trying to kill the people in the car, who seemed to be young girls, too.

Behind him, Grandpa said, "Better reload and save the partial mag."

"Yeah. Thanks."

He swapped out for a full clip, fumbling with it.

Honking sounded down the street, and a black Toyota Land Cruiser with bars and racks raced through the moving obstacles. It stopped on the pavement, the doors flew open, and two thirtyish men rolled out, followed by a redheaded woman. They had black web gear, pouches, handguns, and were holding AR carbines. The woman wore stockings and a miniskirt over combat boots and under a tailored web vest. It would have been hot under other circumstances. That, and when she got closer, she appeared to be a well-kept fifty.

"Reggie, sorry we're late!"

"Glad you could make it."

The two men charged up the steps onto the porch, pivoted, and took positions at each corner. The woman dragged a bag behind her. Once she was up, the men took turns grabbing more gear.

"Where's the heavy stuff?" one asked. "Yes, we've been in Q all week."

Grandpa said, "Yeah, there was a personal issue that got in the way. This is it until I can fix things." He fixed Andy with another gaze. The old man wasn't going to let him forget it.

The man said, "Crap. Well, there's a shit ton of zeds moving this way. We left ahead of them, so you've got a while, but they're probably closing."

"I was afraid of that. But it's looking light for now."

There were perhaps a dozen wandering bodies, though one suddenly started jogging and sloshing toward them.

One of the newcomers put a bullet right through the figure's head.

Grandpa said, "Nice shot, Trebor."

"Thanks. Is it okay to be excited?" The man smiled faintly. He had a very high-end looking AR-15, and an Uzi slung behind his gear. It had Israeli markings.

"Sure. Trebor, Kyle, Kristan, this is my grandson Andy, and that's Sammy. You know Wendell."

"Hey, Andy, Sammy." "Hi." "Sup."

"Boys, these gentlemen and lady are card-carrying members of Zombie Squad."

Kyle pointed to the ID badge on his web gear. "We are America's elite ambulatory cadaver suppression task force." He faced back around with his rifle, a perfectly respectable bolt action with muzzle brake and folding bipod.

Andy said, "You're kidding, right?"

Trebor said, "We were kidding. It was all metaphor for disaster prep and fundraising. But here we are."

"Yeah." He kept twitching over that. Zombies. Guns. But Grandpa really had been overdoing it. Except . . .

Grandpa said, "Wendell, you got it?"

"I do, Reg."

"Good. Boys, Wendell's in charge. He'll tell you when to shoot, what to shoot at, and where to place yourselves. Got it?"

"Uh, yes." "Uh huh."

"Kristan, Andy," he said, with a jerk of his thumb. "Come with me."

"You got it, boss," Kristan said and slung her rifle.

Andy followed Grandpa inside the house, and felt a ripple as the old man locked the door and twisted a second lever. Something clanked like a vault.

"Just in case," he said. "We are going to come back."

Kristan was smoking a cigarette. Grandpa didn't like smoking, but he didn't say anything so Andy didn't. Monica, in the kitchen, looked like she was going to, but stopped. The kids were watching TV and looked very agitated. Lisa was upstairs cleaning. He couldn't see her.

They went down the stairs and into the office in the front. Those windows were exposed at ground level outside, even if they were high up here. They had bars now, but . . .

"Once we get upstairs, there's sandbags out back. But for now, I've got plywood. The back windows have to be done."

Grandpa pulled the closet door, reached in, and grabbed a tool chest. He dragged that out, popped the top and fumbled with both hands.

"Screw gun," he said, handing it over. He grabbed

three pre-cut sheets of three quarter inch marine grade plywood.

"Now we do the back windows and the garage. You know what to do?"

The boards had holes for the screws, which were more like small bolts.

Andy said, "I see. Smart." Damn, the crazy old man really had thought everything through.

"First, help with this stuff."

He started grabbing boxes while Grandpa unpacked the closet. He handed stuff to Kristan, Kristan carried everything through.

Clothing came out, some of it old fashions. Winter clothing came out. Boxes came out. Another tool chest.

"C'mere," the old man said with a wave.

He stepped closer to the closet.

Outside, there were bangs of gunfire, some of them very loud. That must be Wendell's rifle.

Grandpa said, "Christ, we need to hurry."

But he continued moving methodically.

One side of the closet had an inset door. With the shelves and clothes out, that opened. The closet continued under the stairs.

There were more boxes, some of them ammo crates.

"Oh, good." Andy sighed in relief.

"Yeah, it would be, if it wasn't two hundred and sixty troy ounces of silver each. Ammo crates are the only thing strong enough."

Jesus. What did the old man have stuffed down here? He'd unloaded an easy hundred grand in weapons, and still had bullion?

He took the crate and lugged it through to the rear room.

When he came back, Grandpa was down like a ferret, pulling more stuff. He took that, too, and came back.

What the hell is under here? he wondered as the closet kept going.

There was a hole.

So, into the office, into the closet under the stairs, to the left and under the landing, then a short door to the left of that. He shimmied into it behind the old man.

We're under the porch, he thought. Gunfire directly above, muffled through the slab, proved it. It was a concrete block vault with LED lighting and a dehumidifier, under the porch.

More guns. Under here, where no one would ever have seen, Grandpa had more guns.

"I never told you goddam punks how much I really had," the old man said. "You'd have shit yourselves. There are two spreadsheets."

There was another entire rack of AR-15s. Next to that, some old military rifles in red lacquered wood stocks. A rack of those. There was a shelf of Glock pistols. There were crates of ammo. Four sets of body armor and helmet hung on a rail.

"Well, grab stuff and start passing it out."

In short order, Grandpa, the two brothers and Lisa were in armor, though Andy felt very uncomfortable. It was like wearing a fridge. Reggie and the zombie hunters were already armored up.

He was really glad of that, because there were a lot of running bodies out there now.

Back out on the porch, there was a low wall of sandbags. In between surges, the men stacked more while Kristan and Sam kept eyes out. She really was in good shape, and a pretty damned good shot.

"More!" she called, leaned across the railing, and shot.

Kyle leapt back up, squinted through his scope and fired. Wendell stood alongside and fired, his rounds ejecting and tinging off the house.

The defense was layered. They had big bore rifles, smaller rifles and carbines, and if it got close enough, Trebor's Uzi and the shotgun leaned against the doorframe.

Andy hoped it wouldn't come to that.

This was nothing like the movies, either. With all the firing he'd done, he thought he'd hit three. Moving targets weren't easy, he didn't like shooting at people, and they didn't want to let them get close.

Not at all. Several of them bashed through the bay window of a house down the street, then poured into it, scrambling over the frame and each other.

Reggie watched them swarm into the Erdmans' house, and knew there was nothing he could do. If he had some kind of artillery, or could set it on fire, he would. But the poor couple and their baby were either dead, or soon to be worse than dead.

A dozen more followed the first gaggle, and he started shooting into the mass. He winged one, caught a leg, blew chunks of flesh from another, and put one down with two torso hits. They ran on even when shot, like a combination of PCP user and meth head.

That just stirred up several others, who rumbled their way, limbs and skin flapping.

"I count twenty," Kristan said, sounding remarkably calm.

Trebor said, "I'm getting low here."

Andy stuttered, "Oh, y-yeah. Last clip."

"We need more mags!" he shouted and banged on the door.

The mail slot, that hadn't been used in years, opened, and a single mag slid out. It bounced off the ground and a round popped loose.

"Open the goddam door!" he shouted to Monica.

There was a loud clack of the bolts latching.

Oh, shit.

He sprinted off the porch, around the garage, and went in the back. The plan for that was a two by four into metal slots, and she hadn't got to that yet.

But she had locked the door to the garage. He had his keys, quietly unlatched the knob first, turned it with one hand, then unlocked the deadbolt fast and threw his shoulder into it.

She was standing at the bottom of the stairs shrieking, screaming and flapping her arms.

He slapped her hard enough to stagger her off the wall.

"You are an adult woman, get ahold of yourself and act like one."

She stared at him in complete shock.

"Domestic violence!" she whimpered.

"There is no domestic relationship between us and never will be. Now, you can either do as you are told, or I will throw you the fuck outside with the zombies. And

Sammy? That goes for you, too. I realize being a man is alien to you, but you need to learn right now. Your sons need the example."

He turned, took the stairs in three steps, panting in exertion. Dammit, he was old. He unlocked the door and stepped back out. He left the front door open, jammed a bolt into the lockplate, and got ready to shoot. Things had quieted down again.

Over his shoulder he said, "Fill the goddam mags."

Yeah, it was ugly out here. There had to be a finite number of them, but they could get very numerous very quickly before that slowed down. There were near a million people in the city, most of them either unaware or useless.

Sammy joined them, hiding just inside the door. It wasn't as if they wouldn't have warning, but his grandson was a pussy.

Andy, at least, was shooting like a man who was protecting his family. Maybe Sammy would come around.

"How do I use the clip loader thingy?"

The boy didn't know the difference between a charger clip and a magazine.

Reggie reached over and showed him. "This is a clip." He held up the ten round stripper. "This is a loading spoon. This is a magazine. Clip goes here, and press." He showed, and ten rounds slid into the magazine. He pulled the clip loose, dropped it and grabbed another.

"Work on that stack."

"Hey, these clips jam at five rounds."

He glanced over, and saw Sammy trying to press the rounds down.

Shit, those mags.

"Crap! Bring 'em back in!"

He ran for the garage. Bench, where was the drill index? There. Eighth inch. Downstairs, swap driver bit for twist drill.

"See this rivet? It blocks them at five rounds. Drill that out on each. Bring 'em up."

"What happened?"

"Got 'em cheap out of New York. All you have to do to make them work is drill out a stud. Worthless gun control law, but now we're stuck with goddam zombies because of some . . . nevermind, just drill."

He'd erased chunks of the spreadsheet as they went through his collection. He had a backup copy in the vault, under a false name, but he'd completely forgotten about these. They'd been bought online through a gift card, and delivered to a friend in Ohio who'd reshipped them as "used tools."

Drilling each rivet took about ten seconds. Stuffing in ten rounds took another five, and those mags went right up to Wendell and crew. Once there was a small stack, they could start putting two clips in each magazine, then three.

He looked around.

They had the windows reinforced, and wire set. The boys had completely missed the loops of concertina he'd stowed in the garage rafters during their intervention. Sandbags, plywood, those he'd called "Storm supplies."

He'd never understand the mindset that being prepared was somehow immoral or dangerous. He hoped, going forward, to not have to do that again.

He stood on the landing where he could give instructions up, down, and out.

"Okay, tomorrow we toughen things up. More wire and traps, barricades around the property. We have to worry about people who didn't prep who'll be hungry."

"We're not turning away starving people," Monica said.

He gave her The Look.

"We don't have enough for everyone. We'll be charitable, within reason, and these are my supplies. You're welcome to leave if you don't agree."

She wrung her hands and went back to the kitchen.

He figured she'd come around. She wasn't stupid, she was compassionate, she'd just had a very easy life. She was learning.

"Okay, we're secure enough unless they start using prybars, which might happen. We have bars and plywood on all the lower windows, nothing they can climb on, and not much they can hide behind. It's heading toward dark. We need to move inside and bed down. Wendell, can you take the office?"

"Sure."

"Z Squad, how are you splitting?"

Kristan said, "I trust the boys. Will the room with the gun vaults work?"

"Just what I was thinking."

Trebor said, "Yeah, I don't think my wife is gonna make it. I hope so, but she was on business on the West Coast."

"Sorry, man. Good luck."

"Thanks. We can hope."

"Yeah. Kyle, you're a bachelor, right?"

"Since two years ago, yes."

"Then we all bunker down for now. We'll take turns on watch and be ready to respond. Keep a loaded gun with you. Sammy, your boys need to learn the Four Rules of Firearm Safety right now. Bring 'em over."

"Okay."

"Oh, and Sam?"

"Yes, Grandpa?"

"Go make us some coffee. It could be a long night."

He figured the boy was at least good for that.

He looked over their new, small stronghold and started thinking about long-term supplies. Water wasn't a problem, but food and waste would be. They'd need to get on those fast.

Once there was an opportunity, they needed to move out to Russell's farm. He'd take Reggie and Wendell. The ZS people were in, he was sure. As for the others, he'd have to make sure they were up for the task. Regardless of anything, they were family. He couldn't leave them. He figured they needed to leave in about a week.

He was going to miss this place. He'd had it set up just how he liked, and Russell's place was a converted corn crib. They'd be tight in there. It was a lot more secluded and defensible, though, and this might go on for a long time.

Andy sat behind his rifle, twitchy and nervous. They were going to need to have someone on watch around the clock. He hoped he wasn't going to get the middle-of-the-night-alone-in-the-dark-with-animal-noises shift.

Grandpa said, "We're going to take turns packing stuff, and it'll be a lot of food and ammo. As soon as this wave of idiots die down, we'll move out to the country where we can hold them off better."

He said, "I guess that means I'm quitting my job."

Grandpa looked very serious and calm as he said, "If they're going to miss you, yes. Unless you want to hang around in a large city waiting to get infected. The outbreaks are getting bigger, and I expect they're going to get worse. When this current panic is over, I'm going to have to restock. Delivery is going to be a pain. You're paying for any shortages in the market. I expect prices are going to be high."

"Yes. Yes, sir." He flushed again. Really, the whole idea was ridiculous, but it had happened. They were still alive because Grandpa was a devious son of a bitch.

"So you need to close any accounts you've got, cash in stocks while you can, and figure on taking the tax penalty on your IRAs, if there's even an IRS to worry about them by year's end. But right now, lay those last ten sandbags. Then you can have an MRE. Do a good job and I won't make you eat the Tuna with Noodles."

Grandpa was still a crazy old coot.

He was very glad of that.

End

A FIRE IN THE GRASS

Jessica Schlenker and Michael Z. Williamson

Almost every year I submit a story to one of Mercedes Lackey's anthologies, either the Valdemar universe or the Elemental Masters. They're a lot of fun, but they're also very complex and have very deep backgrounds, so I usually have a co-writer. I choose people with extensive knowledge of the books, who can keep my story where it needs to be.

There are many types of collaboration. In this case, they handle the universe, we both handle the story, and I polish the presentation. It's pretty much impossible to tell who wrote what by the time it's done.

Jessica Schlenker helped conclude an arc started by myself and Gail Sanders in two previous shorts, that are reprinted in my last collection, Tour of Duty: Stories and Provocations.

As I mentioned in the Introduction, I've also found that short stories are very good for training your writing to be concise and quick. A hard limit of a few thousand words dictates you set the setting and characters fast, while getting action moving.

KETH'RE'SON SHENA TALE'SEDRIN led the caravan into the trade city of Kata'shin'a'in after a grueling, month-long ride from the Collegium. Even with Nerea beside him, it had been draining. Unlike his trip to Valdemar, however, he had traveled with experienced horsefolk. Not Shin'a'in, but horsefolk nonetheless.

His betrothed, Nerea shena Tale'sedrin, pulled up alongside him. "The younger sibs will be happy to be home," she noted. His—their—clan share had increased during the time in Valdemar, as is the way of horses.

"The ones old enough to remember," Keth' agreed. He took in a deep breath. "It smells like home."

:For you,: Yssanda said, a touch wistfully.

:I hope it becomes home for you, too, my friend,: Keth' soothed.

:We'll see,: his Companion replied. *:At least with Jeris and Halath, I won't be the only one for hundreds of miles.:*

True enough. When Keth' had proposed the plan at the Collegium, his lean and good-humored classmate Jeris insisted on taking part the moment he found out about it. The Valdemaran considered Keth' a dear friend, and Keth' would begrudgingly admit the same. Even after Nerea had travelled to be with him, Jeris remained hard to shake.

:Nor did you try all that hard,: Yssanda said.

:No, I suppose I didn't,: he agreed.

They'd started with a much larger company. At likely points, the other Heralds would arrange Waystations, so future journeys would be both more restful and better supported. Eventually, there'd be other settlements, though most of the Plains dwellers were nomadic.

There was no embassy here; they would have to build one. The first night, they stayed in a small inn amid surrounding tents. Some were the tall, conical lodges Keth' hadn't seen in four years. Others were the long, low desert tents of the deep plains. He was too tired to walk any farther, so they paid at the inn, stabled and brushed the horses, and sprawled on woven hair over fresh straw.

For breakfast, they ate a hearty stew, redolent with the herbs of the plains, with a cup of butter tea. Keth' smiled at Nerea as they held their bowls. They were home. They'd changed, it had changed, but they belonged here. He hoped.

After freshening up and checking on the horses and Companions, Keth' took a walk around the town, gauging the flow of traffic, the people, the districts. Jeris walked with him, and they talked idly. Looked at with eyes fresh from four years in Haven, Kata'shin'a'in really wasn't a town, but everything was represented, just on a smaller scale.

Eventually he found what he sought, between another inn and a stable with a split rail fence at the ragged edge of town. Structurally sound and well situated, the building would do nicely. It needed work, but it had grazing land behind. It fronted a road with several alleys. That it required repair might even work in their favor, as far as hiring help. After all, he had no direct clan here to aid in the effort.

Jeris cocked an eyebrow at him, and Keth' nodded at the building. "It's a good location," he said, "You'll want to ensure the ways between buildings are freshly tamped and graveled."

Jeris said, "I'll want to look inside, but I agree. Can we lodge in the top floor?"

"Typically, yes, with the horses below. Notice the window shutters close from the inside. It can be secured."

They ducked into the pub to ask the innkeeper about the building. At this time of day, they were the only customers there.

"Are you interested?" asked a man wearing the bright, clashing colors of Shin'a'in taste. His accent was heavier than Keth's, but the language was the same, and it came back to him.

"We would like to look at it," he said. "We wish to establish an embassy and trading house."

"Very good," the landlord agreed with a grin. Yes, that would mean more traffic and business.

The building seemed as sound on the inside as it had from the outside, and sufficiently roomy. Jeris' grasp of the language was too rough to negotiate a deal, so Keth' acted as translator. The landlord took the first payment from Jeris on the spot. They paused to confer with the innkeeper as to where most of the craftsmen and laborers could be found. They also asked the price of lodging at his inn until the work was done.

:You're having a productive day,: Yssanda said.

Keth' agreed. *:How is Nerea?:*

His Companion took a moment to respond. *:She is . . . not having a productive day.:* Yssanda refused to elaborate, and Keth' set the question aside until he could ask in person.

After locating the suggested area, a couple of apprentices pointed out the guild building. Once there, Keth' explained the needed repairs and renovation, Jeris chiming in as he could. The guild representative agreed to assess the building and determine a price the next day. They headed back to their current lodgings.

There, Keth' found out why Yssanda had commented about a productive day. Attempting to repeat her arrangement in Haven, Nerea offered to tend to the stabled horses in exchange for lodging, but the innkeeper's usual help were healthy and efficient. She was mildly disappointed. At least, the innkeeper offered suggestions for where she might look. Keth' soothed her by pointing out that they had only been here a day, that it wasn't their actual home, and they'd already made more progress than expected.

They slept on beds that night.

The craftsman who arrived was brusque but knowledgeable. He pointed out several non-structural areas needing repair that had escaped Keth' and Jeris's notice. As this was officially a Valdemar-Herald venture, Jeris kept the purse and had say on the finances.

:He seems to be honest, at least,: Jeris said.

:Yes, he does,: Keth' replied as he concluded the

negotiation. Jeris handed the craftsman the appropriate amount of coinage, while the craftsman wrote up a short agreement and receipt. He disappeared to collect laborers, apprentices, and an extra journeyman. The workers would be building basic furnishings, replacing rotted boards, pounding down the floor with mallets and fill, or refreshing the roof thatch. Tending to the walkways around the building would be a project for another day.

The builder reappeared after a couple of hours, with the first of the crew and materials in tow. They started work immediately. Across the street, young men who should be working idled and made comments, few worth noting.

Among them was a shaman apprentice, who said nothing, but watched the activity closely.

:That one?: Jeris asked Keth'.

:I noticed him, too. Not yet, though. We're not ready.:

:I concur,: Yssanda said, overlaid by Jeris relaying the same from Halath.

A few days later, with most of the work completed, a shaman arrived, the apprentice they saw that first day trailing him.

"You are an Outsider," the shaman said to Jeris.

"I am," Jeris said. "Keth're'son shena Tale'sedrin is not." Keth' noted that Jeris' accent had already improved a touch, and he kept his sentences short.

The shaman turned to look Keth' in the eye. "I have heard of you. The Shin'a'in who was bonded by a Valdemar spirit animal and traveled thence."

"Yes," Keth' said. "Chosen by Yssanda, my Companion."

"Your friend?" the shaman tilted his head at Jeris.

"Is the Chosen of the Companion Halath, and a Herald of Valdemar," Keth' said.

The shaman looked around. "Your pledged sought you out some time ago. She arrived safely?"

He should have anticipated Nerea's insistence on following would become gossip. "She did. She has returned with me, our clan share, and Yssanda."

"It is indeed rare for Outsiders to see true Shin'a'in-bred horses," the shaman said. "More unusual for a Shin'a'in to leave with an entire clan share."

"My training required much time at the Collegium in Haven, and she did not know when I might return," Keth' said. "I learned much." He gestured toward the inn. "I could tell you more about it, if you like, over a meal?"

The shaman agreed. "My apprentice and I would enjoy hearing more of your journey and education."

When Keth' stepped out of the Embassy two mornings later, a small boy was loitering near the entrance, a subdued but anxious expression on his face. He sat playing with some of the gravel that had been patted down to make a better walkway. As Keth' watched, one of the rocks spun from one hand to the other.

Keth' cleared his throat and the boy dropped the rocks as if they had been heated. "You need not fear," he said. The boy's expression remained wary. "Theran sent you, didn't he?" Keth' got the impression the shaman was asking questions with at least one individual in mind.

The boy shrugged, though. "My father was curious as to why the building was being fixed. I thought I would ask for him." He wasn't lying, as near as Keth' could tell, but that wasn't his impetus.

"An embassy for Valdemar," Keth' said. "A place for Heralds of Valdemar and other officials to stay when visiting. Merchants and traders may also visit, to discuss business with Valdemar, if they desire."

The boy nodded and Keth' was on the verge of asking him about the rock. *:Asking him outright may chase him away,:* Yssanda said. *:Ask if he wants to meet us?:*

"Would you like to meet a Companion of Valdemar?" Keth' asked.

The boy shrugged, so Keth' gestured for him to follow to the paddock in the back. Yssanda and Halath waited at the fence. The boy lit up and reached out to the Companions. "They look different from the horses my clan raises," he said.

"They're Companions. They're . . . more than horses, much like a Hawkbrother's bond-bird is more than a bird, but more so," Keth' said.

The boy frowned slightly. "You mean, they know what we say? They can talk to us?"

:Indeed,: Yssanda said to the boy. *:We understand you quite well.:*

The boy jerked back from where he'd been petting her nose, his eyes wide. *:I am Yssanda, Companion of Keth'. You are?:*

"S-Semar," the boy said, eyes still wide. He looked up at Keth'. "She—talked to me?"

"Yes," Keth' said. He patted his dearest friend fondly. "That's not too different from my reaction the first time she spoke to me, too."

:It took a bit to convince him I wasn't just a horse, either,: Yssanda told the boy. *:You're taking it better than he did.:*

Semar frowned again. "My father said that you had to leave the plains and open sky because of it." Underneath, though, his thoughts were as loud as if he had spoken them. *I don't want to leave.*

"That's why I came back," Keth' said, gently. "I had to learn much. I came back to teach, so that others may stay."

The boy nodded slowly, and backed away a bit. "I should go back to camp. Father will be waiting for me."

Keth' agreed, and the boy left. *:He'll be back tomorrow,:* Yssanda said. *:He's curious now.:*

:Hopeful, too, I think,: Keth' said. It was a start.

Nerea moped around the Embassy. By Shin'a'in standards, this was a busy trading center boasting multiple stables for hosting a traveling merchant's animals. She'd offered at three close by, with signs up. All had politely declined. She was also frustrated with how insular folks were here, but then she remembered how hard it had been to visit, adapt, and remain in Valdemar.

Back in Haven, she had been proud of herself for not having been unduly influenced by the different environment. She did not understand why she was being turned away now. Her skill and voice with animals was unmatched, at least in Haven.

Here, she reminded herself sternly, *among my own people, there are others.* That was why Keth' had been Chosen, and taken away from the Plains in the first place.

This task wasn't her calling. Still, she had nothing else to do, not as long as she remained with him.

So she cared for the horses and Companions here. Yssanda, being a person-mind herself, greatly enjoyed proper brushing and grooming. Nerea did a thorough job of cleaning her hooves and dressing them with balm. It had been a long travel. Halath playfully demanded his share of the attention. She got the impression the Companions were humoring her ill mood, and she appreciated it.

They hadn't expected this to be a quick mission, but it might take their lives or longer. She wondered if Keth' had realized they were unlikely to fully return to the plains of their childhood. As much as she was glad to be with him, she needed something of her own, too.

The merchants, at least, were nonpartisan. They sold food and fodder, tools and equipment without trouble. As long as the money clinked, they were happy. Nerea made it her task to check in with them on a regular basis, sometimes with Jeris or Keth' along, sometimes alone. The sellers warmed up to the trio, particularly after approval filtered through the guilds for the respect and prompt payments on the building repairs and furnishing.

In a trading center, it paid to keep the approval and goodwill of the permanent merchants. A week later, a pair of representatives for one of the more distant clans approached Keth', and asked about trade possibilities in Valdemar.

"Kin horses are much in demand," Keth' assured them. "They respect them and treat them well, but need a great many of them for riding, pulling, hauling."

Nerea's tasks slowly expanded beyond ensuring the replenishment of the Embassy. She had no experience as a trader, but was rapidly becoming a sales agent. She spoke both languages and lettered well enough. There was a list of Valdemar interests wanting healthy, young stock, and she could rate a horse by hoof and mettle in moments. She appraised them fairly, and in some cases rather higher than the breeder had asked.

Letters and notes of marque needed to be sent back and forth before the deal was finalized, but he suspected her estimates would be pleasing to both parties.

The interim deal was made, and a letter sent along requesting buying agents from Valdemar, to arrive no sooner than three months hence.

But they still had to persuade the Clans to trust them.

Keth' and Jeris waited patiently as the shaman Theran shena Liha'irden led several older Shin'a'in toward the Embassy. This meeting would, hopefully, allow the Embassy to start functioning in its official role soon. Keth' invited the party into the sparsely furnished public room.

"Keth're'son shena Tale'sedrin, Herald Jeris," Theran introduced them to his companions. "Please be known to Lasara shena Liha'irden, Eliden shena For'a'hier'sedrin, Jelenel shena For'a'hier'sedrin, and D'minth shena Pretera'sedrin. They wish to know more of your idea of an embassy for Valdemar."

Jeris tilted his head. "May I ask what role they might have in bringing it about?"

D'minth, who also wore a shaman's headdress, spoke in accented but clear Valdemarian. "I have long counseled our brethren to be open with k'Valdemar. While we have offered assistance previously, I believe a more official friendship would benefit both. Our companions have previously professed to being like-minded."

Eliden, sharp-faced and tall, settled down on one of the seats, and the others followed suit. Jeris remained standing. "If you are indeed like-minded," the Herald began, "then please let it be known that I speak on behalf of the Queen of Valdemar as her envoy. I have limited ability to make permanent agreements, but I can certainly discuss the issues. Keth' has graciously offered to act as translator as necessary." Keth' was reminded that, unlike himself, Jeris had completed the full Herald training.

D'minth asked, "What purpose does the Queen have in the plains of Dhorisha?"

"She seeks to increase trading opportunities, secure trade routes to decrease the sort of ambush attacks Keth're'son experienced during his travels to Haven, and assist our Shin'a'in cousins, as you assisted us before," Jeris replied. "She has spoken at length with people of the plains who have journeyed and stayed in Valdemar."

Eliden snorted. "Pretty words and ideas. But Theran spoke of this youngling teaching magic to the children of the plains. The rest of this is subterfuge." The man rose as if to leave.

Keth' shook his head. "No, Elder. While it's my desire to help other Shin'a'in learn control of their magic, Jeris' mission here is distinct from mine. With his queen's leave, he and his Companion may assist me in my endeavor, and I in his, but that is all."

"There is no need or reason to teach magic to a

Shin'a'in. The shaman and Hawkbrothers will do as they have always done, and either seal our cursed or take them away." He sneered at Keth'. "For the particularly troublesome, perhaps we can count on these 'Companions' to take them away. As long as they stay in k'Valdemar."

Theran gave Eliden a dark look. "Those with magic are not cursed, as I have said before, Eliden. Furthermore, you know as well as I do that the Star-Eyed has not been sealing the magic away as She once did. There are too many children born with the touch since the Storms ended for us to simply send them away."

Rather than reply, the Elder stalked out of the Embassy.

Into the awkward silence that followed, Jelenel harrumphed. "He would rather the Clans be stripped and barren than admit the world has changed."

"I thought he agreed with the idea of an embassy?" Jeris asked.

"Several of his families could profit with more open trade routes between Valdemar and the Plains," Theran replied. "But he may not be willing to let go of his objection to magic."

Keth' had known it would be a tough task. But he hadn't realized his people were that resistant to change, that fearful of what were really mostly harmless thoughts and ideas.

The next day, Keth' stayed under the awning and watched Nerea negotiate a tough deal with a trader. This one had the colorful cloth of the People, in long, woven bolts.

"I can't set an exact price," she said. "But I can say that our patterns, and that color in particular, are very popular in Valdemar. As there won't be much, the early shipments should command a high price."

She spoke to the man at length about the styles in Valdemar, running inside to bring out two of the dresses she'd worn. At length, he was persuaded. Next was a silversmith.

Keth' wondered if word had filtered through about the desire to teach magic to the merchants. Some faces were new, but others who had been regulars had not shown yet. He wondered, and he worried. He would speak to Nerea later. Perhaps he was overreacting, but Yssanda had been strangely silent on the topic when he mentioned it to her.

Keth' and Jeris were walking back from one of the merchants Nerea had requested they check with. It gave them an opportunity to look for potential students, as well as keep a sense of the town's mood toward them. As people, at least, they seemed to be accepted or at least tolerated, for as long as the topic of magic was not breached.

Then they entered an alley, and were suddenly blocked by a group of men. Keth' felt a frisson of the same fear he'd had in the wilds when the brigands attacked. This time, he had no warning, as he'd been deliberately not listening, as the Heralds had taught him. He was unprepared.

Jeris stepped forward to speak, probably something placating and soothing, and they were both grabbed from behind. *How did they get us so off-guard, off-balance?*

Jeris and Keth' both reacted, and Jeris managed to partially free himself from the men holding him.

Until one of the attackers brought something down on the back of Jeris' head, and the Herald slumped to the ground.

:JERIS!: Keth' reached for his friend with mind and voice both, struggling against those holding him, all of his training forgotten. The Herald was out cold, with only the faintest sensation of thought still there. *:Halath? Can you hear him?:*

:He's alive,: the Companion said, even as he thundered to his Chosen's side. The Shin'a'in attacking them dove out of the way of the charging Companion. Halath looked dangerous, nostrils flared and teeth bared. Yssanda arrived, with Nerea on her back. Nerea slid down, reaching for Jeris.

"I've got him," she said. She glanced at the Shin'a'in, who were gathering back up their courage to face the Companions. "Deal with *them.*"

Keth's eyes narrowed with the reminder. With the Companions to guard his back and Jeris and Nerea, he strode toward the gathering. "This is how you treat friendly travelers and visitors? An envoy of Valdemar, our ally?"

"You want to bring *magic* here. To teach the young things they shouldn't know. To risk the Shin'a'in," one of the older men snarled. Keth' vaguely recognized him, and narrowed his attention to hear his surface thoughts. A flickering image of Semar, protesting he wanted to stay with his family, he didn't want to go to the shaman, he didn't want to lose his magic. *"See, father? I can bring*

water to the horses. I can keep the ill warm. That's all."
An older image, from the vantage point of a child, looking
up at a man obviously related to both. *"I want to stay with
you, father. Please don't send me to the shaman. Seal the
magic away! Just don't send me away!"* Ah.

"Your son has a great Gift," Keth' said, struggling to
keep his words calm and even. "He needs training, like I
needed training. But the shaman are not always the best
place for Gifts like his. Sending him away, when he needs
you as much as he needs his magic, is a cruel thing to
suggest."

The man stiffened and stepped forward, body tensed
to attack. *:No.:* Keth' told him. *:It is* you *who risks the
Shin'a'in, not us. You and those like you, who would chase
all of our gifted away. The world has changed, and if we
are to survive, we must change with it.:*

That may have not been the wisest move on his part,
for the man lunged at him. Keth' halted his progress with
a touch of true magic. *:Sleep,:* he commanded, word laced
with suggestion, and the man staggered to the ground,
snoring before he sprawled.

The others stirred angrily. Keth' looked at them. "He
is unharmed. I simply commanded him to sleep." He
paused. "The first time I was ambushed in the wilds, by
brigands—" *there, that got their attention,* "—it was by a
group similar to you. I knocked them all out, and injured
two of them. They will never be able to tend to their
families again, and must be cared for as infants the rest of
their lives." There was a collective flinch. "I was left
unconscious and bleeding. The girl I was hired to escort
had to tend to me.

"For the safety of the clans, those with Gifts *must* be trained." He nudged Semar's father with his foot. "Take him home, and think. You know where you can find us, if there are questions."

The crowd looked at each other uneasily. After a short moment, two stepped forward and lifted Semar's father up to carry him away, and the others dispersed.

Keth' returned to Nerea and Jeris. "How is he?"

"It's a nasty lump," Nerea shook her head. "But he should be fine with some rest." Halath agreed.

Looking glazed and queasy, Jeris tried to rise, but turned and vomited instead. He stayed on hands and knees, breathing slowly to recover his strength and balance.

"Let's get him home," Keth' said, lifting the Herald up. Nerea assisted on the other side, while Halath danced anxiously nearby.

Keth' didn't need any magic to sense Yssanda's disapproval. He waited until he was sure Jeris's condition was stable before heading back down to talk to her directly. If she was to scold him as a child, he should be there in person.

Nerea stayed with Jeris for the moment. Between her hands-on monitoring and Halath's mental, he should be safe for the moment. Sleep might be all he needed.

Yssanda snorted as he came into the open area the Companions used as their own within the stables. *:You know that was a poor choice of actions,:* she reproved him. *:You possibly have made things* worse. *Beyond the ethics of using your magic in that fashion.:*

Keth' shrugged. "I was concerned for Jeris, and trying to keep things from escalating further. Had you and Halath not arrived when you did, I have no idea what would have happened. We were ambushed, and I didn't . . . *don't* . . . want to hurt anyone." Now that the heat had leeched out of his system, he desperately wanted the comfort of leaning against her. He stayed on his own feet.

:And you know that's the only reason I waited until now to say something,: Yssanda said. *:Your heart is in the right place. However, you must recognize that you cannot simply order the universe into your way of thinking. That is why the Heralds and Valdemar don't believe in "One True Way." You do. And you have never let go of that determination that your way is the true way. Silly Shin'a'in.:*

She sighed, a massive sound in the quiet of the stable, and stepped closer, resting her nose on his chest. His hands automatically moved to rub the velvety skin. *:I believe in you, or I never would have Chosen you. But you cannot be solely Shin'a'in anymore. This incident, if nothing else, should have driven that home to you. Until your people embrace the existence of magic outside their knowledge, you are not, to them, truly Shin'a'in. You cannot let your guard down simply because you are "home." Halath will remind Jeris that he's not among friends, as well. Well, once he's awake again.:*

"Does Halath believe Jeris will recover without incident?" Keth' asked.

:He believes so,: Yssanda said. *:He says Jeris seems to be sleeping naturally at this point. He wishes you to*

refrain from MindSpeaking to him, though, as that might wake or disorient him further.:

"You will . . . remind me, to be more patient, less determined to be *right*?" Keth' asked.

:Of course,: Yssanda said. *:That's part of* my *Task here.:* For once, he felt reassured at the reminder that there were other, wiser heads than his own, who would call him to account. Being attacked by his own people had shaken him more than he realized.

The next morning, Semar arrived, accompanied by his father, as did two others.

"You can teach him to control his outbursts?" the father asked, hinting that there'd already been some events. What had changed, that these powers were manifesting again now? Or had they always been there and just ignored and waved away?

"We likely can," Keth' said. "First we have to find out what exactly he can do." *:Jeris? Semar is back. Listen?:* The Herald kept to his bed today, still dizzy if he moved too much or too fast. His mind was sound, though.

:I'm here,: Jeris responded, and Keth' felt the slight touch of a listening link.

The second boy looked nervous, but proud. He was about thirteen, edging into adulthood for Shin'a'in. The third was a girl, verging on womanhood. *:These two are older than I expected.:* Keth' told Yssanda. Truth be told, the older boy was not much younger than himself.

:You were not the only possibility for the task itself,: Yssanda said on a deeper channel than Jeris would hear. *:Just the one I Chose.:*

Semar's father nodded brusquely. "I will leave him and his cousins in your hands for now. They know the way back to our encampment." The man stalked off, his glower scattering some of those on the street.

Keth' looked down at Semar. "I had expected you back sooner than this," he said softly.

The boy swallowed nervously and glanced at his cousins. "We were prevented. An Elder talked to Father, and Father forbid me returning here to learn what he called 'tricks.'"

:*Eliden,*: Yssanda said, overlaid by Jeris saying the same.

:*Agreed,*: Keth' replied. :*What are we to do?*:

:*Teach them,*: said Yssanda. :*Just like you wanted to. We'll help.*:

Keth' waved them into the Embassy, taking them to one of the smaller side rooms. Nerea watched them carefully while chattering in Shin'a'in with a potential merchant.

"No, there was just a misunderstanding yesterday. It was resolved peacefully," he heard her say.

"Your bonded used magic to end it," the trader said with a touch of accusation.

"Less than a shaman could have used," she shrugged, "and with far less damage than the unprovoked attack on a Herald of Valdemar, an envoy of the Queen, could cause."

The trader flinched, with a sidelong glance toward where Keth' was closing the door. It seemed the trader found other topics to discuss, as Yssanda did not relay any concerns from Nerea while Keth' spoke with the children.

"Thank you for trusting me," he said in opening. "Neither true magic nor mind-magic are something to be afraid of, but like fire or a knife, you have to learn how to use them safely."

The older boy, Stileth, asked, "So we can use it once we learn how?"

"You already can use it, but you cannot *control* it," Keth' said. "Until you learn to control it, it can be dangerous."

Tialek, the girl, asked, "What happens if you do use it without control?"

"You become a risk to yourself and all others around you. You may permanently mind-lame someone when distressed, like I did."

All three children stiffened, glancing at each other. He continued. "Once you learn control, you then must learn *when* to use it. That is why I returned, against tradition for a Chosen. So others would not need to leave to learn these skills."

The older two glanced at Semar. Obviously he'd relayed that part of the previous conversation. "Now." Keth' straightened slightly, drawing their attention back, "In order to gain control of your magic, you must learn focus. Clearing your mind and focusing on the task at hand will allow you to stay calm in uncertain situations, and maintain control of your Gifts." Even as he relayed the concepts drilled into him by his own instructors, he felt a twinge of guilt. Hadn't he lost that focus just the day before?

:*We all stumble, from time to time, even with four feet under us,*: Yssanda said.

Keth' relaxed a bit at that, and proceeded to work

with the children until they were comfortable with the necessary starting exercises. Yssanda assisted, particularly with Tialek, whenever Keth' faltered. Once both of them felt assured the children were performing the exercises properly, Keth' sent them home, to return in a few days.

Late that afternoon, Theran arrived, with Jelenel and D'minth in tow. "There was a street brawl?"

"Jeris and I were surrounded by a group of men, only a short distance from here. They attempted to restrain us. Jeris broke mostly free, and was hit in the head. He went down. Had our Companions not come to our aid, I am not sure what the result would have been," Keth' said, calmly as he could.

"Eliden reported that you were the antagonist, and that you used magic to end it," Jelenel's voice was colder than it had been.

"I did use magic to keep the attackers at bay, and mind-magic on one I believed to be Semar's father. I put him into a deep sleep with magic. I did not wish to cause any injuries. That is all."

:*Indeed*,: Keth' heard Yssanda say, :*he was not the antagonist, nor did he defend himself and Jeris unreasonably*.:

Theran started. "Who was that?" Jelenel and D'minth looked at him askance.

:*Yssanda, Keth's Companion*.:

"May we meet her directly?" Theran asked. "Returning with the story of your Companion will go a long way towards soothing the concerns that have been expressed."

"Of course," Keth' answered.

Yssanda also replied, :*I would be honored.*:

:*As would I,*: Halath added.

The shamans followed Keth' to the paddock where the Companions currently held court. There was a perceptible relaxation in their stances to see the two pairs of blue eyes in stark white faces watching them approach. Halath whickered, stretching his nose out to Jelenel, who rubbed it absently.

"All I have given the children was mental clearing exercises, earlier today," Keth' said. "They need to learn control."

"Yes," Theran agreed. "That's the issue at stake, of course. Yet, Eliden is demanding you forgo teaching the youngsters any magic, even the most basic of control, in order to gain his support for the Embassy."

Jelenel frowned. "He may be one of our Elders, but he is *not* a shaman. He attempted to demand I seal the children or train them before, but Semar's gifts are ill-suited for the shamanic way *or* the Hawkbrothers. Tialek and Stileth are little better. *I* am shaman of our clan, and they need another choice. His support would be beneficial, but this can be done without it as well."

"How well will that be taken?" Keth' asked.

:*She's calling for help,*: Yssanda abruptly said to Theran and Keth'.

"Tialek?"

:*She says they're being restrained. She says flames are burning around Stileth.*:

"Flames?"

Jelenel looked troubled. "He has an unusual affinity for fire, and he's fiercely protective of Tialek."

:The flames are spreading. He's lost control. They need us now.:

:Halath, call Jeris and Nerea!:

"Theran, with me," Keth' said and scaled the paddock fence. "Jelenel, Jeris is on his way down, ride with him. D'minth, our horses are there; Nerea will be there in a moment as well. Gather help!" He swung onto Yssanda's back. She gathered herself for a jump, barely clearing the top bar. Keth' reached down a hand for the shaman as the man swung up behind him.

:No time for niceties,: she said, breaking into a canter. Keth' could feel her frustration that the street, such as it was, bore enough pedestrian traffic that she dare not gallop.

The glow was definitely fire, rising in the scrub and grass. It would head this way quickly. Smoke wisped up and the glow brightened as they approached. Finally, they cleared the densest portion of the town, and Yssanda shifted to a gallop.

"We need to build a barrier between the encampment and the rest of Kata'shin'a'in," Theran said in Keth's ear. "The winds are blowing it towards the city. We need to backburn an area to keep the fire from spreading that direction."

"Can you push the winds away?" Keth' asked.

"Not until we know where Tialek and Stileth are," Theran said.

:Where are they?: Keth' asked Yssanda.

:Near side. You'd burn half of their clan if you send the winds that way.:

:Star-Eyed!: he swore. *:They have not moved away?:*

:I don't know,: Yssanda replied. *:I only know what it was half an hour ago. They're cut off from the main group now.:*

Other riders and some on foot streamed toward the fire as well. *:Halath believes he's catching up. Nerea and D'minth are further behind.:*

:At least it looks like we have hands to help.:

Yssanda halted where those who had run *toward* the fire gathered, talking wildly. Theran slid off. "Go!" he shouted. "Find the children!"

Keth' nodded as Theran began working. Another shaman was among that group, and he felt the tingle of gathering magic at his back while Yssanda homed in on the two children.

The fire had split when it went wild. From what small glimpse Keth' caught, it looked like most of the children's clan got out of the worst of it, but the inferno still raged. *:We will deal with that later,:* Yssanda said. *:The near-side fire may burn enough to block the larger side from spreading that way.:*

They spent a short eternity finding a relatively thin place to break into the fire encircling the children's group. *:Here,:* Keth' finally said. *:We will find no better.:* They could hear the frantic efforts of the trapped clan members to keep the fire from getting closer.

:Looks that way,: she agreed. *:Stay on me.:*

He tightened his grip on her back, and closed his eyes to gather his concentration. He *pushed* at the fire in front of them, imagining a large plow like those he remembered on the farms near Haven. Yssanda, picking up on the imagery he was using to focus his magic, stepped forward slowly. *:That's it,:* she said. *:Just hold that 'plow' in front of us. I'll do the pushing.:*

The "blade" he imagined was three or four times the width of Yssanda, enough to pass through. Even though flames were mostly air, the image, the thought of pushing through several inches of root-thick topsoil strained him immensely. Keth' shook from the exertion as they broke across hot cinders into the center.

Eliden was there, as were the children and their families. Several had suffered burns, including the Elder. Stileth stood nearest the fire, still raging at Eliden for trying to take them away. The fire around this part of the clan was obviously attuned to the boy; the tops of the ring danced with every gesture he made. Eliden's attempts to calm him just agitated him more. Tialek clung to him, trying to convince him to let go of the fire.

Keth' slid off Yssanda, and she pushed the Elder away from the children with her head. *:No,:* he heard her say as she reached out, pressing her nose against the boy's face, much like a housecat might. *:This is not what you want. You risk Tialek, you risk your family. Let the fire go.:*

Keth' tried to get the people out of the immediate area, and did not hear the response. Most turned toward the break in the fire, and it took little effort to usher them out. He felt Yssanda's relief when the boy began to respond to her efforts. The ring of fire began to calm down and shorten.

:He cannot put the fire out,: she reported to Keth'. *:We will have to do that. But at least he will stop* feeding *it.:* Hooves sounded close, now. With her usual recklessness,

Nerea rode her mare into the fire break, keeping low against her back.

:Let's take them back to Theran. He has a fire break like yours now, but we still need to put this out.:

Keth' helped Tialek on Nerea's mare, where Nerea held the girl tightly in front of her. Stileth, face drawn from a reaction headache already, barely protested he should stay and help as he was pushed up onto Yssanda's back.

"You kept the fire from consuming everyone in it," Keth' told him. "That's enough." It may not have been intentional, but he had done that much.

For all Eliden had instigated the problem, he proved his worth as Elder now. He kept his clan moving toward the safe zone. By the time Keth' and Nerea arrived with the children, he'd organized them into groups for assisting each other and the fire fighters.

D'minth and Jelenel were conferring with Theran as Keth' and Yssanda came to them. "Kata'shin'a'in should be safe now, but the fire is still spreading." Theran eyed Keth'. "Do you have strength left to help?"

Keth' nodded. He would suffer the backlash later though, he was certain.

The shamans worked together to call in a dampening storm on the far edge of the fire. It was risky, for the winds could make matters worse. Keth's task was to bottle the winds away, and force the flames down. To do that, he needed to go back to the fire itself.

A thundercrack split the air, and the rain began, soaking the immediate area before shifting over the main body of flames. Keth' and Yssanda followed.

They came up close to the fire's edge, and Keth' closed his eyes to gather his focus. He trusted Yssanda to keep them far enough away. Keth' had learned something while fighting a fire in a wood-framed building, and from watching blacksmiths working. The rain cloud started drenching the center of the fire. Keth' imagined a wall encircling the flames and tied to them. The edges of the fire began to hiss and die from the rain and lack of air. It slowly shrank under the suffocation and drenching, but the spell required Keth' to maintain concentration. He felt Yssanda supporting him.

:*That's enough,*: Yssanda finally said. :*You've done enough.*:

Keth' opened his eyes. The burned zone surrounded them, although the fire was still going. There would, hopefully, be enough of a barrier zone to keep it from growing out of control again. Others could monitor and contain it from this point. They returned to where the shaman gathered. Keth' slid off Yssanda's back, and sank to the ground in exhaustion, pain beating in his skull.

Soot smeared Nerea's face as she slumped down near Keth'. Post-crisis fear flickered in her expression as she stared at the seared grass, and he held an arm open toward her. She shifted over to burrow her face into his shoulder and he pulled her tight. "We were lucky," she said softly.

He made a noncommittal, soothing noise. Yssanda had bolstered his true magic and helped calm the raging Stileth down to the point where the fire could be beaten back. The only luck involved had been whatever drove Yssanda to Choose him.

Jelenel approached, looking as exhausted as he felt. "We will return to the discussion tomorrow."

Keth' agreed, even though he felt tomorrow might not be sufficient to recover from the exertions.

"We are all in agreement, then, that the Embassy will also serve as a training house for those with gifts of magic?" Theran asked the group gathered in the building's main room. Two wore the robes of the Scrollsworn. Several were Elders, and the rest were shaman. Keth', Jeris, and Nerea watched the proceedings as impassively as possible.

Several guests glanced at the injured Eliden as they muttered agreement. His arm remained bound to protect the burned flesh. He was in obvious pain, despite the best herbal preparations available. Not even he dissented, after his lesson in the dangers of an untrained mage.

"How best should the Shin'a'in be represented?" Theran asked.

D'minth said, "Shaman and Elders, in a rotating basis?"

"From *all* the clans," spoke the Elder from one of the smaller clans.

"Of course," Keth' interjected. "Perhaps three Elders, each here for a year or two?"

"Staggered, perhaps," Jelenel said. "Two years for each, rotating, to ensure that there should be one aware of the situations at hand at all times."

Heads nodded. The representatives debated a while before the rotation was settled. They chose two shaman, also rotating, and from different clans as the Elders. Keth' hoped that those who followed the traditional paths would find the support they needed as much as those like him did.

The agreements made, the gathering dispersed from the Embassy. Theran stayed behind with the Embassy staff.

He said, "It will be a long time before those who think like Eliden are convinced this is the right path, before Shin'a'in accept Heralds and Chosen as their own, instead of distant cousins."

Keth' agreed. "I never expected this would be the end of the path. It is only the beginning."

:*Almost profound enough even for me*,: Yssanda said teasingly. :*But it is* our *path*.:

:*Yes, it is*.:

End

MEDLEY

Jessica Schlenker and Michael Z. Williamson

When writing in someone else's established universe, one has the advantage of an extant back story and setting. The disadvantages are that one usually can't adapt any main story characters or events, and have to slip into the gaps. Also, there's usually a strict word count limit. Even without needing to create the overall setting, one has to contend with introducing characters, plot and conflict—fast—and resolving quickly. Our workaround for this has been to create short arcs with some continuity of character or location.

"WHAT'LL YOU HAVE?" the innkeeper asked.

"Blackberry mead, and—what's your special of the day?" Jeris' last trip through here had been personal, before his mission with the Shin'a'in. Blurry memories had prompted him to halt early for the night. Halath, his Companion, had agreed, as they were enough ahead of schedule.

"Mutton stew and bread," the man replied.

"That, please."

"Girl'll bring your stew 'round."

He nodded, and then meandered to an empty corner table.

Lost in recollections, he started when the food was placed down in front of him. He glanced up to meet *her* startled expression.

"Um, hello." He sort of smiled. She was probably married now, her figure softened. She smiled back reflexively, then winced as the owner yelped.

"Excuse me," she muttered, heading in that direction. The tavern owner stood, stiff and angry, scowling at a little girl. Jeris gritted his teeth and didn't interfere. The barmaid—matron now, apparently—stopped beside the girl, obviously interceding for her. The girl nodded glumly, darted behind the counter to gather supplies, and set about cleaning tables.

She kept her head down as she worked, posture sullen and dispirited. Jeris watched her in distant concern.

:Does she look well cared for?: Halath asked.

:Yes,: he replied. *:Just unhappy.:*

:She's young,: his Companion replied. *:No doubt she'd rather be playing than working.:*

However, when the girl looked up and met his eyes, he felt as if he had been slapped. From the earliest he could recall, he'd heard how his sister and he looked like twins. But for the girl's sun-lightened hair, he was looking at *her* twin, twenty years past. *:Lord and Lady,:* he breathed to his Companion. The girl stared back, studying his face.

The barmaid—he couldn't recall her name yet— stopped cautiously by the table. "Is it not to your liking?"

"No, indeed," he replied. "It's all delicious, much as I remember."

She blushed and glanced at the girl. "Finish up quickly, Cara. Grandpa needs help with the dishes."

The girl looked at her mother and back at Jeris, questions obvious in her expression. "But why—"

"Now, Cara."

"Yes, momma."

"She's a pretty girl," he offered carefully once Cara was out of earshot.

Her mother smiled ruefully. "Are you taking a room tonight?"

"Yes," Jeris replied, even as Halath tartly commented, *:You'd better!:*

She smiled again, less rueful, and left to tend to other patrons. Jeris watched her for a moment before cleaning his bowl and stacking it with the mug. He appeared to have given her more than enough work the last time he'd visited. No sense in giving her more than necessary now.

His room secured, Jeris sought comfort with Halath. It could be coincidence the little girl looked so much like his sister . . . Heralds weren't supposed to have *accidents* like this. Their training on the matter was strict, and female Heralds took appropriate precautions.

"How did this even happen?" he muttered. Assuming his suspicions proved correct.

:Well, when a Herald and a pretty, provincial barmaid get together . . . : Halath snarked at him. His Companion seemed both amused and irritated at this turn of events. *:You'd not be the first to succumb to fine liquor and excellent company. You liked her conversation even without the mead.:*

"I wish I remembered more." Fragments of memories flashed—a chime-like laugh, notes from a lute, soft skin, rough but gentle hands. Did she still play?

Cara slipped into the stables. "Oh! Excuse me, sir," she said, hiding an apple behind her back. "I do not wish to disturb you. The horses can wait." She looked doubtful about that.

Jeris shook his head, smiling. "Perhaps they can, but my Companion appreciates frequent meals." Halath snorted his opinion of the jibe. "I can assist you, if you'll tell me what you need."

Cara hesitated before nodding. "Thank you, sir. Our stable hand has been ill these last few days, and that dappled grey in the corner is—" She bit her lip. "—feisty. He tries to step on me."

Jeris glanced at the gelding and nodded. "Certainly. And which fine animal is that apple for?"

She blushed. "I brought it for yours, sir. Momma says Companions and Heralds bring good luck and happiness."

:Oh, I LIKE her. Can we keep her?: Halath stuck his head over the stall half-gate and whickered at her.

"He approves," Jeris said with a grin. "I shan't get in the way of him being cossetted."

She smiled shyly, offering the apple up to the Companion. "The hay's over there, sir," she directed.

Halath's favorite part of their Shin'a'in adventure had been the children, and he missed being feted by them.

Halath delicately took the apple from her and whickered his pleasure.

She rubbed his nose and under his jaw, then politely excused herself.

Jeris took the narrow stairs to his room. The planks jutted from the stone wall, held on the outside with timbers and rails. They were barely wide enough for a man with gear.

A figure came around the wall as he reached the first landing, and they bumped.

"Your pardon," he said.

It was she, the neck of her lute jutting over one shoulder. She half-smiled, gesturing down at the main room. "Retiring already? Cara and I will be entertaining the patrons shortly, as we do most nights."

"I was considering it. You still play, then, and sing?"

"Aye," she agreed, "although Cara has more of a voice than I do." She lowered her voice a bit, "Cara's particularly good at keeping rowdier patrons from causing a ruckus. My father appreciates that enough he even pays another helper for the evenings she sings with me."

"Then you didn't go to the Bardic Collegium?" He felt disappointed on her behalf.

"No," she said, looking only a little wistful. "And Cara upset my father's plans for me even more than becoming a Bard would have." Jeris winced, and she shook her head. "She is my luck and my happiness." More loudly, "Come, you should listen to her sing."

"We need to talk," he replied in an undertone.

She replied in kind. "Later, yes. Which room are you in?"

He told her, and she nodded. "Once Cara's settled for the night." She started back down the stairs. He gave her a moment, then followed.

Another truly excellent blackberry mead complemented the music well. *Her* voice was richer with age, more mellow. When Cara joined the song, however, even Jeris felt hard-pressed to not be sucked in completely. Her voice held the hallmarks of childhood, but the talent remained clear. :*She* must *go to the College,*: Jeris said. :*That much talent, this young? She could be dangerous without training,*:

:*Much like our magelings of before,*: Halath agreed.

"Another, Soressa!" a burly patron called to the pair. *Soressa.*

"Any preferences?" she asked the crowd. Several called out songs, only some he recognized. She conferred with her daughter, then strummed the lute again.

They performed for over an hour before Soressa rose from her seat. "It is late for us, my friends. Time to get this one to bed." She nodded at Cara. Ignoring the muted protests, Soressa gathered Cara up. The girl looked tired, and Jeris wondered if that was from the hour or the exertion.

:*Depends on how her talent works,*: Halath mused. :*I don't know much about the Bardic Gift myself. Just that there's only been a few Heralds with it over the years.*:

Sitting on the edge of the bed, Jeris stared at the walls

of the quaint, serviceable room as he swirled the remainder of his second stein. He should not begrudge Soressa tending to her daughter, but it *had* been over an hour and a half since she'd taken the girl to their rooms.

Anxiety pushed him to his feet, to pace. A light knock on the door proved to be Soressa, and he let her into the room.

"So," he said.

"So."

"You've been well?" *Stupid question.* "And your daughter?"

"Well enough," she allowed. "Cara is sleeping. Some performances exhaust her more than others."

"She sings well," he said.

"She does, and her singing soothes the crowd." She claimed the only chair. "I didn't initially intend her to perform tonight."

"Why the change of plans?"

She looked away briefly. "I wished her father to see her perform. Being a Herald means he may not return for some time."

He swallowed. "So, she is . . . ?"

"Yours, yes."

"I . . . I'm sorry. I had no idea. It's not . . . it's not something I would have needed to think about, with another Herald. You could have sent word to the Collegium. Even if I was away, they would have let me know. Possibly even brought you there."

"I considered it," she said. "But there were other considerations in play, I'm afraid. I'm my father's only remaining family in the area. I felt . . . bound to remain here. Anyway, she upset the plans my father had for me. But I'm afraid he may be renewing those plans, with her in my place."

"What kind of plans?"

"Early marriage, at best. Perhaps even to the man who was my intended eight years ago."

Jeris stiffened. "That's . . ."

"Unacceptable. Yes. He's well to do, but I never felt safe or comfortable around him. He's already *my* elder. He's certainly too old for Cara."

"Cara should be at the Bardic Collegium, Soressa. She's got the Gift, that's why she tires from singing the way she does. She needs training," he urged. "You could take her to Haven, yourself. They may even still train *you*."

"The Bardic Gift? Where would that have come from?"

"Certainly not me," he replied. "I can't carry a tune if it's in a bucket with handles."

She laughed at that. "Can you take her with you?" she blurted. "She'll be safer with you on the road than with me, and I can't leave here. Not yet."

"Possibly," he said nervously. "But Herald missions have a tendency to become . . . complicated, at the best of times."

"She cannot stay here," Soressa insisted. "My father will not agree to her leaving, of course. But she must leave, the sooner the better."

:*What do you think?*.: Jeris asked Halath.

:*Soressa seems worried enough about the girl's safety to warrant concern. We're supposed to just be part of a formal dinner in a week's time? Nothing strenuous, just one of the Lake District's own Heralds attending?*:

:*Supposedly. I expect politicking and at least a bit of Heraldly intervention will be called upon.*:

:*We should be safe enough to take her with us.*:

He reluctantly nodded. "Does she have an animal of her own?"

"No, but some are for sale in the village, at the other stables."

:*I can carry her, too, if necessary. She's not that large.*:

"We'll look in the morning, then."

She sighed, relief obvious. She stood up. "In the morning, then."

"Wait," he said. "I—" he stopped. He knew what he *wanted*.

"I think you're slightly overdressed," she replied.

He stared. That . . . *was* in line with what he wanted. "You don't need to go back to Cara?"

She smiled. "Not immediately." She stepped closer. "That is, if you don't mind? I haven't since you were here last." That was surprising.

"Then I will endeavor to make it worth your while," he said. He bent to kiss her, and found her trembling. False bravado, but not false desire. She melted into the kiss.

"Do you like her?" Jeris asked Cara as she fumbled with the saddle and gear on the pony. The girl shrugged, but sat asaddle well enough. By Shin'a'in standards, the pony would barely rate as an equine, but by the standards of "reasonably healthy, trained, and tempered, albeit expensive," she'd have to do. The girl would travel longer and more comfortably with a girl-sized saddle and animal than on Halath.

"What will Grandfather say?" Cara asked.

"He knows you're leaving with your father to visit your other relatives," Soressa assured her. *Well, he will in an hour or two, at any rate.* "You know how difficult it is for him to wake up in the mornings lately."

Cara nodded.

Intellectually, the knowledge that Jeris was "her father" sat heavy on his mind. Emotionally, he was gauging her against the magelings and other students. By expectations molded by Shin'a'in children, she seemed younger than her eight years. He feared she would be baggage for the mission. She would not add to his image as an aloof, professional extension of the Queen.

"We need to get going," he said. His obligation to her outweighed his misgivings. The girl was his—a result of his actions. *Vigorous actions, much like last night's.* They'd have to adapt. *At least she ought not have a sibling from last night.*

Soressa hugged Cara. "I love you," she said, kissing the girl's nose.

Cara's eyes teared up again. "Do I have to go, Momma?"

"Yes," Soressa said. "You'll be safe. Right now, I don't think you can be so with me."

"What about you?"

"I'll come for you just as soon as I can, my love." Soressa pressed another kiss to her cheek, and Jeris saw Cara trying to stifle a sob. "Be good for your father."

"Okay." The girl's voice was very small.

Jeris mounted the already-saddled Halath. Soressa handed him the pony's reins, which he tied to his saddle horn. "Take care of her for me."

"Yes." What else could he say? A moment more to appreciate the beauty of the woman looking up at him, full lips, full figure, committing them to memory. Her eyes showed distress, but her expression was calm.

Jeris felt heartless as he directed Halath and the pony to the road. He gave Cara what privacy he could by pretending to not hear the quiet crying.

:*She understands that her mother believes it necessary,*: Halath said.

:*I still feel terrible.*:

:*That makes four of us, I think,*: his Companion replied.

From Soressa, he knew Cara's experience outside of the inn was minimal. Running the calculations in his head now, it appeared that, between the slower pace and her inexperience, the week allotted for reviewing the situation in person would become three days.

"Are you angry about me?"

The sudden voice and question jarred him from his reverie.

Well, that was blunt. Though not as sullen as he feared it would be.

"I am not," he said. "Surprised, yes. I don't have much experience, though, so please let me know if you need anything. I'll try to make it happen."

"How long until Momma follows?"

"I don't know. As soon as she can."

"Where are we going? Does she know?"

"She does, yes. The Collegium, eventually, but I have a job to complete for the Queen. I also haven't seen my . . . *our* . . . family in some time, and intend to visit them." He glanced down at her, trying to smile. "They'll be pleased to see meet you."

"What is the Collegium like? Momma couldn't tell me."

She sounded fascinated, albeit nervous. The grief of separation would no doubt return, but for the moment, he could entertain her with stories of the Herald Collegium, and what he'd heard of the Bardic Collegium. He also told her a bit about Highjorune, and what he knew of the troubles there a few years' past.

"We have to go there?" she asked.

"Yes, I have to follow up, but I don't expect any more problems. It may be boring for you, though."

The girl shrugged.

They rode silently for a while, until she said, "I do like the wilderness. I only left town once before."

"This isn't really wilderness," he said. It was a well-traveled road. "But it's not a town, no."

In fact, they were approaching a Waystation. After a stretch and some food, they got back on the road. It was still light, with enough time to make the next inn before it got too dark and she too tired to continue.

The outskirts of Highjorune could be seen ahead. Jeris was proud of the girl. She'd been miserable the second day and most of the third, from muscle ache and homesickness, but she'd complained little. Perversely, the "lack of maturity" in comparison to a Shin'a'in of similar age meant she was less likely to challenge him, but required more direction.

She *was* grumpy and sullen intermittently, and he

occasionally felt inclined to snap at her. Instead, he encouraged her to ask questions about anything and everything, hoping to distract her and draw her out.

He almost rued that decision. Once emboldened that she'd not be snapped at for asking, the questions didn't. stop. even. for. breaths. For *hours*. When not asking questions, she sang. Soressa had taught her a lot of songs, and she had a knack for making up ditties on the go. That pattern continued through most of the third day, as well. This morning was more musical with fewer questions.

"Is that Highjorune?" she asked.

"Yes."

"It's big."

"Indeed."

As they approached, the dull roar of humanity and the change from freely blowing breezes to stale and stagnant air struck him, as it did every time. He glanced at Cara, who was hunched up as if afraid.

They rode through to the larger inn, near the palace. For her sake, he would insist on staying there for the duration of the visit. It would be more homelike, and hopefully less overwhelming than the palace. Once there, he secured a room and a meal for both of them. A messenger was sent to the palace to alert the Herald there of his arrival.

He had clean Whites for official duty. She had her best, if meager, clothing packed as well. Acquiring formalwear for her was unlikely, but he was uncomfortable with either leaving her or bringing her along. The stories of Ancar's treachery ensured most Heralds acquired a distaste for formal dinners, even those Chosen later.

For now, they waited for the Herald temporarily

assigned to the palace. A crowd entered the inn, looked around briefly, and departed. "I've seen that group before," Cara whispered. "They come through our town every few months."

"How do they act?"

"Rudely and very crass, but they have money. They don't fight often. Momma prefers I stay in the back while they're in the dining room."

That was interesting. Were they merchants? Bandits? Something else?

"You should probably avoid singing while they're around, then," Jeris said, still in an undertone. "We don't want them to recognize you."

She looked discomforted. "Not sing?"

"Your voice is distinctive," he explained. "And remember what I told you about the problems here a few years ago."

"But I won't make people do what they don't want to," she protested.

"I know that, and you know that. They do not."

Her expression was somewhere between offended, worried, and distressed at the thought.

They ate dinner in the main room of the inn.

"Herald Jeris?" a woman asked.

He looked up. "Herald Letia. It's been a while."

"Indeed," she said, sitting across from Jeris. "And this is?" She nodded at Cara.

Jeris made the introductions, leaving his relationship to Cara vague. They caught up on the past few years, and Jeris asked about the situation here.

She glanced at Cara and around the room. "Later. I'll eat with you, and we can talk after dinner."

Cara liked to hum or sing quietly during meals while not actively eating. Being unable to obviously bothered her. She perked up when others talked about music, and a patron pulled out a well-worn gittern. Others called out songs for him to play. He invited the audience to sing, and they did. Even Jeris could tell his playing was only mediocre, but Cara seemed riveted to the performance. He nudged her a few times when she started audibly humming. A few songs later, he nodded to Letia and roused Cara from her fixation.

"So, shop talk, I'm afraid," he said when they gained the seclusion of their hired room.

Letia raised an eyebrow and nodded ever so slightly at Cara. Jeris nodded.

"The city remains unsettled, in my opinion. Ferrin did quite the number on the townspeople. When they're not restless about politics, they're terrified that someone who can sing might be out to control them."

Cara shuffled a bit, ready to protest. Jeris spoke to cut her off.

"What's the purpose of this event I am supposed to attend?" He knew his instructions from the Collegium, but it always a good idea to check.

Letia said, "The mayor thought a feast celebrating the improved prosperity over the last two years was in order, now that things are more peaceful. The Lake District had profitable fishing seasons, Lineas better harvests than hoped, and the weather is lovely for early summer. He suggested a couple of Heralds from this area may be of benefit. I was born and raised here, which is why the temporary assignment to the city council," she said. "The circuit Heralds told me you'd come back, so I sent the suggestion to Haven. I hope you weren't already on assignment."

Jeris laughed. "Only the assignment of writing five years of gleaned Shin'a'in culture, language, and customs into archival copies for the Collegium."

Cara piped up, "Will you show me that when we get to the Collegium? I should like to know."

"If you're still interested, certainly," he replied.

Letia gave him another look. Reluctantly, he relayed his belief Cara might have the Bardic Gift, and certainly a strong musical knack. "Oh," Letia said. She knelt down in front of Cara, to the girl's eye level. "I know it's probably hard for you, but for your safety, you need to not sing where you might be heard, okay? Particularly where people might not be on their best behavior or making their best decisions, like an inn."

Cara nodded slowly. "I like singing. I just want to sing."

"I know, sweetie, but here isn't the place. When I see you in Haven, I'd love to hear you, though," Letia said, standing back up. She looked at Jeris. "Is she to attend the feast, or stay here?"

He frowned. "It's likely to be long and boring, isn't it? Not that—" He glanced around the sparse room. "—there's much for her to do here. Cara? What would you like?"

"May I come with you? I'll be good."

"Would that be acceptable to the mayor?" Jeris asked.

Letia smiled. "I'm sure he can find a place for her.

But," she said to Cara, "we need to be sure you're properly dressed. Do you have nice clothes with you?"

Cara pulled her best outfit out of her pack. "Will this work?"

Letia gave it a once over. "Mostly. We'll need to spend a little time on it and you, though, and a little bit of shopping."

Cara looked hopeful. "Can we, d—sir?" Jeris suspected she nearly said "daddy." He wasn't sure how he felt about that.

"I can afford a few *reasonable* trinkets, if my fellow Herald believes them necessary," he said. "Letia? Can you help her?"

She smiled brightly. "My pleasure! It's late, and we have a few days to get you fitted out properly. What say you two come to the town hall in the morning? You can watch the proceedings, and after that, we go shopping."

Jeris nodded. "A sound plan." Cara beamed.

Letia gave directions to the town hall, then left. Cara settled on the bed, while Jeris prepared his bedroll. She broke the silence. "What should I call you?"

A fair question. Jeris took a moment to respond. "For now, either 'Jeris' or 'sir,' is probably safest." A quick glance showed her crestfallen expression. "You're traveling with a Herald, Cara. I'm concerned about the group you noted downstairs. They left after they saw me, which seems odd. If they know *who* you are, well, they might do something . . . dangerous. If nothing else, I promised your mother to keep you safe."

Her voice was small and more child-like than normal. "Okay." The bedclothes rustled as she nestled in.

Jeris felt his heart twist at that word. Was it him? Was it her projecting with her Gift? He didn't know, and Halath couldn't tell him. He tucked her in, and sat down on the side of the bed. "I'm not going anywhere without you, okay? I'll be here in the morning when you wake up. At most, I'll be getting us food." Cara nodded, looking only a little reassured. He gave her a small smile. "Sleep well. Wake me up if you need anything."

She nodded. "Okay."

Jeris settled himself to sleep. :*You sleep well, too, my friend,*: he told Halath.

:*And you.*:

The Council meeting tended toward the dry and boring, as is the wont of such. Jeris felt pleased with Cara's behavior, though. As a preview of a formal dinner, she sat quietly and attentive, with a few questions to him when she didn't understand something.

When the meeting adjourned, they met with Letia near the front dais. Letia introduced Jeris and Cara to the mayor, who—at least to Cara—presented as a jovial, courteous person.

He even issued an invitation to Cara directly. "My friend Herald Letia informs me, young miss, you will be quite lonesome and without escort while Herald Jeris attends a feast at my behest. Would you be so kind to attend? You would be our youngest guest at this part of the festivities, but there will be a Bard to sing."

Cara looked surprised. "Thank you, sir. I would enjoy that."

"Excellent!" the mayor replied. "Herald Letia, I regret I have much to attend to at the moment. Would you be so kind as to escort our guests?"

She nodded. "Certainly, if the Council is done for the day."

"I do believe we are."

"Then," Letia said, "let us be on our way."

A warm, clear day meant the streets were crowded with errand-goers and shoppers. Cara gripped Jeris' hand tightly in the crowd, but seemed otherwise at ease. Letia directed them to a shop with trinkets, and Jeris lingered by the entrance. Jeris noted that, other than a few voices here and there that nagged or bickered, everyone sounded content. It took several shops and carts to find all the things Letia deemed necessary, including boots and barrettes and ribbons.

While they wandered around the food vendors for lunch, Jeris realized the underlying mood of the chatter had shifted. A few notes of music drifted through, and Cara bee-lined for the source. None of the force of Cara's singing accompanied the music being played, but a wary tension could be felt from the crowd. Cara stopped at the edge of the semi-circle surrounding a man in Bardic scarlet, playing a lovingly tended gittern.

The Bard played beautifully, as one would expect from a member of the Bardic circle. Jeris could just barely hear Cara hum along with the song. He gripped her shoulder in a slight warning, and she broke off with a guilty glance up at him. When the song finished, she stepped into the cleared area. "That was lovely," she said.

The Bard smiled, glanced at Jeris, and then over his shoulder. "Ah, Herald Letia! Are they with you?"

The two Heralds engaging with the Bard palpably lessened the tension Jeris felt in the crowd, and those uninterested in the music milled around and past. "Indeed, Ralin. Jeris came from Haven for our feast, and Cara travels with him, to visit family nearer the shores. Jeris, Cara, please be known to Bard Ralin. Like me, he grew up in Highjorune."

"Quite. Although my home has been less warm these last few years," Ralin agreed, almost affably, with just a touch of emphasis on "home." "But perhaps the feast will restore the town's good humor. And you, young Cara? Will you be at the feast? I noticed you singing the words of the ballad just now."

Cara nodded shyly. "I was trying to be quiet."

"You like to sing?" She nodded. "Do you play at all?"

"A little. Momma plays the lute. We only had the one instrument."

"Well, perhaps if you are in town for long, I may show you a few tricks?" Ralin glanced at Jeris, who nodded slightly. Having her interact with a Bard could only be to her benefit, despite the townspeople's discomfort. Perhaps he could advise on her unwitting use of her Gift.

"I can direct you to them later," Letia put in. "But we came through to eat. Would you like to join us, Ralin?"

"It would be my pleasure," he bent to put away his gittern, and Jeris leaned down, ostensibly to help pack Ralin's folding chair. For Jeris' ear, Ralin murmured that it was to his advantage to be seen with the Heralds.

"I thought so also," Jeris replied.

Jeris and Cara selected their meal at the suggestions of Letia and Ralin. Jeris noted how much more at ease the crowd seemed after Ralin put away the instrument. Over a filling, tasty lunch, they agreed Letia would escort Ralin to their inn.

"It's not that I don't know where the inn is," Ralin commented. "It's just that it seems prudent lately."

"The last bit of trouble was a few years ago," Jeris said quietly. "Is it still such a concern?"

"It had faded for the most part, so said the previous Bard. Stories surfaced from travelers about another one, and the town is tense again. Most would prefer to forget the recent wars altogether, and certainly a bed of treason."

The answer discomfited Jeris more than he liked. Why would the stories resurface now?

As discussed, the Heralds and Cara arrived at the feast together, the two Companions walking side by side, in step. Jeris smothered a smug smile at the awed expressions. No matter how many times a pair of preening Companions were seen, the reaction was the same.

The trio dismounted and joined the amorphous blob, nominally the entrance line, leaving the Companions to themselves. A pair of city-liveried people checked names and directed parties to their seats. Despite the numbers, they were quickly seated near the mayor and council.

"My compliments on the organization so far," Jeris offered to the mayor.

The mayor smiled and declaimed any credit. "I am fortunate in the quality of citizenry."

A liveried woman scurried up to whisper in the mayor's

ear, and he murmured back. Standing, he gave a short speech, welcoming the guests and introducing the Heralds. The servers started circulating as soon as the mayor seated himself.

Ralin's playing accompanied fine food, acceptable wine, and pleasant conversation for the first half of the feast. Jeris half wished that Soressa were present to observe Cara's youthful enthusiasm and awe.

About an hour in, Ralin took a break, relieved by a string quartet while he rested. He was seated on the other side of Cara, across from Letia. Cara peppered the bard with questions about what the quartet were doing. Jeris gently reminded her to allow the man to eat as well. Looking chagrined, she obeyed.

Jeris should have expected the event was going too smoothly. Towards the end of the quartet's third piece, the first sounds of discord started on the far side of the room. He recognized the man who stood up and gesticulated wildly as being the loudest member of the group Cara had pointed out their first night in Highjorune. The volume escalated, and he and Letia traded glances. "I'll go see," she said.

"I will go with you," the mayor put in.

Before they got there, another man had risen, obviously angry. Jeris didn't see who threw the first punch, but it shortly didn't matter. It seemed the crowd Cara warned them about had arrived to this event itching for trouble. Half of the room was in full brawl in seconds. Children and startled women scattered toward the walls.

"Go," Jeris ordered Cara, pointing at the stairs. Getting

her out of the melee area was his first responsibility. She
went. He ran to help Letia and the Guard separate the
brawlers. There were too many. *This isn't working,* he
thought as a stray blow grazed his chin. He reached out
to Halath, to ask the Companions to intercede with mass
if nothing else.

A small, strong voice chimed through the brawl. It was
Cara, standing mid-stair. He recognized the lyrics of a
prayer song to Astera, high, clear, calming. Her hand
clutched the railing.

A hush spread out from the bottom of the stairs and
across the room. Some stopped and turned to see her.
Others just untensed and ceased fighting.

In a few moments, they were all listening to her bell-
like tones. *She is amazing,* he thought, *so clear and in
pitch, despite her age.*

A deeper voice joined hers, Ralin's voice, and Jeris felt
the *pull* of the two, as the Bard picked up the harmony on
his gittern.

:Get her out of there,: Halath ordered, breaking some
of the hold of the music.

He abruptly realized that Ralin was trying to distract
the crowd from Cara's display by overpowering it. He
shook himself out of the lulling song and dodged through
the crowd to Cara's side. "You need to drop out of the
song," he urged at a whisper. "We need to get you out of
here."

Her eyes widened and her chin dipped in bare
acknowledgement. She softened her portion, dropping to
silence at the end of a verse. Ralin's voice strengthened
further, a pulling, lulling sound which Jeris found he could

only barely resist. He gathered Cara, carrying her down the stairs.

Catching Ralin's gaze as the Bard played and sang, Jeris gave him a sharp nod of acknowledgement. The Bard quirked an eyebrow at him without losing a note or beat. Letia moved to Ralin's side, Jeris assumed for the purpose of taking over the attention of the now-lulled gathering, as soon as the song ended.

He carried Cara out to Halath as fast as he could. She started shaking, even as he hoisted her on to his Companion's saddle. He swung on behind her, and Halath cantered for the inn.

Halfway back, she asked, "Am I in trouble? I just—I didn't want anyone to get hurt. It's what Momma's always had me do during a brawl."

"No. You did your best in a not-good situation. But others may not see it that way," Jeris told her. "That's why you have to go to the Bardic Collegium. They can teach you when it's . . . acceptable."

He offered a brief, silent prayer of his own, hoping he hadn't left Letia and Ralin to an unruly crowd alone. *:Drayl says they're safe, for now,:* Halath relayed the message from Letia's Companion.

Cara was still shaking when they arrived at the inn. Jeris left Halath to the stable hand for care with Halath's agreement. Getting her upstairs and into bed was a priority. He could see the reaction headache already setting in.

He got her settled in, prepped headache draught, and insisted she drink some before she fell asleep completely. It was the best he could do for now.

:That was more people than she's likely ever seen in one place in her life. She must have poured everything she had into it,: he told Halath.

:She kept it from getting bloody,: Halath replied.

Hopefully the Guard and Letia would be able to sort out the incident and individuals without his assistance. For now, he needed to care for a little girl due to be in a lot of pain, even with a preemptive draught.

Jeris woke up, disoriented. A small, warm body cuddled against his, and he snapped alert before recognizing it was Cara. Color had returned to her face, unlike earlier, when she had been violently sick from the reaction headache. He'd coaxed more medicine into her, and cuddled her to sleep while she whimpered.

He gently disentangled from the clutching girl, who murmured a protest which sounded like "daddy." He gritted his teeth and took care of a few necessities. He tried to nudge her awake to gauge her recovery, but she just murmured something incoherent and didn't rouse. He went downstairs to order strong tea and breakfast. He found himself thinking longingly of the Shin'a'in morning brew as morning fatigue set in.

He was groggy enough that he didn't register the loud voices arguing outside of the tavern until he entered the main room, while the innkeeper stood in the doorway.

"No, you may not disturb any guests under this roof," the innkeeper said.

"She's the little brat from Soroll, the one who squirrels all my deals," a man shouted. "Can't have a little fear to make a bargain go well, not while she's around. Can't even have a healthy brawl. She's a witch!"

Other angry voices joined his at that accusation.

Jeris didn't remember going back up to the room to get her. He realized he was shaking her awake. "Cara, you have to get up, you have to get up *now!*" He was about to pick her up to carry her, still asleep, down to Halath when she opened her eyes blearily.

"Am I late for work?" she asked, still groggy.

"No, yes. You have to get up now, there's trouble."

She tried. She really did. She hadn't recovered from the night before, and was tiredly clumsy. Jeris swept her up, and bounded down the back stairs to the stables. Halath whinnied as they burst in. "You've got to go. Halath will take you to Letia."

She was awake now. "Da—Jeris, sir, please!" She looked scared, but didn't resist being hoisted on Halath's bare back.

"Cara, some of the people recognized you last night. They're angry, and they're likely dangerous. You have to go to Letia, and tell her that. Halath can find her or her Companion, who can take you to her."

He put her hands up to Halath's mane. "Hold on here if it helps you feel safer. Grip with your legs. He'll keep you on his back as long as you try to stay there. Got it?" She nodded, fingers working into the fine hair. He pressed a kiss to the back of her hand. "I'll see you soon." He flung the stable door open, and Halath left at a canter.

Jeris ran around to the front of the tavern from the stable entrance. The angry crowd huddled at the front of the inn. He wasn't in his best Whites, but these would have to do. "What seems to be the problem?" he asked loudly, in full Herald demeanor.

The individuals closest to him turned, and upon realizing a Herald was at hand, looked a bit cowed. Some started edging off to the sides. The loudmouth at the door, however, didn't turn around, still haranguing the innkeeper. Jeris caught the eye of one of the men slinking off. He hadn't been with the group Cara originally recognized. "You there. What's the fuss about?"

"We, ah, were just concerned, sir, about a guest at the inn," the man stammered.

"And why might that be?" Jeris prompted.

"She's a witch!" another spat at him.

"She caused trouble last night!" a third person said.

"Oh?" Jeris replied, arching an eyebrow. "Please elaborate."

Several people threw out wildly different stories of the events. The voices overlapped, but Jeris got the gist. He raised his hands to quiet those nearest him down.

"How many of you were in attendance last night?" Heads shook, and the quiet spread toward the inn. "Most of you weren't, it seems. I was." The crowd quieted further, drawing the attention of those nearest the troublemaker. "In fact, the . . . *gentleman* over there was near where the original altercation started." People started edging out of the way between them.

Once called out, the man seemed ready for a fight, along with a couple of his bullyboys.

Jeris didn't want to fight, not if it could be avoided. He just had to delay. Most of the crowd were spectators, easily stirred up, and just as easily deterred. Many expressions showed second thoughts about a riot against the Queen's representative. They might join in, though.

The three had work knives on their belts, but hadn't drawn them yet. Jeris had not drawn his sword, either. They were gauging him, considering their chances, and in a moment they were going to charge. The lead man would be in front, of course, and the others would flank. Jeris prepared to move and draw against them.

Down the street to his left came shouting and clatter, above the noise of the crowd.

"Clear the street! Make way!" a voice shouted.

The crowd parted again, now broken into three smaller groups, and split by the approaching party.

It was a dozen men of the city watch in leather armor with halberds, clubs and swords. Letia was behind but catching up fast, astride her Companion, with Ralin seated behind. With them were another dozen levied volunteers with staves and bars. They fell into a skirmish line across the street, behind Jeris.

"What is the meaning of this?" the Guard captain demanded.

"It appears," Jeris replied, "we have a less than honest merchant who is irritated by his strong-arm tactics being thwarted in more than one town."

The Guard captain gave the loudmouth a baleful glare. "We were looking for you, as a matter of fact, for the disturbances last night and previous complaints. It'll be best for you to come with us quietly, instead of slipping off again." The man looked to be weighing his options, still leaning towards a fight.

"That girl is a witch!" one of the others said.

"No, she's a Herald's daughter. *My* daughter," Jeris said loudly.

A ripple went through the crowd, and glares began to go in the tough's direction. The changed mood appeared to be enough to convince him to take the easier option. His posture relaxed, and the other two stood down. The Guard collected them, and the crowd dispersed.

"We came as fast as we could," Letia apologized. "Thankfully, as everyone was already *at* the council over last night, it was faster than it might have been."

"You came in time," Jeris shrugged. "Cara?"

"Safe," Ralin answered. "I'll need to have a few more words with her. Some guidance, until you get her to the Collegium."

"I'd be grateful."

"Remember, you've promised to sing for me when we're in Haven," Letia said, helping Cara onto her pony.

Cara smiled, still shy about it. "Yes. But we're going to father's family first, right?"

Jeris nodded, tying her pony's lead to his saddle. "Yes, Haven after that."

"And I'll be able to sing there?"

"Any melody you wish."

End

OFF THE CUFF

At Pennsic, 2014, a young lady heard from someone else that an SF writer was on site. She came to my store, and inquired if I might assist with a project.

She was competing in the GISHWHES contest. GISHWHES is The Greatest International Scavenger Hunt the World Has Ever Seen. The profits go to different charities, but typically Misha Collins' charity Random Acts. Since the scavenger hunt has been going on there have been 3,423 senior care facility visits, 2,872 volunteer hours at food kitchens, 954 donations to women's shelters, 2,038 blood donations, 842 bone marrow donations, 456 beaches cleaned, and 1,473 coat drives held.

Her task was to "Get a previously published sci-fi author to write an original story (140 words max) about Misha, the Queen of England and an Elopus (Elephant/Octopus mashup)."

Twenty minutes later, I handed her this:

✛

SO, NO SHIT, there I was, thought I was gonna die. I was sitting in the Europa Hotel in Blastfell, excuse me, Belfast.

In comes the Queen of England with her entourage and guards, accompanying some bizarre creature that looked half octopus (the top half) and elephant (the bottom half), and let me tell you, I've seen smaller barstools. He said his name was "Misha," but he had a Swedish accent.

So, anyway, Queen Liz orders a Tom Collins and Misha the Squidboy offers up a toast to Cthulhu.

I'm guessing that was a mistake. Next thing, the whole place erupts in hypergolic violence. A flaming penguin arced through the air and impaled a beaver. Really.

I got literally peppered with spare punctuation marks. (Sorry.)

I'm dead serious. I stayed completely sober and the bar got bombed.

End

BATTLE'S TIDE

Bill Fawcett called me and said he had an outline for a shared universe, did I want to write? He'd pay me.

Well, obviously, the answer is yes.

He sent me the background for the universe. It's one in which the dinosaurs didn't largely go extinct, and continued to evolve, but so did mammals. We find our setting to be an alternate Bronze Age, with sentient felinoids and theropods, around a Mediterranean undergoing a Messinian Salinity Crisis. It's a deep, dry, scorching desert surrounded by highlands, in turn surrounded by seas. The felines don't wear much in the way of armor, and no one has bows, but they do have spears, wagons and other accoutrements.

Then I saw the two included stories already written by other contributors. Possibly you've heard of Harry Turtledove and S.M. Stirling.

Certainly I'd met and talked to them at conventions, but to be included in a collection with writers of that level of reputation was quite a thrill. It made me feel I'd "arrived," as they say.

Bill did have to offer some direction, as my health was not great at the time—lingering breathing issues from the Middle East. But I like how it turned out.

⊕

NRAO OF THE VELDT liked his wagons and his spies.

He sat under the broad shade of his residence in a wicker chair, enjoying a drink of grer, fermented arosh milk. It refreshed the body and let his mind think clearly. He had much to think about. So did his advisors, seated in a ring with him on carved wooden chairs. His son Nef benched quietly attentive off to the side, learning actual rulership along with the parchment lessons he took. The boy looked distracted, his long tail twitching impatiently from side to side, but Nrao understood that was partly an exploitation of his age. He was wiser than many suspected. He was tawny and handsome, certainly his mother's son as well as his. Nrao's warm, golden coat was striped with black on cheeks, wrists, tail and ankles. Distinctive markings, the seer Ingo said, for a male of distinction.

Nrao's neighboring Mrem sometimes mocked his taste in politics. They preferred decorated Dancers and large warriors. His corral of wagons, the extended wall and defense works around it, the shapers who maintained all, and the monies spent on distant rumors amused them.

He had Dancers and warriors, too. His warriors knew several fighting styles and tactics. His Dancers studied a variety of dances and incantations. When a fight came, the wagons moved his warriors rapidly, and he could place them in superior position to the enemy.

That was why his steading was larger than any within knowledge, and why he was amused at the mirth sent his way. Hidebound traditionalists would fall by the wayside. His clan was one of the first to take southern land from the Liskash. The ancient enemies were still licking their wounds. This meant he had some of the best water and grazing. They held a large if dusty savannah with three large rivers and numerous wells and oases. Clan herds beyond count browsed the tall grass. So it had been for over five years, an ideal home for a growing clan, but now . . .

When the sea broke through to the Hot Depths, he'd dispatched scouts, diplomats and spies to draw maps and tell him all they saw. They were here now, to counsel him on all they knew.

Nrao began, "I would like updates on each aspect. Talonmaster Rscil?"

It would be hard to miss the talonmaster, with his oiled fur looking darker than its natural tan tones, worn and abraded harness he seemed never to remove, and flat but heavy muscles. Next to him were spear, javelin, battle claws and knife, neatly leaning against the bench. He had come directly from fighting practice.

Rscil spoke in his deep, confident voice. "The refugees continue to gather and approach. One large band has gathered the remnants of several clans. Few are a threat directly, but all need food and water. I still suggest guiding them east and then north to the cool streams and woods. It is not long before we will have to do the same within a few harvests. Isolated there is no question that eventually we will fall." One ear twitched as he finished.

Nrao said, "While I bear them no ill will, sending them ahead provides useful information, and has some effect on the cursed Liskash."

"Yes, Clan Leader." The talonmaster was practical, of course.

"Seer Ingo?"

His elder philosopher, aged but spry, his fur tufted and ticked in white, leaned against one arm of his bench and said, "Land itself, the Hot Depths, was taken from the Earth. It was not prime land for anyone with fur, but all of its dwellers must find a new place to live. The weather is still changing, and more than we expected. The Sun will draw much rain from this large new sea, and drop it to the west. This will improve growth, but will also cause new rivers and erosion."

Nrao nodded acknowledgment. "Will that cool things enough to hinder those annoying Liskash?"

"I don't know yet." Ingo did not lower his ears in shame. It was safe to be unsure around Nrao. He knew not all answers were cast in bronze. "It may enable or hinder them."

"Can we use that land?"

"We can. It could prove rich eventually, but it would take development of grass, then scrub, and repeated burnings to make a rich soil. We'd need to transport earth borers, naked tails and goats to provide dung and dig it in with claw and hoof. Also, the Liskash will object."

Nrao smiled and said, "They'll object, but it might not be an issue, if the climate is not to their favor. Watcher Tckins?"

His head spy leaned forward slightly. The Mrem was

slim and very average looking. His dull gray coat was healthy but ordinary. He wore harness of a trader, the pouches stuffed with items and valuables. It was a suitable disguise for his comings and goings.

"Nrao, there is much going on between the Liskash and other Mrem. People fled the flooding in all directions, some to be captured by Liskash, others crowded and displaced. They caravan and fight, as the talonmaster has said, to seek homes further north, and west around the New Sea. Liskash fight with them, and each other. I can't speak to the long term of the region, but movement west is our only option. East is desert and sea, south is Liskash, north is the New Sea."

Nrao said, "That is certainly an issue. Do you believe it's worth it to move now, though?" Tckins trembled slightly at the question.

"I believe we can find good position early, run wagons to small strongholds to keep them supplied, and build a solid steading. The Liskash are fighting amongst themselves. We might find a defensible position north of the hills, without needing to fight our own kind."

"That would be good, but is not the only consideration. We must have enough people to occupy and hold the land against violent Liskash and displaced Mrem. Priestess Cmeo?"

The only female present, the priestess had the circling symbol of the Sky Lord around her neck. The bronze of the medallion stood out against her glossy black fur. She stretched out a hand. The very grace of it attracted the attention of all the males, but it was what she said that mattered. Her round, gold eyes were sincere with concern.

She spoke, "Aedoniss does not speak directly. We must infer. If this is to be a new, rich land with a broad sea to fish in, and has caused much distress for the Liskash, it is clear he is offering us an opportunity. He does not guarantee it will be easy, or successful, but I feel he wants us to try. Challenge is what makes Mrem great, over those indolent, lazy Liskash."

Nrao saw it, too. There was risk, though it was manageable with preparation and forethought. There was also the chance of great expansion. Rich territory, plentiful food, and perhaps a secure border against the slimy Liskash.

"Then first, I will have the wagons checked, and meat dried."

Oglut was excited and nervous, though he'd never let the underthings know that. His fathers had built this palace of carved marble and scented wood through the power of their minds to control others. His limits had always been those who could also force others to their will. Now some of those who had lived in the lowlands were gone, or had lost their slaves. He sat on his throne and thought.

There seemed no end to the water. Where there had been rich holdings now there would be nothing. His own lands had been considered too high and cool. But now his holdings were intact and these riches he had coveted lost. Where he had once ruled at the edge of the lowlands, now he would control the far side of a new ocean. At least if it stopped rising before the whole world was flooded.

There was potential for great expansion, with Sassin

and Ashala dead and their holds in tatters. Then, those accursed Mrem who had challenged them in the warm jungles were also fleeing ahead of the New Sea. Most went north to the cold lands they had been spawned in. The few heading directly west would be easy to incorporate as they reached the range of his mind. It was a silly game they played, but what could one expect of semi-sentient mammals with no mindpower? They weren't good for much, but could serve as a buffer against other attacks, rather than waste more valuable lives.

The New Sea would also bring rain and growth. More food meant more slaves, and a finer godhold. He needed to move quickly, to secure it before someone from far south did so, or it got overrun by those accursed hairy Mrem from the north.

He pondered it all while sitting on his favorite throne, comfortably fanned by slaves, caressing the new female he had recently acquired, and occasionally sipping from a golden goblet of wine. He enjoyed his godhood. He put that aside and chose action. Yes, it was time the boys grew up.

Oglut wished for his servants to appear, and shortly they did.

"I am moving to secure the empty godholds of Sassin and Ashala, to claim the slaves and resources that they abandoned. I need my chariots and guard ready. My sons will lead the campaigns."

Then he called his sons.

Mutal arrived, young and eager with trappings worthy of himself. He had had his scales gilded and painted in handsome colors to resemble a mosaic. His garments had been woven of the finest cocoon strands and dyed regal purple. Behind him, dull-eyed Mrem servants carried his gilded weapons and armor on plush pillows. Buloth didn't appear at once. He was big enough now to be a slight challenge. That was another issue for Oglut to address.

He waited for Buloth, who arrived with hints of incense and sage smoke. His costly blue and yellow raiment was askew. Had the boy been breathing dimweed again?

Oglut spoke to him first.

"I have decided to annex the lands left vacant by our departed neighbors, all the way to the coast of the New Sea. Once this is done, there will be a large godhold for you, so you need not wait for my demise."

"Thank you, Father." Though the boy, now grown, didn't seem appreciative, but smug.

Oglut frowned. Perhaps he did not understand the gift he was being offered. "Rather than you fight me for control, you can have a new holding, and larger than this one. Mutal," he said, shifting his gaze and his power to the younger male, "you will have my holding, or a large part of it, what you can control, when I am too old to rule. If we expand further, it may be larger as well."

"Thank you, Father. It is a great offer, but I wish you long life." The younger one, at least, was sincere.

Oglut dismissed the comment with a wave. "Of course I will live long, but I am older than you. We will plan now to secure our new lands. I will have Buloth ready at the east with an army, to expand as far as possible along the new coast against the furry pests as the weather warms. Mutal, you will go south. Success awaits us. All we need to do is be ready for it."

His sons smiled in approval, as did he. No backstabbing or mind-forced retirement as a helpless elder needed. They could have three large holdings now, and his sons would expand after he died. If one of them died in the process, it would just mean more for the other, and for himself.

Oglut was pleased. Some of his hatchlings would die. Those who survived would have lands of their own that would take them many seasons to secure. They would have no time to turn on him and try to claim their inheritance early. And by the time they were strong, he would be much stronger.

"By the end of this season you will all be lords of your own lands," the Liskash finished.

No need to offer them his already stable holding. He hadn't lived this long through trust. They could create their own. Their triumphs would reinforce his own borders and set them up as shields for his realm.

If the Mrem and their beasts showed up after things were secure, they'd just make useful slaves.

The massive hide tent that served as both the residence and command center for the clan was nearly full. None could twitch their tail without hitting another. There was a strong scent off the moist fur of the nervous Mrem as those Nrao had summoned stood and sat inside, sheltered from a light rain. The two dozen Mrem waiting were of every size, color, and type. They seemed to have nothing in common; none carried himself like a warrior. But then that was the idea. Most appeared to wear the tools of merchants or tinkers. In reality they were the eyes and ears of the clan.

All were strangers to each other; Nrao had never before called in so many of his scouts and spies at one time. Ears and tails twitched as the normally solitary and cautious Mrem watched each other with calculating eyes. None were armed, but all labored to keep their claws sheathed.

The clan's spies usually sent messages in code, or brought reports back after a tour of merchanting or as envoy. Rarely did they report in person and always in private. Just being known to the others put them at risk. Nrao had ordered them all in quickly when the full extent of the water's rise became apparent, sending replacements with the call. Those Mrem were not as experienced as the existing spies, but this is how they learned. Those who survived. Nrao and the clan needed every fact now, but still had to keep up their guard, even at a cost.

Also, Rscil's scouts were on a steady rotation, to map the New Sea and watch for migrations. Nothing but Liskash had lived in the very bottom of the Hot Depths, but the river courses were lush and fertile, to the point where they evaporated. With the flood, a few tribes had moved north, more south, an unknown number west, where they would be massively outnumbered by the Liskash.

Every eightday, he met with Rscil and the incoming scouts personally, and received updates from his advisors. He would not move until he knew conditions were right, but then he'd strike like lightning to exploit the opportunity.

Today, he had both a spy from Afis's domain to the west, north of the Liskash, and the scouts from the coast.

He waited on Ingo, while Nef sprawled on his bench and stropped his claws. Annoyed, Nrao reached out one of his own claws and dug it into the post between the boy's. Nef flared his ears back, nodded and sat up.

"That is better," Nrao said. "Now, pour wine for the guests."

"Yes, Father," Nef said. He might be young, but the trappings of courtesy came easily to him. He should make a good leader one day.

Refreshments and a casual atmosphere, Nrao found, made information more forthcoming. Some rulers demanded strict formality and adherence to rank. He was first among them, and deserving of respect, without the need to be ego-fluffed. When all were served, he sat among them, his pupils spread wide to show friendliness and interest.

Sicht, the spy, wore a well-made harness, as befitted his position as one of the trade ministers to Afis's holding. He was comfortable enough with Mrem of status, and politely took a drink and a sweetened meat chew, pounded with honey and dried frusk. They were unhealthy, but delicious.

The two scouts were politely subordinate, but their smell and the proud set of their ears said they knew they were trusted to report honestly. Hril and Flirsh brought out their notes, and stood to consult with Seer Ingo. The old male unrolled his larger map, cut from the whole hide of a draft-bred arosh stretched out, and the three gathered to mark it. Nrao sat back enough to let them work, while watching.

Shortly, Ingo glanced up at him. "The flooding of the

warm lands is causing more rains, and dampening the hills. They are green with growth. It has drowned many Liskash and those Mrem who were passing through."

No Mrem chose to stay in what had been stale and hot lowlands. But through that desert had been the shortest route to the rich, open lands in the south. Nrao's father had led the clan through, though not without losses to the heat-loving Liskash that thrived there.

The scout's tail flipped with concern, flapping against two startled spies behind him. He seemed to not notice. "The water has come quickly enough that the great lords there are destroyed, but thousands of Liskash fled ahead of it. They can only reinforce those who were already trying to destroy us."

Nrao let the tip of his tail lash as well. "Obviously we must stop that before it commences."

Hril, as senior scout, said, "The rise is measured in handspans a day, but it has spread over a huge area, and periodically inundates a depression with great force. Everywhere as it rises and the rains come the land is thick with muck because nothing has time to grow where once there was desert. The water slows, but still claims more land every day."

The scout's concern was obvious as he finished. "We searched every direction and route. Deep water blocks every path back to the lands of our ancestors. It would have taken days to run at the narrowest point. But there is no crossing the swirling sea that covers those routes now. To sleep near the water's edge is dangerous. One scout who ventured too far out into what we thought were shallows was pulled away by powerful, hidden currents.

No more clans will come to reinforce us: no one can cross. Those of us south of this new sea are alone."

Nrao had never seen a sea. He would have to correct that. He did understand there were plants that grew submerged, vicious reptiles in the depths, and even primitive animal-like things, fast but edible, near the shore. That was something else to explore. If they lived long enough to explore anything, the clan leader reminded himself, stroking a whisker.

Rscil traced roads and paths on the broad parchment with the tip of a claw. Two disappeared into the new coastline. Three others were very close. All those routes north were broken. That particular bay would have a lot of shore traffic, if they could secure the area. If there were some way to cross it on water . . . but it was far too broad and stormy.

"Ingo, what about crossing the water at some later time? Can boats be made larger?"

The sage tilted his head in assent. "With heavier timber, yes. We have none now. That might come from the hills as thicker forests grow."

"I am not worried about it now, but after this campaign, I think it a worthy pursuit for our artificers to ponder."

"Noted."

Nef, leaning over their shoulders, suddenly pricked up his ears eagerly.

"Father, what of caravans? Should we have more warriors along that route, against conflicts or bandits?"

Nrao was proud of that. "A good question, Nef. Most insightful for your age. Rscil?"

Rscil nodded and raised his ears. "The caravans can support each other in proximity, and I don't foresee them fighting, although water could be an issue. But it's not a bad idea to reinforce the garrison on Steep Slope. They can conduct escorts and patrols. Outpost Master Shlom is one I well trust."

"Please. I will arrange supplies for you."

Rscil said, "But this is all temporary. All of us must move, and I concur on doing so soon. The later we wait, the more desperate we will be." His ears showed his agitation.

"Soon, Rscil. We must be prepared."

By midday, Nrao had updated his strategy and plans with the new information. He offered all parties a lunch of fresh roasted mottlecoat liver with salt and ground sharproot, and gave orders for following spy missions.

It was time to discuss stopping the Liskash mind threat.

The clan leader wondered how even sitting the Dancer could look graceful. Cmeo was beautiful and moved with a deadly grace that entranced all males. Nrao also reminded himself she was the second most powerful Mrem in his lands. He wondered what she saw sitting there with even her slitted eyes still as she waited for him to speak.

"Cmeo, the spies bring me disturbing news. Oglut is the name of the Liskash godling in the east. From reports, he is powerful in his mind magic. He bound even Mrem warriors in the fight."

She stared at him, subtle changes in posture and a twist of her tail showing she was attentive and clearly listening.

He realized Dancers rarely engaged in the skirmishes that his warriors had faced as they moved south.

"Once a warrior is actively fighting with an opponent, he should be intent on the task and not susceptible to distraction. So it has been for generations. Oglut overcame that. My scouts saw him enter a battle against those fleeing the waters and bind the warriors to his mind. The Liskash then turned them against their own clan brothers."

"I see."

"That means we must bind them back. Priestess, what can we do?"

Cmeo sat back and stared at the panel behind him, the black pupils spread so wide they swallowed up the golden irises. He let her do so, realizing the meditation for what it was. He often stared while thinking himself. Hers, though, was much more intense, even to watch. She fingered the symbol around her neck and her eyes slackened, then focused sharply on nothing.

He sat still also, not wishing to disturb her. These things worked in their own time.

She blinked and said, "We must strengthen the dance."

"Very well. How so?"

"If we have more Dancers, and closer to the warriors, they can exert more power. Distance is very important. The power weakens quickly."

"Closer, you say. That's awkward, in a battle formation." He twitched his ears.

She said, "Ideally we would need to be in the formation."

That was a striking and uncomfortable suggestion. It made his fur bristle, and he wanted to forbid it at once.

However, he had to consider it fairly.

Mixed with warriors. It hadn't been done. That could mean there was a good reason not to, or that it hadn't been thought of.

He took a sip of his drink and said, "I will summon the talonmaster. Return in an eighthday."

"Yes, Nrao." She bowed respectfully and left.

A messenger ran for the talonmaster, but it took time to clear the field and arrive. He used that time to consider. A central clearing in the formation for them? Several smaller ones?

Talonmaster Rscil arrived shortly, his fur puffing in sections as the muscles underneath twitched. His face remained calm, but his body betrayed his tension.

"Welcome, Talonmaster," Nrao greeted him. "I want to explore the idea of putting the Dancers into the warrior formation."

Rscil fluffed and said, "Clan Leader Nrao, have I given you cause to doubt my abilities?"

Nrao hastened to reassure him. "Not in the slightest, Rscil. I could find no finer warrior. This undertaking of mine seeks to provide you, and the greatest warriors of Mrem, with stronger shields against the Liskash. Do you have doubt in *my* abilities?" He asked it without rancor, but it was a test. Not of Rscil's loyalty, but of his willingness to argue against Nrao.

"None. My concern is that battle is traditionally a male pursuit due to strength. Females fight well, but are better in defense. Also, Dancers will not be fighting. They will be dancing. If we lose large numbers of Dancers—females—the entire steading suffers."

Nrao dipped his head in assent. "I agree with that assessment and its logic. However, by combining your strength with their resistance, and with a goodly support of wagon drivers, we can take and hold a deep piercement into Liskash territory. Desperate times may be ahead. Any tactic we can add that will forward our aim is worth exploring."

"Then I propose we test it as we go, and use known, working tactics if it proves unsuccessful."

Nrao had that exact thought, but decided it made a good bargaining point.

"A sound idea. We will discuss this, Cmeo and you and I and others, in a few days. For now, I wish for both groups to become more familiar."

Rscil's ears perked out and he twisted his mouth. "I will try. It's an untested concept, and requires adjustment to our formations."

"We will discuss it now, then," Nrao decided. "Rscil, I offer you some grer."

"Thank you, Nrao. I accept."

Nrao sat patiently. Rscil calmed down as he first gulped, then sipped the cool, tangy fermentation. A scribe stood back, waiting for attention, and Nrao gestured for him to approach. The Mrem did so, and hesitantly proffered a bark tablet of provision accountings for the pending expedition. It was more than Nrao had planned, but a reasonable amount. He marked it, and dipped a claw in ink to make it official, then handed it back.

Shortly, Cmeo returned.

"Greetings, Nrao and Talonmaster Rscil."

"Dancer," Rscil said.

Nrao nodded. "Welcome, Cmeo. Rscil has urgent matters to discuss on our plan, so I moved the meeting. I hope this is workable."

"I will make it so," she said. She curled into the bench opposite him and drew her feet up onto the seat. Her tail wrapped up around them.

"Good. This is a private meeting," he said, and looked over at the recording scribe, who nodded, stood and left the hall. He looked at his son, who stood poised as if to depart, but he looked as though he would like to stay. "Yes, Nef, you may remain. Remember this is a most secret meeting, not for discussion even with Ingo or your other teachers."

Nef was so solemn and earnest that Nrao almost smiled.

"I understand. It is a matter of the steading."

"It is." He turned back to Cmeo and Rscil. "I wish you both to be free to raise objections and offer input. My concern is that the plan work, not that my ego be assuaged."

His advantage, of course, was that he meant it. He was hard to sway from a course, but did accept reason, and appreciated argument even if it distressed him.

There was silence for a moment, then Rscil said, "Clan Leader, Priestess, with respect, this is what I find: My warriors are unused to the presence of females. This causes them to either loiter as near as possible to the females, hoping to attract attention, or to cavort and exhibit, for the same. I fear that in battle, they will uncontrollably lash out to prove their heroism, or gather around the females to protect them. This means they will not be fighting the enemy in a coordinated fashion. They'll fight more like scaly Liskash, not like Mrem."

His ruff was raised in agitation.

Calmly, Nrao said, "I understand the problem and believe it. We must find a way around it. Cmeo, please explain your plan."

Cmeo said, "I will assume we can resolve this problem." She looked irritated, too, however, grasping her tail to stop it from twitching. "As I explained to you, by having the Dancers closer to the warriors, I believe we can provide a stronger protection against spells. This means we need some warriors to protect the unarmed Dancers. I thought it easiest for both to put the Dancers in the middle, surrounded by warriors."

Rscil said, "The logic is sound, but you are not a warrior, nor are you used to dealing with warriors, and the special mindset they need. It is one of brotherhood, not of a male for his family, or a potential family."

Nrao intended to ask, but Cmeo beat him.

"Then what do you recommend as a solution?"

Rscil's ears popped, but he calmed down and replied, "How close must you be? Would behind a rank of wagons be close enough?"

"It might," she replied. "But my thought was to be close enough for the warriors to hear and be inspired by the chant. There's more power in it. It's hard for me to explain, but during practice, I can feel the power of it, and the closer, the stronger, and being part of it is of course so much more."

Rscil said, "It's logical. There's also the logic that warriors don't do well that close to females."

Cmeo cocked her head and her pupils narrowed. "Yet the Dancers don't have this problem. Are you suggesting your warriors lack this discipline?"

Rscil's fur brushed up all over and his claws twitched.

Nrao said, "Careful! This is a conference, not a challenge." He eyed them both. Aside, he saw Nef wide-eyed in worry at the clash of wills. The boy was still for once.

Cmeo's pupils spread out to normal. She said, "While I meant that to be provocative, the question remains. Are not the warriors disciplined enough to keep their positions?"

"What?" the talonmaster snarled.

Rscil needed a moment to calm down, and Nrao allowed it. He sipped his drink and waited, without indication of unease. It occurred to him that his own ability to choke down his instincts might be a large part of what made him so effective. He never rose to a challenge unless it suited his purposes, and ignored jabs and pokes that others dueled over. His neighbors slapped at him hoping for a reaction, but also afraid they might get one, and so kept their distance.

Rscil drank his grer and shook his head. "It is not so simple as it sounds, Priestess. Yes, my warriors will take my orders, well and willingly. What I am describing is their nature to protect females, and to seek mates. This will cause them to shuffle in close to keep the females from harm, and to be aggressive, within the limits of their orders, but not at the ideal level, to show their bravery. Females encourage what is best in the male, but an army is not about one warrior, it is about the whole."

"Fair enough," she said. She turned a hand over, the

picture of feminine grace. Nrao understood well what the talonmaster's concerns were. "Then the question remains, what can we do to make it work better?"

"I don't know," he said, with a toss of his ears. "Any concentration of females is going to cause this, I fear. This is why they are used in the defense, while the males campaign in the offense."

Cmeo offered, "What about several concentrations, then? It's not ideal for our trancing, but it might be done."

Rscil pondered, as did Nrao. He didn't understand the workings of magic, the Dancers, and trance. As a former talonmaster, he understood how to place warriors. This would be complicated. The idea was a sound one, but was implementation possible?

Rscil finally spoke. "It is possible. I advise against it, because it means manipulating each element by itself, or requiring the warriors to manage greater details, and fallback plans if one should take more casualties than another."

Nrao said, for Cmeo's benefit, "Yes, it is best they have only their fist of fellows to move and be concerned with."

Cmeo drooped her ears and slumped. "That is all I can offer. We will do our best wherever you will have us, but closer is stronger."

Rscil seemed genuinely unhappy to have won the debate. Nrao appreciated that. So when the idea hit him, he felt sorry for what it would do to the poor Mrem's mind.

"What then," he said, "if we evenly disperse the Dancers?"

Both stared at him. Rscil's tail twitched. Cmeo arched

her mouth and flexed her ears. They were both too surprised to respond.

He continued. "The original idea didn't go far enough. Everything Rscil says is true. But, if we mix the Dancers throughout, there's no clustering, and the warriors can show their best mettle without pressing the formation."

Rscil said, "It might be the whole formation will surge forward. It also means the females will be exposed to attack, especially by thrown weapons. There will also be arguing for position."

"Not from my Dancers," Cmeo said tightly. "In this context, you must think not of females, but of Dancers. They are as necessary to the fight as warriors, and not all females, nor even more than a few, can serve thusly."

"Necessary, but not necessarily on the battlefield!" Rscil roared.

Nrao held up his hands for calm and said, "No plan is without flaw. Can this be done? Does it solve more problems than it creates?"

Rscil growled a sigh, and untensed his ears.

"It means a great deal of work, and drill, and instruction for the warriors."

Nrao regarded him sincerely. "I can think of no one more capable, and worthy of the songs afterward, than you, Rscil. Call your drillmasters. Cmeo, prepare the Dancers."

"I shall, Nrao." Cmeo faced Rscil fully and said, "It appears we will be working together." She extended one claw.

Rscil smiled, propped his ears up, and hooked her claw with his own.

"Thus are legends created," he said.

✧ ✧ ✧

Oglut supervised his sons' preparations in the fenced field outside the keep. They had a tendency to loiter before acting. That was so animal. It was best to keep them a bit hungry, and a bit aggressive. He set Buloth's forces against Mutal's in a war game. The young males set up their battle lines for Oglut's approval. Buloth needed to be ready first. His target was farther away, so Oglut concentrated upon his preparations.

"You place the Mrem at the rear," he called, seated on a comfortable bed on the back of a trunklegs, a behemoth mammal with leathery gray skin and a prehensile snout. "So they can eat anything that dies on the way, either by falling out, or native life stirred up by your passage. Remember they must eat meat, unlike our more advanced digestion. If a creature is lamed, kill it and give it to them. It motivates the others, and also keeps them aware of the vileness of these hairy beasts."

Buloth said, "Yes, Father. Also, I will put the mammal herd beasts in front, where they can eat grass before it is trodden. They make good emergency food."

Oglut nodded. "They do. Not the tastiest, but adequate nourishment for slaves."

Buloth's gray tongue darted across his lips. "I have decided I will kill and roast a Mrem before any battle. The smell will motivate them to my desires."

That was very amusing. Oglut chortled and flicked his tongue. A whiff of breeze brought him the smell of a cook fire at that moment. No Mrem, but something savory. Yes, that was a fine suggestion.

"Very good," he said.

Buloth said, "I have enough food for me and my assistants. The rest will scavenge as we go." He sounded most eager.

"They are well fed to start. They will have good endurance and be pliable."

"Thank you, Father."

"Are you ready to take control of them now?"

"Yes, Father! I am ready and privileged."

Oglut felt his son probing, enveloping. He was strong enough, but not confident. That would come. He also had mixed feelings to find his son was not as powerful as he. Less of a threat, yes, but also somewhat inferior in mind. He might improve with practice, though.

In a few moments, his son had taken command of a two-thousand-creature army, plus a few personal retainers and some stupid beasts who only needed a vague prodding to haul carts. All their wills were bent to his. It was not as complete a command as Oglut would have had, but it would do.

It was time.

He thought rather than said, *Go, son, and teach the furry little turds a lesson. You may start on your holding now.*

His son's mind-voice came back clearly. *I hear you, Father, and am grateful. They will be brought into the whole.*

He turned to Mutal. "See what your brother has accomplished, and learn."

"I will, Father," Mutal said, earnestly. In his mind, Oglut picked up a well-developed sibling rivalry and ambition of his own.

Success was within their grasp. He had bred well.

The warriors were of two minds. Either the females were a too-welcome distraction, or they were a hindrance. Rscil felt as if he could pluck out every hair on his body in frustration. His tail was constantly moving as he watched his subordinates mediate arguments and order the warriors back into line.

He found himself in daily conference with Cmeo, starting the first day. They used his chariot, with an erected sun shade, as a platform for observation of the drill field.

"This is not going well," he sighed.

"It will. It is a new thing, and will take getting used to." Cmeo sounded confident. Her eyes were bright and calm, and her expression serene.

"Indeed," he said, wiping sweat from his eyelids. "How are the Dancers?"

"I don't know entirely. I see one substantial problem, though, that must be resolved."

"Yes?"

She fluffed slightly, and her ears flattened. That was surprising. She had very good control of her elegant body, usually. It must be significant.

"Several of the warriors have been most condescending to the Dancers. It is not only rude, it will undermine their confidence, and their empathy."

"Yes, that must be addressed," he said at once. Indeed. That would not build a cohesive force, and as she noted, could undermine what they had. "What is the nature of these comments?"

"Several to the effect that females are not suited to battle, only to defending the house. Others that they can't possibly manage to keep up with such powerful warriors."

Rscil couldn't help but grin.

"That first would be from the older ones, the second from younger ones."

Cmeo couldn't suppress a smile in return. "It was."

"It will be hard to break," he sighed. "I have some ideas, but you must support me."

"Of course," she said with a cordial lay of her ears.

"I'll start on that in the morning." He could start now, but he wanted time to think, and it was a hot day, dusty and gusty and more suited for a nap. He'd have to call a break shortly.

Cmeo said, "Well, I must thank you for your understanding."

Rscil regarded her evenly. "You are welcome, Priestess, but I must be honest."

"Yes?"

"I share some of that sentiment myself. However, my clan leader has given me orders, and I will comply as best I can. I expect as much from those I command."

She almost sighed, and her ears drooped slightly. "I understand. I also will do the best I can. Of course, I'm not happy with such . . . instinctive behavior." He knew she'd wanted to say *undisciplined*, though she did not. "I will trust you to address it."

"Thank you," he said. Fair enough, and he'd continue to give her the benefit of the doubt.

He wasn't sure she'd feel the same way tomorrow.

♦ ♦ ♦

Barely after dawn, the training resumed. Rscil watched from atop his chariot as the drill masters motivated the warriors in the cool air and dew-damp earth.

"Crawl! On your bellies. There are leatherwings overhead, and hurled spears and rocks. If a filthy Liskash sees you, you'll drool and do his bidding. Now up and run! Run like the filthy Liskash wants you carnally. Down! And crawl!" The nearest leader clapped his hands together to make his warriors move faster.

Rscil had talked to his drill masters, and by "talked," he'd told them bluntly what behavior was acceptable to him, and thence to Nrao. A general lesson and motivation now, would be followed by individual attention to any comments, and further group activity would continue until the problem was resolved. As an additional incentive, he'd spread the snide word that any warrior who didn't feel capable of marching with females had his leave to return to the herds. That resulted in hundreds of flattened ears, but no desertions.

They might hate him, but they would obey.

Cmeo looked rather nonplussed at the warriors crawling through sand and brambles, jumping, charging, diving. It was painful and exhausting, and mildly degrading. Still, it would enforce the rules.

They drilled all day, and there was clear resentment, but better response. One side benefit, Rscil thought, was that no warrior would quit if the females didn't first. Nor was anyone foolish enough to challenge the clan leader, the talonmaster, or even a drillmaster on the matter. He was satisfied.

Two days later Cmeo reported, "The comments have

stopped. Muttering, however, continues. The Dancers are dealing with it, including joking about it. With respect, a warrior of great ability need not boast. His skill is apparent. The boasting only serves to point his insecurity. Especially with Dancers, who can read feelings."

"I will relay that," Rscil agreed. "Some of the warriors will feel put upon, that they have been felt in such a manner." It struck the talonmaster that he had watched the graceful Dancers and their movements had inspired the occasional less than chaste thought. Had Cmeo or the others sensed this? He dismissed the concern and plunged ahead.

"I have a suggestion, a delicate one, if I may," he said. His proposal was a bold one, and could have repercussions if not taken well.

She raised her brow hairs and said, "It's necessary that we agree that we are not enemies, and can share sensitive things."

He hoped Cmeo was referring to what he was about to propose.

"One matter, which I feel is legitimate, is that this will be a long march with stiff battles."

"Go on."

"The warriors fear the Dancers are graceful but not strong, and I use that term in the physical sense, and will not be always able to keep up with the army."

"I see," she said. "Yes, I understand the context. And what do you propose?"

"I would like to conduct training routes as well as drill. A few hundredlengths at first, building to greater distances."

"That makes sense," she agreed. "To make it interesting, I propose three thousandlengths to start."

Rscil took a moment to eat that. While not a great distance, it was a healthy route for warriors, and a fair approach to battle. Eventually, he'd like twice eight or more thousandlengths. Cmeo proposed starting at more than an eighth of that at the start. Of course he appreciated the offer. It would speed training, and make a better showing for them. Could they do it, however?

"Are you confident of that?" he asked.

She sniffed. "Warrior, what do you think females in camp or town do? They butcher meat, haul wood, walk herds, fight predators. It has been years since we fought to defend the town, but you've heard and seen herding station battles. Besides, I will guarantee none will drop out. If they fall, it will be from exertion, and demonstrate they have the courage to give all. Surely that will serve some measure?"

Rscil admired her assessment of the situation and appreciated the cooperation. "Either will serve great measure. I admit to knowing little apart from war, and I value your advice," he said.

She chuckled and rumbled in her throat. Her eyes twinkled.

"This information is a lack of your warriors, and ironic being as we know so much of our neighbors and enemies."

"It is," he agreed. "Does any male ever understand a female? Or the reverse?"

"I understand you better than you think, Rscil." Her eyes bore a flash as she raised a gourd for a lap of water.

Her glint made him most delighted and uncomfortable at the same time.

To cover his confusion, he said, "I will see to the plans for these routes."

As he left, he heard her growl a much louder chuckle.

Before dawn the next day, Rscil looked over the warriors at morning gathering. Some were stolid, relaxed, attentive. Some were eager and itchy to start. A few looked disdainfully at, or away from, the Dancers who were clustered together at one side of the field. Everyone's tail twitched with impatience.

Cmeo stood nearby, a bundle next to her. It was smaller but similar to his, with water gourds and dried meat for meals. She had a dagger and short javelin, to his full panoply.

"Today we march," he shouted, and the drill masters echoed him. "Follow me!"

He turned and picked up his bundle, then started at a brisk but steady pace toward one of the well-worn paths of the settlement. Cmeo matched him and fell alongside, with Senior Drillmaster Gree on the other side. Gree had counting beads, and a very reliable pace. He also had a very craggy face with claw scars and torn ears. He'd fought in many border raids. Cmeo looked like an unearthly being in comparison, glossy black, trim, dainty and graceful.

It was early and dark, cool and misty, but would be warm soon enough, from exercise and the sun. His chosen route was south, between several copses that led to the Great Desert, many days' walk south. There had been forest here, until Mrem had harvested it for building, and to clear grazing land.

Nothing was said for a time. Gree kept count, shifting beads on the string. They were drilled copperstone, the rich blue that became ore when heated. Rscil shifted his pack slightly, to relieve pressure on his back. Cmeo kept pace well enough. She took more steps with shorter legs, but seemed unbothered by the exertion.

Behind, the lines of warriors and Dancers stepped off, with drums beating a time. The rearmost ranks had to wait in order to move. There were noises of shuffling and shifting, occasional curses from the drillmasters, but shortly, it evened out and they were all en route.

Gree counted aloud as he reached the first mark. "Seventy-six, seventy-seven, one hundred . . ." Then he resumed a barely audible mutter under his breath.

Rscil said, "Gree can be trusted with all information. So, Cmeo, did you advise the Dancers on our plans?"

"Only as you did the warriors. A route march, with water."

His ear twitched acknowledgement. "Very well. I hope it turns out as it should. Though I do wish Mrem had the endurance of arosh. Even a few thousandlengths is barely a morning's work for them. It would last us all day."

She said, "In exchange Aedoniss has given us our brains, and not as slaves to Liskash, but as individuals."

"Indeed. Our tools are our strength." He gestured slightly with the javelin he carried over his shoulder. It was cast and hammered, ground to a fine, gleaming edge, decorated with etchings and chiselings of praise to the Sky God. He observed that hers was as well made, though it had not seen service.

It was a hot day, and dusty, with little wind. Despite

that, Rscil could smell the army. The whole didn't smell too fatigued yet, and he could tell the females by their different scent. They managed. Behind, the arosh hauled light carts for any injured. Inevitably, someone would step in a rut, take sick from the sun, or otherwise need to be carried. The Liskash usually left casualties to crawl or die. Mrem made sure to recover them, both for practicality and in compassion.

Gree counted, ". . . seventy-six, seventy-seven, four hundred . . ." The tempo was perfect.

A while later, a thought struck Rscil. He turned to his companion. "Cmeo, it seems to me that a good route march is a bit like a dance. Ideally, every warrior should have the same stride, the same speed, and move in an even line."

"A bit," she said. She sounded a little breathy, but still fit. "This is another benefit of mixing the Dancers. We can help keep the time, with our drummers." She signaled behind her to the female drummers at the head of the file of Dancers. They stopped playing their complicated rhythm of worship and changed to a rapid double-beat that matched the pace the marchers were keeping.

Rscil found it lightened his step. "The drums are enticing. Once they are steady, I look forward to them and walk with them."

"That is part of the magic," she said. "The dance, the drums, the chants, all reach the brain, and keep it focused and free from distractions and mind magic."

She sounded somewhat winded now, as Gree reached a thousand paces. Rscil used that as an opportunity to say, "We are halfway to our turnaround today. Yes, I will arrange for the drummers. Let us be quiet a time. I wish to listen to the army and hear for trouble." Quiet would also save breath.

They strode on, Cmeo occasionally quickening to catch up. She didn't fall behind, but she did have to work at it. Rscil made a point not to slow his pace. His warriors knew how he moved, and this was to prove a point.

When Gree counted one thousand five hundred lengths, Rscil stopped and raised his arm. He turned, shouted, "Circle and rest!"

It was obvious the Dancers hadn't seen this maneuver before. Some warriors broke out of ranks, formed eight points with spears jabbed into the ground, and the rest swarmed through brush and behind rocks looking for threats. In beats only, the area was secure, with watchpoints on a few rises to supplement the defensive positions, and a clutch of small lizards, rodents and eggs piled next to a fire lay and ready for Rscil's orders.

"In rotation, eat and rest!" he shouted.

One of the drill masters struck a fire plunger, coaxed out the tinder, and blew it under the lay. The fire caught, and there was a frenzy of skinning, skewering and placing of meat for a quick roast. Someone placed a pot to boil leaves, and the groomer-surgeons dropped tools into another pot to boil clean. There were some blisters and small lacerations to attend to, male and female both.

Across the warm, hummocky field, that scene repeated with other groups, each of eight fists. The Dancers watched with growing admiration. Rscil was pleased.

Satisfied, he sat himself, on his pack. Gree was already comfortably squatting, and Cmeo cautiously stretched out on a blanket. She stretched the pads of her feet to ease them.

"They will take turns on watch and eating, then?" she said.

"Yes, with a few mouthfuls of fresh meat to improve this harness leather," he said, holding up a flat, translucent piece of dried mottlecoat meat.

She tightened her face and flattened her ears. "Are some of them eating . . . those?" The plants the warriors were chewing on looked like weeds, unappetizing weeds at that. The brown seed packets looked very different from the rich crops Mrem raised in more peaceful times.

"Emergency training. Some seed pods contain enough substance to keep one alive a few days. The spies and scouts practice that in case they have to escape without supplies."

"I see. It just seems so unappetizing."

"It is, and causes digestive trouble without practice. They eat a mouthful now and then for preparation."

The females had grouped themselves apart from the males, which he approved of. There was some mingling, but it seemed courteous and appropriate. Two latrine pits were dug, one east and one west, to allow some modesty. Those would be filled as they left.

He allowed an eighthday for food and rest, with light naps in the sun. It was arid and clear in their part of the world, but not too warm. To the north, though, he could see clouds above the New Sea. The sun drew water that would fall to the east. With Gree on guard nearby, he allowed himself to take a short sleep. Cmeo had already curled up on her blanket to nap.

On his order, the warriors rose, drew in the circle and formed into ranks. The Dancers shuffled among them, and did so fairly quickly. They were learning.

He felt a little stiff himself, being no longer a youth. Still, this was something he could manage, and he led off with a shout.

The day would be pleasant at rest. It was hot for striding, and they all panted and sweated much of the way back, but almost all made it without issue. Before supper time, they were within the low stone walls of the city.

At the warrior compound, fresh towels aplenty waited with clear water for wiping fur and cooling down. Gree immediately acquired a large bundle from the caretakers, and brought them over. He handed a large one each to Cmeo and Rscil.

"It went well, I think," Cmeo said, neatly cleaning dust from her coat. She was most careful to wipe around her eyes and in her ears. "Only three Dancers fell out, and all are older. So did two warriors, both saying they were injured."

"Yes, some Dancers are older than any of the warriors. An old warrior becomes a smith or farmer. That is something I had not considered." He scrubbed his face and drew his whiskers through the soft cloth.

"Acceptable?" she asked.

"It is," the talonleader assured her. "Have the comments lessened?"

She smiled. "From what I've heard, they lessened throughout the march. It was my Dancers who had comments. They found the exercise boring."

"We must do this, as boring as it may be, regularly before we begin the long walk to the war. Though Nrao tells me it won't be many days. He awaits more information."

"So I was told also," she agreed. "Do you prefer more practice?"

"I always prefer more time to drill," he said. "However, there's a point where it's more important to get on with the task, rather than boring and tiring the warriors."

"I understand."

Once clean, they both walked up the cobbled road to Nrao's broad house. Rscil pondered that he typically ate with the warriors except when the clan leader called him. As a warrior himself, he was not mated, and never bothered with a servant. His own house was small, with a sleeping bench, sitting bench and a hearth. Someday, perhaps, he might settle down. He glanced speculatively at Cmeo. What would such a one be like as a mate?

Nrao greeted them, and he nodded in courtesy, ears out.

Rscil offered, "Our training goes well. A little more is desirable, but we stand ready to leave on your word."

"Excellent, Talonmaster. And you, Priestess?"

Cmeo said, "The Dancers are fitting in better, I think, and there is less unrest with their presence. I will defer to the talonmaster's advice, but I believe they are ready."

"I concur," Rscil agreed.

"I am glad to hear it," Nrao said. "I have word from one of our observers. There are Mrem held captive by the scaly worm's accursed mind magic. He saw them without harness. They differed in height and face, as well, so two clans. Oglut binds them to his bidding and forces them to the basest of chores."

Rscil said, "I think Aedoniss speaks to us. Territory, improved land, two Liskash tribes eliminated and the third made easy. Succoring our fellow Mrem from such desolation is the pointing star. How are the preparations?"

Nrao said, "Eight eights of wagons threefold, each with five eightyweights of meat, darts and tools."

Rscil did some mental calculation. "It will be enough. If you wish, let us plan to move an eightday hence."

"I do wish. Aedoniss guide you, Talonmaster and Priestess." He looked wistfully around at the dusky horizon, dark to the east and mottled pink in the west, his tail flat against his body.

"It will be a challenge to leave our home for new lands."

Hril checked the time. The moon was full and almost full high. It took some study, as it rose lower here toward the north. It should lower again to the far south, if the philosophers were right. They claimed the world was a ball 29,000 thousandlengths across. A huge distance. More than three times that around.

All he knew was that they'd wagoned, walked and now slunk and crawled 650 thousandlengths. They had spears, slings and large packs of dried meat, and would have to return unseen. They would be heroes; no scouts had traveled this far and fast. Spies took their time and sent missives of gathered stories. Scouts watched directly. It was thrilling to be so far, well within Liskash territory, but unseen. Their splotched coats of brown and tan were supplemented with crushed ochre and bark, so they blended with the ground. More importantly, though, were their abilities in stealth.

The river below flowed into the New Sea, helping fill it, ripple by ripple, as the massive waves tumbled in from the far east. Oh, to see that. Reportedly, it was a waterfall two hundredlengths high, four thousandlengths across, acting like a hose for a waterwheel, blasting across the former Hot Depths, flooding villages and driving herds before it.

But the river was their current task. It would have to be crossed on the way north, and they needed an easy ford. The hills were a poor choice, for the thin air, steep slopes and rocky terrain, not to mention being much closer to several Liskash strongholds. Lower here was less predictable, constantly shrinking, but probably the only practical choice.

"River" was charitable. It probably was one farther down, where it was inundated by the New Sea, now only a few thousandlengths away in a pointed bay. Here though, it was a broad stream over rocky shallows, filled with cobbles and pebbles and a few larger rocks from uphill. It would be easy to ford across. He had to decide if they should do so, and explore further, or just record this location and report back.

The rocks were a bit odd, and looked tumbled and displaced. He'd have to consider what had caused that. Large beasts pushing? An army? Earthquake? Recent heavy flooding? Perhaps that. The banks were scoured. The rocks seemed not to match, though.

It was a cool evening, slightly damp, and quite pleasant

on the whole. His fur was slowly soaking up dew from the air, but it wasn't so cold as to be a problem. The wind brought wet, pungent smells from the east.

His musing was interrupted when Flirsh whispered, "Do you hear something?"

Hril flared his ears and listened. There was something.

"Thunder?" he muttered back, but it went on and stayed steady, but got closer.

"Earthquake?" Except there was no shaking.

Then there was a little tremor. Only a little, faint and again, oddly even.

"Downstream," Hril said. He couldn't believe what he thought he saw.

"It is the sign of Aedoniss," Flirsh hissed reverently.

The river was flowing backward, in a solid wall of water.

Hril stared, still outside but shaking within, as a wave four lengths high rushed below in an almost sheer wall, the air seeming to hold it straight. He saw rocks tumble before it, weeds and branches thrash.

Then he understood, for once he had seen the Great Sea.

The moon called the sea to her, causing it to rise on the beaches. The sea broke in waves, twice a day, retreating in between.

Here, though, the New Sea narrowed in a long indentation caused by the river's former valley. It was quite deep farther along, and looked like a water funnel. When water was poured into a funnel . . .

The moon poured all the water of the sea into that small funnel twice a day. It rushed higher and deeper up the long valley, tumbling rocks, disturbing growth, ripping mud from the ground. Nor would it move in waves; there was nowhere for it to go with the weight of a sea behind it. It would stay here, retreating slowly over a quarter day, gradually releasing back into that long bay. The reeds and grass would look scoured by flood, but the rocks would remain upstream and tumbled, in odd contrast.

He realized that as the sea continued to rise, this whole plain to the mountains could flood. It would become impassable, and make a great strategic barrier against attack.

It was even possible some of these foothills would become islands.

"Let us go," Hril said with a faint smile. "We have seen what we need."

If they could move the Mrem army across it soon, they would have a sea to protect their rear.

It certainly was lush, Buloth thought. The rains greened things up tremendously. They also cooled it down somewhat. Hopefully, that would change once the New Sea was full. For now, he kept a wrap over his shoulders, and ate nuts for the fat. Tonight he'd have another warm fire and tasty meat. He had to eat almost as much as a mammal did in this climate.

The soarers said there were Mrem to the east, and moving west. That was serious. It was his territory, not even mapped yet, and the vermin were moving in. He praised the flying beasts, bid them wait their time, and find out more. There were also Mrem in the south, trying to move into this territory.

Buloth enjoyed the campaign. He could feel his mindpower increasing with practice, and he was grateful to Father for this opportunity. As they advanced, he drew in more animals, a few stray workbeasts, and even the population of a small village by a stream, all to add to his army. At times, he could even feel insects and snakes drawing to him. He rewarded his fighters by causing many rodents and digging lizards to stand up and wait to be harvested. He'd learned that well-fed slaves were happy slaves. He attributed his gains in power in part to that. His father was frugal to the point of stinginess, and kept them hungry. Distractions like hunger, though, weakened the grip on their mind. There was a positive side of that as well, though. He had no desire to be mind-linked to a slave upon its death.

Later that day he did feel the ugly touch of Mrem to the east, scrabbling through the hills. They were refugees from the river valley into the Bottomlands, distressed, tired, sore and hungry. That would make them hard to manage. However . . .

Yes, they'd eat well on the rats he'd just suggested present themselves. That would settle them down in a camp for a time. He determined where to the east they were, and maneuvered the army that direction. Their camp would make a convenient place for his army to rest, after he incorporated them.

The trunklegs turned in that direction, and he decided to take a nap in the swaying carriage, atop the fluffy mammal-hide mattress he'd brought.

Nrao received the scouts in his home, and made sure

they were offered good refreshments, of grer brew, honeyed mottlecoat livers, and less rich, overbearing fare, like the delicate graygull stewed in arosh marrow and water.

They sat at his bidding, drank copious amounts of brew in guzzle rather than lap, followed by even more herbed drink. He didn't mind. They needed water and energy and salts. Formal manners were for formal occasions. This was about information. He let them make a start on replenishing their withered hides while he called for Ingo and Tckins.

The scouts were eager to report, but did so between mouthfuls of soup and meat.

Hril pointed at the spot on the map with his spoon and said, "The water rises, slower, but steadily. It occurs to me that as the ground flattens and widens, the rise will be slower, but it doesn't mean the far flooding is less."

As he limped in the door, Ingo said, "That is correct. I am awaiting an architect with measuring sticks to return from the coast near the Great Flood. That will tell us more."

Flirsh said, "All is chaos. The sea also comes and goes." He indicated the movement with his hands.

Ingo said, "That is the tide. As the moon circles overhead, it draws water up toward it. It should be a footlength or so different, but that can matter in the marshes."

Tckins said, "It is more than that in the narrow valley here," he pointed at the map. "This used to be Cracked Mountain Pass. Now it is a stream, as Hril has said, and water beats against the rise twice a day."

Ingo said, "Yes, with nowhere to go to spread out, the water must splash high, much like in a bathing tub."

Tckins said, "Any advance will have to work around it, higher up the mountains or around, or time the approach carefully. It's like a flash flood in the desert hollows, twice each day."

Nrao tapped his chin with a claw. "This interests me greatly. It's a predictable barricade we can hide behind and sally from, that can't be removed. It's intermittent, but impenetrable during that time." *And more than that*, he thought.

"We will find more," Hril said eagerly. He and Flirsh were justifiably proud of the information that they had brought home. Nrao nodded.

"Please. An accurate schedule is most desirable," Nrao added.

"At once," the Mrem agreed.

They drew on the map, told of their observations, then Nrao gave them leave to go rest.

"You serve well," he said, placing a hand on each of their shoulders. "We will all be grateful to you."

Once they departed, the clan leader grinned to himself, and scratched his ear in thought. He sent a messenger for Rscil. It was time. Aedoniss had given them the tools they needed.

He turned to Nef, watching from his favorite bench.

"Do you see what I do, young one?"

Nef was maturing quickly. He'd sat still for most of the council.

"Father, the water has power. If it moves rocks, can be harnessed to move rocks for us, or to cut more ground."

Nrao was proud of his insight. "Yes, cutting ground is what I have in mind for now, and moving rocks later."

Then, with no one around for the moment, he grabbed the boy in a tussle. They laughed and snarled and sweated until the days' scribe rumbled a reminder. They sat back and recovered their breathing.

"Scribe, you may take a break for an eighth. I thank you."

"Thank you, Clan Leader. I will return." The Mrem bowed slightly and walked out.

Rscil arrived, dusty from training. Yet another reason less formality was good. There was no delay while his talonmaster cleaned and put on a polished harness. He took Rscil and led him to a bench in the corner of the enclosure.

"Rscil, this is in private, because I have a most exciting strategy in mind . . ."

Talonmaster Rscil was pleased with how the long march was going, given that they were leaving the Veldt forever. He was not a sentimental Mrem, but he had felt a pang turning his back on their home for the last time. From that moment forward, they would be strangers anywhere they went.

They were far north and west, well into the foothills. Drizzling rain and cool temperatures prevailed, which wasn't particularly comfortable, but was much better than dust and heat.

The first three days involved a lot of wagons interspersed with walking, and some minor coordination problems with replacement wagons. The station masters simply hadn't

believed the numbers involved and had assumed error.
Rscil's presence had been all the motivation they needed
to sort it out quickly. They furnished what they could, and
soberly accepted the orders that they'd move out with
Nrao's large caravan.

They'd passed through the territory of Rantan Taggah
and Jask the Long, who were gone leaving ghostly camps
and empty keeps. The spies reported their progress as
somewhat successful, but desperate and harried. The
Veldt clan would not be so scattered. Rscil's army would
be followed by Nrao's, also heavily supplied and prepared
for a long journey. They gathered and hunted to improve
their rations, not simply to survive.

Their people numbered fifteen thousand and more, a
staggering count. Two thousand of the best were with
Rscil, entrusted to break trail for the families, young and
elderly. It was good, he thought, that warriors weren't
permitted to mate until older. It was one less distraction.
Of course, that was the reason they found the Dancers
interesting, even out of season.

Once past the road shift caused by the bight in the New
Sea, they'd turned north, dismounted and walked. Days
passed eating dried meat and berries, a little honey,
supplemented with stew of wild game and chopped
tubers. It was nutritious enough, though not satisfying.

The Dancers managed well enough. The warriors bore
it stoically. The drovers and others in support made no
protest. Each day's march, though, was a struggle, with
some shorter than others to allow recuperation.

Water was the main thing. When it rained, all the
wagons opened to let cones gather it into barrels. They

filled at every stream and pond. It rained on the third night while they bivouacked, and broad leather sheets became catchments for every container possible. The water would hold.

Which only left how they'd work and fight.

While it was easier to hide in low areas, dispersed, a good high ground was stronger and more defensible. This land was rolling and hummocky, but there were a few viable positions.

Rscil considered the location of his battle stronghold carefully. His force was limited and casualties had to be minimized. That was necessary for Nrao's wishes, and his own survival. He would not waste his Mrem.

He chose a broad hill, not very high, but with steeper sides. It would be hard to approach, hard to attack, except by the accursed leatherwings. Spears would do for those. To counter ground troops, they would construct a fortress, but one with many surprises for the enemy.

Under his direction, the warriors, drivers, haulers and the stronger females went to work. The drillmasters snarled in friendly fashion, indicating placement. Everyone dug, making a low rampart around the hill, surrounded by a now much steeper approach. There were two entrance ramps, one facing the territory ahead, one back toward their holding.

The younger warriors used the large bronze tube hammer to set their stakes into the rampart, and the fist leaders followed along, each with their rope and thong, lashing them into a solid defense. The wagons, their wheels blocked, made a defensive inner circle. A large, frontal assault might still overwhelm the post, especially if the attacker was willing to trample his own warriors, but it would give enough time to mount and depart, or at least flee on foot. The wagons were left packed, and items only withdrawn as they became essential.

It was tough, panting work, and might have to be done several times, but it would leave them with a trail of defensible positions. All Nrao's group would have to do to augment it was drive their own stakes in the existing rampart.

That done, watches were set, well-hidden firepits dug for food, and latrines cut to drain downslope, rendering those areas even less approachable. If there was time, more earthworks and stakes might go in. It was not nearly as good as a stone castle, but stronger than the natural terrain.

Once done with that, they rested a day. Progress would be slow. Nrao's neighbors would laugh at this, as they had at many of his practices in the past. They'd prefer to rush headlong. Nrao and Rscil preferred to minimize risks. Those left in camp would be charged with reinforcing it daily until no longer needed, starting with more earth, then adding any rocks or timbers they found.

Buloth took great delight in the acquisition, or near-acquisition, of more slaves for his army. He was somewhat nervous, and fought not to let it show in front of his senior servants. Ahead were the Mrem escaping from the Hollow Lands, numbering some two hundred. He cautioned his lead slaves to restrain themselves, and they simply trudged over the landscape, like the mindless beasts all non-Liskash were. He prodded his drivers and beasts to move ahead, to give him range. He sat back in his padded seat aboard the trunklegs and patted his hands together in gleeful anticipation.

One hundred and ninety was his improved estimate. A little closer.

It was exciting. He could feel their minds, feel them becoming distinct entities, and knew they were unaware of him. They were beyond that next ridge. Some suggested they were on watch, but they were not atop it yet. He knew of them, they not of him. He grinned.

Suddenly it clarified in his mind, like melted sandglass. One hundred and eighty-eight exactly. Three of them approached the crest of the ridge. He continued to approach but focused on them. They were near the peak, he could feel their unease and then . . . he had them. He felt for the symbols, but could make nothing of their harsh, unorganized language. He pushed what he needed, though, and one of them turned and signaled below. Then they began back down.

A little while later, he felt the minds of the others in his circle. He stretched out, felt a mass shriek of panic and fear, then a huge swell as their minds fell under his. It was almost sexual, the warm flood of power and anguish, and then they were his. They could not withstand him. They must see their new master!

His beasts topped the ridge, he looked down on his new vassals. The dull eyes of the Mrem refugees stared up at him. It was not the welcome he would have liked, but he loved the sensation that all the creatures he could see belonged to him. With a casual hand, he suggested his army build its camp for the night around his new charges.

To drive home the point, he set the filthy furbags to work digging cesspits.

Buloth could feel his power growing day by day. It was a combination of practice and distance from his father. That made sense and also proved the need to set his own godhold a safe remove from Oglut's domain. They could be allies. They could not be cohabitants. The weaker Liskash didn't matter; he could control them if he wished, or ignore them to their peace. Only a few were worthy of godhood, though, and while they must mate to keep the lines pure, otherwise, distance was needed.

He'd been directed northerly, and there were allegedly Mrem that way. He wasn't keen on north. North was cold, and hard on people. However, it was now a lot more moderate, and humid, than the previous time he'd been here with Father. It seemed to be true the weather was changing with the New Sea. He'd have to make sure to see it, after he secured a godhold. He'd have to go to it to assuage his curiosity, he thought wryly. Creatures would take his orders. The sea would not.

A few more gis of distance should be enough for now. That would put him beyond the Low Mountains, and create an easy border at a safe distance. He could always relocate his capital at a later date. The labor was free, after all.

He pondered the power his mind gave him, to take peripheral information from entire gis away, if one of his slaves saw something, and then to integrate it into his plans. The future belonged to Liskash.

It was at that moment that he saw a flash of a Mrem wagons, well within the borders of his godhold. Buloth growled and grew tense, and sought the source of the vision. There. That one, and through it he saw the filthy creatures had even constructed a crude fortification, of sticks and mud. Somewhat like ants they were, but far too clever for stupid beasts.

He flicked a finger in their direction. That excrescence would have to be dealt with at once.

He directed the slaves to abandon their digging and walk. If he was satisfied with their progress, they could eat tonight.

In a crack in a grassy hillside littered with fractured rocks, Hril felt the vile punch of Buloth's mind. He focused on the grass in front of him, absorbing its smell, its color, its springy coils, fighting to be one with the grass, not that mind. It worked. He wasn't enslaved.

To his surprise he realized he had gained information from that brief but intrusive touch. He knew that mind was sending a large army toward them, based on something seen by a creature in thrall to it. That spy had to be one of the browsing pebbleskins they'd passed earlier, or even one of the leatherwings drifting overhead in lazy circles, may Aedoniss curse them. Given all that, it would be best to wait for dark for him and Flirsh to move. The reptiles were not only slow and cold, they couldn't see in darkness, either.

He gestured to Flirsh and they both crawled deeper into the crevice to await the night.

It took all their training not to panic. Their fur fluffed in fear as well as for warmth, and they huddled like kits. Hril listened and felt the thud of footsteps. He lost count of the number of reptilians who came past, from little scavengers to herd beasts to adult, armed Liskash in singles and small groups. Even a trio of bedraggled, half-starved Mrem caught in the spell wandered not far enough away for comfort. He and Flirsh didn't speak, but he knew they were both terrified of winding up just so—brainless, pitiable slaves of a scaled monster. He wasn't sure if it would be better to rescue those Mrem or kill them in mercy. All he and Flirsh had were knives and hand axes, though, for food and shelter.

Eventually, dusk gave way to darkness. They eased themselves out of the crack in the rock, and he led the way, fur stiff and heart thrumming, in a low, silent slink between rocks and tufts, toward the distant fortification, which didn't feel as safe now.

After a few hundredlengths of aching muscles and grueling fear, he deemed it safe to rise and walk erect. When he was sure there were no other creatures about, they ran.

Rscil received two panting, dirty scouts, and served them bowls of water and a plate of soft meats at once. They guzzled and lapped the water, and smacked down the meat between comments.

Hril said, "The Liskash approach, or at least their slaves. Too many reptiles to count. A trio of starven Mrem. Eights of small beasts, with that look of mindless focus."

"How far away are they?"

While Hril drank some more, Flirsh said, "Over the next hills. They will arrive within two days, if they continue west."

"You didn't feel the spell?"

Hril nodded. "We felt it. We avoided it by thinking like plants. It felt angry, focused. I believe he knows we are here. He intends conquest."

Rscil flattened his ears.

"That was inevitable, but perhaps it's a little early. Still, the world is what Aedoniss decrees. We will get to try our new tactics soon, it seems."

It was then that a distant shout was relayed by a closer watch. "Liskash are sighted on the hill!"

The scouts rose, but Rscil gestured for them to stay. "Drink, eat, sit a few breaths. Your bravery is needed again, but I would have you in best health."

He turned and stepped out of the tent to give orders.

When Rscil shouted "Form up!" Cmeo shivered in thrill and fear. This was it. They were going to test her belief that Aedoniss' dance and chant would protect them from reptile mind magic. If she was wrong, they would all be filthy slaves of a filthy lizard. If she was correct, they only had to fight for their lives against them. She gathered her females together, waking a few from sleep.

Many of the Dancers were agitated, and their smell, fur and ears reflected that. A few even lashed their tails in fear.

"Hurry now!" she cajoled, urging them toward the sound of the talonmaster's voice. "The warriors need us in place." She didn't say "depending on us." That seemed too heavy for the moment.

Warriors sprinted past her, with shields, javelins and swords, some with daggers and pouches, a handful with stiff leather visors against sun or stones. They fell into line surely, and with a few shuffles were in perfect formation. Despite eightdays of practice, the Dancers didn't look nearly as neat or skilled. It was nerves. That, and perhaps Rscil was right about the different ways males and females fought.

They looked it, too, with their fur and ears like that. A few warriors betrayed eagerness, or trembliness. The Dancers, though, were nervous or afraid. She had to stop that.

She waited for the initial orders from the drillmasters to echo down, then called out herself.

"Dancers, now is the time to be put your trust in Aedoniss and Assirra and the Dance. We are here to fight as warriors, to make the males even more powerful and sure. We act as their shield against the filthy mindrape of reptiles. Stand fast and ready."

It wasn't a bad speech, though not entirely what she'd wanted to say. Rscil had coached her carefully in how to phrase it so the warriors wouldn't be offended. It increasingly was obvious to her that the warriors were rather sensitive Mrem, and needed constant reassurance. Still, they were expected to wade into battle and perhaps die. She would hold her tongue and phrase it to honor them, if it helped

It did seem to work. The eldest and youngest Dancers steadied a bit, and that spread throughout the troupe. The eldest of them had some experience with violence, but the youngest had no grasp of it. In between were the many with enough knowledge to know fear, without the practice to handle it. Together, though, they had their years of training, and the eightdays of practice they had with the warriors. It might not be enough, but it would have to do. Cmeo nodded to Rscil. They were ready.

He nodded back.

Buloth sat at the peak of the hill and looked below. He had an excellent vantage point of the entire valley. The terrain here was drier and coarser than farther south, due largely to this being out of the old cloud line before the New Sea. His godhold would end not far from here. Still, these filthy furred things were in his territory, and would never go away of their own accord. They were intruding now, from the desolate wastelands they spawned in.

He sat under the awning of a comfortable tent, with a bed stuffed with fluffpods and dressed in trunkleg hide, tanned to supple softness. He had a fine clusterberry wine, delicious shoots and tubers, and a delicate stew of some fast running bird his domestics had brought for him. Nothing could be finer, if he could only eliminate the rotten mammals.

It was amusing to see this stronghold of theirs, all mud and sticks and rocks. No carving, hewn stone, no buttresses. They showed the sophistication of savages generations past, as he'd seen on a hill near his father's capital, that had been a Liskash holding lost in the dawn of time. That was all this kind could aspire to.

Still, they might eventually learn to build, and that would be problematic. The time to eliminate a pest was when it was first found. That meant now.

He could see them frantically running around, and forming neat little squares. They really were like birds or insects in their simplicity, unable to work independently and lacking the mind to control others. He smiled faintly and pushed his army forward.

Upon boarding his chariot, Rscil first made sure his warriors were arrayed as they should be, then that the Dancers looked right, with Cmeo nodding approval from the ground. After that, he checked that those defending the followers on the redoubt were on the ramparts with arrows, stones and javelins, and the gates ready for instant blocking. Only then did he turn his gaze to acknowledge the enemy. It was a thought-out policy, and it was also a visible display of his respect for his own and contempt for the scaly ones. He checked his own weapons by touch. He had a fistful of javelins, a heavier stabbing spear, and the bronze gripclaws he'd use up close, if any lizard survived to reach the chariot. It wasn't wise to wish for that, but he'd enjoy it if it happened. In front of Gree was a box of heavy, weighted darts.

Up the hillside were creatures. He couldn't tell precisely what type since they wore enveloping leather armor and helmets with spikes or crests, and clouds of dust surrounded them, but their arrangement made it clear they were organized, and therefore hostile. They were either Liskash or controlled by them.

He knew he had the best scouts because he was not surprised, knew the approximate terrain, and already had his warriors ranking up. Against that was foreign terrain with a much easier supply line for the enemy, but he'd maximized his chances.

Rscil watched his warriors stand unmoving in

formation, and the Dancers hold their now familiar places among them. The terrain was clear, but uneven, with rills, dunes and rises, occasional patches of scrub and a bare fistful of trees. As battlefields went, it was excellent. However, it would take maneuvering, and besides the usual unblooded warriors, there were the Dancers. He was concerned, but they could not be his first priority.

Rscil watched the attackers' movements to determine their strategy. Quick was good. Planned was better. They were a loose formation, but steady at the low end of a charge as they advanced down the hill. Probably, they were at a brisk walk, and their weight and the slope pulled them forward. Loose, though, and not a proper square of ranks.

"At the pace, advance!" he ordered. Gree heard him, and tapped the chariot's fast-running arogar into a trot. They were valuable beasts, and could speed him anywhere. These two were well-blooded and as experienced as any old soldiers.

Rscil decided they might as well take the fight to the enemy. There was no advantage to waiting further, and he hoped to disrupt the Liskash formation, if it could be called that. It was a tight group, but rabble. They wouldn't fight with heart; only with enforced and reluctant desperation.

He was concerned that some of them might be Mrem. In a perfect world, Aedoniss would let those be captured alive. In this world, they would likely have to be killed. His warriors had had some border skirmishes with other steadings, but not against mind-gutted slaves. His best and most veteran were in front, and some mixed among the rest. He trusted them to do what was necessary.

Still, it would not do to underestimate that force. More dust rose as they advanced, and they were on higher ground for now, coming down from the mountains. They would be motivated by whichever Liskash styled himself their "god."

The drillmasters kept up a steady, encouraging shout as they advanced, until Cmeo started her chant. In moments, the other Dancers voiced with her, and the drumming caught to match the footbeats.

It was an inspiring sound. It looked . . . odd. Even after long practice, to see the Dancers twisting forward between paired ranks of warriors was disconcerting, and felt slightly wrong, and even unmasculine. If it worked, though . . .

There were some slight ripples in the ranks as the enemy became visible. Liskash in plenty, some mounted on several eights of beasts, behind a charging wall of literal meat—herdbeasts including mottlecoats, pests, scavengers and some lupins, anything the ruling Liskash could stir up. Yes, there were Mrem in the van, with body language and fur showing extreme distress. Poor creatures.

Then the smell of the mass hit him, and he realized that was part of the ripple of bother. The reeks of fear, anger, despair, anguish and the stench of unwashed bodies and uncared-for animals, because the Liskash didn't care about their slaves, all rushed up his nose. He winced, sneezed, and shook his head.

"Forward!" he shouted.

The horde came on fast, and there were more ripples, and he realized one significant problem. The chanting of the Dancers drowned out the encouragement and orders from the drillmasters. The formation was more ragged than he liked.

He pointed, and Gree cropped the arogar into motion. He wanted to get alongside to offer personal encouragement.

He shouted as he went, matching the first drillmaster he passed. *"Keep your spacing! Keep your spacing!"* He hoped to turn that into a chant itself. A couple of others caught on, and it spread.

It worked. Fist leaders within the ranks echoed it, and order improved. He neared the front, and hefted his bundle of javelins, then checked the bronze claws at his side. He would be in the battle directly. The front two ranks tossed their first volley of bronze darts, and it had some effect. It would have more effect against a cohesive force of thinking beings, rather than against a disorganized gaggle of dull-witted slaves.

Then the oncoming wall of enemy smashed into them, and a fistful of leatherwings dropped from the sky to clap their wings low over the ranks, while cawing and snapping their jaws.

The Dancers in the third rank hissed and snarled and lost the dance. A couple froze, the rest fluffed and arched and poked at things running between their feet and flapping overhead, dancing around in disgust or surprise. One stretched her claws and ripped a tear into a leatherwing. Two others tore at a small beast until it came apart in gobbets of flesh and bone.

That was manageable, but their aggression caused a complete break of the two ranks of warriors behind them, as they hesitated, unsure if they should shove their way past or wait. Several tried to rush in front to form a block around the Dancers, leaving a gaping hole in that line. Some farther behind ran to join that mass, exactly as Rscil had feared. The sensation of calm that the drums and chanting had instilled was fading.

Drillmasters shouted, lost in the din as the first rank thrust and stabbed the leaping Liskash. They left the spears impaled and drew swords and claws, as the second rank poked their points between for support.

Well enough, despite the chaos behind them, but the enemy flowed and spread and would envelope them if he didn't get things reined in fast.

"Fifth and Sixth, split and wing!" he ordered, and nothing happened. The chanting was distracting at this point, and didn't seem to accomplish anything. He heard his order relayed, and long moments later, those ranks parted and ran, to take positions on the forward flanks.

This wasn't something they'd practiced enough with the Dancers. Upon seeing those warriors battle run, rather than jog into position, those females in the Seventh reacted in fear, drawing up, fluffing up fur and claws for a fight, and disrupting the last two ranks, which he needed for support. Cmeo and some others shouted and gestured at the laggards, and he felt the spell in his mind. It was one of exasperation and motherliness, or perhaps big sisterliness. It helped, and he saw them gingerly move back toward some semblance of order. Swiftly, the peace in his mind was restored.

Then he had more to worry about, as he was in front right of the formation, with Liskash, stomp lizards and a pawful of ragged, sickly-looking Mrem charging at him.

Gree was ready as soon as Rscil slapped his shoulder, drew up fast, and grabbed his own weapons. They each tossed four darts in quick succession, and one from the Liskash flew close between them from somewhere, its fletchstring brushing his whiskers and making his fur puff even more.

The flankers fanned around him and chopped their way forward, which was good, as the arogar were crippled and dying in whinnies, riddled with spears and cut by blades. For now, though, it was a platform from which to direct the fray.

They had a good front, and could manage an envelopment, but it was thin, only the two ranks. The third and fourth had recovered, and he pointed and shouted for them to be general reinforcements to replace casualties.

The Dancers had pulled back, or rather, Cmeo had pulled them back. They were a few lengths away, but seemed comfortable enough there, and their chant was in full, deep resonance, an angry snarl of defiance. The drums were abandoned, and it was clear that Cmeo and three of her senior Dancers were holding the rest together.

The drillmasters at either end, realizing communication was impossible, and seeing opportunity, began enveloping. That slowly put more blades against less Liskash, and they clambered over the bleeding green bodies. That also disrupted the lines, but that was for a positive reason.

There were more coming, though. A lot more. On the crest, another thick rank of javelin-waving Liskash waved and shouted in their guttural, hissing equivalent of speech.

"Arch back and fall back!" he shouted. *"Arch back and*

fall back!" Others picked up the shout, and with dignified poise, the army drew back, while curving on the flanks to maintain a defensive perimeter. They formed a deep V that gave them lots of room to attack at the flanks of the Liskash, as they retreated on an oblique step.

A handful of the enemy realized what the formation was, and tried to get behind the V, but that meant running back against the rush of their own fighters, and then they'd have to hope to advance again. It was more exercise than lazy lizards were prepared for, even with their brains controlled by that distant slug.

The Dancers formed two clumps, one each side of the point of the V, and moved smoothly back, a good distance behind the warriors.

At least the retreating army left a good crop of bodies for the scaly beasts to consider.

By the time the enemy reinforcements reached the place where the battle had been, the retreat was four hundredlengths back and still moving, still leaving a lot more dead lizards than Mrem, and stable in movement. Then the attack broke up, and the Liskash desultorily retreated, just turning and bumbling off. A few darts and javelins took a few more in the back, until the drillmasters ordered a halt to it.

"Hold javelins!" one drillmaster shouted. The cry was immediately taken up by the others.

"Why, master?" a warrior yelled back. "There's more of these overgrown pests to kill!"

"We'll need them for another battle, lad!" the drillmaster bellowed.

The warriors shrugged. One of them stooped to the

dusty ground and came up with a fist-sized rock. He heaved that at the retreating Liskash. A lizard caught it in the back of the head and sprawled face first on the ground. His fellows cheered and felt for more stones.

While not as effective, a certain amount of damage and several casualties were inflicted before the staggering Liskash were out of range.

It was a grueling march back to the fort, but they were left in peace, for the moment.

Buloth was delighted, lounging on his comfortable bed in the fading light. He'd lost slaves, yes, but he'd beaten back this force of individuals. Most amusing that they thought lining up in rows would match the power of his mind. It organized them, but they gave up some of their vaunted independence. More than his own slaves gave up; all he cared was that they attacked the enemy. How they chose to do so was their problem. These creatures, though, had voluntarily crippled themselves, and relied on shouted voice orders.

It might take several battles, but the outcome was inevitable. The stronger mind—his— would win and acquire more slaves.

Thinking of that, he tried to tally old slaves, new slaves, and any casualties. He could feel the latter whimpering and hurting, but lacked the strength to twist them into death. They'd just have to suffer, so he shut them from his mind. Surviving slaves were down a bit. That was annoying. Buloth wondered if it were possible to count casualties in the even lines of the mammals. He'd remember that for next time.

Meanwhile, he should regroup his force, feed them enough to carry on, and then advance on the furry beasts again.

This whole venture of developing his own godhold was quite exciting, and very informative. Once done with his, he shivered in anticipation that he might even be on terms with his father.

Mutal wouldn't matter, nor even hinder, if he managed to absorb his father's holding. When the old Liskash died or was frail, his slaves were his for the taking. Then a simple advisory to his younger brother that he was assuming the minds should do it. There wouldn't even be a need for fighting. Yes, that was a good plan.

With that settled, it was time to quickly crush these encroaching creatures and secure as much space and as many minds as possible, both for the prestige, and for the practice.

But first, dinner. He'd vowed to roast a Mrem. Now would be the time. He called his cook.

Rscil's tent was imposing in presence, even being no larger than the others. Perhaps it was the finer weave of the russet-colored fabric, or the small but comfortable and beautifully carved benches. Perhaps it was the guests, or just the presentation, but those within felt a sense of awe.

They had much to discuss. They were alive, with some casualties and low morale. That was first. Cmeo, Rscil and Scout Hril were all dusty and worn, but alert and waiting.

"I will start with my assessment," Rscil said, not

ungently. "It was bad, but to be fair, not terrible. The Dancers panicked when battle joined, recovered somewhat and stayed out of the way. Obviously, we could not practice real combat beforehand. Cmeo?"

The priestess looked somewhat embarrassed. Her whiskers slicked back and her ears lay against her skull. The tip of her tail twitched back and forth.

"Yes, they were scared and are. I saw the warriors stuck behind them, but couldn't move fast enough to help clear the way. It did not go as we had hoped."

"What do you suggest?"

"More practice is needed," she said without hesitation.

He was impressed. She asked no respite, but was eager to press on. Was it safe to do so, though?

He said, "I don't dismiss the idea, but I insist on proven tactics for future battles. Let the Dancers be close to the rear—they proved comfortable in that position—and let my warriors have their cohesive mass."

Cmeo said, "Rscil, I understand your caution, but we are less effective further away. We must make this work." She gripped her tail to avoid fidgeting, and her ears betrayed agitation. She felt that strongly about it.

"With respect, I saw no effect to speak of. Morale was higher than normal, but much of that was taken away in the confusion. Then a number of warriors rushed to worry about the females instead of the fight, exactly as I warned." He finished and braced for the return.

Cmeo was remarkably calm in response.

"Rscil, how many did we lose to the thought stealing of the Liskash?"

"Why, none, that I'm aware of."

"Very well, it has worked that much," Cmeo concluded.

Rscil said, "That was with Dancers in the rear, as I propose."

"I prefer that they stay with the warriors. We will train them not to hamper the battle."

"We will see," Rscil said.

Hril said, "I have a little favorable news to add."

"Yes, Hril?" Rscil asked, his ears betraying his curiosity.

The scout stood and paced, tail twitching. "Battle Master, Priestess. First, let me offer that this godling of theirs appears inexperienced. He let his warriors loose enough to retreat, with no thought for gleaning or the wounded. I have other scouts and a few teamsters recovering javelins, swords, harness, and there are some wounded we can treat. We have mercied several, and there will be more. When convenient, we also mercied the Liskash wounded, regardless of their condition. I feel pity for them as slaves, but have no desire to friend such creatures. Their javelins, also, are being taken to the bronzewrights to be straightened and sharpened. We will use them. Some arosh and arogar have been butchered. I included yours, Battle Master. With no disrespect to fine animals, but they are meat." He bowed slightly.

Rscil said, "Of course. I would expect no less." A fine scout, and a potential master of some kind. Hril's pupils swelled with the compliment.

"Thank you. Also, just before this council, we sighted eight and four Mrem who were held by the Liskash. They fled west and slightly north, back toward the New Sea."

"They broke the mindbinding?"

"Yes, apparently when our retreat started."

Cmeo said, "When our voice was surest. As I predicted."

Hril twitched as Rscil leaped to his feet, but it was not a threat.

Instead, the battle master said, "Cmeo, we will drill our warriors and our Dancers so that we do better next time."

Rscil knew it would not be quite so easy, but he would take the risk. He, all of them, would be remembered for generations once this was done. He only hoped it wasn't as spectacularly brave failures.

Cmeo raised herself tall and said, "Talonmaster, as if things are not complex enough, it seems the Dancers can fight if they must, without weakening their voice, as long as they are in the formation."

"Yes, we have agreed," he said. What was she leading to?

She seemed a bit hesitant as she said, "How many javelins have we recovered from the Liskash?"

That was a striking notion.

"I see we must drill the Dancers as well."

The warriors were not entirely happy with the decision to continue with the Dancers. They let it be known. Drillmasters reported hearing angry comments from their fists of warriors, and voiced their own complaints.

On the one fist, Rscil understood both their need to release anger after the battle, and their frustration at a formation broken, with fellows left dead. Some two eights had been succored and would probably live, though many would never be fit to fight. Eight other eights and three had either died, or needed mercy. There would be other battles, and they were only two thousand and a few.

On the other, it must be driven to the haft that they were bound together.

Rscil called the army to order. "If you are unhappy, you may walk back to our steading in defeat. The warriors will remain for our glory. We'll wait to begin practice until those who wish to leave have gone."

The complaints quieted to mutters, and there was much shuffling, some bristling, and flattened ears. None wished to abandon the others, nor bear the shame attached. It was also clear there was no retreat, except as a whole. Individuals wouldn't manage the trip, except a few hardy scouts, all of whom stood with Rscil. They could form parties, but what if they were attacked, to then die unknown in shame and ignominy? And if this campaign were successful, what chances would they have of mates and land?

He and Cmeo watched from his chariot, led by two precious replacement arogar. The practice, no doubt spurred by the threat of disgrace, was much more vigorous, and the Dancers moved with urgency.

A drillmaster shouted, "Step Aside!" and the Dancers gathered in pairs, leaving gaps for supporting warriors to use. It was also hoped this would be their default movement if agitated, with enough practice.

Gree took over, ordering, "Advance!" and the supports flowed through the Dancers, who resumed their normal spacing.

"Retreat!" "Flank Right!" "Flank Left!" "Envelope!"

Rscil watched with satisfaction tempered by caution.

They knew the moves, and with better relay through the fist leaders, the orders propagated across the field in heartbeats. It was going much better since they understood the faults of the first attempt.

Cmeo said, "I am more confident, now that they've seen battle."

"Only a little," he said. "I wonder what will happen the first time one dies."

The Dancer hesitated. Her lovely eyes turned sad. "I don't know."

"Pardon me if I seem brusque. There's some increase in resentment, given that the Dancers were in some part a hindrance, while suffering no harm. Even the benefit of spells is hard for a warrior to grasp and see."

"I understand," she replied. "How did the retreat go? It seemed to me to be orderly."

"Surprisingly so. The Dancers moved well enough, and the warriors were busy focusing on line and fighting."

"I felt the Liskash was happy with it. We retreated from him. It built his ego."

He felt rage fill him as it had not at the end of the battle. "Is this something you see as a positive?" he snapped. "Because I don't feel the benefit."

Cmeo laid a long, very soft hand on his arm. "Please bear with me for a moment, Rscil. I need information."

"Go on," he prompted, corralling his temper.

"How did our casualties do in retreat?"

"If I understand your question, we gave a lot more than we took, but there was very little succor for those we had to leave."

"Would a further advance have meant more?"

"For us? Yes. For the enemy? It's hard to say. Cursed Liskash don't retreat as they should, and killing them seems to only lead to more of them."

"What if we planned to retreat?"

He flared his nose, ears and eyes at that, then considered the question as a matter of strategy.

"I think I see," he said. "We face off, take a smash, fight an orderly retreat killing as many as we can. We stay cohesive, and the scaly godling believes he is doing well."

Cmeo's eyes danced eagerly. "Could we repeat it?"

Rscil considered. "Possibly. If we could fake an actual panic . . ."

"How often must we do it, or can we do it, to even the odds?"

It shook him from his pondering. He took a breath of the rich, fresh air and remembered the story he had heard.

"Oh, that. That's not the goal. The goal is to get near the godling and kill him, which destroys the entire army's will to fight. Our task is to protect the clan as they move along the shore. We will all meet up in good time."

"Does that mean a concerted thrust?"

He tensed and felt his fur fluff. "There is a specific plan for that, but it is not for sharing. I require that you not try to read it from me." He bristled his whiskers and hoped she'd comply. Now was not the time for any such intimacy.

"I understand your caution. Of course I would do no such thing." Rscil chided himself for not trusting her. She was diplomatic, and honest, and a fine companion.

He said, "So let us continue to improve the legend."

Upon next daybreak, the warriors were in much better spirits, and slivers of sweetened dried fat for breakfast boosted their morale. They'd worked hard in attack formation, and been praised.

That changed when drill started. The first few practice retreats were accepted and went well. Obviously, it was important to be able to disengage.

However, with each iteration, the fidgeting and fluffing of fur increased.

Between the Fourth and Fifth, one of the drillmasters, Chach, approached the chariot, sought assent, then came close.

"Talonmaster, with respect, when will we return to practicing attack? The warriors feel they are being punished."

He shook his head firmly. "No punishment, Chach. We will practice attack shortly. The Dancers need more drill than the warriors to ensure things work. At least one retreat is likely, and significantly important if we are to save our fellows. Attack will follow. We need an orderly retreat, and we can fight as we do so."

"Mrem warriors are not much for retreating, Talonmaster."

Rscil acknowledged his warrior's brave soul. "We do when we must, and we do so well. In this case, think of it as a planned strategy to bring us more lizardlings to kill. We will kill as we advance, and again as we retreat."

The Mrem grinned, and reached to flick his whiskers. "That I like. I don't like, and can tell you the warriors don't, having to leave wounded fellows behind."

Rscil nodded. "It is a terrible burden. However, we lost

fewer in retreat than in advance, and less than in a prolonged clash. Remember, our enemy is the godling. His slaves are nothing without him, and merely obstacles."

"It's a hard idea, Battle Master, but a bold one, in its twisted, backwards way."

"You may spread the word that I am confident in our ability to attack, but want to make our retreats equally painful to the scaly pests, who are twisted and backward themselves."

"Thank you, Talonmaster. I shall." He nodded in respect and strode away.

Rscil kept the exasperation from his ears. He didn't care for it either, but it had to be done. As they moved north, they'd certainly be attacked from behind.

The warriors were most disgruntled at the idea, even in acceptance. Rscil, with plain harness, loitered upwind of a fist campfire that night. An honest appraisal of one's support was necessary.

Someone grumbled, "I don't care if it does inflict casualties. Retreating is just un-Mremly. Do we retreat the whole way north, guiding them with us, leaving our fellows in a trail for the rest to follow?"

Another replied, "We'll advance as well. We just have to draw the damned things out. Remember they have no endurance."

"They have numbers. We should be striking through their mass like a spear, to destroy this godling."

"Well, Talonmaster, why don't you tell us how it's done?"

"Hish," the second Mrem said dismissively. "I don't need to be a talonmaster to know that hurting enslaved lizard things won't win this. Poor, disgusting bastards. Lesser animals and not even the dignity of being themselves."

Yet a third offered, "Well, honestly, I don't like it much either. It'll be a sad day if our proud claim is that we retreat better than anyone. But if we win that way, I suppose eventually that will be the respected thing to do. At least when fighting Liskash."

An older, raspier voice said, "It's like that always. My mentors lamented the loss of individual bravery into this cohesion, but we beat everyone with it. Theirs lamented the longer ranged javelins as cowardly, and detested slings. Styles change and advance."

"But do you like it, Frowl?"

"No, I don't. But while I'm fist leader, we'll do as the drills and the talonmaster says, and do it well. Forget that we're retreating. Just plan on being the smoothest, neatest, proudest fist, with the highest pile of lizard bodies."

"Urrr, I guess a pile of dead lizards rather proves the point."

Rscil smiled. A snarling warrior was a happy warrior, and would do as he was ordered. As the old timer had said, this wouldn't be possible with the styles of Nrao's grandfather.

At two other fires in other areas, the grumbling was the same. The warriors didn't like it, but they'd do it.

As he returned to his tent for another late-night council, there was a hissed alert from a sentry.

In moments, warriors rose, clutched whichever weapons were closest, and dropped low to spring lightly on all fours.

They moved quietly, more so than untrained people in daylight. Seasoned warriors, good warriors. Rscil was proud of them.

In moments several impromptu fists formed up. They might not be of the same fist, but they would make it work. Some moved to the edge of the embankment. Others prepared to defend the gate.

At the same time, a drillmaster took several other fists to the far side, and as other warriors were apprised, they filled in around the perimeter. A noise could be nothing, or a threat, or a feint.

A warrior awatch on the rampart gave signals. Past each side of the guard post a fist flowed through tunnels made for the purpose, and sought to envelope the gate.

Rscil watched the signs while seeking a spear himself. One of the warriors recognized him, stiffened silently, and offered his spear while drawing his claws. Rscil took the spear, twitched eyes and ears at him, and turned back.

Several warriors were atop the traps, prepared to block the zigzag entrance with tumbled rocks.

Rscil was talonmaster, but the sentry on the rampart was the Mrem in charge. It would be foolish to step into the middle. He watched and waited for a signal. A secret part of him hoped for a small scuffle in which he could be only a warrior. He missed that part of his life.

Then the sentry raised his hand for a hold, while gesturing with his javelin for a foray. The two fists in the tunnels scurried from sight. Beats later, they returned through the gateway, leading and surrounding thirteen prisoners.

They were Mrem. Scrawny, scraggly, unkempt, but

Mrem, carrying Liskash-style spears and very crude rawhide harness. They stared around in nervousness and fear, tinged with a scent of despair and shame.

One of them acted as spokesman for the rest.

"We tank you of our rescue. I be Trec."

The fist leader asked, "You were held by the Liskash?"

Trec nodded nervously. "Liskash, yes. Held in bond and contempt."

"How did you escape?"

He opened his hands and gestured at the others. "At battle ending mind helding break. I gather we and walk, intent normal."

"Are there others?"

"Might so. I hope."

The fist leader said, "I must take this to Rscil."

"Rscil will come to you," the talonmaster said, coming into the open. "I am still a warrior, after all."

The fist leader—Ghedri, if Rscil remembered correctly, nodded in respect and stepped slightly aside. He addressed the newcomer.

"Trec, I am Rscil. We move to conquer the Liskash, and occupy this territory."

Trec looked wistful and sad.

"If we can only live to see that."

Rscil knew what he was asking, and it fitted his needs to have insider information.

"You might. Will you serve under me, as we smash them?"

Trec looked him up and down. "How addressed you, leader?"

"I am titled Talonmaster."

Trec extended his hands, palm down toward Rscil.

"Rscil, I accept as Talonmaster mine."

The others held hands forward in agreement.

"I welcome you," Rscil said. "Mrem, see that they are fed lightly but often, clean water, help them bathe, and find them rest. We will march again tomorrow."

He turned and walked back to his quarters.

On the whole, it had been a good day.

With the power of his mind, Buloth threw a pitcher at one of his senior attendants. The Liskash picked it up without a word and took it away with him. The young noble wasn't happy at losing slaves. The stress of battle had to have done it; he was not as strong as his father yet. That was a good lesson for him. Not just the mind magic, but the ability to retain it in harsh conditions. That would come with practice. Today, he meant to get practice. Those retreating Mrem would not find it so easy this time.

He wanted to pretend he wasn't concerned about the escaped Mrem. He didn't need to pretend. No one here was aware of it, nor concerned. He enjoyed this lone power. How would he manage that with mates and children? That would be something to think on later.

For now, he didn't have to worry about the nasty creatures, and he found his mind focused sharper when it only had reptile brains to manipulate. They were cleaner, more advanced, less chaotic. He could control them better, and it felt as if he had more. That might be something to examine, too. If he could select the best, most tractable slaves, he could do more with them. The rest would have to be used for more menial tasks until they broke properly to his control, or used where they could die heroic deaths for his greatness. Yes, he liked that notion.

There was much to explore here. First, though, he would flank and crush those nasty little vermin.

He selected a wine for his victory, and had his handserver put it aside.

He also decided Mrem did not taste good. No amount of seasoning made that gamy meat palatable.

Rscil had doubts about his strategy. His warriors didn't like retreating. He had new, untested weaklings, to be honest about it. He had most of the clan's Dancers and warriors and their lives or independence to lose. There was no par, no gracious drawing of lines. Either he crushed the helpless slaves of this Buloth, and that creature himself, or he and all his people became mindless shit-handlers for the thing.

Still, it had worked once by accident. Hopefully it would work again by design.

The warriors were drawn up, with the thirteen new recruits mixed among them, and the Dancers. The warriors looked more concerned about the newcomers than they did about the Dancers. Rscil found that a relief.

This time Cmeo rode with him, with a spear to defend herself in need, and a loudcone like his own for directing her priestesses. All knew it would be a retreat. None yet knew the whole story on why.

It started as before, with a steady march toward the encroaching force that swarmed down the hill at a run.

This time, though, the clash did not cause the Dancers

to snarl and panic. Many flinched or fluffed in aggression, but all kept their positions. The line held, and worked, and hordes of slave fighters fell squirming in reptilian death. It took so long for them to die. Eights of beats they'd thrash and twitch, long after their blood and their life had left them. Did they have no afterdeath to retreat to? Was that what kept them tied to the dead flesh? Was the mind magic grip that powerful?

He was almost distracted by those thoughts, but a javelin whipped past again, the bronze scarred from edge-to-edge combat, and bright as it missed his eye. He swore, and Gree galloped them closer to the line as a taunt to the enemy and a salute to his own. He would be closest during this retreat. Cmeo chittered slightly from nerves, but gripped the bound edge of the chariot and stayed still.

Then his divided attention returned to realize another mass of Liskash were spreading to flank them. Advance, retreat made no difference. There were thousands of them. Possibly an eight of thousands.

He raised his cone and shouted, "Drillmasters, divide at the middle and retreat in two elements! Divide at the middle and retreat in two elements!"

He burned and cringed inside. That was a complicated maneuver they'd never trained for, but it might give them enough frontage to save themselves. This was not to be a winning battle. He must hope for an attritive one.

It worked to start with. Five and six, and seven and eight spread out to match the flanking forces. Three and four split in two and clustered behind the lead ranks. The Dancers stepped aside, and they formed two shallow arcs that deepened into broad Vs. Once again, the slaughter started, leaving clumps of twitching bodies for the attackers to maneuver around. It broke their advance and slowed them, and the Mrem butchered them as they came.

It worked so well it was an advance, slightly. Rscil flared his ears. *That* was useful. Perhaps that could be developed. Instead of a flat front, a dagged one.

Several Dancers broke from the mass and dragged wounded warriors to the rear, where a wagon waited to haul them far back. Some of them might survive, with herbs and washing and fire.

Then the retreat started in earnest, and it didn't look as if the warriors were faking fear. They were massively outnumbered, but laying about with claw and shield at any limb offered. Not many Liskash died, but eights of eights were crippled or maimed and would never fight again. He watched a leatherwing beat down, attempting to disrupt them with its wingtips. One warrior slashed off a tip with a keen spear, and a Dancer hurled her javelin just right, into its breast. It screeched, beat away, and collapsed into the Liskash lines.

Cmeo hopped down from the chariot and ran toward the formation, leaving him to wonder what had taken her. She didn't act bespelled, and she ran toward the battle, so he waited to see what happened.

He shouted for more reinforcements on the right flank, which was taking the brunt of the assault directly in front of him. He and Gree hurled their barbed darts into the encroaching mass in rapid succession, scoring an eight of wounds each.

The retreat suddenly erupted, with those cursed

refugees turning to strike defending Mrem marching beside them. Rscil snarled. Once a slave, always a slave. His warriors responded instantly to the attack. The refugees were no match for warriors on guard against them. He watched one smashed in the head from behind, another stabbed, others beaten and driven to the ground. The damage was done, though. Brave warriors had been outflanked and died, and the formation damaged. Some areas had but a single line of Mrem now. The snarls had turned to pain and fear instead of anger and challenge.

The Liskash were winning, and looked ready to press the attack all the way back to the fort. He sensed this was their end, and determined only that they'd all die before being turned into plants waving in something's mind breeze.

"Shallow the Vs and retreat!" he shouted. That would expose a wider, thinner front, but there was no choice. They couldn't make it narrower. The nasty Buloth had seen their maneuver and planned to defeat it. He was not so stupid as he seemed before.

"Reinforce the Vs in twos!"

They would also leave many brave warriors wounded or dead. That was too much to think about.

At that moment he felt Cmeo's presence.

Courage, warrior, it said, and he felt it directed at him. The snarling song, the waving javelins, the shifting dance, gave him a calm measure of strength.

He heard her again, giving orders through their minds. Yet it was not unpleasant. *Dancers, heed the dance, heed me, and advance.*

Then something amazing happened.

The retreat continued, with bloody precision. The Liskash charged, were slashed, stabbed and tossed into small heaps that became obstacles. Occasionally, a Mrem fell, sometimes in death, but more often from a crippling but treatable wound. The scouts had recovered some last time, but many had been lost.

Rscil stared in bemusement and spine-fluffing appreciation as the reserve line of Dancers chanted and danced right through the defensive rank, which drew aside briefly in surprise, then locked behind them. Two warriors made to follow, remembered their orders, and stayed.

But for whatever reason, the magic worked. The Liskash didn't notice the Dancers walking right through their mass. They even seemed to step aside for them. The dance wove taillike through them, twisting past wounded Mrem who were offered two shoulders each. The chant continued, while their dance disrupted a little, but seemed to hold.

They worked their way across the Vs, then the Liskash parted to let them back at the Mrem line. Two warriors stepped aside for them, and they twirled right back through with the wounded in arms, right past his chariot. Cmeo flared her nose and spread her ears as she passed.

There was one tragedy, made worse for its uniqueness, as they finished. The spell weakened as they reentered, and some hulking, green-skinned thing noticed them, enough to jam a blade into the spine of the last, and youngest Dancer. She convulsed and died with a shriek.

Then the Liskash weakened again, and drew back. This time it was orderly. They fought their way out of reach, fell back in groups, hurled rocks and javelins, taunted the Mrem, then ran.

"Let them go!" Rscil ordered.

He decided not to discipline a few eights of warriors who hurled javelins into the retreating masses. A dead Liskash was a dead Liskash.

Rscil shuddered in relief that the battle was won. The line had been so thin, so frail. Any rush from the Liskash would have smashed through and destroyed them all. The godling seemed to know only the crudest of tactics. Advance, envelope, reinforce. He lacked any skill in maneuver or strike. It proved they weren't particularly bright, just possessed of an evil grasp.

However, it would be foolish to assume another wouldn't be better. This one might have been a child or a fool. The next might not be.

The message dispatched to Nrao with his swiftest runners advised of their situation, tactics, supply level and location. The plan to swing around the hills was not sustainable. Instead, they'd have to move north fast, and try for the river valley the scouts found. They'd have to cross between surges of sea, and hope not to be pinned by it if they were attacked. It was like a gate that opened twice a day, and moved along the fence a bit more each day.

With luck, the messengers would intercept the resupply wagons and have them divert. Even with gleaning, javelins had been lost or broken. Wrighting took charcoal and fine clay. They could hammer damaged ones straight, and treat them in the fire, but there were limits to repair.

With all that done he had to address the aftermath of the battle. The warriors fed and drank, as did the Dancers. He heard the discordant snarls of Cmeo and her senior Dancers performing rites over their youngest dead, and two others. He gave them credit, though: they'd fought well and bravely when death came to their ranks.

Rewards and accolades would come after one uncomfortable matter. Punishment. Outside, the drillmasters, several fist leaders and a fistful of Dancers awaited as witnesses and advisors for him. He stepped out of his tent into the improvised parade field, where Trec and four surviving refugees waited. Refugees? Escaped slaves? Inadvertent traitors? What status should he give them?

For now he settled on name.

"Trec, you and your Mrem betrayed my warriors in the midst of battle. I will hear your argument."

Trec staggered and shook his head. "Oh, my Talonmaster!" he shouted, and fell to his knees. "Buloth's power did us caught, into mind squirming beneath and within. I stabbing one of your warriors ere I knew, then to strain against, tried." He held forward his left leg, lacerated by his own javelin edge. "Resisted, but not enough. Shamed I survive, that your warriors beat me down alive, not dead."

He turned to address Trec's appointed commander. "Fist Leader Chard."

"Yes, Talonmaster." Chard was stiff-faced, dirty and twitching in the after tension of battle.

"Tell me of Trec's fight."

Chard twitched his whiskers as he took a breath, and

said, "He fought weakly due to his health, but with eagerness. I know of three wounds he inflicted on Liskash, and perhaps a death. Then he turned on Cysh, and was beaten down with hafts and fists."

"Fist Leaders, is this true of the other four?"

Nods and ears of assent said that was so. Fist Leader Braghi said, "This one, Cir, killed three and wounded two. We saw him turn and stopped him before he did more than inflict a scratch." He held up his forearm. The bandage indicated it was somewhat more than a scratch.

Rscil wanted to be diplomatic, and to encourage others to defect, mostly for the information they'd bring. A few more spears, wielded by half-starved, untrained drifters, whose minds were bent to a lizard, were not of much military consequence. He couldn't have them near him, though.

"Trec, Cir, Gar, Hach, Leesh, stand and hear my ruling."

The four of them stepped, or rather, limped forward, and stood proudly. They were scared but determined, and would die like Mrem for their shame.

Rscil said, "Your mind was not your own, and you fought to maintain it. I hold no charge against you. I will move you into the van, however, for your courage. At worst, you may earn an honorable death. At best, perhaps you will turn back to yourselves, and put this false godling beneath you. Until then, you will be guarded by others, with respect and in support."

Trec spoke for them all. "We will honor in live or die, and thankee for mercy and wisdom."

He nodded, flared his ears, and said, "Priestess Cmeo,

is there anything that can be done to strengthen their minds?"

She spread her ears and said, "Perhaps. I will work with them."

"Now I will publicly praise you and your Dancers for saving twenty-seven wounded warriors with your dance through the battle."

There was a snarling cheer.

She bowed with a smile, erect tail tip twitching. "Thank you, Talonmaster. It was a proud privilege for us."

He went on to praise eight and six warriors who'd shown remarkable courage when reduced to a single rank without nearby flankers, fighting with the inspiration of Aedoniss and holding the line. Two had done so when Trec's Mrem had attacked their fellows. He discreetly referred to "wounded in battle," not "stabbed in the back."

"That is all for now. I respect you all for your fight and magic, and you, our drivers and handlers, for your tireless work. I must coordinate our withdrawal from this fort, though all things willing, we will return and garrison it, build it and declare it a town before long. All be sure you are prepared to move tonight."

Cmeo caught up with him as he entered his tent.

"Rscil, if I may ask, what did you see of the spell this time?"

With only a little reluctance, he said, "The chant and dance broke the spell. It does work." He waved to the other bench.

"Yes," she said as she sat.

"I noted that Trec and his cohorts were furthest from

you, and ceased hostility as your dance left the formation, surrounding them on all sides."

"It does work," she echoed him.

"You have no more Dancers to add, and we may face larger armies. How will you manage?"

"Stronger spells and louder songs," she said. "Think of it as complement to your warrior shouts."

"I see," he said. He had an idea. "Would more music help?" Cmeo's eyes widened with curiosity.

"It might. There are spells that incorporate layers of voice harmony, of horn."

"We have used baghorns in battle. They are great for signaling."

She brushed her whiskers and smiled. "I remember those from the route here. Why aren't they used in battle? You could choose tunes for messages."

That was a startling idea. Music was more about feel than thought, but of course Dancers felt things differently.

He clamped down on his interest in this shapely, brilliant female, and said, "I will add that to the long list of things to study, after we have won this war."

"Thank you, Talonmaster," she said, with a warm lilt that had to be purposeful, and meant to tease him. "Then can you arrange a meeting with your horners? I'm sure we can develop something."

"I will do so. We will win in our next engagement, I am sure."

"As am I, needing only my faith of spirit. And in you."

She stood and pulled the curtain as she headed for her own tent.

✦ ✦ ✦

Buloth shivered in elation, riding his bulky steed at the rear of his army. There they were, the hairy mammals, in their crude, dusty, smelly little hilltop camp, and here he was, with a thousand warriors a bare gis away, approaching in foggy darkness step by measured step, each creature in a slow, methodical advance. If he'd got the trick right, they felt pain for making noise, and nothing for proper advance. With practice, he might offer them pleasure, as disgusting a concept as that was, but it would improve motivation with simpler minds. That wasn't a subject he intended to discuss with Father. He'd save it in case of need.

They approached closer and closer, and he heard scrabbles and voices and movement. He couldn't read the Mrem, though. There were a few, but not enough. Those cursed priestesses of theirs. They interfered with his mindspells. He'd not only kill them. He'd humiliate them first, in the most carnal ways possible, with the filthiest beasts.

Then the mental fog cleared and he realized he'd been cheated. There were less than fifteen Mrem in the camp. He silently and angrily ordered the charge, and flogged his trunklegs into speed. He would be first, and take vengeance personally.

He dismounted and ordered two large stilts to carry him up the slippery slope. Twenty warriors flanked him against attack, and they burst in bounding turns through the back and forth of the gateway.

Rocks crashed and smashed into his guard, he tumbled and rolled to the slippery, sharp ground as the stilts were crippled, and found himself and six guards facing the Mrem. He reached out to grab their minds.

Nothing happened.

They were drunk. Something fermented, something smoked and something eaten. They were wailing, insane, mindless hairy beasts, armed with rocks and javelins and frothing at the mouth as they slashed and beat at his guard.

In moments they were all dead, though one moaned and twitched. Perhaps not dead, but what did it matter? It would be soon enough. Let it enjoy its pain for daring to attack a Liskash god.

Buloth staggered around, realized he'd been hit stingingly in the leg, and recovered his composure, outraged at the events. Then he saw the bandages on the dead Mrem.

These were all wounded, left behind drunk and drugged to fight him, with no purpose other than to kill a few Liskash before they succumbed to their injuries. They lacked even the grace to die with dignity.

But the rest were gone. He could chase them through the dark, but he suddenly realized he was afraid. He was in a furious panic and knew it. Those fuzzy beasts were better than they should be. How could they do this? They were stupid, barely intelligent, with no mindpower. They couldn't know what he planned, yet were ready for him. They'd retreated and slaughtered his slaves on the way. The second day, he'd spread for envelopment with a massively larger force, and they'd split to match it, then retreated again, and destroyed more. Now they retreated entirely, and with little loss.

The slaves lost in the first bout had come back to him

in the second, then he'd lost them again. Were they so mind-damaged? Had he done that? Too much hold, too little? Part of this was Father's fault for not giving him more instruction. The servants taught him literacy. They could not teach mindholding. Father's fear had caused him to fail.

The toll in slaves and beasts was terrible. Nor had he acquired replacements. It felt as if he'd lost numbers in the last day. How? Why was his mindpower slipping?

The numbers were so bad he'd even made an attempt at having the wounded bandaged and carried, in hopes they'd heal. Limping slaves might not look the best, but at least they could stop javelins for the others. That he was reduced to this shamed him to a yellow tinge, even without other gods to see him.

His only recourse at this point was to retreat home and beg for reinforcements, and ask for advice on his failure.

He might not be ready to be a god yet. It hurt his ego, but he was a realist, as Liskash were.

He let the servants strike the pavilion and the banners, douse the fire and pack the wagons. He would ride home proudly but without fanfare, and ask Father to help him fix it.

Buloth reported in his best manner. Father sat on his carved and padded throne, listening in annoyance.

"Father, as I noted, I enslaved a hundred and eighty-eight Mrem, and pushed two strong attacks—"

"And botched them disgracefully," his father said, vocally.

Buloth swallowed. That was not a good sign.

"I tried my best, but I need more counsel," he said, diplomatically, and willed himself to present that way in mind.

Father snorted and took a swallow of wine. "More counsel? You need more intelligence. Unbound animals outfought you."

"They did not bind. I tried surely. The ones I had bound also broke." He kept it as factual as possible, but he was afraid it sounded insufficient.

Clearly your mind is not strong enough, came the reply.

It is, he said. *I felt them, counted them, even turned some traitors back once amongst the enemy. There was interference. Their priestesses . . .*

Priestesses? his father roared. *Animals don't have religion. They have superstition at best.*

As you wish, but that is how they presented.

Buloth knew it was fruitless. Father would not believe until he felt himself, which hopefully wouldn't happen, as it would mean Mrem here, in the stronghold. But Father was not finished.

You have wasted my slaves, shamed me in front of the world, and made it necessary that I now do your job myself. Your younger brother will take my place. He has proven worthy.

Buloth had earned his father's scorn. *I abase myself, Father.*

You'll do more than that.

He felt a warm little trickle, then a crushing weight.

Buloth gasped and spasmed, fell to the ground and described a running circle with his feet as his own hindmind crushed his heart.

The last thing he heard was his father's voice.

"Even a son has a price in slaves."

Rscil felt vindicated. He'd pushed hard for them to move north and east, then east along the side of the hills. Behind, the setting sun reflected off the New Sea and turned the water crimson. That was all anyone talked of, once it came into view. It also kept them moving, too excited to want breaks. He insisted, though. Rest was necessary for good health. They might be in unending battle soon enough.

They camped on a hummock, with a hasty berm reinforced with stakes they'd hewn en route. Those had taken the last four days to gather, with the scrubby trees hereabouts. Hunting parties brought in some game to stretch their salted and dried rations. There were even some tubers that worked adequately in stew, if there was enough frusk and other fruit to cover it.

They could smell the New Sea, and hear faint rushes of water. At first it was disturbing, but quickly it became familiar and relaxing. The smell was of muck and rich earth, and some musty mold. This would be productive land.

The next morning they were afoot, moving quickly and eagerly to this New Sea, larger than any lake. At midday they reached it. Even seasoned veterans halted in wonder at the sight. Rscil was as awed as the others.

Gree said, trying not to sound too eager, "Talonmaster, I propose we allow a rest and play time."

Rscil grinned at him. "I agree. In shifts of three, an eighthday each." Not that he didn't think it was a fun idea himself, but he recognized it would be a distraction until they all got it out of their systems.

Then they'd move north, and try this most bold of tactics, based only on information from scouts. This was a new way of war, and he wondered how it would be fought generations hence.

Cmeo was very beautiful, erupting wet and slick from the water, her glossy black fur clinging to her form. He looked away to avoid being distracted. Perhaps after this campaign he could consider a mate, but could any female compare with one as brave and intelligent as she?

The water was turbid and lukewarm, like runoff from a camp station for watering beasts, not at all refreshing. Bits of plant floated in it, and bubbles of deep decay rose occasionally. It was shallow, except where it dropped off suddenly, this being a plain at the edge of the hills, with the former Hot Depths east and below. It took only a short time for the polish to wear off for Rscil.

He formed them back up, and had the scouts and watchers move out to clear the way. They still had a long way to go on this new route, and at least one legendary battle.

There was surprisingly little grumbling, and the break seemed to have refreshed the Mrem, as well as inspired them, with this mucky, bitter water that lapped at the land. In short order, they were moving north. He studied the narrow but obvious tidal flat. How did one decide where the land ended and sea began? Especially with the sea changing?

Rscil walked, though he could ride. Occasionally he'd mount chariot and patrol around the army, to offer encouragement. Then he'd dismount to walk again. It saved the beasts, and let every Mrem know he walked with them, not above them.

It was good that he did so. It helped keep the pace even. Stragglers would be at risk, though he did urge them to greater speed.

"Dancer, I saw you fight. This is but a walk. You are well up to it!" "Wright, you hammer bronze all day. Move that strength to your legs." "Warrior, you don't want to be late for the glory."

They were in good spirits, just fatigued. A long march could do that. He kept up the encouragement and had Gree at the van slow their pace slightly. Faster was preferred, but arriving all together and fresh to fight was more pressing.

Before night, a message came from ahead. A watcher sprinted back through the lines of wagons, slowed for the approach, and came alongside Rscil.

"Talonmaster," he said, "we have sign. Drag and trail of an army, and fresh filth marks of Liskash scouts."

"Thank you, Arschi. I will note both and send all the scouts out."

Indeed he would. This was almost the end.

Oglut was very, very annoyed. Mutal had been unable to secure the south against the remains of Ashay's godholding. Several offspring warred for position, leaving the entire area a shambles of discord and starvation. It would take time to resolve, and would have to be rebuilt from the bottom. However, Mutal had marshaled his creatures and brought them back largely alive. His report indicated that much fighting went on between the new aspirants and the stray Mrem. That was something that should be left for now. They could kill each other until Oglut was ready to move on them.

It had not been a great campaign, but it hadn't been the disaster that Buloth's was. There were now reports from his distant eyes of two Mrem mobs near the New Sea, south of the hills and moving north. This was after the ridiculous behavior of moving west. The new environment was prime for reptiles, not the steaming, stinking furries. If he didn't know better, it seemed as if they'd meant to conquer his territory, and now were fleeing north. There were tens of thousands of them.

If Buloth had done his job, at least one of those packs would be slaves, scattered savages or slaughtered now. Instead, there were two, and he'd have to deal with them personally. One son was a former incompetent and now corpse, the other competent but untrained.

What annoyed Oglut most was it was his own fault they lacked in such skills. Still, there'd been no way to trust them with that power until there was expansion room. Between the cool continent to the north swarming with mammalian vermin, and the two strong, warring factions to the south, there'd been nowhere to go. Now there was, but it was a mess.

He called for his beasts and handlers, and pushed the army and loose auxiliaries into movement. This would be an excessive slaughter.

Rscil pushed the army on into the night. They

grumbled and snarled under their breaths, but he could tell they were at least as excited about meeting with Nrao's force. That would make them stronger.

The original plan was for Rscil to drive around the hills, north of Oglut's city, drawing that army along. He'd have the advantage of speed and a good map they couldn't know he had, and that would free Nrao's force, with the civilians, to move north unmolested. With river, sea and hills, they'd have all the terrain advantages.

Now, they had to guard Nrao's rear, and challenge the approaching Liskash. He hoped it would work. It had to. They still had terrain, and from scout reports, the Liskash were heading to meet them.

It was profound how this sea had changed the world. The filling of a ditch, albeit a large one, was destroying entire kingdoms not anywhere near the Hot Depths.

Shouts from ahead roused him from his musing. They'd run into the tail of Nrao's army. Warriors sent up cheers and yelled greetings to their mates. Drillmasters had to shout them back into order, but they had smiles on their faces as well.

It took most of an eighth night to actually find the clan leader. There were that many warriors, and Dancers, and wrights and drovers. Add in the dark and few lamps, and it was a chore. Eventually, though, he heard Nrao's gravelly voice nearby.

He called, "Clan Leader, I greet you."

The golden-coated male turned suddenly, and a smile spread across his face.

"Talonmaster! Well done!"

Rscil bowed his head as the failures of the last several

eightdays rushed into his mind. "Not so well. We are forced to an alternate plan."

Nrao put a hand on his shoulder. "Still within our plans. I have your reports, but would share grer and hear first hand."

"Certainly."

It felt good to sit on a bench in Nrao's tented wagon. It was big enough for four to talk or one to sleep. The grer drove the damp and chill from Rscil with its fermented warmth. Nrao waited patiently until he was ready to speak.

Comfortable, and with big slabs of fruit-laden dried fat at hand, Rscil told his tale. Their body heat warmed the small tent, though the humidity clung to their fur.

Nrao sipped his own drink. He was polite and attentive, and seemed eager for the upcoming fight. When Rscil finished his story, he spoke.

"I am pleased by this. You have found a tactic that will work well in this position, even better than we planned. The Dancers have proven their worth. We can beat the lizards' mind magic and their army. I am sympathetic to the former slaves, but I agree they should be offered the chance to die bravely, or win through. It is the only way for them to be free."

"Thank you," Rscil replied.

"It is only days until this comes through." Nrao warned.

"Then a new home?" Rscil hardly dared consider it, it was so far out of his plans. Nrao understood. He smiled.

"Yes, then a new home, but I will need you behind until we are out of danger. Then you will build a fortress. Do you still prefer Outpost Master Shlom?"

"I do. He commands well without supervision, and I will leave seasoned drillmasters with him," Rscil assured Nrao.

The clan master's throat hummed with approval. "Excellent. Our welcome in the north will be better if we leave a strong position here, I believe. Then let us rest and prepare for the fight. Are the refreshments to your liking?"

"It is good grer," Rscil said agreeably. "How are Nef and Ruhr?"

Nrao's pupils spread with pleasure at the courtesy. "My son and my mate are far ahead, with a trading caravan bound for Grachs' city. He has accepted Ingo as our envoy and will at least grant us passage. He did not promise it would be secret passage, though."

"So long as they are safe."

Nrao stretched, shifted and curled again on his bench. He tilted his cup and drank thoughtfully.

"Safe is relative. You do realize, Rscil, that we could have left in small caravans and likely been unseen, most of us, spreading out across the north. We would sacrifice our steading and our past, but our bloodlines would continue. My son suggested it, in fact."

Rscil was uncomfortable with the idea.

"A bloodline is more than just blood," he said.

"Yes, that is why it is only a desperate last plan. We must remain a people," Nrao emphasized by slapping the wood. He raised the crockery bottle for a refill as shouts came from outside. He placed it on the table and scooped up a javelin. Rscil followed suit, and both were outside in moments, with Nrao's guards and servants falling in around them.

There was a Liskash present, but only one, looking somewhat bruised and worse for wear. Two scouts held him by his scaly arms. He was greenish yellow, and well concealed in darkness.

Nrao spoke at once to Rscil. "Do you have anyone who speaks their oily tongue?"

Rscil said drily, "I rather hoped one of your spies did."

"They are busy elsewhere," Nrao said, without elaborating.

Rscil thought. "Then no, but wait." Possibly . . . He turned to a scout. "Send for Trec, among my camp."

Nrao said, "Ah, the escapees you spoke of. Good."

The Liskash didn't fight, and his expression was creepily blank. No ears, no smile, little way to tell what they thought, if they thought. Though at least some of them built castles. He did seem to twitch whenever the grips on him were lightened, pondering escape.

"Hold him well," Rscil said.

The warriors nodded and all but sat on the cold-skinned thing. He struggled a few beats, then seemed to accept his position.

Trec arrived in short order. Despite the long route and field rations, he looked fitter and fuller than he had when he'd dragged his worn self into their camp. That said much.

"Greetings, Trec. Are you skilled in the tongue of these creatures?"

"Talonmaster, and you are the lord?" he asked, turning that toward Nrao.

"I am. I greet you, Trec. I will meet with you later."

"Understood, lord," he nodded and turned back. "Talonmaster, no one I known speaks language this. Do not the commoners project thoughts. They only hear, and not much."

"That is unfortunate. I am reluctant to kill him in case he is expected. He may also prove useful to send a message back, as well, if we knew what to say."

Trec said, "I can translate you thought hearably, I think."

Nrao didn't want to think overly on that. The poor Mrem had had those disgusting creatures in his mind. That by itself helped color his response.

"Tell him this: 'Go tell the slimy lizard we await him.'" He gestured, and the guards hauled the lizard upright.

Trec strained, gripping his head and shivering until he drooled. He sank slowly to his knees. Suddenly, though, the Liskash stiffened and recoiled, whipping around and reacting in horror, even while on the ground.

Trec stood and said, "I did my best."

"For us?" It was harsh, but a valid question.

Trec nodded and took it like a Mrem. "I did, Talonmaster. My mind is breakable to rulers of they, but not here, and not of things like that." He pointed at the now panicky Liskash.

The sentries looked to Rscil for assent and, receiving it, prodded the creature with the butt of a javelin. The Liskash trotted unsurely away, before increasing to a run into the damp, foggy darkness.

Rscil smiled and said, "Aedoniss and Assirra willing, we shall meet this Oglut in a day or so. For the first and last times."

Nrao said, "I hope that optimism is well-placed, Talonmaster."

"It is. You will be impressed."

Nrao said, "It's near dawn. We may as well awake and on with it now."

Rscil was exhausted, but concurred. The sooner they arrived on their chosen terrain, the sooner they'd be ready for battle.

The next day, they reached a wide, shallow river in a loamy plain, and Hril assured them it was the one he and Flirsh had observed. It flowed steadily over the rocks, and they certainly did look disturbed. They were wet, as the tide retreated.

"On this side we have a wall to stand against," he said. "Across, we have a barrier against attack."

Rscil nodded. Though it was more than that.

"For half a day at a time, yes. It is as you describe." Timing was critical, though. "We will bivouac here," Rscil ordered. "I want stakes and pits."

Then they'd await this creature who styled himself a god. In this terrain, they had a steep hill to east and lapping water to the west. With a river as a third side, they'd pin him down regardless of his meaningless slaves, and eliminate him.

Oglut was in his tent at a meal when his servants brought a messenger to him. The creature was worn, abraded and weak. He also seemed reluctant to speak.

"Out with it. I am in a hurry," he said. The roasted trot bird was most tasty. He belched up its essence and inhaled it.

The Liskash trembled. "Great Oglut, the message is unpleasant."

Tell me.

"The message was . . . speak to slimy reptile of our presence and impatience."

Oglut grew cold. His entire body grew still from that comment.

The messenger cringed and huddled, awaiting a terrible backlash. Oglut stared down at him.

"I will not kill you," he said. "That is the message. If the furry filth wish to meet me, they shall." He ripped the location from the scout's mind, enjoying his flail and gasp as his mind was violated. "I must go to the New Sea anyway. I will do so to drive their broken bodies into it."

To his servants he said, "They are at the steep mountain creek, above what used to be the cataract. We go there now. Toss scraps to the slaves and get my carriage."

He looked down at the nervous, hesitant creature before him.

"Stand. Get ready to march with me."

One didn't kill messengers. One could, however, move them to the front.

"They come!" was the call.

Rscil woke to it. He'd had a couple of eighths of rest at least. It would have to do. It was morning, but he'd been up most of the night, conducting his own reconnaissance, placing stakes to mark key points, and examining approaches.

"Form up!" he shouted as he sprung from his cot. He

heard Nrao shouting, and Cmeo, Gree, several other drillmasters calling out their orders in response.

Once out in the sun, he checked its position. If the chart the scouts had was correct, it was a full eighth and a quarter until the river filled. Behind them was a wide, muddy flat, strewn with rocks, deadwood and debris, with a shallow river splashing leg-deep down the middle. It was poor protection, though harder for the enemy to cross while under defensive fire. If the Liskash came down from the heights, though . . .

Ingo's report had detailed times based on the position of the moon, and a prediction of eventual depth. This narrow beach would soon be a shelf under the sea, probably within a month. The hardscrabble cliffs above and west would be the shore then.

The warriors were well-blooded, and all his Dancers too. Nrao's army somewhat less so, as they'd marched straight here. Between them, though, it should be fine, he told himself. They were side by side, filling the beach from cliff to water, as the drillmasters had been instructed. The line between them was apparent to him, but probably not to a reptile. It was a weak spot. One of several.

Several fists of scouts scurried up the cliff, to hold high ground against a flank. Nor had a force come around the mountains. South was the distant, dusty mass of a Liskash army, led by some godling or other, hopefully Oglut himself.

Whoever it was approached slowly. Rscil realized they might be standing a long time. Given that, he ordered, "Rest in place!" and indicated to the nearest drillmasters to give Mrem turns to relieve themselves, drink water, grab a chunk of meat, even if they weren't hungry.

It was almost a stately advance, of a formal meeting. Except neither the Mrem nor Liskash cared about dignity or formalities with each other, only about killing the other as a threat.

Dust in the distance informed him that the enemy was close. Here they came, in the advance, moving to a faster walk. They were perhaps five hundredlengths from the south bank.

"Watch for leatherwings and attacks from the cliffs!" he ordered.

It was none too soon. There were leatherwings all over. High above, the scouts shot arrows and slung stones at them, but the enraged beasts stooped and dove at them. That kept many away from the army on the ground, however the flocks seemed endless.

Several soared down the cliff and over his formation, only to be slashed by warriors and Dancers. They quickly gave up and retreated, cackling and cawing in pain. The warriors on the cliff kept up a barrage to speed them. Sending a prayer to their bravery, he turned back to the approaching Liskash.

"Steady!" he ordered, as a stampede of wild animals bore down on them, ahead of the approaching army. It was large, mostly lizard and all ugly, until the lead beasts piled into the narrow-angled trenches they'd cut across the ground. Shrieking and stumbling, they piled up in a wreck of bodies and dust, flinging grass and debris. It was an abattoir of legendary scale, with the smallest animals racing through to be speared, the half-sized game lamed and injured in the pits, to be smashed under the hooves and claws of the tumbling, trumpeting wall of large meat.

If they survived this battle, the Mrem would all eat very well indeed.

Oglut seethed. These too-clever furballs did seek to challenge him. He gurgled gleefully as a soarer flung one of them from the rocks to dash to its death below. He would send them to gang up on the cliff-scaling creatures one at a time, if that's what it took.

But ahead, madness. The stampeding animals were to smash this neat little box, crush the stinking beasts under claw and foot, and leave only scattered, panicked individuals for his army to finish off.

Some had made it through near the water. There, the Mrem slashed and fought, their proud formation broken into groups who could only prod at trunklegs with their bronze spears. Oglut had his mind and the trunklegs' weight.

Farther inland, though, where those pits were, was a shambles of broken, screaming things. If he could kill them with thought he would, not from mercy, but to shut their wails. They were beyond distracting, they were painful.

However, the mammals numbered a few thousand, and he had tens of thousands. They cared for their lives; his slaves did not. All that was necessary was to advance past the blockade of dying meat, then charge. If they could be stuffed into the river, they could be drowned.

The beasts were actually in advance. He laughed to himself.

He would not fall for the tricks his worthless son fell

for. For one thing, they couldn't get past the crippled stampede or their own traps.

He gave his orders slowly and carefully.

Rscil, now aboard a wagon, which was sturdier if slower than a chariot, studied and planned while the advancing army wove cautiously between and over dying, kicking beasts. That said all that was needed about this godling. Death and pain of others were tools for him, with no compassion at all.

But Aedoniss and Assirra had brought them here at this time. They guided their Mrem.

He raised his loudcone and shouted to Nrao. "Now, as we agreed!" Then he raised it to his drillmasters. "Slow retreat!"

This wasn't a fighting retreat. This was a maneuver for position. They maintained line and spacing, though it was awkward while stepping backward on rough ground.

It was unnerving to see thousands of Liskash moving cautiously, slowly, across the beaten ground, under the mesmerizing spell of their master. However, that made it clear it was Oglut they faced, not some lesser lord.

Next to him, Cmeo raised her cone and said simply, "Dancers, now!"

Their wailing, resonant song rose instantly to full volume, with a tight chatter of drums that resolved into a strong beat. The borrowed baghorners sounded off, punctuating and reinforcing the song.

Oglut gritted his teeth. First the shrieks of the beasts, now the wauling song of those cursed Mrem. Was it their death song? He hoped so. Even here, it hurt his mind, made concentration difficult. It must be horrible up close. A quick check into the mind of a forward warrior indicated it was so. Ugh.

His army made it through the obstacles, and had only a quarter gis to go reach them. Soon enough he'd hear them make other noises, ones no more pleasant, but much more enjoyable for him.

Now the fuzzy things changed direction and advanced again. Whatever they were doing, it wasn't going to help them. With these gone at last, he'd solidify to the north and send Mutal south. It might be time to sire a new brood for the future.

He took a gulp of a good wine for fortification, rose up on his carriage's dais, and ordered a charge. He'd follow right behind them to enjoy the view.

Rscil had told Nrao he would be surprised. Indeed he was.

The band advanced with precision, for these were not slaves. Each one was a willing, trained Mrem, their minds and actions linked in a joining that could only be called magic.

The Mrem kept the pace and the beat, in a steady, mesmerizing thump of left feet. The warriors advanced in identical, perfect pace, their rows as straight as an engineer's string. In and among them, the Dancers moved in their own special way, arms punching and flailing at the air in unison, the motions rippling in waves from van to rear. Their unified chant inspired even at this distance. Under it all, the drone of the baghorns buzzed like angry bees, simultaneously adding to the power whilst distracting from anything else.

Those head tosses looked flamboyant and artistic, but meant each Dancer stared down the length of her row every two steps, and did not look long enough at the advancing Liskash to be distracted. For the warriors, the gyrating Dancers were visible peripherally, and gave them reference points for their own lines. It didn't hurt that they were lithe females, either.

Ahead, the mass of Oglut's army advanced. They came now in a cohesive, but uncoordinated group, with a little forward swelling in the middle, a dip of less brave or driven to the sides, and a slight swelling at the flanks. The narrowness of the new beach throttled them into a tighter bunch. They moved well, not hindering each other, and with some shuffling, the braver moved to the front.

The main concern was some flanking maneuver on the high ground to the east. Nrao squinted up that way, his pupils narrowing to slits. The slingers, archers and javeliners had been tolled heavily by the leatherwings. He hoped enough remained, though the ground up there seemed inhospitable to most, strewn in boulders and clumps of stalky grass. A few stray beasts and a fistful of Liskash scrambled up, to be shot down. It was the far side of the battlefield, but not far enough.

A good battle was won before it was engaged, by having all avenues accounted for, and good position and movement. This was a good position. The fanning Liskash slipped down the bank and piled up again, sorting themselves out, but wet, muck-sheened and visibly frustrated.

There was always that fear, though, that it wasn't enough. It only took a wobble in the front to create a gap that became a hole. How would this formation fare? Rscil reported very favorably, but Nrao hadn't seen it in person. Trust fought with insecurity. He gripped his own chariot rim. Oh, to be in the fight. But now as clan leader, he must defer to others. He led them all, not just the warriors. He had the sea flank, Rscil the hill flank. He'd rather they were reversed. The gooey ground underneath hindered the chariot. It might be best to dismount. With a nod to his drover he did so.

It worked well, so far. The warriors in the first two ranks seemed calm, collected, and held the best spacing he'd ever seen. They strode and strode. Diagonally behind them, the Dancers waved those short spears overhead and side to side, keeping a perfect line. Their motion was almost mind magic itself. It drew one in, commanded one to watch. There was good and bad in that, as the enemy approached rapidly, already across the river's shallows and climbing the bank.

Then it was on.

A wave of leathery reptiles charged forward, swelled out against the Mrem, broke and tumbled and fell. In beautiful, glittering, musical balance, the warriors struck the incoming bodies, tossed them aside to the females. The Dancers' spears twisted, flashed and resumed their shaking flutters. The scaled beasts thrashed and twitched, their bodies reluctant to release souls already dead.

Forward momentum stopped, each rank pulling up and trying to maintain spacing from the one in front. The ranks stacked up, but kept even for the most part.

With only minor ripples, the Mrem came to a stop and kept a solid, impenetrable front of shields and spears. The oncoming enemy could only advance and try to overwhelm them frontally, past broken bodies and across a pot-holed savannah.

The tactic worked. The reptiles and a handful of sad Mrem under godling control advanced again, as the cajoling demands in their minds fought with their fear. They were many, and directed, but not inspired. They arrived in a ringing clash, and fell in clattering heaps. The Mrem were many, and were inspired and each an eager, thoughtful self building a greater whole. No single death could stop them; were Nrao or Rscil to die, the battle would continue. As some few warriors and Dancers fell, others stepped forward. The formation was built of courage, discipline and art.

And magic. Oglut put forth his will. Nrao could feel it, a mighty darkness clutching at his mind, his spirit. He shuddered himself, this far away, and watched in fear as a ripple swept through the combined band.

But that was all. A ripple, then nothing. The over-whelming force of a lizard who styled himself a god was no match for the proud minds of cooperating Mrem. His grasp for control evaporated. Then it slipped from those he already held. His entire army could be seen to hesitate, shiver, stop for a moment, then collapse on itself. Some few pressed half-livered attacks. Others cowered down where they stood, trembling in abandonment and fear. Most retreated from a walk to a panicked sprint, ebbing back in a softer, weaker wave than the attack.

The Mrem advanced slightly, but only slightly, holding

the perfect dance, the perfect advance and moving forward in step on step across the plain. Rscil shouted, as did the drillmasters. The energy, the power, the motion and sound of the dance, let the bristling spears add to the magic, and nothing Oglut had mattered.

It was time, though. To the west, the lapping waves built, and the gravelly loam between it and the Liskash narrowed quickly.

"Retreat," Nrao ordered the nearest drillmaster, and his flank began to withdraw. Others caught it, and the order flowed forward and through the mass. Rscil nodded and shouted it. The other drillmasters echoed it, and the formation marched through itself, with the lead warriors now holding the face of the V.

It was a struggle to keep aligned as they backed across the river silt. Nrao had never been so proud in his life.

Oglut felt a surge and a shift. That was odd. His power felt suddenly much greater. He seized it and pushed his will, urging all his slaves into the attack. He was sure he'd acquired a number of Nrao's warriors, who would sow chaos in that very pretty formation, and bring it to a boiling incoherence the rest could overswarm. His warriors and beasts hesitated, regrouped and charged.

It hit him too late what he'd felt. It was not the sudden gain of the attacking Mrem. It was the recovery of some of his slaves, who had actually broken from his mind. He cursed, and flogged them mentally, demanding they charge or face even greater agony. They slowed, but continued.

That was fine, even for the mindweak, because the Mrem were in retreat. They were pulling back across the river now, and lacked the heart and spleen to face his mind and his warriors. He would press now, then pursue. The muck and water would slow them. Their care for their skins would be their end.

Rscil felt strangely calm, despite hot sun, sticky mud and the sun beating down on him. Then he sloshed into the river and felt chill. He sought gaps between pebbles with his feet. A fall now would be disastrous.

Even though their plan called for abandoning the carts and chariots, temporarily, his guts flopped as they did so. The drovers and javeliners dismounted and ran, to fall into rank where they could.

Ahead, hundreds of soulless eyes stared at him from Oglut's mind-ravished slaves. They took little care as they slid down the gullied bank, from tangled grass to sodden mud, then onto loose rocks. They crashed through the growth and over downed limbs, to splash into the water.

It was up to his waist now, and he looked around to monitor progress. It went well enough, but the lines grew ragged as bodies fought the current. The water was cool, though, and cleaned his fur. That probably wasn't fair exchange for hindered movement. He was in a deeper, slower pool at the bottom of some cascades hissing above him. Others were ankle-deep in rocky, tickling shallows. Some were in rapids between the two.

The other problem became apparent. He cared about holding formation. The cursed Liskash didn't. They high-stepped and waded and dove into the current, eager to reach the Mrem because the monster in their brains told them to. They threw themselves against javelins, to die and drag those into the water in their bodies.

"Darts!" he shouted, and a flurry of bronze-tipped and weighted points arced from the front rank.

The water ran red downstream of him.

Then he was knocked under and felt a point tear past him, slicing his arm. Some had made it obliquely up the hill and across the rocks above. He felt three or more, and he struck out with his spear, while clutching at his waist for his battle claws. Another jab missed, but he was still under and being held. His arm burned and his lungs started to.

The spear was jammed in the riverbed, so he could only use it for support, as cold water shoved at his nostrils and throat, sloshed in his ears and pulled at him. He got a fist in his battle claws, though, and raised them with a grin that he restrained just in time to avoid choking.

With a firm thrust and shove, he accomplished two things. He pushed his head above water, and he sliced the guts of his rightmost antagonist into tatters that leaked and bled in a boiling surge of color.

He swung them gleefully around and watched for just a moment as a Liskash's expressionless face shredded like a wind-ripped tent. The thing convulsed and thrashed and at last made a squealing sound as its feet kicked and it fell away. That freed his spear, but he left it in the chest of the third, that clutched at it and drooled blood as Rscil swam downstream, spitting gory water.

Quickly, he assessed. There were other melees in progress, as Oglut's slaves tried to overwhelm them by sheer numbers. The live used the twitching dead as stepping stones, and seemed determined to catch every Mrem point they could.

It would work, he realized. They'd run out soon enough, and then, regardless of claws and teeth, they'd be buried under revolting lizard flesh. He watched one catapult itself over its predecessors, clear a gap in the First where no one had any longarms left, to land amid the Dancers, who snarled and howled and ripped it apart with javelins and claws.

Three beats later they were back in formation, panting and glazed red, but singing and waving.

But a glance back showed that Eight and Seven were scrambling up the north bank, reaching down to help the Dancers ahead of them. There were holes in the front, where the bravest had died, but Aedoniss, and especially Assirra willing, the rest would get up that bank, and have high ground from which to stab the disgusting lizards.

We'll be heading north soon enough, he told himself.

Then he ordered, "Quick now, and even! Thrust and block! and thrust and block! and step! and thrust! and step! and thrust!"

At least the nearest heard him over the din of dying Liskash, and swung their points in unison. It worked, creating a wall of bodies again, that hindered the advance, until the water dislodged some into the shifting ripples.

Then they were all on the silt and debris of the north bank. Sharp gravel had never felt so wonderful. He gratefully dragged through mud, pulling at the nearest warrior and Dancer, shouting, "Keep position! And keep dancing!"

He could hear left feet stomping as the retreating army took back its position. Those farther back passed forward their spears, keeping their javelins for themselves.

There was a roar. Rscil hadn't heard that sound before, but he knew what it meant.

"Retreat at the double!" he shouted. *"Retreat at the double!"*

He heard someone echo it before the sound was lost.

If they could only get up that slippery bank . . .

Oglut saw victory. A sheer wave of dispensable slaves, petty criminals and mindweak inferiors hurled themselves against the lead Mrem. They might hide it from his sons, but he saw that the front rank had all the stoutest and best. Beyond that were lesser-built males and even females. Crack that facade and the rest would flee.

They were moving faster, already, eager to retreat from him. They slipped and clambered backward up the bank, using their spears for support and traction. He had them, and now for the kill, and once he tasted their anguish, he would draw them into his fold and make them his. They would entertain him, clean the herd beasts, scrub latrines, all the lowest tasks.

He urged his trunklegs on, drawing his high-wheeled chariot, bedecked in its glittering silver and bluestone, in a bumpy ride down the bank and across the mud. It wasn't dignified, but none would notice. With enough speed, the animals managed not to mire, though they did struggle. His wheels sank, but dragged and rolled, and then he was in the river, up high, looking down on the puny victims. A wounded one waved an arm before him, and he steered to crush it under the left wheel, feeling a rise and crunch as he ran over its ribs.

It was then another distraction caught him, to the left and west. He glanced over, and froze in wonder. Was it magic? Some trick of a storm? But the sky was clear and blue, and a rushing wall of water roared toward him, brown with dirt and spitting froth and weeds.

Was their damnable god real?

The far flank disappeared under it, others turned to run even before he gave the order, and a handful of Mrem scrambled farther up the bank, as one slipped and submerged. He had no time to balance that small frisson with the searing hatred and disgust welling up inside. The water was easily twice his height as it rose over the chariot, tumbling him with it and bruising him with heavy river cobbles that smashed and burned. He sealed his nostrils and grasped for support, but the chariot was atop him, the trunklegs thrashing upside down and tangled as they drowned, and he knew he was to follow in moments. He recalled he'd wanted to see the New Sea. It had even come to him.

He pressed forth his will for his surviving slaves to fight in reckless, unending abandon, but knew it was pointless. Stupid creatures. Many had run from the far dry bank right into the path of this flood.

He felt them crying, panicking, dying, and a swell of elation from the cursed mammals, then the odd burning of water inside him.

After that, there was only the sighing of the waves.

End

TIDE OF BATTLE
PROVOCATIONS

THE DISTANT PAST: A SETTING FOR SCIENCE FICTION

This is a nonfiction article I wrote about the details and process of my novel A Long Time Until Now. *Eric Flint emailed me and told me I was working far too hard on research, and suggested a comfortable library would be better. He's probably right, but I'm terrible at taking advice.*

⊕

MY UPCOMING NOVEL *A Long Time Until Now* visits the far past rather than the far future.

A military convoy is interrupted by temporal chaos, and once it's over, ten soldiers find themselves . . . elsewhere. Eventually, they find enough clues to place themselves in the distant past, with only hints as to exactly when. They have their personal gear, the contents of two MRAP convoy vehicles, and their wits.

While the market for action-adventure is bigger than for hard SF, I've always been a fan of the science-oriented story. The limitations of reality, combined with speculations within them, is a rewarding challenge.

Of course, I didn't realize when I started writing *A Long Time Until Now* that there hasn't been much research about Paleolithic Central Asia. I also had an almost impossible time finding knowledgeable people to talk to. In fact, even with introductions from friends in other sciences, I didn't hear back at all from most of the scholars I was referred to.

I sought professional papers on the subject. They're sparse. Still, I read what there was, and quite a bit on other parts of Eurasia. I found one academic in the field who'd respond to my requests for help: Michael Williams, PhD (no relation) of the UK was helpful with some other sources and papers. His site is http://www.prehistoric shamanism.com/. My friends Jessica Schlenker (biologist) and Dale Josephs (research librarian) found a few more. Ross Martinek (petrologist) had some information on terrain and climate. I gathered what I could from all these.

I may have read most of the scholarly papers on that location and era, which tells you how few there are. Other parts of the world have been studied extensively. Large chunks of Asia are still wilderness, as far as prehistoric study goes.

So then I had to fake it, which frustrated and concerned me. This is supposed to be hard science fiction, not fantasy. Then I realized that if we don't know what happened at given times and places, I can't be expected to be exact. So I did the best I could based on the nearest cultures and environments to that timeframe and location.

Next, I started experimenting. I learned or refreshed quite a few skills while writing this. I made fire by friction with a firebow and fire plow. I tried several types of bugs, and prefer them cooked. Emily Baehr brought a bag of weeds (that's plural, okay?) and showed me how to find an entire salad's worth of greens in temperate biomes, even in residential lawns. I used primitive weapons to bag a few targets. I use bows regularly, and have thrown spears. I tried atlatls and slings. I knapped some bottle glass.

Then I developed several recipes that will appear in my next collection of stories and articles. How do you cook a tasty meal with minimal spices and no cooking utensils? Well, it turns out you can create quite a few spices and seasonings from plants in the carrot family.

There are a lot of edible plants and quite a few spices in the Apiaceae family. In fact, almost all edible plants come from about six families, and do so in the last 7000 years or so. Before that, there's some evidence of rice and wheat, and occasional possible evidence of fruit domestication (versus actual agriculture).

However, it's obvious from the evidence that vegetarianism is just a modern ideal. No matter how many believers bleat about it being "natural," it not only wasn't natural then, it was a complete myth. There just aren't plants in the temperate or boreal latitudes that you can gather for enough protein, fat and calories to stay alive.

Even if you could, you won't find them in December. This is a world nothing like our own. No domesticated grains, no herded animals. Even modern "wild" berries are usually contaminated, and sweeter, because of cross-pollination with domestic breeds. I've had vegetarians insist we were mostly vegetarian at the time, but they're unable to name the plant species we allegedly derived our calories from, especially fat, particularly in winter. I'll save you time: There are almost none. Gathering non-fruit comestibles is a net calorie loss and a waste of effort.

Most of the Paleo diet people won't be happy either. There was a lot of meat, but most of it was stringy and lean. Humans need fat for brain development and to maintain the skin, among other organs. When you can't get gorged, winter-ready animals with a layer of fat to eat, you wind up eating brains, livers and kidneys. These also provide salt, minerals and flavor. Hunter-gatherers cherish the organ meats for nutrition. You'll want a lot of fatty fish, too.

After a week of this diet, I was ready to kill someone for some french fries or a peanut butter sandwich.

Food preparation is another matter. Rocks work well for cooking, as do sticks, and of course, a military convoy has ammo cans, but are the painted surfaces non-toxic even when scoured? More research.

Ten people can't live for long in the backs of two trucks. If they don't want to be adopted into a Paleolithic village, they need shelter. Since most animals and no predators really fear humans in an environment like that, it needs to be protective shelter. Then, how much can you trust your neighbors?

But, how much can you do with ten people, when you

need watch-standers and hunters? With hand tools only, and damned few?

A tepee is easy, and variations on it or the wickiup are universal. There are actually quite sophisticated building foundations going back 30,000 years, of rocks dug and set to make a solid lintel on which to place struts and poles for any number of lodges. You cover them with sheets of bark, or with hides that you then smoke to shrink and preserve. Then there's a way to produce leather that might have been found by accident. I put that in there. (I've since had actual paleoanthropologists tell me I may have discovered a new hypothesis on how leather was developed.)

But a palisade is a useful thing, though a lot more labor intensive. It blocks vision from the outside, wind, animals, foes, and provides a lot of comfort and safety. All you need is a thousand logs . . .

. . . and then a few more for log cabins.

So where do you put your midden heap and latrine? How do you reach the stream and the well?

All these issues pile atop each other. You have to eat, stay warm, stay sheltered, get clean, plan ahead.

This led to the next problem: sheer volume.

There's only so much room in a book, and it has to be story, not background, but that background is an essential part of the conflict in a story like this. Man against the environment is one of the classic literary struggles. There's more I could have put in, but I had to leave some areas unfulfilled. I was at 212,000 words.

For example, the troops have melee weapons aboard the vehicles on convoy, against potential boarders—tool handles, broom handles, bats. Being American troops, I guarantee someone will have a glove and ball to go with the bats. But there is no Stone Age ball game, because I couldn't find anywhere to place one. I didn't go much into the care and feeding of penned goats. It's not dissimilar from today, and there wasn't room to address it.

There have been some initial reviews from people who wanted more action, and missed the lack of a named villain. But nature herself can be the ultimate opposition, especially when resources are short. Nor could I find anywhere to insert epic battles between time travelers or Paleo natives. However, there's plenty of possibilities for those in a sequel.

Of course, realism only goes so far. I learned that long ago, during a Dungeons and Dragons campaign where the Dungeon Master insisted on excess realism. We players each rolled six sets of three dice for our attributes and gamed from there. The results weren't impressive. Normal people don't adventure. If they try, they die. We did.

Military members at least have basic standards of fitness and training that are above normal, which is disturbing to think about—half the population are below average, and I've commented sarcastically that I think that's being generous. Especially when it comes to any training outside of the narrow scope of a person's culture and society.

But, that military training is specific, and the standards can vary by circumstance. I didn't cheat, but I did optimize some of the characters' backgrounds and gear. You will find people in the military with all of the skillsets and training mentioned within. You won't necessarily find them all in one location, but it's not impossible. You will find all the described equipment, and more, on trucks in war zones. Troops take what they think they need for engagement or comfort.

Even with that, the characters have only what they had with them when it happened. I gave them a little help. They have proper pioneer tools, not the multiple-headed "Max" monstrosity that is issued. There's a decent tool kit aboard one vehicle. They have plenty of knives. They have some rechargeable batteries and two chargers. The rest of the gadgets will die as their batteries do. Lighters only last so long, and of course, caffeine and tobacco will run out in days. A good axe and spade can be worth their weight in salt when you cannot replace them, and salt can be almost priceless. All these things do occur in theater, and I gave the troops just enough to make them miss the rest. Hearken back to that role-playing game: if regular people go adventuring in street clothes, the story is boring, because they die.

The troops, however, can't approach things with a combat mindset, because their ammunition is very finite, and megafauna are not impressed by 5.56mm. If you are lucky, the wooly rhino won't even notice the attack. If you're not lucky . . .

I liked the characters, even the ones I didn't like. I knew where I wanted them to go. I knew their feelings and motivations. They were consistent, and they were human.

They're a mixed bag. They're not all Soldiers—two are borrowed from other branches, known as ILOs in some documents—In Lieu Of. Only one is Combat Arms, the rest are various flavors of support. Two are women. Two aren't in great shape, because they're older and broken, and panicking over what will happen when their medication runs out. Stay in the military long enough, you'll get broken, too. They are urban or rural and technical or intellectual. There's not really a "typical" service member, with a nation of a third of a billion to recruit from, and several territories and protectorates. That's what a unit looks like these days. That required research, too, since I'm an immigrant myself and don't really know what any "typical" American is like at an intimate level.

Some are religious, and while I'm agnostic myself, I was raised Anglican. There would be serious matters of faith for a believer in these circumstances. They have different politics, which are of no immediate matter, but color their perceptions. I always hated cookie-cutter military characters, and I try not to write them. Those I served with were of a broad spectrum.

Then, what's it like being the minority group in the world? What's it like when you're the minority among that minority? The closest I came was deploying with an element that was about half and half Puerto Ricans and Guamanians. The rest were mostly Mormons from Utah. I was not only the token Mid-Westerner, I'm an immigrant one at that. Even if people are supportive, it's lonely. When there's no one else in the world like you, it's going to have a deep emotional bite.

I knew the plot, the story, the challenges. I even had most of the technical gear in mind. I know what people can do with limited resources when they have to, and how they adapt tools to fit their needs.

These characters are Soldiers, though, not scientists. They know some of what they need, they can learn the rest, but some of it they can never know, and will not be able to learn within the story.

So there are mistakes in this book. They're not a problem. They make it better, and they're by design and intent.

There are two types of errors in this book. Errors of knowledge, and errors of memory.

The characters are suddenly about 15,000 years in the past. One of them has enough knowledge of astronomy, and others some training in archeology and climate, to make that estimate. I know the exact date, and even what the stars look like at night (thank you, stellarium.org). I may tell you in a future book.

But they don't know a lot of other things. None of them know ceramics, for example. Molding clay is easy, but how do you fire it? What do you use for glaze? Possibly some combination of sand, ash and salt? They don't know, so in this story, they don't try. If they have long enough, they might experiment.

There are skills they just don't have, and there's no Internet to research it even at a cursory level. They have to guess about some aspects of the Romans and their culture. They have to develop some skills from pure theory or hazy memories. Their ongoing frustration shows. The Internet may be the greatest information tool humanity has ever developed, and most people use it to post pictures of kittens and scream, "Fuck you!" at each other. You don't miss what you take for granted until it's gone. They have laptops, and access to all the critical military software such as porn and PowerPoint, but no way to retrieve any other data.

I deliberately didn't research any areas the characters didn't know, and wrote about those from my memory (or from the characters' memories, based on deliberately incomplete notes). Two of them know about the Younger Dryas and the 8.2 Kiloyear Event, but is that 8.2 kya or 8.2K BCE? And how much are they before or between those events? If you know in theory how to extract iron ore, do you recall how to make a reduction furnace? How do you feed air to it? If you know edible plants in the modern US, how much do those resemble Paleolithic Central Asia? Which nuts are edible before agriculture, and which have toxins? How do you use an animal's intestines to make sausage casings or rope? Various groups wear armor and clothing you can use to ID them, if you know what it is. Otherwise, direct discussion is necessary. The Romans know who their emperor is. The Americans don't recall his reign dates. So when exactly are they from?

As far as interacting with the displaced Romans, I had an expert translate the actual Latin. The Americans fudge their Latin from English words which I reLatinized from memory (and I'm sure for inventing that word, some schwastika-wearing grammarian is going to chase me down and hurl books at me). It's a butchered lingua franca, but comprehensible.

So names, dates, technologies and skills are sometimes wrong, because the characters would have them wrong. Nor would they have any way to ever check. If you find those errors, they're there because I meant them to be, and did not allow any corrections in the copy-edit process. The characters can't know all these things, so they don't know them. Still, if you want to talk about those areas, it might make for a great conversation. I prefer red ales and single malts, just in case you need to know.

The story is about people, stuck in a world that's partially familiar and sound, and largely alien and terrifying. You probably have no idea how dark it is, under an overcast sky, when there are NO cities. These days, the glow can be visible for hundreds of miles. With nothing but a small fire, a cloudy night is literally as black as a darkroom. Then the trees creak, and something predatory makes noises . . .

As to the science, I'm sure the little research done in that real-world location will be expanded upon in the coming generation, and our overall knowledge of the era will change and improve dramatically. Sooner or later, the story will be technically dated.

Consider that *The Quest for Fire* was hard SF when it was written in 1911. I wonder how my novel will hold up in a century. I can only hope the character story survives better than the science story will.

In the meantime, here's two recipes to get you in the mood:

First, prepare your cooking utensils. You will need:
    A flat rock.
    A clean, empty ammo can.
    Your knife.
    A fire.

Be careful with your rock. Granite is best. If you have to use slate, heat it very slowly to make sure the moisture is out before cooking. Fast heating can cause . . . explosions. If you have nothing like this, you can use a cast iron pan, dry. I take no responsibility for your actions.

To prepare an ammo can, remove the lid and put aside for use as a cover and as another prep/cooking surface. Scour the paint off the inside with sandstone, using a stick and sand in the corners, or by heating over a fire, then dousing remaining paint with water so it bursts loose. Season with nut oil or animal fat over a low fire. Avoid wild almonds—they're toxic.

✧ ✧ ✧

Stone Age Chicken:

Salt (colored rock salt preferred)

Wild onion. You can probably find it in your lawn, if you haven't sprayed everything dead with pesticide. Otherwise, go to the park and find some. It's endemic. It looks like tall, green shoots, and smells oniony when crushed.

Greens from wild carrot or something in its family, but be careful with Queen Anne's lace.

Black sesame seed (sparingly)

Build a fire and let it burn down to coals against your rock.

Crush the salt against a rock with your knife blade. Repeat with the sesame. Catch in a canteen cup, ammo can lid or clean leather.

Crush and shred the greens and wild onion. Mix with the salt and sesame in the ammo can lid or on a flat stone.

Slice the chicken into thin strips. Peel meat off the bones. Drag them through the herb and spice mix.

Let them age while the stone heats. Rake the coals around the rock and let it warm (keeping in mind the safety warning above). You can also do this on a good charcoal grill if you are an apartment dweller, using real hardwood charcoal, not those plastic-bindered "briquets".*

Once the stone has had a half hour in the fire coals, lay the strips on it. They'll sizzle and steam and if you cut them thin enough, will cook in a matter of seconds. You want the outside golden brown.

My teenagers swear by this and I have to make it every week or so. If you have a little fat, suet or seed oil, you can follow up with shelf fungus (you'll need to research how to ID and ensure it's safe. It's easy, but I take no responsibility for what you acquire), sautéed until crisp and brown.

Now, try it. I think you'll agree, that does not suck.

By the way, I had Jane Sibley, PhD, make up a batch of a similar spice combination for ongoing use. If you're interested, contact her at http://www.auntiearwen spices.com/index.html and ask for Crazy Einar's spice mix.

*(NOTE: Try the hardwood lump charcoal. Most hardware stores and good groceries have it. The bag weighs less, but contains about the same heat value for cooking, burns a lot cleaner with less ash, and makes the food taste much better. Tried it? You're welcome.)

☙ ☙ ☙

Field Pot Roast Stew

Required: Carved or turned wooden bowls treated with butternut or walnut oil.

Ammo can or other deep metal pan.

Your cooking rock and fire.

Take a joint or a chunk of beef or antelope roast, rub

all over lightly with salt and let rest for a couple of hours. Keep the flies away using a tepee of sticks and a shirt.

Brown on all sides on your hot rock.

Place in a roasting pot or your ammo can. Take several wild onions, chop off the roots, rinse off the dirt, and chop into chunks. Smash the root bulbs against a rock with your knife. Place in pot. Add another sprinkle of salt.

Add several rinsed root bulbs of dandelion or carrot-family roots, small and fresh. As they age, they'll go tough and woody.

Finely chop some pine needles or scrape out some pine nuts. Add a little more salt. Add about a half inch of water.

Simmer over or next to a bed of coals for two hours. Add water as needed to maintain level.

Chop, slice or shred beef into chunks.

Chop up several small apples and add as a starch and thickener. Cook another 30 minutes.

Serve in bowls.

Chicken strips on a hot rock.

Notice the shattered slate. Moisture in the rock causes this when heated. Any water bearing rock must be preheated while you stand well clear, but I recommend not using slate, shale or similar stone. Granite is much better, if you can find flat pieces.

The chicken cooks quickly, and can be peeled up with a knife and eaten directly. The black specks are sesame seed.

The stew in the ammo can.

Shelf fungus was added as well as the ingredients above.

The ammo can works for baking, pot roasting, or stewing. It's also a good idea to season the outside with meat drippings periodically. Since it's sheet metal, it won't take as much heat as cast iron. Don't overheat it.

WHY NO ONE WATCHES MOVIES WITH ME

I like to analyze a movie for its meta-meaning or undertone. This seems to perplex a lot of people. For example:

Madagascar:

This is the story of four naive urban socialists, unfamiliar with the processes that feed and support them, winding up in "The Wild."

The Wild is a libertarian paradise where no one has toilets or toilet paper, and occasionally feral creatures eat one of the residents due to the complete lack of national defense or police functions. They throw some bitchin' parties, however.

The socialists, in classic fashion, demand to talk to "The People," code for the bureaucrats they expect to handle all their life issues for them.

Meanwhile, a group of right-wing extremist penguins hijacks the ship and heads for their native paradise, only to find it sucks a lot more than an industrial society in the temperate zone.

They head back to Madagascar, where the socialists have finally learned to somewhat fend for themselves, but are still dependent upon others for the necessities of living.

Ultimately, everyone winds up On The Beach, with no drinking water, toilets or way to get home, but declare a win because the party is a lot of fun.

Over the Hedge:

This is the story of RJ, a raccoon (Quisquiliae Ailuropoda) who is a textbook thieving socialist. We start the movie with him stealing from a hibernating bear. Despite cautioning himself to only "take what he needs," he tries to steal everything on hand, including the food from the bear's paws. Once a socialist has an opening, they will always go too far, and RJ does.

RJ gets caught, and resorts to fast talking and promises of extravagant returns if only the bear won't kill him, arguing that if the bear does, he'll have to repeat all that labor himself. The bear grudgingly grants a grace period for compensation of RJ's crimes, and releases him on parole.

Denied a Have to leech off, RJ scavenges through trash for food and finds little. He takes his bag of minimal possessions and goes stalking a new subdivision of Haves he hopes to exploit for the debt he's already acquired, and the resources he needs moving forward. This uncannily matches every Five Year Plan the USSR ever had.

Without shills, socialists starve, so he also seeks

accomplices. He finds them in the form of a motley band of foragers just waking from hibernation.

Being a dedicated socialist, he goes full Bernie Sanders, persuading the foragers that they can have all the good stuff for free, just by taking it from the leftovers of the Haves. They do so, oblivious of the wreckage they leave behind. RJ is aware, but doesn't care. There's always more loot to be had.

Vern, the patriarchal conservative tortoise, loudly denounces RJ as taking advantage of the gullibility and stupidity of the group. Offended by his presentation of documentable truth, they turn away from him entirely, and hug socialism to their bosoms. Hilarity and disaster ensue, as they always do, because socialists are gullible and stupid and never learn.

When an exterminator, representing capitalist power, is brought in, they realize they should retreat to safety and live within their means. However, once again RJ the Politician persuades them that enough just isn't enough, that they must enter the very homes of the people and steal goods directly.

Keep in mind this is to enrich himself personally by his position, and pay off the bear who has a legal claim against his very life if he doesn't furnish compensation. The bear represents a bank or investor who acted in good faith, but was screwed over by claims of "fairness." RJ is a textbook democrat, stealing with one hand, lying about it, and feeding his sponsor with the other hand lest he become lunch himself.

The house is a shambles, the homeowner imprisoned for attempting to defend her premises, the exterminator deemed a villain for attempting to enforce the rules of society, and the bear is forcibly removed from the home where he was doing nothing wrong. What was a functional system is totally destroyed.

And the socialists retreat to the life they had before, enhanced by the rotting remains of capitalist production, blissfully unaware that when it runs out they'll return to the edge of starvation. Then they'll repeat this pattern of behavior, and wonder why it never works out in the end, and why exterminators keep coming to kill them.

AFTERNOTE: It does deserve credit for showing the dangers of energy drinks on excitable youth.

WHY MY ENGLISH TEACHERS HATED ME

YES, I really turned in reports like this in school.

Alfred Noyes' "The Highwayman":
   The prose was a ribbon of purple, over the puke green page . . .
   Okay, what is it with this poem? Sure, Loreena McKennitt's version has her ethereal vocals. Love it. But the poem itself . . .

$$\oplus$$

LESSEE, this poofta-dressed, bitch-boot-wearing, career robber rides up to the inn to tell his tawdry tart he's going to relieve some honest landowner or businessperson of his gold. Oh, jolly good start.

   He can't actually reach her, and her father apparently knows the score because this waste of breathing air isn't allowed in the front door (smart man). So we find out said

Highwayman (We don't ever get his name, so let's call him . . . Horace? Finnegan? How about Lamar? Hell with it: Bob) has some kind of hair fetish that gets him off. (Okay, I'll admit I tried it once or twice. But certainly not while astride a horse wearing thigh highs, leather pants and French lace. KINKY.) Then he gallops away to rob someone. Asshole.

Then the beta-cuck "nice guy" who works in the stable figures he can get some sloppy seconds if he arranges for Bob to be tossed into the hoosegow or otherwise disposed of. After all, doesn't every landowner's daughter dream of getting it on with the help?

The lawful peacekeepers of the time arrive to put down this dog, as he's later correctly referred to, though Noyes makes that out to sound like some kind of tragedy or loss to mankind. Oh, boody-fricking hoo! The soldiers shot an armed robber. But I digress.

Knowing the worthless trollop will open her fat yap, they tie her, accessory before and after the fact she is, to the bed, along with a musket. They could have just hanged her, heels kicking and eyeballs popping, from the nearest stout elm, but they showed a measure of compassion. And her father lost nothing but a barrel of ale for his cowardly quiet nod to this scumbag looting the local economy and banging his daughter's headboard on the side. What's the problem?

Okay, so she has a musket angled under her breast. This would be the Land Pattern musket, or Brown Bess. As every third grader should know, this has a 42" barrel and an overall length of 59". The trigger is about 43" from the muzzle.

Her hands are TIED BEHIND HER! She manages to scourge them free of the ropes with much blood, which would cut her to the tendons and make manipulation impossible, but hey, it's romance, right? Then, this mutated orangutan is able to reach the trigger. The weapon is either to the side or in front. Her arms are BEHIND. The distance in question means her arms are 38" at least, maybe 50", and that's not from the center, that's from the shoulder seam. Maybe Bob does her while she swings from the wrought-iron chandelier. I dunno.

Splat! Angst-filled proto-emo bitch blows her heart out. No wiggling so the musket falls and thereby brings the trigger within arms reach of someone normal, like an NBA player. No, she wants the dark goth effect. Well, she's an accessory to felony, so what's the big deal or the loss? Waaah!

So, glam-boy Bob Hood (he's got the stealing-from-the-rich part down), somehow surprised and angry that his brachiating wench is dead, openly charges a musket squad while brandishing a rapier. This shows little tactical or common sense, but definitely suggests hidden Freudian compensation issues that go with his clothing fetishes. The Inedible Shrinking Man, maybe? Boo hoo. The soldiers shot a criminal who brought a knife to a gunfight. These days, he'd win a Darwin Award. Back then, a poetic eulogy full of purple adjectives that is inflicted on middle-school students to this day.

And they say our schools aren't liberal.

SLAUGHTERING SOME SACRED COWS

I can be an ass.

Yes, really. Ask around.

I've been known, on occasion, to log into a firearm forum, say something like, "I don't get the scout rifle concept," then back out and watch as people argue themselves hoarse over stuff that was intended to be purely hypothetical.

A lot of people seem to miss the relevant point that military and civilian shooting needs are different. Civilians can't rely on a truck or chopper to bring more ammo and spare parts, and shouldn't be shooting that much even defensively—if you're in a fight where you need that much ammo and can't retreat, and don't have military backup, you planned poorly.

Conversely, military troops need a lot of suppressing fire to pin the enemy in place, and usually won't have the luxury of finding a tall stand, a clear view, and the chance to take a long, relaxed shot at a slowly moving target. Combat is fast, ugly, messy.

So, what gun you need for a particular purpose varies, just as a Ferarri, a Toyota Hilux and a Dodge minivan all fit different criteria for cars, and don't really compete with each other for a "best." Your needs dictate your parameters.

Watching firearm aficionados argue over these points can be hilarious, boring, frustrating and even angering.

Then we get to the military, where scientists and engineers have to provide products to combat officers who aren't usually scientists or engineers, and know what they want in the perfect world, but are frustrated when it's impossible.

So I threw together a post to remind them they're all idiots.

If you aren't "in" the firearm community enough to get the humor, you really haven't missed anything. This is sheer gun nerdery.

And please don't write to complain about my stereotypes. That's how humor works.

⊕

ARMY, sometime in the 1920s: Most of the technological militaries are going to 6.5-7mm cartridges, with good success. John C. Garand, design us something like that.

Garand: How about a self-loading rifle in .276 Pedersen? Easy to shoot, reliable, effective.

Infantry officers: I wanna be an engineer! Let me tell you my ideas.

MacArthur: I've decided that since we had lots of .30, the rifle should be in .30. Just because we're changing doesn't mean we should . . . change.

Army: This rifle can't handle full loads of .30. They bend the op rod. Reduce the power of the .30, call it M2. And the en bloc clip Mannlicher came up with in the 1880s is pretty cool, so modify it for that, too. Just like the Carcano.

GI: OW! M1 thumb,hurts! Good rifle, but OW! And yeah, the op rod bends sometimes. Still, there will NEVER be anything better than this!

Army: Yes, there will never be anything better, so let's improve it. Turns out, you can pull off the base plate and with a few minutes of milling, fit a BAR magazine on it. How about that?

Army leadership: That's too simple! We'll research this for a decade, and expect improvements in another decade. A new, improved Garand, magazine fed with its own PROPRIETARY magazine. Because, you know, the rifleman and automatic rifleman should NEVER have commonality of magazines.

Garand: I've designed this bullpup rifle. Short, light and compact.

Army: WTF?! That doesn't even *look* like a rifle! Forget it.

British MoD: We figure the mid-caliber is the way to go, and the bullpup concept. Here's the EM-2 in 7mm.

Army: What?? A smaller caliber? Only .280? We need a "full power" man-stopping .30 that's capable of killing a man at 2000 yards, even if the sights are limited to 460. After all, without .30, you can't properly jerk your co— . . . anyway, it HAS to be .30! Screw you, NATO. .30 or nothing.

Belgium: We call this the FN-49. Now exporting in .30, 8mm and .308.

France: Unh hunh! We shall convert our MAS-49s.

Spain: Ve could do ze (cough), sorry, señor, didn't meant to sound German. I'm not, you know. No former Nazis here. Anyway, here's the CETME, in .308, sort of. We'd wanted a bit lighter cartridge for this roller lock, but it'll work, if you load the ammo light enough.

Belgium: This is the FAL. Stamped steel, and broach cut receiver, and quite cheap to produce.

Eugene Stoner: ArmaLite. I have this idea, considering what the Army's doing. AR-10. Change uppers, and it's rifle, carbine, machine gun and sniper platform.

Army: OMGWTFBBQ! That looks like a ray gun! Not a REAL rifle! We can't have that! But, the carbine/rifle/MG idea in one platform is good. Let's steal that. Springfield, can you do that?

Springfield: Uh, suuuure. Yes, we can. Mass-produced, too, so you don't have to worry about those commie union workers.

Infantry: Wait, what's this about the Russians, Chinese and Koreans having a rifle that holds 30 rounds and is select fire? Screw that. GARAND! GARAND! GARAND!

Springfield: Here's the rifle. It's basically an improved Garand with a magazine, just like we discussed in 1934, and it only took us until 1954. This is almost as cool as that Beretta the Italians have out, based on the Garand.

Army: That's great. What do the Italians know? Ours MUST be better! It's American! And .30 cal! And it only costs $240 to the Garand's $80. Well, so it's a bit more expensive. Okay, three times as expensive. But it replaces the BAR and M3 and M1 carbines as well! Okay, it doesn't REALLY replace the BAR. Too much recoil, not controllable, and too small a magazine. Crap. Well, take the M60 GPMG and tell people it's an automatic rifle! Problem fixed! $240, 9 lb rifle replaced with $750, 26 lb machinegun. And it still replaces the grease gun and carbine. Well, not really. It's heavier, bulkier and kicks too much to be a carbine. No problem, we'll just hang onto the grease gun and carbine. The point is, it's better than the Garand, so it's better than perfect! Three times better, in fact, which is why it costs three times as much!

. . . Okay, so it's not great in the jungle, with its dirty gas system and long length. But that's because those damned commies won't fight like men! What's this AK-47 thing, anyway?

So, Europe, whaddaya think now? Huh? Huh? Isn't the precision-milled, by skilled, master union machinists, M14 better than your cheap stamped and broach-cut FAL? Eh? Aw, screw you. Hey, Springfield, didn't we discuss that this was supposed to be easy to produce without master craftsmen?

Scientists: See, you can't actually see a man past 500 yards, and 98% of engagements are under 300. If you use a smaller round, you can carry twice as much ammo, inflict twice as many casualties, for the same weight of system.

Infantry: But . . .

DoD: Shut up, you dumb grunt. Here, take this stick and go hit the enemy.

Infantry: A stick! Cooooool!

General Lemay, SAC: Holy crap, Eugene, this downsized AR-10 of yours kicks ass. Crap tons of capacity, twice the power of the toy carbine, what the hell was the Army thinking with that 6 MOA squirrel shooter? I want these for the APs tomorrow. Here's a check from my personal account.

APs: Cooooool! Off to Tan Son Nhut.

SEALs, Green Berets: Wait, you've got a rifle we haven't seen? That's not allowed. Gimme. (Shoots Gook. Gook blows in half.) Holy crap, this freaking rocks. We'll take lots. And it's LIGHT. That means we can carry more ammo. Cooool!

SAS: A new rifle what? That also takes a grenade launcher? YOU SEND ME NOW! YOU SEND RIFLE! Israel, Singapore, Canada, you wait your turn!

Army: Alright, we'll do as the scientists say, mostly because the M14 really isn't doing anything a Garand doesn't, and not as well, really. Sorry, Springfield. But, we have to IMPROVE this new rifle! Change that bolt! Change that rifling rate! Change that ammo! Add some doohickey to the side! Whaddaya think of THAT, Eugene?

Stoner: Er, I kinda hoped you wouldn't do that. See, this was designed as a unit to—

Army: No, no, you're supposed to say you LIKE what we did!

Stoner: I guess we're both disappointed, then. (Actual paraphrase)

Infantry: Screw you, Stoner! This rifle you designed—

Stoner: *I* designed?

Infantry: Basically, yes. It's jamming all over the place!

Especially when we put it back together with pieces missing! (Actual quote) What's this about it never needing cleaned?

Stoner: No one said it never needed cleaned!

Army: Someone at Colt said it was self-cleaning.

Stoner: WTF? NO, NO! The GAS TUBE is self-cleaning. Only.

Infantry: Huh? But I've been jamming sticks and rods and stuff down that gas tube to clean it. And it BREAKS! Luckily, I hear they're going back to the .30 before 1970.

Stoner: Yeah, you're not supposed to do that.

Infantry: Who the hell are you to tell us what we're not supposed to do?

Stoner: The enginee . . . oh, screwit. I'll go design the AR-18/180/SA80/L85/G36 platform, the Stoner 63, bunches of other guns these imbeciles at ArmaLite will never market successfully, and someone else will get rich off. See ya.

Civil War vet: The problem came when you pansy whippersnappers went away from the full power .58 Minié! That was a man's cartridge. Those .45s and .30s and .22s will NEVER replace the REAL American rifle!

Infantry: I Want .30 WANTWANTWANT! .30!

DoD Logistics: Dude. Supply chain. You cannot possibly carry enough .30 for a modern firefight, anymore than you could carry .45-70.

Infantry: WANT .30! WaaaHHH!

Scientist: 5.56mm will stop the enemy, and will do so better than the Russians' 7.62x39mm.

Infantry: That's impossible! See, .30 is BIGGER than .22. So there! I hit this guy forty-seven times center of mass and he didn't fall down!

Neutral observer: With a thirty-round magazine?

Infantry: Screw you, you're not Infantry so you don't know nothing! I don't care about a guy in the lab. I was the man in the field!

Neutral observer: Did you do side-by-side comparisons, in different environments, with cameras and controlled media and—

Infantry: Didn't you hear me? I WAS IN COMBAT! That makes me smarter than you! Luckily they're going back to the .30 before 1980.

Marines: Okay, we want to upgrade this rifle. Heavier barrel. More robust stock. Stronger receiver.

Marine infantry: And three-round burst, because taking

your finger off the trigger is haaaarrrrddd! And it should be able to shoot through a helmet at 800 yards! Just like a .30!

Scientist: As we've discussed before, you can't even SEE the enemy at that range, the sights aren't good for that range, you can't shoot accurately at that range in combat, and this is an ASSAULT RIFLE, not a SNIPER RIFLE.

Infantry: Who cares? This is only temporary anyway. They're going back to the .30 before 1990.

Colt: We'll do it. We can always sell it to camo commando survivalists.

Army: Um, this new round isn't as lethal as the last one.

Colt: Well, yeah. You wanted more range and to punch through steel at that range. That requires a heavier, tougher bullet. Heavier, tougher bullets don't fragment as well, for several reasons, including—

Infantry: Aw, screw all of you! It's a good thing we're going back to .30 before 2000!

Colt: Anyway, we made this carbine for some Arabs who wanted a carbine with grenade-launcher capacity.

Army: Sweet! We'll just issue that to everyone. What's the range on this? 1000 yards?

Colt: Er, no. 400.

Army: Awesome. 1000 yard carbine! With armor-piercing-explosive-fragmenting-incendiary-nuclear-ammo that will stop a Muj with one shot every time, even if it misses!

Colt: Look, basically you have a light carbine. Two hundred yards yes. Four hundred with a good marksman and planning.

Army: Colt, why aren't you giving us what we want? We'll go talk to HundK! They promised all that from a twelve-inch barrel with a hundred-round grenade launcher, too, in a five-pound package.

Infantry: Boy, I'll be glad when they go back to the .30 by 2010! Or at least that new 6.8, like the Brits came up with after WWII!

HundK: Ja, weighs twenty-five, like we agreed. Twenty-five kilos. Three rounds grenade, und pistol mit no sights.

Army: Look, we started the SPIW program in 1960. It's been forty years, and now you're calling it OICW. Any other progress yet?

HundK: Ja. Gif us more money.

Fanboi: We should have stuck with the Garand! And the Sherman tank! Patton loved them, which proves something!

DoD: So, special ops guys, what do you think of the 6.8mm?

Special Ops: Well, it's good for what we do. Definitely more punch. The problem is, there's not enough more punch to offset the reduced ammo load. Fine for us, of course, but those grunts will just shoot dry. It'll do a fine job of replacing .30, though, for a smaller, lighter series of support weapons with more ammo.

DoD: Sweet. We'll get cracking on that, then.

Infantry: Boy, it's a good thing they're going back to .30 by 2020!

. . . to be continued . . . endlessly.

THE GARAND: ALMOST AS GOOD AS A REAL RIFLE

I actually own a Garand. I have an M1D Sniper variant for my collection. The reasons I don't own more are detailed below.

⊕

AH, I CAN FEEL THAT HATE NOW. Fanbois always hate it when you inject facts into an argument.

Let me start by saying I have nothing against the Garand for what it was—a forward-looking design for the 1920s. John C. did a fine job with the technology of the time, and it's not his fault what happened after.

Mr. Garand designed a stripper-fed, gas-operated self-loading rifle in a mid-sized caliber. It was very advanced, and the only advantage it lacked was a detachable magazine, which was still a subject of discussion at the time—the SMLE had it. The Mausers and Mosin Nagants did not. As designed, it had moderate recoil, and could be topped off by shoving extra rounds into the top of the action, as with every other battle rifle of the time.

Then the Army took a crap in it. I can't blame Garand for this, because the Army crapped in almost every weapon it got given in the twentieth century, then complained about the taste.

MacArthur made a logistical decision to stick with .30 caliber, as it was the Depression and all the loading equipment was set for that. Now, I'm not blaming him for that decision . . . except that I'm blaming him for that decision. "Gee, I like your Corvette, Mr. Earl, but it really should run on diesel." Then, of course, we found out that infantry officers aren't really very smart about such subjects as metallurgy or physics (or counting above twenty-one, but I digress), and that the op rod couldn't take the punishment of "full power" .30 cal loads (that term is meaningless, by the way, but fanbois love to toss it around), so the loads were reduced in power to baby the system. (So, the fanbois' definition of "full power" was changed to meet the lighter load, and again for the .308. There's nothing more consistent than the apologetics of this crowd. They're now conceding that .276, as Garand originally intended, or 6.8mm, might be considered "full power." Another eighty years and we'll actually bring them into the 1950s.)

But wait! That en bloc clip Mannlicher came up with in the 1880s is all the rage with the Italians! Let's use that instead of stripper clips! Why? I dunno. It makes the action more complicated, and means SHOVING YOUR HAND INTO THE ACTION TO LOAD. Cue fanbois' whine of, "If you know the proper places to hold each of your fingers, the proper motions, and dance steps, you can insert it WITHOUT injuring yourself!"

Google the term "M1 Thumb." Then Google "Garand Thumb," just to make sure you've got the full report. You'll find about THREE MILLION hits. Now Google, "thumb jammed in M16." I'll wait. Google "thumb jammed in FAL."

If I have to stick my hands into a heavily sprung action that is capable of smashing my fingers, and risk smashing my fingers, to load the weapon, IT IS DEFECTIVE. There is no argument you can make to the contrary. If a car required reaching under the fan belt to fuel it, and might spontaneously start, smash your fingers and set you on fire, IT WOULD BE DEFECTIVE. If a gun might smash your fingers to paste on the off chance you might happen to want to put ammo in it, it is defective. Don't tell me you can avoid it with the proper dance card and samba lessons—I'm in the middle of a firefight. It's not a "design feature." It's not a "beta improvement." It is a CRITICAL FUCKING DEFECT.

To be fair, I will at this point dispense with the largely myth theory that the "ping" of the ejecting clip will tell the enemy where you are. I suppose it might occasionally be an issue, but in the midst of a firefight, that's not likely to be an issue—the enemy will be keeping his head down as much as you are.

But it does bring us to the other matter of loading. I've had fanbois insist against reality that "the Garand can be loaded with one hand without losing sight picture."

Really? You can secure a clip, reach up over the action

RIGHT IN FRONT OF YOUR FACE, press it down in so it hits the release, avoid smashing your thumb and still have a sight picture and finger on the trigger? Well, no, actually you can't.

M16: Reach forward with index finger, press release to drop empty mag. Pull finger back to trigger. Use left hand to insert fresh magazine, roll hand and slap bolt catch. Eyes still on target, finger on trigger before the round loads, and no need to stick fingers into the fanbelt. Any other modern rifle is similar.

But wait! There's more on this loading ritual. The Garand has some cute little quirks, and by quirks I mean "additional Army-mandated defects." That en bloc clip holds eight rounds. Because it's a double stack, it ONLY holds eight rounds. If you have really new, springy clips, you can get away with seven. Say it with me: "Eight shall be the counting, and the counting shall be eight! Count not six, unless it be followed by seven and eight. Nine is right out!" If you're down to six rounds of ammo, it's a single-shot rifle. You could refill your clips, except its other cute trick (see above) is to throw the empties across the landscape. Hah! Why would you need to reload? Certainly, in the modern world one dumps mags if one has to. It's nice, however, to have the OPTION of sticking one into your belt for later reuse. Or, going, "gee, I think I've fired more than eight rounds out of my rifle. In fact, I think I may have fired twenty-five. Why don't I drop, load and continue shooting with another thirty rounder, and redistribute those remaining five later?"

Good luck with the Garand. Now, as he designed it, you'd just slap another stripper of five in the top and be done. But no! That made too much sense for the Army. Cue fanbois: "Just release the partial clip and put in a fresh one."

Really? Ready? Alright then. Release, PING!, rounds and clip scattered all over the landscape, because once that clip is out of the weapon, it won't retain less than eight rounds. Congratulations! You won't be recovering that clip, OR THE PARTIAL LOAD OF AMMO IT HAD! (I get the impression that most of these fanbois have never actually tried all these clever tricks. I have. They don't work. Really.) (You actually can release and retain the clip, load it half out of the action, then press it back down. But that's more complicated than stripper loading or detachable magazines.)

This now brings up the minor but relevant side issue of sighting. Before detachable magazines, military bolt actions loaded through the top for speed. They eject the same way. Fair enough. In the twentieth century, though, they eject out the side. Now, most of the early bolt action sniper rifles loaded single rounds under the scope, and fired the same way.

Nope. The Garand is TOO AWESOME to play by those rules. Remember: you must load an eight-round clip. It must go through the top. It must eject the same way. You'd LIKE to actually have your scope inline with the barrel, wouldn't you? BWUAHahahaha! Silly sniper! No, you'll have your scope offset to one side, bringing a whole new adjustment to the mix. The fanbois will argue that if you're a real, true, sniper you ENJOY having an extra adjustment to your point of aim. Well, I'm not a sniper . . . but I have beat them in competition. So on the subject of precision shooting, I'm adequately knowledgeable. No, really, the less adjustments the better. You want that scope directly above the bore and as close to the same plane as possible, not in a completely different plane requiring juggling windage and elevation even before gravity and wind come into play. I'm sure someone will argue the Garand was not intended as a sniper rifle. This is bull. All military rifles are intended for precision shooting when needed. The Garand just brings all its special quirks to the table, and leaves them there in the middle of dinner. And as sniper variants exist, that argument is silly.

The Garand club can always rely on power and accuracy though. Or, at least they could rely on accuracy, until the M1A and AR-15 started making it their bitch at the National Matches. These days, if someone brings a Garand to the NMs, you think, "Oh, good. So I don't have to worry about him taking top." And power . . . ah, yes, it's more powerful than . . . well, not really more powerful than .308 military loads, nor more than 8mm Mauser. It's more powerful than most twentieth-century loads, but that's because when actual science displaced Freudian symbolism, it was determined that being hit by a Caddy was just as lethal as being hit by a Mack Truck. The Garand does have those awesome iron sights, though, so you can shoot 1000 yards. Well, okay, the manual says the sights are rated for 460 yards. Still, that beats the M1A, which is rated for . . . 460 yards. Well, at least it beats the M16, which is rated for . . . 460 yards. Unless it's an M16A2, which is rated for 550 meters, or 601 yards. Well, I guess an extra 50 years of development was good for something.

Ah, but the body count! The Garand killed Germans 15:1!

Well, not exactly.

The Russian casualties are due to Stalinist leadership at least as much as German marksmanship. And it looks like 5.2 million Germans and allies versus 6.9 million Russians and allies KIA, so hardly 15:1 on the Eastern Front, where Mosin Nagants were in use.

Germany's total military deaths were under 5.5 million. So, that's three hundred thousand Germans in the West and North, by Garand, MAS-36, Lee Enfield and Springfield combined. Oh—and Mosin Nagants in some of the European and Nordic nations, and, of course, Swede Mausers and such. Oops.

So it looks like the Mosin Nagants killed about twenty times as many Germans as the Garand. And the Garand may have scored even fewer than that—the Brits did a serious number, and the French really did put up a fight (check the casualty figures for major battles before you start smirking and looking like a moron), and let's not forget the Canadians. Oh, and those bombing campaigns and artillery and tanks.

The Garand does really well against charging 4'9" Japanese with stamped-steel swords, though.

Lessee: 2.1 million Japanese military deaths, and probably half of those by naval gunfire and aircraft. Then some Marines had Springfields. And Johnsons. And M1 carbines. And Thompsons. And artillery. And tanks . . .

So, the Garand's military accomplishments are largely hype, much like the rest of its capabilities.

It sure looks classy and elegant, though.

Well, then you won't like this: We used completely re-arsenaled Garands for about three months on base Honor Guard. Inside of a week, we had SOP of firing in three volleys of two, with the seventh man in reserve, so that WHEN, not IF, those pieces of shit both failed at the same time, we could manage to get off a bang.

These were completely refitted and speced, and looked wonderful. In theory, they were to exact tolerance. In reality, they were jamomatic garbage.

At which point, we went back to M16s, which didn't look as historically classy, but at least went bang every time we pulled the trigger.

The Garands also jammed on loading. Regularly. I remember one time the clip refused to seat, then did. So there I am, traumatized, blood seeping into my white parade glove, next to a deceased veteran, trying very hard to stay in formation, not wince, not cry, not curse, and not fall out of timing for three volleys. I managed.

(Some guy on Facebook responded with, "Sorry about your parade glove." I guess he missed the part about TRYING TO HONOR A DECEASED VETERAN while my rifle did more damage to me than the enemy ever did. I'll charge it off to him not reading thoroughly. I'd hate to think he was mocking a military funeral.)

Really. We were burying WWII and Korean War vets, and the vaunted rifle of that era couldn't manage to reliably fire three times in a row in tribute. We even had clips springing across the landscape when the action cycled, which really didn't make a good impression.

Now, I've handled good Garands as well. I'm just pointing out that we had a dozen of them, tuned to what should have been perfect spec, that often couldn't get off three rounds in a row from any combination of seven rifles. The order to change back to real, working guns came after we tried to bury a colonel and had to completely reload to get off the third volley. Yeah, that went over well.

Ah, but the Garand was the first of its kind—a self-loading battle rifle.

Well, no, not really.

John Browning had the Remington Model 8 in production in 1906. The police model had a 15-round magazine, beating the Garand. It even fired in .30 Remington and .35 Remington, more than enough to be "full power."

The French Meunier came out in 1914, and was in production when the war started. Wars being what they are, it only had a few thousand pieces produced, but they fired in 7mm, with outrageous velocities. This even made a second development into the RSC 1917.

MEXICO had the Mondragon in 7x57 Mauser, patented in 1907, built under license by Sig, and used by some Germans. Mexico, being smarter than the US Army, started with the en bloc, and then went to the detachable magazine in an 8- . . . and 20- . . . and a 30-round drum for the Germans.

And, of course, the Russians had the Fedorov assault rifle before the Revolution. Again, that revolution screwed a few things up, and production was limited. However, it did exist.

This doesn't count a dozen other designs around 1910-1920 that didn't get developed beyond early tests. So, yes, the US Army does deserve a little credit for thinking ahead, but only a little. Because when one John C. Garand designed them a mid-caliber bullpup in the late 1930s, the T31, beating everyone to the concept to the best of my knowledge, they kicked him out on his ass.

So, the M1 Garand is not the Model T. It's more like the Volkswagen. Historically interesting, rather quaint, beloved of a certain set of collectors, but really not a replacement for a Corvette TR1, a Ford F-150 or a Buick Rendezvous. Louis Blériot's monoplane was more advanced than the Wright Flyer, but I'd not want to take one across the Atlantic. My TRS-80 was a really cool computer . . . in 1982.

Seriously. The Garand was fielded in 1934. Soviet Simonovs were out in 1936, Tokarevs in 1938 (and I'm referring to rifles with both of those, so some of you don't embarrass yourselves). The Johnson, which could be topped up in mid-load, was out in 1941. And then that pesky MP43, StG 45, SKS and AK-47 came along, rendering the Garand a museum piece in under a decade.

But, wait, there's more! You CAN fix several of the Garand's defects in a machine shop in a few minutes—a bit of grinding lets you fit BAR magazines to it, which fixes the not-enough-rounds-to-engage-a-squad-of-Japs-with-swords problem, and the smashing-the-thumb-on-loading problem. Of course, the Army did this . . . eventually . . . with a special program that took twenty years until 1954, used a proprietary magazine, and became one of the biggest turkeys of the twentieth century—the M14, which, I believe, still holds the record of the shortest service life for a primary issue rifle in US history, because the flaws were so apparent even the infantry couldn't pretend it was worth a damn. (Occasional DMR use by very heavily modified M14s, while awaiting more AR-10s to replace them, does not constitute "primary issue" of a rifle. So stop emailing me and looking stupid.)

And that's where it should have ended, sometime in the early sixties, with AKs, FALs, G3s and other, much superior designs in plentiful use throughout the world. But almost fifty years later, you just can't get the stake into the heart.

Now, the Garand is arguably better than the Mauser K98, but it's not better than the three Mausers you can buy for the same price, nor the ten to twenty Mosin Nagants you can buy for the same price (these days, only four to five). When it comes down to it, it's a mass-produced, multi-million-number milsurp, which should cost about $300. At $300 it would be well worth having. And, of course, unusual markings, history, etc., might justify more.

Hah. You wish. To touch a Garand, even a "service grade" with a bore that gauges more than 3 (meaning "well used") is going to cost you $500. A pristine Mosin Nagant is about $80-$100 in 2011. A pristine Garand is about $1500 or more. For that price I can buy a really nice AR-15, AR-10 or an FAL and a stack of magazines. So if you want a using rifle, you're buying an antiquated relic with critical design defects for the price of something state of the art. Don't try to explain your logic. You have none. FAL beats Garand, for less money, any time. AR-10 beats Garand. AR-15 beats Garand, though you'll throw a frothing temper tantrum and fabricate or perpetuate all kinds of BS before you'll admit it.

The final, and perhaps most amusing bleat of the

fanbois is the appeal to authority. They like to quote one George S. Patton, to whit: "I consider it the finest implement of battle ever devised."

Indeed he did say that.

In 1943.

Well, you know, I have documentation (shut up, yes I do), that in 25,347 BC, Ung the Hunt Leader of the Upper Cave of Mucky River said, "I consider the chert-tipped spear to be the finest implement of battle ever devised."

So there! Who are you going to argue with? The general giving a pep talk 75 years ago, or the leader giving a pep talk 27,358 years ago? Huh? HUH?

All hail the Garand! The most overrated firearm in history!

Your hate mail WILL be mocked and derided.

CALIBERS

You may be aware there are thousands of calibers of ammunition. Some of them do have distinctive names—.44 Magnum, .44 AMP (for Automatic Magnum Pistol), .38 Special. Occasionally there's a neat one like .577 T-Rex or .600 OverKill.

But I think we can do better than that.

⊕

I PROPOSE NAMES that suggest the massive capability of the caliber in lurid, instant imagery.

Let us consider in inches:

.2 Pac: Guaranteed to stop a rapper.

.420 Stoner: This would be perfect in an AR-15, and the recoil is so mellow.

.451 Fahrenheit: It sets things on fire with the muzzle flash.

.499 Feinstein: I always wanted to cut a .50 BMG rifle down by a couple of millimeters so it won't chamber the standard caliber, then use this, named for one of the antagonists of Freedom of Recoil.

.50 Cent: When the .2 Pac isn't enough.

.6000000 Holocaust: It just kills everything. All at once.

.65 Extinction Event: Really, a big-game cartridge should be named this.

And then there's metric calibers:

9mm Doubletap: It's a perfectly normal 9mm. We just want you to remember that.

7.93mm Viking Raid: Used for slum clearance when entering Britain.

10.66mm Conquest: You'll be the only one left standing.

11.25mm Charging Moro: Wait, this actually existed. We know it as .45 ACP.

IT'S TIME TO ELIMINATE THE GUN CONTROL LAWS. YES, ALL OF THEM.

If I can get serious for a bit, here's an article I published in several firearm magazines in 2016.

I've been a Second Amendment activist for decades, and I'm a small part of why Handgun Control, Inc., had to change its name to The Brady Campaign. I provided snark and satire to a friend who lambasted them mercilessly in parody on his websites. It seems they registered HandgunControl.com and .org, but not .net. By the time it was over, he had parodies of their sites in the US, Canada, UK, New Zealand, South Africa and Australia. The sites featured numerous feeds about "guns in the news," which were all defensive uses, parody interviews, links to the DoJ statistics and some of my commentary, which I let him use for free.

Their first response was to threaten legal action for simply having similar site names and appearances, *claiming it infringed upon some implied ownership of the term "gun control." This is certainly a novel legal theory.*

Mark responded via his attorneys, suggesting we'd love to hear a federal district case hearing of "Handgun Control, Inc. v. Free Speech, Inc. of Indiana"—his nonprofit.

They declined, and secretly changed their organization name instead.

And now you know.

Regardless of your political position, I hope to persuade you that the laws in question are pointless and irrelevant. Prohibition in whole or part never successfully changes human behavior.

⊕

BEHAVIORAL LAWS require three components to be effective: They must accurately describe an action that causes harm to others. They must propose a penalty that disincentives the activity. They must be enforceable.

Let's consider the laws against murder. The harm done is obvious. The penalties range up to death. They can be enforced by an examination of the evidence during trial, and punishment.

How about "disturbing the peace"? If you plug in a Gibson ES-335 guitar and a stack of Marshall and Hiwatt amps at 2 AM and start playing Black Sabbath's "Iron Man," there's a good chance your neighbors will complain. If they do, we have a clear report of harm done (minor harm, but relevant), and can again have an examination, trial and punishment, probably a fine.

Of course, we could prevent some of those incidences

by licensing guitars, having waiting periods on amplifiers, and requiring proof of need for any amp over 20 watts.

Wait, how would that work exactly? And why should we exercise prior restraint on an otherwise lawful activity? How would a waiting period stop anyone from blasting the neighborhood?

Let's look at a global issue, and management: driving.

Most nations have speed limits in various areas, typically from 25-35 mph in residential areas, and typically from 55-100 mph on rural highways, depending on traffic load and conditions. Stop signs are almost universal, as are yield signs. Traffic keeps to one side unless passing. Cars have brake lights, headlights and turn signals. Most nations will let foreigners drive on their own nation's license. You can go between the US, Canada and Mexico and the rules are fundamentally identical. Europe's are not dissimilar. Parts of the old British Empire and Japan drive on the opposite side, but that's adaptable. Driving laws on the whole suit a consensus of what is reasonable, and serve valid purposes in reducing and preventing accidents and damage.

We've had cars for a bit over 100 years.

We've had guns for 800 years. It would make sense, then, for firearm laws to be as consistent and uniform across the world.

Before getting into that, what other 800-year-old technologies are restricted from the populace? We don't restrict printing presses and broadcast, despite the obvious incidents caused by their unfettered use. Generators don't require licensing to own, nor do engines. There are occasionally laws against knives, which are sharpened pieces of metal, and it's obviously a lost cause to ban the fabrication of something so basic. Guns are slightly more complicated, but can be mass-produced using cheaply available machinery of the nineteenth century. Why have we deemed such a basic tool to be some sort of mystical demon?

There are countries with far more murders than the US, committed with or without the use of firearms, where weapons are almost completely banned—Mexico[1]. There are others less violent where they are even more almost completely banned—Japan[2]. There are nations with far fewer murders than that and fewer restrictions on firearms—Switzerland[3].

The US has a category of weapons called "Curios and Relics," weapons of historical value and interest. The Russian SVT-38 and 40 rifles fit the definition of this category, and weapons contemporary with them are readily available. The SVTs, however, are banned from import. Yet, in neighboring Canada, with theoretically stricter laws, those rifles are unrestricted from import.

Most countries ban suppressors ("silencers"), but some encourage them for hunting. In the UK, once one has a firearms certificate, the suppressor is unregulated. In New Zealand, they are completely unregulated. In Canada, they are banned. In the US, they require registration and a $200 transfer tax.

One of the more glaring examples is in "deactivated" weapons. An M16 properly deactivated in the UK, for

1: https://en.wikipedia.org/wiki/Crime_in_Mexico
2: https://en.wikipedia.org/wiki/Crime_in_Japan
3: https://en.wikipedia.org/wiki/Crime_in_Switzerland

display and collecting, has the barrel destroyed internally and plugged, breech welded and/or cut, the bolt face cut and welded, and the firing pin disabled.[4] Yet, in the US, it would still legally be a machine gun, since the receiver is intact. Conversely, the US would require torch cutting or crushing of the receiver, which leaves the bolt and barrel intact, thus making them firearms under UK law[5].

Where guns are banned, people still acquire them:

https://amodestpublication.wordpress.com/2009/05/08/loyalist-paramilitary-improvised-machine-guns/

http://www.thefirearmblog.com/blog/2014/04/04/australian-motorcycle-gang-diy-firearms-surface/

https://homemadeguns.wordpress.com/

Many countries prohibit people owning firearms for the legitimate use of self-defense, but permit them for "sport" and "hunting." In other words, guns are too dangerous for you to use for their intended purpose, but perfectly okay to play with.

And then there's the State of California, with laws that are beyond Byzantine:

http://www.calguns.net/a_california_arak.htm

The wild inconsistency and observable illogic of these laws reveals them for what they are: hysteria-driven reactions to panicked demands to "do something" about

---

4: http://dwsuk.org/epages/057184c7-2fa2-4321-880c-a30e87657239.sf/en_GB/?ObjectPath=/Shops/057184c7-2fa2-4321-880c-a30e87657239/Categories/Deactivated_Weapons__FAQ
5: http://www.ima-usa.com/legal_info/#machineguns

"gun violence." As if guns can commit violence—reference Switzerland vs. Japan.

In California, offering an illegal "assault weapon" for sale without even actually using it is as severe a crime as raping a police officer[6,7].

Alcohol, which serves zero non-medical needs, is involved in more crimes than guns, and in many crimes involving guns. Half of all crime, in fact. Yet we understand what happened when we attempted to ban booze. I have had people insist to me that alcohol serves "legitimate social functions." If you believe that reducing inhibitions and judgment is legitimate, I won't argue with you. You know you're wrong and are being defensive. You most certainly have a right to consume it, but it's not a consequence-free act.

Stepping into sensitive zones, AIDS kills as many people each year as die from gunfire. Half of all AIDS deaths still come from unprotected gay sex. With gay men being perhaps 2% of the population, that means they cause twelve times the deaths per capita compared to gun owners[8]. But suggest "reasonable" laws regarding gay sex—mandatory condom usage and education—and you'll be called names by a horde of angry, mouth-foaming "liberals."

Canada has learned slightly. After tremendous expense, they admitted their firearm registry was a complete failure and largely abandoned it[9]. They also "fixed" the "problem" of hollow-point defensive ammo:

6: http://www.leginfo.ca.gov/cgi-bin/displaycode?section=pen&group=30001-31000&file=30600-30675
7: http://www.leginfo.ca.gov/cgi-bin/displaycode?section=pen&group=00001-01000&file=261-269
8: https://en.wikipedia.org/wiki/HIV/AIDS_in_the_United_States

1. Importation of hollow-point handgun ammunition is governed by the Explosives Act.

2. "Safety cartridges" (ammunition) come under the Act, but are generally exempt from almost all provisions.

3. Many years ago, citing the Hague Convention (which only relates to bullets used by soldiers in war), some dolt in the Explosives Branch put a ban on the importation of "hollow-point handgun ammunition" in place, by classing each such cartridge as a "prohibited explosive."

4. The importation of hollow-point rifle ammunition is not prohibited, say, for the .44 Magnum Ruger rifles, the .357 Magnum and .38 Special and 9mm and .40 Marlin rifles, .22 rimfire rifles, etc., etc.—so many people have imported hollow-point rifle ammunition in those calibers. Sometimes, they have been required to attach a little sticker to each box of cartridges, saying, "For use in rifles only."

5. The sticker has no effect. Once the ammunition has been legally imported, it comes in as a "permitted explosive" which is not and cannot be a "prohibited explosive." That being so, it cannot be retroactively made a "prohibited explosive" by a person loading it into their handgun. Therefore, ammunition in boxes with that sticker can legally be fired in handguns, because the only possible charge is possession of a "prohibited explosive" and both the Explosives Branch and Canada Customs certified that each cartridge in the shipment was a "permitted explosive" and not a "prohibited explosive" in order to let them into Canada. It is not possible to prosecute a person for using hollow-point ammunition in a handgun because they would be found innocent as a result of "official misdirection." (Points and references here: [10])

Maryland has realized their ridiculous notion that fired cases in a database could ever be relevant to a criminal investigation was flawed, after it never helped solve a single crime[11].

As for the "reasonable" demand for registration, let me help: 180235. You now have the serial number of one of my pistols. What are you going to do with that information? What *can* you do with that information? Its only purpose is for the government to have a means to harass me. It will never prevent nor solve a crime.

The recent catchphrase is some variation of, "Well, you gun nuts need to come up with something, because doing nothing is no longer an option."

In response: People who make this statement have been doing "something" for over 150 years, to the tune of 20,000 federal, state and local laws. Despite all that, they are insisting "nothing" has been done, an admission that they believe it was all worthless, pointless and to no effect.

They are absolutely correct.

This demonstrates two things.

First, that people with no knowledge of the subject shouldn't be attempting to create legislation.

Second, that all those laws should be repealed.

Every single one.

10: https://nfa.ca/resource-items/hollow-point-handgun-ammunition
11: http://www.baltimoresun.com/news/maryland/bs-md-bullet-casings-20151107-story.html

ASK MAD MIKE

My Crazy Einar's Viking Advice Column spawned a contemporary partner on Facebook. Here are some of the important ones:

❖ ❖ ❖

Dear Mad Mike,

The other day, a group of us were arguing over whether "Native American" sports mascots should be banned. I pointed out, "Americans name things for Winners because they hope some of the Winning Spirit will rub off — have you ever seen a sports team named for Africans?"

Was this wrong?

—**Troublemaker**

Dear Shit Stirrer:

Following your logic, we do not find any teams named after liberals, urbanites, poets, barristas or the French. Or the Nazis, Francoists or Argentines for that matter.

Since we do in fact find teams named Vikings, Apaches, Spartans, Blackfeet and Highlanders, among others, we can confirm your theory of naming teams after things that scare the opposition. But it does have to have a context and pronounceability to Western lips.

So as far as Africans, names like Mau Mau, Massai, Tuareg, !Kung, Xhosa and such are just too hard for your typical American to pronounce, even if they could place them on the map and understood their awesomeness. And no one has called their team the Zulus because if they lacked sufficient badassery, Shaka's ghost would arise to gut them personally. That's like naming your team the Chuck Norrises. Choose wisely.

⊕ ⊕ ⊕

Dear Mad Mike,

I was just shaving and I noticed something about myself.

1. I am a handsome son of a bitch.

2. Even though I am Mexican by descent, I have decidedly European features (light skin, curly hair, brown/hazel eyes (mostly brown but noticeably hazel in the right light), distinguished cheek bones and nose, and dashing chin hair and pencil mustache when trimmed right).

I'd like to plunder, enslave and possibly exterminate some Mesoamerican people. I am wondering if I should trim my facial hair to resemble something more befitting of my Spanish ancestry?

—White Hispanic

Dear Guy Who Wouldn't Be Allowed Within 50 Miles of a Klan Gathering:

1. Damn, you're a wordy narcissist, but, I guess that fits.

2. Stop, you're turning me on.

3. Van Dyke, definitely. With sneering mustachios. Do please report back on the plundering. I take 5% commission.

✧ ✧ ✧

Dear Mad Mike,

Does it count as "Stolen Valor" if the uniform and medals one is wearing are from a nation which hasn't existed in a long time?

—**Cosplayer**

Dear Poseur:

That depends on the nation. I doubt anyone will complain if you're wearing Vichy France decorations. If it's the Nazis, that's considered cosplay some places, the height of evil others. If you're wearing decorations of the USA, a lot of people may not realize it's a nation that no longer exists and take it personally.

✧ ✧ ✧

Dear Mad Mike,

What is the deadliest firearm in history?

—**History Nerd**

Dear Geek:
FN Model 1910 in .380 ACP is the most lethal handgun on Earth. It killed 37 million people with two bullets . . . fired into the Archduke of Austria.

Second most lethal handgun: 1895 Nagant 7.62mm revolver. It killed 14 million people, most of them kneeling 6" from the muzzle.

❖ ❖ ❖

Dear Mad Mike,
I am currently looking to purchase an OTF auto knife to compensate for my tiny micropenis. The knife laws in my state are vague and should be void, yet every law enforcement member I have spoken to has given me a different answer as to the knives' legality. My question to you is thus: should I go with grey body, black blade or grey body, polished blade? Also, serrations?
Thanks in advance,
Small but Sharp

Dear Dickless:
Colt 1911. What was the question?

❖ ❖ ❖

Dear Mad Mike,
What is your favorite scotch, favorite bourbon, and favorite Tennessee Whiskey?
—Aficionado

Dear Drunk:

I'm actually really enjoying Ardbeg for its peaty smokiness. For bourbon, I've always liked Elijah Craig. For Tennessee Whiskey, it depends on whether I'm cleaning corrosive or non-corrosive residue from the rifle bore.

◆ ◆ ◆

Dear Mad Mike,

Now that Barack the Maleficent and his lovely wife have been evicted, er, left office, their Twitter accounts have had to be changed. Now Mr. and Mrs. Trump are using the handle POTUS and FLOTUS. Could we expect the appropriate new Twitter accounts for Mr. and Mr. Obama to be FLOTSAM and JETSAM?

Confused in Flyover America

Dear Red Blood:

Those are good choices, though I might also lean toward IMPOTUS and . . . sorry, who's the other one?

◆ ◆ ◆

Dear Mad Mike,

My friends call me a mixed-up luddite because I prefer the SMLE over the Mosin Nagant. Are they right?

—Colonial

Dear Represser:

Boy, this is a tough one. On the one hand, we have

the Glorious Empire. On the other hand, we also have the Glorious Empire. I say you should reach a compromise where you bring one and they bring the other.

❖ ❖ ❖

Dear Mad Mike,

I've been wondering. If I get shot by a mugger with a .25 Lorcin, is it ok to rip his head off, or is that just a little too pissed off for such a puny round? I don't want to overreact!
   —Urban Cowboy

Dear Streetwalker:

I feel you have a moral obligation to discourage rude behavior. If he can't be bothered to dress nicely and shoot you with something tasteful—say, a Colt Python or Inglis contract Browning Hi-Power—you should definitely correct his behavior.

❖ ❖ ❖

Dear Mad Mike,

At 54, several health issues, a mostly lead-free pencil, and very few friends, should I just plan on living the rest of my life as mostly a hermit? I know you have a very active social life; how does one go about finding friends, especially possible romantic ones, at this stage of life and with several issues?
   —Senior Citizen

Dear Old Fart:
Money.

⬧ ⬧ ⬧

Dear Mad Mike,
Visiting all 50 states is one of my goals in life. What should be done regarding California, given what amounts to a ban on firearms and ammunition, performance cars and overall freedom?
—**Traveler**

Dear American:
There are 49 states.

⬧ ⬧ ⬧

Dear Mad Mike,
Is it possible to understand why John Moses Browning was taken from us? Why? WHY!?
—**Distressed**

Dear Penitent:
God needed him to craft weapons for Armageddon. We will again witness His greatness when the time is right.

⬧ ⬧ ⬧

Dear Mad Mike,
My neighbors of questionable immigration status

persist in having loud parties where their friends of equally questionable immigration status join them in making unpleasant noise into the night. However, I also live in a sanctuary city. What is the best way to make this problem go away?

—Sleepless in Seattle

Dear Lameo:

I don't understand. If you don't like Dos Equis, take your own beer.

◈ ◈ ◈

Dear Mad Mike,

A person approached me in my shop today. This person was 6'2, and wearing a dress. They had a closely cropped beard and mustache. They were wearing makeup, consisting of lipstick and eyeliner, what appeared to be mascara, and blush where their beard was not full. Their hair is fairly short, but had flowers braided in it. They informed me their pronouns are "xie/xir/xirself". I'm writing to ask, in what way can I get across that this is bullshit?

—Clerk

Dear Serverbot:

I guess it depends on if you might get your ass kicked, and how much money they want to spend.

◈ ◈ ◈

Dear Mad Mike,

I love the feeling of walking around in a kilt. What do

I need to do to prevent myself from looking like a tool in public?

—**NeoScot**

Dear Wannabe:

Make sure it's long enough to cover your tool.

✧ ✧ ✧

Dear Mad Mike,

I have a tendency to wake up in my backyard wearing nothing but a boonie hat and H-Harness with a knife in my hand. Is this normal, and why do my neighbors avoid me?

—**Veteran**

Dear Hardcore:

I do recommend boots.

✧ ✧ ✧

Dear Mad Mike,

My wife wants to celebrate International Women's Day in the bedroom. Should I be worried?

—**Wade**

Dear Loudmouth:

I guess that depends on what you want to get into. Or what she wants to get into.

INAPPROPRIATE COCKTAILS

This is a thing I started on Facebook and collected in my previous collection—Tour of Duty. *It has now become a Thing and my fans expect me to provide one for most events, incidents, disasters or celebrity deaths.*

A proper Inappropriate Cocktail is politically incorrect or sarcastic in nature, but also delicious to drink. The latter, though, is secondary to the former. Many but not all commemorate people or events.

If you are crazy enough to try all of these, I would prefer not hearing about it.

✧ ✧ ✧

The Full Broadside

For the Old World
>   A glass of port
>   A glass of sherry

For the New World

> Shot of light rum
> Shot of dark rum
> Shot of mescal
> Shot of tequila

Then, RELEASE THE KRAKEN!

Pretty much guaranteed to sink you.

✥ ✥ ✥

The Company Commander

50 different good shots of liquor for the good troops
5 cheap beers for the layabouts
5 chocolate bars to represent the unit turds
Mix it all together because "a unit is better
    than individuals."
Mix it in a Coleman cooler.
Leave it out in a trench overnight to chill.
Let it warm up in the sun.
Shout "Hooah, sir!" and drink from a canteen cup.

✥ ✥ ✥

Mazeltov Cocktail

Mogen David wine
Everclear
Serve in a bottle with a rag on top.

✧ ✧ ✧

The Officer Friendly

5 ounces MD 20/20
1 ounce White Dog
1 ounce Bulleit Rye
Sprinkle some powdered sugar (evidence) on the bar
after drinking.

✧ ✧ ✧

NOT A DRINK

Dessert Burrito

Chocolate chip cookie dough ice cream
wrapped in a pancake.

✧ ✧ ✧

The Boston Bomber

Sam Adams Summer Ale
3 ounces Irish whiskey
2 ounces Fireball
Serve in a runner's water bottle.

✧ ✧ ✧

Chechen Pressure Cooker

Baltika No. 2
3 ounces potato vodka
1 ounce cinnamon schnapps
Serve in an aluminum coffee cup.

❖ ❖ ❖

The Boston Marathon

1 ½ ounces London dry gin
1 ½ ounces apricot brandy
½ ounce grenadine
Juice of ½ a lemon
3 ounces ouzo
You're never going to finish it.

❖ ❖ ❖

Chechen in a Boat

Sam Adams Summer Ale
1 shot cheap vodka
1 shot Bacardi
½ ounce grenadine

❖ ❖ ❖

The Teamster

A Budweiser, but you have to pay for 8 of them, and it
shows up 20 minutes late, dented and warm.

❖ ❖ ❖

Trayvon Martini

3 ounces Arizona Tea
2 ounces vodka
Garnish with Skittles in the bottom of the glass.

❖ ❖ ❖

The Midway

Hawaiian Punch with a shot of pineapple vodka and sake

❖ ❖ ❖

The Pearl Harbor

Glass of Arizona Tea
2 ounces dark rum
Drop a sake bomb . . .

. . . followed by a torpedo.
1 ounce rum
1 ounce vodka
1 ounce cognac
1 ounce white crème de menthe
Mix the liquors, and garnish with a cherry,
cucumber slice, and twist of lemon peel.

❖ ❖ ❖

The Johannesburg Car Bomb

Float Jenever on Amarula in a shot glass,
drop into a glass of Fat Tire.

❖ ❖ ❖

The Apartheid

Light rum
Dark rum
Light and pour into a Fat Tire.

❖ ❖ ❖

The Hiroshima (Nuclear Kamikaze followed by Atomic Fireball)

1 ounce vodka
1 ounce triple sec
2 ounces sweet and sour mix
½ ounce Maui® Blue Hawaiian schnapps
Mix sour mix, triple sec, and vodka in shaker with ice.
Strain into cocktail glass and add Blue Maui to mixture.
¼ ounce 151 proof rum
½ ounce Dr. McGillicuddy's® Fireball Canadian whisky
¼ ounce grenadine syrup
Pour the grenadine syrup first, then layer the
    Fireball on top of it.
Lastly the 151.
Drink and enjoy. Tastes just like candy.

❖ ❖ ❖

The Dresden Fire Bomb

Rumple Minze dropped into Hefeweizen

❖ ❖ ❖

For Tom Laughlin, The Billy Jack

Billy Beer chased with three shots of Jack
Feels like you've been kicked in the head.

✦ ✦ ✦

For Dave Brockie, The Oderus Urungus

A green jello shot with rum, vodka, kiwi fruit,
and bits of gummy worm to look like tentacles.

✦ ✦ ✦

Fred Phelps #1

4 ounces bourbon
3 ounces sour mix
½ ounce Angostura bitters
2 tablespoons crushed pineapple
Fill rest of 12-ounce glass with prune juice.
It's sour, bitter, fruity underneath it all,
and you'll even hate yourself in the morning.

✦ ✦ ✦

Fred Phelps #2

Crushed pineapple
Prune juice
Bitters
Tequila (he hated Mexicans)
Ouzo (he thought all Greeks were gay)

Layer with a rainbow of Blue Curaçao, red raspberry
liqueur, orange liqueur, melon liqueur, lemonchini,
passionfruit pieces, and suck through a twizzler straw.

It's a FABULOUS! drink with a crappy finish.

✢ ✢ ✢

The Ukrainian Rebel

Vodka
Bloody splashes of grenadine and cinnamon schnapps
Stir with a miniature nightstick, light on fire.

✢ ✢ ✢

The Sochi Olympics

A White Russian without vodka served in a dirty glass.
That'll be $15. Shut up and enjoy our Russian hospitality,
you decadent Westerner.

✢ ✢ ✢

The Dead Giraffe

2 ounces Grand Marnier (because giraffes can reach the
top shelf)
Several drops of brown coffee liqueur
Bloody red splash of grenadine
1 ounce vodka

✢ ✢ ✢

The Mikhail Kalashnikov

Ice cold Stolichnaya while riveting AK receivers together.

✧ ✧ ✧

The Peter O'Toole cocktail

Double gin and tonic, staples of the British Empire
2 ounces sangria from Spain (*Man of la Mancha*)
A splash of Brandy (*The Lion in Winter*)
1 tablespoon Date syrup (*Lawrence of Arabia*)

✧ ✧ ✧

The Europa Hotel

You have to drink 28 shots of Irish in 23 hours.

✧ ✧ ✧

The Malaysian Plane Crash

2 ounces ginger ale
2 ounces orange juice
2 ounces pineapple juice
Twist of lime
1 ounce triple sec
Float 151 on top and light.
Extinguish with a vodka bomb.

✧ ✧ ✧

The Robin Williams

A triple espresso of Vietnamese coffee with 3 shots of
amaretto and 2 shots of vodka

Top with whipped cream, a dusting of powdered sugar,
a cherry and a slice of cucumber.

✧ ✧ ✧

The Ebola

Chop berries into the bottom of glass and add an ounce
of white rum.

Pour in 3 ounces each Irish cream and Kahlúa, drizzle
with grenadine and chocolate.

It looks like you exploded and died.

✧ ✧ ✧

The Charleston Church

9 shots Kahlúa
1 shot coconut cream
Serve with a Colt 45 chaser.

Of all the offensive drinks, this one got hundreds
of demands that I apologize for "racism."

If I treated this incident differently than I treat any
others, THAT would be racism.

(There will be no apology.)

✧ ✧ ✧

The Godzilla (in memory of actor Hiroshi Koizumi)

Dust rim with wasabi powder.
2 ounces melon liqueur
1 ounce saké
1 ounce orange juice

Serve over crushed ice and fruit debris
(or Lego bricks of a broken cityscape).

Light 2 ounces 151 rum and pour on top of the wreckage.
Splash of grenadine for the blood of the victims.

✧ ✧ ✧

Charlie Sheen's Tiger Blood

Red Bull with 12 cherries
2 ounces Everclear
½ shot grenadine

✧ ✧ ✧

For David Bowie, the Ziggy Stardust

2 ounces Goldschläger
Coke
Serve with ice cubes containing plastic spiders.

❧ ❧ ❧

The Alan Rickman

1 ounce Beefeater Gin
A couple of mealy worms (for Doctor Lazarus)
1 ounce Herbal Schnapps (for Hans Gruber and Professor
Snape)

❧ ❧ ❧

The Glenn Frey

A Tequila Sunrise with pink champagne on ice
Put on your headphones and take it easy.

❧ ❧ ❧

The Lemmy

3 fingers of Jack Daniels, splash of Coke
Stir using middle finger while holding a cigarette.
Use the Ace of Spades as a coaster.

❧ ❧ ❧

The Abe Vigoda

Vodka, sour mix, Manischewitz, prune juice
Serve with a side of goldfish crackers.

❖ ❖ ❖

The Donald Trump

A light beer in a Red Bull can so your hands look huge
Tell everyone it's top shelf scotch.
Compliment everyone on their hats.

❖ ❖ ❖

The Bernie Sanders

Top shelf scotch in a light beer can
Tell everyone you're one of them.
Ask them for donations to make beer available to everyone.
Stash it all to buy more scotch after you leave the party.

❖ ❖ ❖

The Purple Rain (for Prince)

2 ounces vodka
4 ounces Chambord
Fill champagne glass the rest of the way
with sparkling wine and garnish with a raspberry.

❖ ❖ ❖

The Punch Drunk (for Muhammad Ali)

3 ounces Kentucky Bourbon
Lemon juice
A swirl of grenadine syrup and a dash of Angostura bitters
Shaken, not stirred.

✧ ✧ ✧

The Gordie Howe Hat Trick

Gordon's Gin with Canadian Club, bloody red
grenadine and a splash of maple syrup.

Serve on ice, and punch the customer.

✧ ✧ ✧

The Gene Wilder

Chambord, Godiva, Irish cream, chocolate syrup,
and drink with a shaking left hand.(Commemorates
Willie Wonka, and the Waco Kid.)

✧ ✧ ✧

The Election Night 2016

Vodka, Cointreau and bitters

✧ ✧ ✧

The Janet Sterno

Everclear in large glasses
Light on fire.
Serve to small children in a locked room.

✧ ✧ ✧

The Red Tail (for Willie Rogers, the last surviving original Tuskeegee Airman)

Drink a German beer with a cinnamon schnapps chaser.

✧ ✧ ✧

The Fidel Castro

A large glass of dark rum with a fat cigar
Best served while standing on the backs of several low-level workers.

✧ ✧ ✧

The Green Hornet (for Van Williams)

1 ounce each melon liqueur, orange liqueur and vodka

✧ ✧ ✧

The Hillary

3 ounces Russian vodka
1 ounce bitters
7 sour grapes
1 ounce sour mix
Serve in private. If your guests complain, ask them what difference it makes.

✥ ✥ ✥

The George Michael

1 ounce each orange, apple, melon and pear liqueur
3 ounces sangria
Top with champagne and add a slice of passionfruit.
Chug, and WHAM the glass on the table.

✥ ✥ ✥

The Carrie Fisher

Coke and vodka and a lot of ice
Serve in a Solo cup. It's your only hope.

✥ ✥ ✥

The Father Mulcahy (for William Christopher)

A cheap gin martini, followed by some sacramental
wine, some cheap Italian red and a Virgin Mary.

✥ ✥ ✥

The Chestburster (for John Hurt)

A triple shot of Fireball, Jägermeister and 151 Rum

✥ ✥ ✥

The Apollo (for Richard Hatch)

Peach mead with vodka (ambrosia and rocket fuel)

✧ ✧ ✧

The Johnny B. Goode (for Chuck Berry)

Johnnie Walker Black Label and Peach Fuzz on the rocks

The rocks are not optional.

✧ ✧ ✧

The Don Rickles

A short shot of Goldschläger
Bitters
Served on a hockey puck
Follow with a swig of pickle juice.

✧ ✧ ✧

The Powers Boothe

Kool-Aid with Southern Comfort

✧ ✧ ✧

The Black Hole Sun (for Chris Cornell)

8 ounces Sun Tea
2 ounces Kraken Rum
1 tablespoon dark molasses

✧ ✧ ✧

The Sir Roger Moore

A bourbon, for his Bond character
(who drank that in lieu of vodka martinis)

A scotch, neat, for Ffolkes, his best character, in my opinion

And a Cannonball Rum (Cannon Blast)

❖ ❖ ❖

The Ramblin' Man (for Greg Allman)

3 ounces Southern Comfort
3 ounces Coke
Best served in the back of a Greyhound Bus. Hey, it's better than being tied to a whipping post.

❖ ❖ ❖

Zbigniew Brzezinski

Potato vodka
Predict major political change.
Laugh last when you are correct.

❖ ❖ ❖

The Manuel Noriega

Rum and Coke served in a hollowed-out pineapple
Add a banana.
Crank some Metallica.

✥ ✥ ✥

The Peter Sallis

No cocktail. Just a selection of cheeses.
We did a Wallace and Gromit marathon with all the
cheeses from the show one year at Windycon. For "It's
like no cheese I've ever tasted," I brought in a vegan
"cheese." In fact, it remains untasted, even by the vegans.

✥ ✥ ✥

The Rock Bottom (for Kathy Griffin's career)

2 ounces vodka
2 ounces tequila
2 ounces gin
1/3 ounces lemon juice
1/3 ounce lime juice
1/3 ounce pineapple juice
Mix all ingredients except tequila,
which you pour in slowly over crushed ice.

Dig it out with a fork. Keep digging until you reach the
bottom.

✥ ✥ ✥

The Bat Punch (for Adam West)

1 ounce Grey Goose vodka
1 ounce blackberry liqueur
1 ounce Bacardi 151 for the *POW!*
4 ounces champagne for Bruce Wayne

✦ ✦ ✦

The Whiskey Tango Foxtrot

2 ounces Four Roses
1 ounce Frangelico
Fill glass with Tang.

✦ ✦ ✦

The Vegas Shooter

Shots for everyone.
More shots.
No, still more shots.